REQUIEM'S JUSTICE

A Dark Fantasy Adventure

THE SPLINTERED LAND
BOOK III

RICHARD PARRY

Requiem's Justice

The gods have turned away. The demons have not.

Geneve and Meriwether are cast across the sea by a relic of the ancients, torn from their allies and flung into lands on the brink of ruin. **Geneve finds herself in a city ruled by a devil king**, where every deal has a cost. **Meriwether awakens in a cursed temple**, where echoes of the last great war refuse to stay buried.

The gate between worlds stands open. **Demons pour through, hungering for conquest.** If Geneve and Meriwether cannot reunite, the world will fall—not just in battle, but **in blood and fire, swallowed by an army from another plane.**

The gods may have abandoned them, but Geneve will not.

This is Requiem's justice.

You're Awesome

You could have picked any book, but you chose this one. That means a lot.

Your support keeps independent authors like me forging ahead, writing the stories we love (and hopefully, the ones you love too). Whether you're here for the characters, the worldbuilding, or just a little escapism, thank you for being part of this journey.

You. Kick. Ass.

Roll for Narrative

WHERE WORLDBUILDING AND OVERTHINKING COLLIDE

Love stories that linger in your brain long after The End? Ever wonder why some books hit like a natural 20 and others critically fail their way into the 1-star abyss?

Join *Roll for Narrative*, my hub for sci-fi and fantasy lovers. I explore storytelling like a rogue casing a dungeon, review movies, books, and games, and dish out writing tips like a chaotic-good bard with a grudge against bad prose. No spam, just good stuff.

Join the quest:
https://rollfornarrative.parrydox.com

For my Rae, always.

Dramatis Personae

KNIGHT CHEVALIER GENEVE

Geneve serves the Three: Cophine, Ikmae, and Khiton. She is a Knight Chevalier, master of the Storm.

She knows the heft of Requiem better than the lines on her palm, but the demands of the Tresward now seem foreign. Her order commands death to sorcerers, but her dearest friend is one of their kind.

Geneve will use her blade, and the Storm inside her, to protect the innocent, and hold the guilty to account. She only need work out which is which.

MERIWETHER DU REEVES

Meri has found a friend in the unlike-liest of people: a Tresward Knight.

His modest skills with illusion have stood them in good stead, but his journey isn't over. He will go with Geneve on her quest to uncover the rot within her order.

If the world gets saved on the way? So be it. But that's not why he's here. Red hair and a pure heart call to him. He used to be smarter than this.

It's time to stop doing the smart thing, and do the right thing instead.

SIGHT OF DAY

One of the secretive Feybrind, Sight of Day leaves his forest home on a mission to the human kingdom of Or'sen.

Skilled with a blade, bow, and wit, he is friend to all except the hated Vhemin. Sight of Day is a craftsman of great skill, whether making weapons or pancakes.

He has lived many years longer than even the oldest mayfly humans and Vhemin. The Feybrind can't talk, so he communicates with the People's beautiful handspeak.

ARMITAGE

Vhemin. Hunted. Hunter. That's Armitage.

Some jobs take longer than others. This one might take him the rest of his life. And that's fine, because his tribe's gone. Too brittle to find another, he'll stick around with the Knight, runt, and cat until the end comes.

He's got nothing better to do.

VERTILINE

Knight Chevalier Vertiline commands the Storm in one hand, the bitter whip of sarcasm in the other.

She's in the Tresward for the wrong reasons, but she's still the second best swordswoman the world has ever seen. If she can hold on to her courage, Vertiline might just stop stupid people from doing stupider things.

If not, well. She wasn't a proper Knight anyway.

Revelations

The lightning brought terror.

Omrar was on his way home from the town fountains. He'd collected water for tomorrow, the heavy pole holding jugs swaying across his shoulders. It didn't pay to linger or to look idle. Idleness was a sin. It wasn't healthy to appear sinful, so he carried his water with short, hurried steps. His eyes were down, measuring his tread on the smooth, worn stones paving the streets of Imshir.

Sinning was rife, if the Arm were to be believed. It was the cause of all wrongdoing in society, and the Arm made sure everyone knew it was sinners that stole the moons from the sky. The Three had watched Omrar for as long as he could remember, but now ... they were gone. The Arm's watches tripled. People were dragged from their homes, strung up in the town square in front of the temple, and flayed alive before the baleful gaze of the Precept. His neighbor Lily, who supplied Omar's store with fresh bread, had been missing for two days. He'd heard screams in the night, and her ovens were quiet and cold the next morning.

So: water, quick steps, and straight home. Omrar remembered when the fountain held the sound of laughter along with splashing water. *That happened a lifetime ago. Or to another, in a different life. This life is fear.*

A rumble made him pause. It sounded like what came after lightning, but the sky held no flash. He looked toward Heaven's Gate. The mighty mountain shouldered the sky to the north. It was a natural wall against invaders, its rugged slopes vigilant but friendly. The setting sun left the mountain half in shadow, half-baked by waning rays.

Rumbling came again, longer and louder, and *then* came the flash. Not a simple lightning strike, but a pillar of twisting, incandescent light. It hammered the side of Heaven's Gate, rock exploding into the sky. From this distance they looked like slow-tossed pebbles, but Omrar knew the stones to be big as houses. The lightning wasn't a simple strike, one and done. The cloudless sky unleashed fury in a twisting column for ten seconds before stopping.

The town answered with screams of panic and the metal clamor of an alarm. The Arm were mobilizing, and being on the street—even with water for his store—wasn't a good idea. Omrar didn't want to tangle with the Arm. He had no wish to know firsthand what happened to Lily.

She made such good bread.

People emerged from their houses, some at street level, others on the rooftop gardens Imshir was famous for. All eyes were turned toward Heaven's Gate. Most had missed the cascade of rocks, but none could mistake the gout of lava that spewed forth from the mountain's side, as if the earth was injured and magma its lifeblood.

The rumble sounded again. Somehow smaller, but no less ominous. A second twisting pillar of lightning reached down, striking north of Heaven's Gate. The destruction it wrought was hidden by the mountain. Omrar clenched his teeth and put his back into the task of hurrying home. *The streets aren't safe. They were* never *safe, but the Arm will be looking for sinners to blame. I'm no sinner, but I'm ... convenient.*

Omrar had a small business that sold food, but no powerful family, or patrons in the Precept's palace. He knew if someone needed to die to appease the people, or the gods, he'd do just fine.

His store was the ground level of his home. The whole affair was a simple three-story building surrounded by adobe walls as tall as a man. The garden out the back held the day's laundry. Omrar imagined what the clean white cotton would smell like, or the coarseness of linen sheets against his skin. *Move, old man, or you'll never enjoy simple pleasures like folding washing again.*

The pole across his shoulders rattled against the chains suspending jugs of water. He should just leave it, but he needed the water. A man could be judged for sinning by inaction as much as the wrong action. Wasting water was a crime against the gods. Imshir was a paradise in a wasteland of desert, and the gods' gift shouldn't be wasted. So, he kept his burden, and hurried as best his old, bent frame could manage.

He was four blocks from home when a third rumble broke the air. Omrar managed to ignore the sounds of screaming as citizens cried panic or were dragged away by the Arm, but there was no ignoring the thunderous tolling of heaven's bell. A third pillar of twisting fury lanced from the sky, this time hammering the ground no more than a block away.

Omrar was tossed from his feet, water urns breaking as they crashed against the ground. He landed on his hip, feeling a twinge of pain. The air tasted of burnt copper and rage, as if the gods were accusing all Imshir of crimes unimaginable. The lightning twisted and curled, stealing away Omrar's sight with night-blindness. A fourth rumble sounded, and despite not seeing it, he *felt* the lightning impact. His body bounced, and he cried out.

Then, it was done. His hearing was gone as was his vision in the wake of the gods' might. He pawed across the ground, dragging himself to the side of the street as near as memory could guide him. *Please let me see. Please, just a glimpse of color.* There was no place in Imshir for the broken, the frail, or the helpless. There was barely enough space for a tired old man. He felt sick, desperate, his heart laboring like the old workhorse he was.

In fits and starts his hearing came back. The bells of alarm, overlaid by the hammer of horse's hooves drawing closer. His vision came back as splotches first, then a blurred image of the street, like an artist's watercolor, but drawn from a memory of a long time ago.

A contingent of the Arm cantered past, the metal shoes of horse's hooves sparking the cobbles a meter from Omrar's face. He scuttled back, drew his knees close, and urged his old body upright. It obeyed, but not without complaint. The Arm continued on past toward the lightning strike's site.

I should go. Get more water, or just get gone. Omrar knew the wisdom of a hasty retreat, but couldn't turn away. Before the gods stole his vision for a moment, he could've sworn the lightning brought something with it.

I saw someone come down in that pillar of fire. A person, even a godly one, might need help.

It was old habit talking. Time spent in the Arm before they'd passed from law to disorder, after the Precept took the good things from Imshir and bottled them inside his palace. But habit wouldn't be ignored. *I couldn't help Lily. Perhaps I can help ... whomever this is. A castoff from heaven will find no help from the Arm.*

Omrar hurried down the block, journeyed west for another, and rounded the corner to see a crater torn from the bedrock of Imshir. No one stood by, because unlike Omrar no one was stupid enough to go where the Arm would follow. He scuttled toward the crater. It was perhaps twenty meters across. The heat was intense, the ground flickering with tiny flames as released gasses caught. There was nobody here.

The crater destroyed the whole width of the street. The lightning caved in the wall of a house to the east and destroyed a wall to the west. That way Omrar caught movement. A figure, hunched low, daring a backward glance. His eyes weren't working well enough to make out more than semi-imagined details.

Omrar tried to follow as fast as his old bones would allow. He hobbled around the smoldering crater, heading after the figure. He passed through the broken fence and through a smoking garden. Ahead a gate banged closed, beckoning him on. *Old man, you should run, and not after that figure. I should get away before the Arm arrives.*

His feet didn't obey. It was as if they said, *What if the storm brought terror, but for the Arm? What if the figure is sent to save Imshir?*

"Stupid feet." Hand on the gate, he paused, listening. Horses drew closer, and with them, the harsh sound of men's voices raised in anger, fear, or the heady mix of both that would drive one to unthinking madness. He looked at his sandals. "Feet, stop talking and start hurrying."

Omrar made it through the gate into a small garden typical of Imshir. Stone fruit trees vied with ground vegetation. He spied turnips, and what might have been silverbeet, but he hated the stuff. He helped himself to a date no one would miss and pushed through the gloom. The garden was fenced like the rest, encircling this little Eden. A two-story house waited to the north. A line holding linens swayed.

There is no wind.

He headed for the line. A gap in the laundry the width of a large shawl or small sheet showed the figure's intent. *Camouflage.* The back-door was locked. He wondered where the figure got to when a strong grip spun him about.

He was faced with a woman. Her skin was lighter than his. Not white like ghosts and the ridiculous savages from Or'sen, but not the earthy tone he'd carried all his span. Green eyes hard as emeralds watched him. Young. Barely twenty summers, if that, but those green eyes held cares and demons aplenty. Her hair was red, perhaps dyed, cut short, but not short enough for modesty in Imshir. She wore the missing sheet, wrapped like a toga about shoulders that were broad and strong. Her hand didn't leave his arm, but neither did she use her obvious strength to push him around.

Her voice was even, calm, like riding lightning was a thing she did each Tuesday, right before lunch. She spoke, voice rising at the end in a question. The language was beautiful, melodic, and unfamiliar.

"I don't know what that means." Omrar shifted, nervous, but curious. He'd never met a god before. "Did you come with the lightning?" He pointed above.

Another series of words, cut short as she spun at something crunching beyond the gate. It gave him time to think. He recognized a word.

"Trebani? Yes, this is the Empire." He shook his head. "It's seen better days." Then he realized what shaking his head meant and nodded. "This is Trebani."

Her eyes narrowed. Another question in that gentle, soft language.

The gate he'd come through crashed aside, and the Arm walked in. Three were burly men, the fourth a slender woman with officer's banding on her arm. They saw Omrar, then the woman in the sheet. The officer's eyes narrowed. "Sin."

"It's hardly a sin for someone to be lost and alone." Omrar snapped his mouth shut, unsure of where the words came from.

The officer's face twisted to a sneer. "Old man, we'll deal with you in a minute. Take her. The Precept wants a word."

Her three men marched forward, curved blades coming from their sheaths. The green-eyed woman pulled Omrar behind her, then strode to meet them. Omrar goggled. *She has no armor. By the will of the gods, she wears a* sheet. *No blade's in her hand. She's going to die. The savior from the heavens will bleed out in this nice yet small and insignificant garden.*

She took two more steps while his brain tried to keep up. *I should help. I should get in there and do* something. *I used to be good at this, but all I'm good for now is making other people lunch.*

The green-eyed woman didn't care what he used to be good at. She stepped for the first of her attackers, hands wide, stance lowering. The blade hungered for her neck, but somehow she wasn't there anymore. Omrar wondered if it were his eyes still not working right, because she didn't seem to step, but rather flow. A hint of a golden luminance dogged her heels as she stepped behind the man.

He spun to follow her, but she hadn't finished moving. The gods-warrior made the officer, taking the woman's sword before she'd drawn it half-way. Whoever this Three-given fighter was, she didn't waste time with the monkey, going straight for the organ grinder. Officer's saber in hand, she kicked the woman in the gut, then spun back to her original attacker.

Or not. The green-eyed woman didn't look where she was going. Her sword seemed to guide itself, swinging an arc that glittered gold. *Wait, what? The saber is steel. Not brass or bronze. I'm going to die here, but I'm going blind first!*

The blade took the arms off her assailant, the sword meeting no resistance. It didn't make sense. No Arm blade was sharp enough to shave with, and she worked it one-handed. The sword cut through steel-banded armor, flesh, and bone as fast and slick as his own pairing knives dealt with tomatoes.

Like tomatoes, red gushed, and she moved again. The blade swung about, taking the head from the second man, who'd only just begun to register what his comrade's screams meant. Startled eyes stared at Omrar from the ground where his head landed, before life's light left them.

The third Arm, perhaps unused to seeing two of the Precept's best killed in less than five seconds by a previously unarmed woman in a sheet, checked himself. The officer looked about to move, so the green-eyed woman kicked her in the stomach without turning, as a mule might. The officer dropped, the air going out of her like it had better places to be. The green-eyed woman held her stolen saber cross-guard, waiting.

The last Arm lunged, and lost his hand for his troubles. He grabbed the stump, trying to stop the fountain of blood coming from it. Shock or blood loss took their toll and he sank to his knees, to be run through with the saber.

The gods-sent woman turned to the officer. She asked a question, her tone hard.

"You will die, and it won't be a good death," the officer wheezed.

Green eyes flashed, lips pressed in a line. More words, but one repeated more than others: *Meri*. A weapon? A person? Perhaps a place? Omrar knew of nothing wearing that moniker.

The officer tried to regain her feet. The gods-warrior let her, blade never wavering. "I swear by the gods you will die."

The saber flashed, and the officer fell, but in two places, sheared from shoulder, through ribcage, and out the other side. Another sentence, this one final, but also forgiving.

Omrar looked at the bodies, and listened for horses. He stole another sheet, moving toward the gods-warrior. "Here." She spun, blade ready. Omrar held his distance. "Your clothing, uh, sheet. It's covered in blood. This one isn't." He offered the sheet again. She looked to it, then her own, and nodded. More words, Meri repeated again, and again. It was unlikely Meri was a clothier, so... "Meri's a friend of yours?"

She touched her chest, over her heart. Omrar understood. "We best get you off the streets. If Meri is precious to you, the Arm will find him, and they will use him to break you."

The green-eyed warrior looked to the sky, then tossed her saber aside. Omrar led them from the garden, and to home.

Chapter One

"What do you mean, they're gone?" A vein on the side of Heser the Cheg's temple throbbed, angry and insistent.

Vertiline almost rolled her eyes. It was only through years of Tresward training that kept her face in check. If that kind of emotion ran rampant, she'd not be great at sword-fighting. *And if I roll my eyes, they'll spin so much I'll tumble across this fine throne room floor.*

The throne room was like it'd been the day before, except there was no Geneve, and no Meriwether either. The sinner had grown on her, but Tilly worried for her sister in battle. Not because a single day had passed without her. *I'm concerned she's dead. I'm worried she's done something stupid, because she's young, and when I was her age I signed up for a life of service to the Tresward, which was a terrible idea.*

In the throne room was the usual suspects. Morgan was on her throne, leaning head against hand, eyes closed in a way that suggested a migraine. Vertiline knew *exactly* how she felt. Picotee lounged in a chair toward the back of the room, eyes locked on the ceiling, the very picture of *this is a boring conversation*. Eyeballing Heser the Cheg was Armitage. The monster—

He's not a monster.

The Vhemin hadn't been himself since the battle. The injury he'd sustained left him moving with great care, as an ancient man might. Tilly had seen men hurt before, and what happened to Armitage wasn't a thing you walked off. Yet he walked, a challenge to common wisdom, and was spoiling for a fight, despite looking like his spine was a single piece of wood that didn't flex.

Sight of Day stood with hands clasped, golden eyes bright and patient. Morning Song was by his side, her emerald eyes brilliant. A scattering of Queensguard held attention by the queen, most of their focus on Barret, who looked like she had zero fucks to give.

Heser the Cheg was making a great show of being distressed, but Vertiline didn't understand why. Vertiline cleared her throat. *Better jump in before this takes up more time in my life I'll never get back.* "I don't see why you're upset."

Heser the Cheg, about to burst into another tirade, checked himself. "Because the Savior of Ravenswall is missing."

"Don't forget the runt," Armitage said. "He's important."

That vein on Heser the Cheg's temple pulsed again. "He's not—"

"He's not *here*." Vertiline's hand found the hilt of her sword, not because she wanted to skewer Heser the Cheg, but because swords were useful in conflicts, and this felt like one of those. "He is also the person who suggested she," Tilly pointed at Barret, "take your job, and the cat," her finger wandered toward Morning Song, "corrupt your intelligence network from within."

Heser the Cheg's mouth opened and closed a couple times before he found his mental footing. "What?"

"At least, that's what you're thinking." Vertiline's fingers tapped a casual medley on her pommel. "Without Lord du Reeves you might stand a chance of getting your job back, protecting your queen, and getting all the non-human interfering scum out of the throne room. It won't work."

Queen Morgan looked up at this. Face framed by raven locks, eyes like glass, voice like the hush before an earthquake. "It won't?"

"No." Vertiline sighed. "The sinner's worthless with a sword. He can barely run a block before his breath gives out. His magic is border-line useless. But what he's good at is *thinking*. He's already worked out there's a bunch of assholes," her arm pointed to a window, through which a shaft of sunlight bravely tried to face her, "out there, trying to get us killing each other, rather than killing them. So, if we get rid of the Vhemin and the Feybrind, we're on our own. Worse, we'll spend time murdering each other instead of the people who *deserve* murder. I've no time for that kind of lunacy."

The queen looked slightly put out, as if she'd been thinking along the lines of getting her kingdom back under lock and key and didn't like being called a lunatic. "There are other ways we can do this without positions of power being in the hands of, of..."

"Say it," Vertiline encouraged. "You know you want to."

"The enemy?" Heser the Cheg's voice held a questioning tone, like his eyes saw a trap but his brain hadn't interfered fast enough, lips already on their way to saying something stupid.

"The enemy who saved us all." Vertiline nodded. "The cats held the waterfront. They died in hundreds they couldn't afford there, on the battlefield proper, and all through the streets. The Vhemin fell in far greater numbers, some under the command of an evil man, others trying to get a little payback. All of us," she touched her chest above her heart, "practiced *dying* while others cackled in glee. If you're," she swung toward Morgan, who looked agitated enough to interrupt, "thinking of reverting to tradecraft with people who never responded when the need was dire, what do you think will be different this time? The lords will return with hugs and flowers?"

"Keep a civil tongue in your head," Heser the Cheg warned. "You address the Queen of Or'sen."

Vertiline snorted. "I've got no quarrel with her majesty, but she and I both know the Tresward don't bend the knee. This isn't about me versus the kingdom. Don't you see? That's the whole point. You've a Tresward Chevalier here, getting involved in *politics*," she spat the word, "because this is bigger than any faction. It's all of us."

"All of us, or none of us." Morgan nodded. "We agree."

Heser the Cheg frowned, stroking his chin. "Your Majesty—"

"Not today, Heser the Cheg." Morgan stood. "Picotee du Parneer, your queen needs you."

Picotee jerked upright. "You what?"

Morgan clapped her hands. "Find them. All available ships. I need to know where the Savior of Ravenswall is."

"To ... bring her back?" Picotee guessed.

The queen offered the eye-roll Vertiline had been dying to make. "No. So we can help them." Morgan turned to Morning Song. "Isn't that right?"

{Don't bring me into this.} Morning Song tried to slink back, but Sight of Day put a gentle, anchoring hand on her shoulder. It didn't look welcome.

"Tell us what you heard."

"I thought there were no witnesses," Heser the Cheg said.

"The reason I called you here was my spymaster woke me at an hour that is frankly impolite." Morgan smoothed her gown. "She witnessed everything."

{I wouldn't be a good spymaster otherwise.} Morning Song's emerald eyes found the floor, as if realizing she'd just formally accepted her new job. *{The dragon said they were going to where the demons were strongest.}*

"Then we need to get there too," Armitage said. "I don't like the idea of Geneve getting all those kills without us."

Sight of Day blinked. *{That was your outside voice.}*

"What's your point, cat?"

Vertiline cleared her throat. "We've got work to do, then."

Picotee tried to feign disinterest, but it didn't stick. "Doing what?"

"Barret, for recruits." Tilly swung her gaze to the Lady du Parneer. "Picotee for ships. Maybe the Tresward, to see if they can spare glass or steel. Lords and ladies. Barkeeps and weavers. We will go everywhere, and we'll do it fast."

Armitage winced. "There doesn't sound like there's a lot of room for food and booze on this trip. What makes you think the Tresward will help? Or Barret? Or the sea-bitch?"

"Watch it." Picotee's tone turned ominous. "It's easy to fall overboard, and the embrace of sea is mighty cold."

"Sounds just like your—"

"Anyway," Vertiline clapped her hands. "Let's get on."

Sight of Day stroked his chin. *{What makes you think anyone will help us?}*

"They're a part of this world too. We all face the same demons. And ... they owe us." Tilly looked at her feet. "Or Geneve. No one in this world is where they are without her. Not the queen." Morgan nodded. "Not the Tresward. And definitely not the sea-bi—"

"I get it," Picotee growled.

Vertiline touched her temple in salute, then strode for the door. She allowed herself the guilty pleasure of a small smile, feeling a spring in her step. *I forgot what my old family was like, but my new one is ... better?* "Heser the Cheg's not going to have *all* the fun."

Chapter Two

When Meriwether woke, he wished he hadn't.

If he were Armitage, he'd have said his mouth tasted of ash and ass. Geneve might have winced and stood up, but otherwise walked it off. He could imagine Vertiline holding up her metal hand, the gift given at agony's knifepoint, asking him, *Do you think it hurt more than this?*

Sight of Day might have given him a hug, then said, *{Get a grip.}*

He was alone, which made everything worse. *We were supposed to check out a platform, then fly back for a quiet night's rest.* Meriwether found himself on the ground, coarse and unyielding. Tiny pebbles scratched his skin, some sharp as knives but of a size fairies might use. The ground wasn't the type he was used to, with grass, or even sand beneath him. There was no convenient boulder to use as shelter from the sun.

Meriwether lay in a curved hollow set in the ground. It sloped evenly from all sides to meet him at the center, or bottom, depending on your point of view. The surface of the ground was worn smooth like the inside of a shield. The tiny pieces stabbing him mercilessly were chips of a glass-like material. It looked like he'd landed in a crater caused by great heat, every surface sloughed to a smoother, less definite form.

Also, he was naked.

Meriwether eased himself to his feet. A mountain lay to the south. It looked high enough to dissuade the casual climber, but didn't seem studded with cliffs or other unforgiving bastions. He scratched his back. "If I had to guess, where I need to go is on the other side of that huge hill."

A bird chirped from its vantage point of a low tree, but no one else seemed to be about to voice an opinion on the matter. Meriwether climbed out of the scorched depression in the earth, stretched, and looked around.

Grass, the odd tree, and no one for miles. The grass wasn't healthy, most of it dry and withered. Between the clumps of mostly-dead foliage lay rock and sand, which explained why he'd found himself stabbed by glass. *Take sand and enough heat, and glass is the eventual product.* He sighed, eying the mountain. *Maybe I should get it over with. Just climb it. I know I'll need to be on the other side, because it's the hardest place to get to.*

The smart regals said he'd be better off finding clothes first, and maybe a horse. But even before that, he needed to find a huge dragon and what was no doubt a very angry, red-headed Tresward Knight. If everyone arrived in a pit of fire without clothes, the people who first met her better be polite.

His mouth quirked into a grin as he thought of Geneve. Meriwether wasn't worried about her. Of the three people the ancient device transported to whatever-this-place-is-called, she was the best equipped to deal with demons, sword-wielding maniacs, or ancient terrors of the world. The dragon would probably be fine. *Truth, but I should be worried about myself.*

He squared off against the bird, which returned his regard with head cocked. "But I'm not. Worried, I mean. I'm in a place I've never seen with no clothes. I don't even have the book of High Magic. I should be terrified, but..." The bird hopped to the left on its branch, watching him. *But I'm not scared. I'm ... free.*

He didn't recognize this land at all. Not the mountain, the plains, or what looked like the shimmer of sea to the west. Which meant the land didn't recognize him either. No one knew the du Reeves name. Unlikely they'd heard of Leander, and the merciless crimes he'd perpetrated on the Kingdom of Or'sen. *Maybe they don't have Vhemin, Feybrind, or the endless war between us all. Could be a nice place to settle down. Now, if only I could find the dragon.*

A dragon seemed the best thing to aim for. "Giant flying lizard. Can't miss it." He turned another slow circle but saw no dragon. *Maybe Ormeon's on the wing.* He looked up, but didn't see a dragon there either. Something that looked like a vulture circled, but he didn't look near dead enough for it to come closer. "Ormeon!"

Nothing.

Clothes, then. He closed his eyes for a moment, concentrating. When he opened them, he was attired in his usual garments. A cloak about his shoulders, a shirt—complete with sword rent—above pants and boots. None of it was real, but it meant if he came across anyone other than a bird they probably wouldn't murder him for perversion. Foreign customs were tricky to navigate.

Meriwether walked in widening circles from his crater, trying to find any sign of ... anything, really. Aside from his feet getting sore, because walking on gravel, hot sand, and rock without shoes wasn't the easiest thing in the world, nothing changed. No Geneve, and no Ormeon either. No craters showing where they might have landed. Just the damn bird, which didn't seem concerned about him anymore. It followed him as he walked, moving from its original branch to another tree as he paced.

Time to get to the mountain. Meriwether faced the tree-studded edifice and set out. He took it slow, his desire to hurry, thus avoiding sunburn, governed by the beating his feet got. The bird kept pace well enough. It was small, about the size of his clenched fist, with bright-blue feathers covering everything except its chest, which was white, and around its eyes, which were a bright green. He had no idea what kind of bird it was, but it didn't have a poisonous barbed tail or breathe fire, so pretty much he was good with it following him.

The mountain drew closer by degrees. He smelled woodsmoke, and oriented himself slightly west, the breeze from that direction guiding him in. He walked until he found a small decline, too modest to call itself a hill to anyone but its friends. At the hill's bottom was a hut about ten meters a side, well built from long planks that might have been cedar. A fire pit lay beside it. The flames barbecued what looked like human bodies. Two Vhemin stood next to the fire, eating from skewers and warming themselves.

So much for no Vhemin. Meriwether backed up, nice and slow, right to the point where he hit something. He glanced over his shoulder at another Vhemin. The monster was about a head taller than him, and twice as broad in the shoulders. It wore half armor like a gladiator might, or someone who liked to show off their massive chest and ripped abdomen, which the creature had in spades.

"Hello," Meriwether said.

The monster slugged him in the side of the head, then tossed him over its shoulder. It walked to its fellows at the bottom of the not-quite-a-hill, tossing him to the ground beside the fire pit. It pulled out a wicked-looking knife about the length of Meriwether's forearm, curved in a way that promised it would hurt more than the regulation amount if it entered your gut. The Vhemin's friends grinned their shark-toothed smiles, snake eyes bright and feral.

"I see you're not up with the play. Allow me to explain." Meriwether curled over with a gasp as the monster kicked him in the gut. "Please. Let me explain," he wheezed.

The monster growled words in an unfamiliar tongue, brows furrowed in confusion.

"Right," Meriwether said. "The thing is, we're not at war with the Vhemin anymore. Big battle, lots of arrows and swords, and yes, there was a dragon, and demons too. After that, we decided murdering each other wasn't as useful as murdering the demons. Did no one tell you?"

The Vhemin pursed his lips, thinking hard. More incomprehensible babble. It sounded like Tebrani, if you sieved out the meaning and left nothing but swearing and death threats.

"No idea," Meriwether admitted. "But I think we should come to an accord before you die." The monster gave a guttural sigh, almost a snarl, then readied its knife, perhaps to plunge it into Meriwether's heart. "Don't say I didn't warn you."

Ormeon the Redeemer landed with a jarring *whump* that toppled the three Vhemin from their feet. She snatched the one with the knife in a clawed hand, raising the struggling figure to her jaw. She *crunched*, juices squirting, then chewed twice before swallowing. *//HOW DID YOU GET YOURSELF IN TROUBLE SO QUICKLY?//*

The other two Vhemin bolted. She whipped her tail around, swatting one into a smear, then snatched the other and gobbled it in three bites.

"Well. To be fair, it's been some hours since I woke." He blanched. "Do you have to chew so loudly?"

//THESE VHEMIN ARE FOR EATING.//

"Sure, help yourself." Meriwether stood, dusting himself off before remembering he wore no actual clothes. "Why am I naked?"

//BECAUSE NOTHING WORKS ANYMORE.// Ormeon sighed like a windstorm. *//WE'VE MORE IMPORTANT THINGS TO WORRY ABOUT. I CAN'T SEE THE DRAGONRIDER.//*

Meriwether felt his heart stumble. "What do you mean?"

//I MEAN, SHE'S GONE FROM MY SIGHT. ALWAYS I CAN SEE HER, BUT NOT NOW.// Ormeon crouched low. *//COME. THERE'S AN OLD TEMPLE ABOVE. WE CAN GET YOU SOME PANTS.//*

FLYING THE DRAGON WITHOUT GENEVE WASN'T EASY. NOT THAT Ormeon did anything *wrong*, per se, just that … well, Geneve was something to hold onto. Without her, his hands tried to grip Ormeon's scaled hide, with varying levels of success ranging from *By the Three, I'm going to die* through to *I might just be getting the hang of this.*

"Tell me why you don't have a saddle!" Meriwether hollered over the wind.

//TELL ME WHY YOU'RE NAKED.// The dragon gave him an over-the-shoulder emberfire smile. *//I THINK I GET THE WORSE PART OF THE DEAL.//*

"How so?"

//I'M NOT RUBBING MY JUNK ON YOUR NECK.//

"Fair point." Meriwether might look like he was clothed, but there was nothing really there except a few stray moonbeams and a little imagination.

The dragon banked around the mountain's crown, her wings dipping to afford Meriwether a stomach-clenching view of trees and rocks below. A massive crater sat like an old wound in the mountain's side. Scattered about, looking like charred pebbles at this distance, were huge rocks. A massive, burned stretch lay like a river of ash down the mountain's flank.

I wonder what happened there?

//I HAPPENED,// Ormeon said.

"Are you reading my mind?"

//DID GENEVE NOT EXPLAIN THIS TO YOU? IT'S NOT MIND READING. IT'S ... NEVER MIND. YES, I'M READING YOUR MIND.// She descended toward a vertical basalt slab of rock, leaving Meriwether's stomach in the clouds above. Ormeon extended her feet, landing with a crunch Meriwether would feel in his spine for months.

"Nice landing."

She snaked her head around. *//WOULD YOU LIKE TO WALK HOME NEXT TIME?//*

"I said it was a nice landing!" Meriwether slid from her back, trying not to cause undue injury to himself.

//I'M READING YOUR MIND.// The dragon pointed a clawed hand at the basalt surface before them. *//BEHOLD.//*

Meriwether walked toward it, shoring up with his hands on hips about ten meters back. "It's a nice piece of rock. A little weathered, I'll allow, but with a certain," he waved his hand, "striation that lends character."

//I DON'T KNOW WHY SHE KEEPS YOU AROUND.// Ormeon dipped her head to be next to his. *//THIS IS THE DOORWAY TO AN ANCIENT TEMPLE.//*

"It's not a temple. The ancients didn't really have temples." Meriwether scratched his beard which, unlike his clothes, was real.

//COPHINE GRANT ME GRACE.// Ormeon closed her eyes, sighing a great dragony sigh. *//I KNOW THAT. BUT YOUR PRIMI-*

TIVE FORM OF REFERENCE THINKS ABOUT TEMPLES, SO IT'S A TEMPLE.//

"What is it? Really, I mean." Meriwether put his hand on the stone surface. It felt old, as old as time itself. "Like, what did they call it?"

Ormeon gave him a little side-eye. *//THEY CALLED THIS PLACE SAFE. HOME. HAVEN FROM PERSECUTION.//*

"And they died?"

//AND THEY ALL DIED,// she confirmed. *//TO YOU, IT'S A TEMPLE. FULL OF WONDERS AND HORRORS. I'M ALSO CONFIDENT THERE WILL BE PANTS OF MANY SIZES INSIDE.//*

"Cool," Meriwether said. "How do we get it open?"

//IT SHOULD HAVE OPENED ALREADY.// Ormeon's voice held doubt. *//I AM A DRAGON.//*

"You say that like dragons can go anywhere."

She turned ruby-red eyes on him. *//DRAGONS CAN GO PRETTY MUCH ANYWHERE.//*

"Another fair point." Meriwether's hand strayed to his belt, where the tome of High Magic used to sit. The clutch was a nervous tic, nothing more. He'd memorized it. Remembering every symbol was different to understanding them, though. "The ancients would have a code word."

//THIS IS NOT A FORT CHILDREN PLAY IN.//

"Work with me here."

//THEY WOULDN'T HAVE HAD A CODE WORD. THE TEMPLE KNEW THEM FROM THE SMALLEST PARTS THEY WERE MADE FROM. CODE WORDS CAN BE STOLEN, BUT WHAT MAKES YOU REAL CAN'T BE FORGED ANYWHERE EXCEPT THE HEART OF A STAR.// Ormeon nudged the basalt with her nose. Aside from a grating noise, nothing happened.

"You mean, demons can't get inside?" Meriwether nodded. "Makes sense. They couldn't get into the place you were... made, either." He sniffed, remembering Tristan, and Geneve's love for the horse.

//HE WAS A GOOD MOUNT. I DIDN'T WANT HIM TO DIE.//

"I know, beastie. Anyway. The last temple opened to Red and me without any trouble. Like it knew us."

//IT KNEW THE RECIPE-MAKERS. ONE DRAGONRIDER,

ONE HOLOMANCER.// She sat on her haunches. //IT WAS MADE FOR YOU, SO YOU COULD MAKE ME.//

"What was this one made for?"

//KILLING DEMONS.//

"Good talk." Meriwether crouched beside the cliff face, examining it. His inner eye could make out no magic. Nothing barred their path except good, honest rock. Movement caught his eye as the bright-blue bird landed to his right. It cocked its head at him. "Hello, bird."

The dragon looked at the bird. //THAT'S NOT A BIRD.//

"It looks like a bird." Meriwether held up his hand. "I know, I know. It's probably a death-dealing horror. Capable of killing ten men with a single chirp."

//IT'S NOT A DEATH-DEALING HORROR. I'VE CORNERED THAT MARKET.// Ormeon slunk behind Meriwether, nosing toward the bird. For its part, the bird didn't fly away in terror as Meriwether expected. //HELLO, BUILDER.//

Meriwether scoffed. "It's a *bird*."

//IT CAN OPEN THE TEMPLE.// Ormeon stared at the bird, the blue-feathered creature staring right back. //YOU DIDN'T ALWAYS WANT TO LOOK LIKE THIS, DID YOU?//

The bird shook its head. Meriwether took a step back. "It understood you?"

//I CAN BE VERY PERSUASIVE.//

"I mean ... your words." Meriwether crouched down, hand out to the bird. It eyed his fingers with more suspicion than it had Ormeon's maw. "Come on, friend."

Meriwether could've sworn it rolled its eyes, but it bounced closer, then flitted to his hand. Two small claws gripped his finger. He held it up to his eye line. "Where'd you come from, then?" It looked at the rock face, then back to him. "In there? But this has been sealed for..." *Hundreds of years*, he thought. *This bird doesn't look a day over thirty*.

//EIGHT HUNDRED YEARS OR'SEN HAS BEEN WITHOUT THE THREE'S GRACE.// Ormeon chuffed. //THE NOT-BIRD IS VERY WELL PRESERVED.//

"I'll admit, an eight-hundred-year-old bird is cool and all, but how does it open the temple?" Meriwether winced. "Sorry. I don't mean to imply you're a tool ... oh, Ikmae's sometime balls. I'm talking to a *bird*."

//PERHAPS YOU SHOULD ASK THE NOT-A-BIRD TO HELP.//

"Okay. Bird, can you open the door?" The bird cocked its head, turning a beady black eye in his direction before alighting and flitting to the door. It touched it with a bright blue wing, then returned to Meriwether's finger.

All three looked at the rock face expectantly. *//I ADMIT, I EXPECTED SOMETHING IMPRESSIVE.//*

"Maybe eight hundred years as a bird has taken some of the magic out?" The bird chirped, a tiny angry sound, then it flitted to touch the basalt again. With a groan like the sound of an earthquake, the basalt cracked down the center. Dust rained, causing Meriwether to cough and squint. The doorway opened wider, showing ... darkness. Meriwether cleared his throat. "I bet there are a lot of spiders in there."

Ormeon chuckled like a thunderstorm. *//THERE ARE WORSE THINGS THAN SPIDERS.//* She shuffled into the entrance.

Meriwether watched her hindquarters for a moment. "You think that's supposed to make me feel better?"

//IF IT HELPS, I THINK IT MORE LIKELY THAN EVER PANTS ARE TO BE FOUND WITHIN.//

The bird flitted from Meriwether's finger to his shoulder. He barely felt its weight, but the sharpness of its claws pricked his skin through his illusory shirt. "Pants would be good," he allowed. "Come on, bird. Stop holding me back."

With a glance at the sun, as if hoping to memorize it in case he never saw it again, Meriwether stepped into the dark maw of another temple of the ancients.

Chapter Three

Geneve wished Meri were here. She felt his absence like the ache of a pulled tooth. Something was missing in her life, and the hole left nothing but pain. Which meant she needed to find out where he was, and how to keep him safe. Problem was, Geneve wasn't sure where *here* was, let alone where Meri could be. Or Ormeon for that matter, but the dragon wasn't the sort to need concern.

The moons were missing. Gone, ever since she'd killed the demon Ahkiban and his summonings. *And I used a dragon's demand to pull my love back to me. Was that wrong? Did I break the rules, causing the Three to turn their faces from the world?*

It didn't feel right, not least of which because life went on. Wherever *here* was, folk might have skin of a darker hue to hers, but they ate and slept just like everyone else. And they lived in fear of tyrants.

The old man who'd taken her in was kind. She'd felt his well-meaning intent like the heat of old coals nearing the end of life. Geneve felt he must have served before the world beat it out of him, metal over-tempered in a too-hot forge. Omrar wasn't made of Tresward Smithsteel, or too many things had been alloyed with his basic nature for him to raise his eyes in challenge anymore.

That didn't stop him trying, in his small way.

He'd taken her to a house set above a small shop. Delicious smells lingered in his store. A frontage with glass cabinets would offer tasty wares to hungry patrons. A kitchen at the back held ovens and big hearths. Geneve remembered huge Tresward kitchens feeding hungry Knights, and Omrar's establishment looked similar. He'd make bread, perhaps, or cake, alongside more savory things.

Narrow steps at the rear wound to living quarters spanning the levels above. The floor was old, well-worn wood. Furnishings were modest, tired even, but kept with care that suggested Omrar hoped for more visitors than he got. The first level was a space where a person could take tea, coffee, or whatever passed for that here. He didn't take Geneve to the upper floor, shaking his head, eyes down when she pointed.

It's his bedroom, then. And he doesn't want me to get the wrong idea.

Geneve liked Omrar even more for that small courtesy offered across language barriers. She imagined Meri might have the same foresight, and it made her worry for him even more. Omrar came down from the top level with blankets and pillows, pointed her to a worn-comfortable divan, and left her for the night.

She shouldn't have slept, but she dropped into a dreamless slumber.

Morning came like it did in Or'sen—with a spread of sunlight, tossed like Cophine's blanket across the world. Soon enough Ikmae would barter the transition to Khiton's nightly shroud, and the cycle would begin again.

Will it? I can't see the Three watching from above anymore.

Geneve couldn't help but notice the smell of bread, drifting skyward on heavenly feet. She tossed off her blanket, finding clothes by the foot of the bed. They were cut in what would be a man's style in Or'sen, but the colors were strange. Pants of dark green, a shirt of faded red, and a dust-brown scarf she wasn't sure what to do with. She dressed. The clothes were a good enough fit across her shoulders and hips. She draped the scarf around her neck and headed downstairs. Her fingers itched for Requiem's hilt, but her skymetal sword hadn't been in the crater with her when she arrived. Neither was her armor, her scattergun, or glass shield. Whatever took her here stripped her back to her bare essence.

If an ancient device destroyed my sword, I will hunt its maker through time and end them. Requiem was a gift from a dear friend. The memories caught in its silver-bright length couldn't be replaced.

Noise greeted her in increasing waves as she went downstairs. The hustle of people, voices raised not in anger, but negotiation. She understood nothing of what was said, but her nose beckoned her on. The kitchen waited, but wasn't dormant like the night before. The ovens radiated heat, and large pots bubbled on the stovetops.

A covered plate was left beside a mug and pitcher of clear, cool water. Geneve whipped the cloth away, guzzled the water, then wolfed the food. Fresh flatbread and a spicy stew she couldn't place kept the beast from howling at the door. There wasn't a fork or knife, so she used the bread as a spoon. While she ate, she let her eyes roam the kitchen. A curtain separated it from the shop's front. Kitchen accoutrements were not in short supply, but she noted there were precious few knives. The serrated edge of a longer blade best used for carving loaves sat by a board, but the bright promise of flesh-cutting steel was hidden.

Either Omrar didn't want her using knives, or someone didn't want him having a weapon close to hand.

The curtain twitched aside, and Geneve was on her feet faster than thought. The plate was in her hand, cocked for a throw, mouth frozen mid-chew. Omrar goggled at her pose, and she wondered what she looked like. *Skin the color of amber honey, not the deeper luster of coffee. Plate held like a disc, eyes wild.* Geneve relaxed, setting the plate down. "Sorry."

Omrar bustled to her. He wore an apron, well cared for but worn like everything else. He touched her left hand, in which she still held bread. Omrar said something in that wonderful language of his, gently prizing her unwilling fingers from the bread, and transferring it to her right hand.

Right hands are for eating. Got it. "Thank you." She bobbed her head.

He smiled, and she felt the warmth of it, like sunlight creeping through a fog's shroud. He held his hands toward her scarf, then paused. More words she didn't understand.

He wants my permission for something. This old man is very careful not to touch me inappropriately—is he afraid of what I might do to him? No. He wouldn't have me if terror guided him. He's showing me courtesy his words can't. Geneve lowered the bread to the plate, then dropped her hands. "Please."

Omrar teased the scarf aside, shook it out, then put it over her head. He was gentle, the fabric not tight like a shroud. After a few turns, Geneve felt her head—and hair—were hidden from view. He spoke to her like a frightened animal while he worked. She caught just one word: *Tebrani.*

"I wish Meri were here. He has a gift with language." Geneve looked aside. "I lost him. We were together, then..." She trailed off, unsure of what happened. White, blinding light. A sense of speed, a rush so vast it felt impossible. Then she'd fallen, hitting the ground ... *here.* "I should go. It's not safe for you with me near. There are demons, Omrar."

The old man didn't seem to mind all this talk about demons or missing Meris. He nodded, smiling, busying himself with things to fetch or carry in the kitchen. Or he'd understood her meaning well enough, but knew there'd always been demons. Today wouldn't be any different.

Geneve sat, resuming her meal. She took care to use her right hand with the bread, removing the scarf so she wouldn't chew cotton with her breakfast. The stew was hearty but didn't seem to have meat in it. *It's no wonder Omrar is small and thin, if his people eat nothing but weeds.* She gritted her teeth. *I am a stranger here. Or'sen knows almost nothing of Tebrani. Listen. Watch. Try to help.*

She didn't know how long she sat in Omrar's kitchen with its delicious smells and comforting sounds, right up to the point where the sounds went away. They didn't trickle out with customers leaving the shop, but silenced as if sound came from a faucet and someone closed the tap. Geneve heard silence like that before. It was noise banished by fear.

A man's voice, harsh and loud, in Omrar's language. Then, a

woman, not as loud but with blades between her words, sharp and vicious. In the middle of her speech, one word rang out: *Tresward.*

She understood. They hunted *her*, and she'd brought them to Omrar's shop. Geneve wanted to stay, to find out who they were and how they knew her. To know her was to know her armor, and perhaps her blade, and she needed both. But this city didn't feel as kind as Omrar. There were no knives, even in a kitchen. People didn't run to help when disaster blasted lightning into the street. They ran, hiding, keeping faces from view.

To be here is to doom a kindly old man.

She slipped from her stool, then took her plate to the sink. She set her chair straight, as if no one were here at all, then swept out into Omrar's backyard. Geneve was blinded by the sun and squinted to make out details. No one stood in the yard waiting for escapees. *Good. They don't suspect Omrar; they're looking for me, but looking everywhere.* She slipped behind billowing white sheets, making the door to the back street beyond.

Tugging her scarf close to her face, she lifted the latch and stepped into chaos.

It felt like a thousand people walked the streets. Animals like horses with long necks pulled carts. Men and women shouted at each other with an urgency as if their single conversation would determine life and death. They used the melodic language Omrar introduced her to, but with more enthusiasm.

Geneve turned right, slipping into the flow of traffic, eyes down, but shoulders wide. She didn't know if green eyes were unusual. Omrar's were brown. But the one thing that marked sinners the world over was a furtive posture. *I should know. I hunted so very many of them.* It felt wrong to be on the other side of justice. The gods seemed fickle here, and someone who was less sure of their existence might have called them perverse.

Hells with it: they're perverse, all three of them. The moons are gone. Cophine, Ikmae, and Khiton no longer watch this world. It can't be my fault, can it?

She made good progress, Tresward training keeping her feet sure. Geneve dodged carts as one born to the streets. *I need to know if any follow me*. She took the next right down a narrow laneway between houses, then paused at the end. A glance left showed an armored pair exit a building that looked like a trader of something like coffee, their customers seated in tables out front with small cups beside them. Geneve glanced right toward Omrar's shop. A couple of soldiers exited, wearing the same armor as those at the coffee shop.

The same armor as those I killed last night.

Geneve noticed they each held a sheet of parchment, showing it to anyone without the sense to drift clear. *Perhaps it's a picture of me. No, that makes no sense. I left none alive to describe me.* She faded back into her alley as the woman's eyes swept the street.

As the pair headed further away, Geneve slipped back into the thoroughfare. Traffic here wasn't as strong as behind Omrar's store, either because it wasn't as busy, or because people feared the law in these parts. *Meri would say those aren't mutually exclusive.*

I miss him. I hope he's okay.

Geneve shook her head. *Focus, Knight Chevalier Geneve. You have a world to save.* She kept her strides even, as relaxed as she knew how, keeping up with the pair in front. They prepared to go into another store, then the woman rapped the man's armored back, pointing into another alley. They turned like a single person, heading with shark-like focus into the laneway.

Faster. There will not be another chance like this. Geneve picked up her pace, following them into the shade between two old alabaster edifices. The pair had a third person held against a wall. The stranger was a man of middle years and extensive paunch, his skin not the dark of Omrar's but a lighter shade like Geneve's. His hands were up in the universal *don't hit me* gesture, but that didn't stop his persecutors.

The woman sneered. Omrar's beautiful language turned rancid on her lips.

Geneve didn't slow, her feet whispering along the smooth, old stone the city was crafted from. She marked the man being extorted as a merchant, his fine clothes and girth drawing the eye of those who wanted more than they had and weren't afraid to ask impolitely. The merchant didn't lower his hands, protesting, *pleading*.

The male soldier raised his fist, perhaps to make a more effective point, and then Geneve was on them. She grabbed the man's wrist, dragging it over and behind his shoulder then pulling down. His legs went out from under him as gravity lent its own help to their conversation. When the soldier hit the ground, she hit him in the face. Her timing was perfect, catching his nose on the bounce-back from his head hitting the street.

Geneve rose, stepping backward away from the sure-to-come strike the patterns promised. She wasn't disappointed, the other soldier swinging at nothing but air. Geneve kicked the back of her knee, then hammered her fist into the woman's skull. She dropped on top of her comrade with a clatter of armor. Geneve crouched, turning the woman over. Now she had more time to examine the guards she noted their armor wasn't solid steel like Geneve's Tresward plate. It was combined with strips of leather and lacings of chain. *Lighter, and more flexible. Worth noting. Also, cooler, important for this heat.* She rubbed her face, already pricking with sweat from the sun's furnace and her activities.

She liberated a scroll of parchment from the unconscious soldier. Unrolled, her eyes were immediately drawn to a burnished sun. It sat center of the page, surrounded by an artist's rendition of her Tresward armor. *They found my Smithsteel. They're looking for me.*

Geneve stood. "Be on your way. It won't be safe for you here." *He won't understand me, but I have to try.*

The merchant's eyes widened. "Or'sen?"

Geneve raised her eyebrow. "I hail from the Kingdom."

"You're a long way from home." The merchant's words were accented but easily understandable, like he'd learned the language as a child. He spread his hands. "I'm afraid you've traveled to Tebrani at a bad time. The end of the world has come."

Chapter Four

They had a lot of pants.

"Dragon, I don't know what they were thinking." Ormeon wasn't with Meriwether, but when you walked the halls of an ancient structure that could no doubt kill you at any moment, it was good to remind denizens of the dark you weren't alone. Even if you were. "I'm sure we'll find something for everyone here."

Nothing but silence met his words. It was like being in a tomb, without the bodies. *Same sense of loss, foreboding, and eternal presence.* Meriwether shivered, rubbing his arms. The place wasn't cold, but he felt chilled. The air was cooler than the heat outside, but it didn't have the frigid overtones of old rock. The walls were made of the ancient's pale stone-like material. He'd seen no cracks or other obvious signs of wear. Not a cobweb, dust bunny, or mouse dropping anywhere.

The blue-feathered bird flitted to his shoulder. It pointed its beak into the doorway Meriwether considered. Within was a long room of pants, shirts, jackets, and other accoutrements. The room looked like it would clothe the entire Vhemin race, each rack holding at least fifty garments, and there were hundreds—no, *thousands*—of racks.

The room itself faded into gloom. The light of this place wasn't everbright; the darkness loomed at Meriwether's elbow, threatening to barge in. The pale stone walls glowed, but no brighter than luminescent moss. He felt they might have been brighter at one point, but age robbed them of will.

The bird *cheep*'d at him. The noise was startling, but no imagined denizens of the dark leaped out to eat their faces. "Bird, hush. If something comes to kill us, it'll eat me, because I'm both slower and larger." It was hard to make eye contact with something on your shoulder, but Meriwether tried all the same. No doubt how he angled his chin, it still felt like the bird was looking down on *him*. "Wait. Did you just roll your eye at me? How's a bird even learn to do that?"

With another *cheep*, the bird fluttered into the room in a flurry of bright blue the dim lighting couldn't subdue. It settled on a rack with long coats, hopped a couple handspans further along, then dipped its beak. Meriwether sighed, wandered inside, and fingered the indicated coat. It was smooth, a fine-spun fabric only ancients could make. They'd even taken the manufacture of exquisite clothing to their graves. "At least you've good taste." The bird cocked its head in a, *well, of course, I'm a bird* gesture. The plumage wasn't to be denied. Meriwether shouldered into the coat.

It wasn't light. Not heavy, like it was made of furs, but also not billowy and graceful. *I'll burn alive outside in this.* The bird didn't seem to care, fluttering to another rack. This held shirts, all pale spun elegance. "This is more like it."

It didn't take long for the bird to select clothes for him from boots to hair. They found a tall mirror, and Meriwether admired himself. Dark gray pants below a shirt that might be white in real light. The coat hung above all, falling open at the middle, with a complicated set of buttons and straps down the front. The boots were the finest he'd ever owned, comfortable as soon as his feet called them home.

His blue-feathered friend watched from the mirror's lintel, then flew off. *Everyone's a critic.* He followed her, unsure how he'd settled on a gender. *I'm not good at sexing wildlife. Perhaps it's because I miss Geneve. I'm projecting my need onto this creature. I'm sure she won't mind, because she's a bird.* He hunted for the bird about the lines of clothes, drawn on by insistent *cheep cheep*'ing. Meriwether found her through another door toward the rear. Within was a tile-lined room with a wealth of mirrors.

Stalls lined the walls opposite the mirrors. His boots made almost no noise against the smooth floor, the barest squeak coming forth as he turned a circle. "Eons be damned, I'd know this kind of place anywhere. This is a toilet."

The bird flew from the top of a cabinet by the mirrors, completed a lap of his head, then went back to the cabinet. Meriwether scratched his beard, then opened the cabinet. Inside was a collection of killing irons that could only be shaving devices. He fussed with various blades, salves, potions, scissors, and oils until he got the hang of how to not slit his own throat with them, then eyed a mirror.

The beard had to be tamed.

He squared off against his reflection. Water trickled into a shallow stone depression before him, seeming to exude from the rock. The moss-dim light around the mirror brightened momentarily before giving up. He smiled. "Mirror, I like that you tried. It's the best any of us can do."

Meriwether's reflection nodded back, smiling, and he almost screamed. He scrambled back, but his reflection stayed put. Meriwether landed on his ass, hit his coccyx, and wanted—just for a moment—to cry. His reflection leaned forward, as if peering through a window at him. It didn't break the mirror's surface, but Meriwether felt it *wanted* to.

Meriwether's reflection cleared its throat. It spoke in a fluid language but in a voice that wasn't Meriwether's. It wasn't anyone's, really, unless that person was faint and far away, their words crackling with the hush of rain and distance. The words sounded a little like Tebrani, but Meriwether only knew enough of the trader's tongue to order ale and ask forgiveness for a dishonored sister, not necessarily in that order.

Meriwether stood, brushed off his new pants, and squared against his seeming. It wasn't an illusion; he detected no magic. His hand reached to his belt where the book of High Magic used to rest, the motion reflexive, resigned. "Okay. I'll ask the obvious question. What the fuck are you?"

The reflection vanished, the mirror turning opaque. A moment later, the mirror beside it held a Meriwether. *"Ahlaan bika. Velkommen. Bienvenido.* Welcome."

"That one," Meriwether said. "The last one."

"Adjusting," not-Meriwether agreed. "Dialect calibration in process. Data store incomplete. Would you like to learn to shave, see an ideal cut, model different styles, or close this simulation?"

"The *fuck*," Meriwether breathed.

"Sexual activities are available at a separate terminal in concourse B, sublevel twelve."

"I want to not kill myself shaving," Meriwether said. "The bird thinks I need a trim, and I agree."

Not-Meriwether eyed the blue-feathered creature now on the sink beside the tools of facial hair destruction. "That's not a bird."

"I know," Meriwether said. "The dragon didn't think it was a bird either, but what closed the deal was getting fashion advice."

"You seem to be taking this in remarkably good spirits," not-Meriwether said. "My database indicates no one's shaved here in seven hundred and thirteen years."

"It's a long time between trims," Meriwether said. "So. How do I not kill myself?"

"Basic shaving tutorial initiated," his reflection said.

"I know how to shave," Meriwether said. "I've done it before."

"Without killing yourself, too." His reflection appraised him as if he'd made an error of judgment the first time. Its voice grew stronger the longer it spoke. "Would sir like a styling guide?"

"You know what? Maybe I'll skip the shave." Meriwether leaned in. "What can you tell me about this place?"

"You're in a bathroom."

"And the bathroom is in a..." Meriwether left it hanging.

"A building."

"And the building is a..."

"Ah!" His reflection snapped its fingers. "You're an intruder! I should alert security. Please wait." Not-Meriwether looked to the left, as if addressing someone standing there. "Um."

"Security's not answering?"

"Security is *missing*. What did you do?" His reflection sounded scandalized.

"I arrived several hundred years too late, I think." Meriwether sighed. "Reflection, have you ever been in a situation where you feel totally out of place?"

"I'm getting that feeling right now. It seems as if we're at the limits of this simulation's capability."

"Work with me," Meriwether suggested. "I came here in a bolt of lightning. There's a dragon, and a dragonrider. The dragon, whose name is Ormeon, is waiting in a big room hoping I'll find pants." He scratched his chin. "We came with a dragonrider, who's missing. And this bird found me."

"That seems a lot to take in."

"I wish I could talk to someone about it. Someone who knows something. A someone who could help fix it." Meriwether leaned on his hands. The ancient stone bench still trickled its endless stream of water. "Can you do any of that?"

"I'm excellent at personal grooming." Not-Meriwether spread his hands, eying the bird. "She's better at that other stuff than I am."

"The bird?"

"It's not a bird. It's a ... *corrupted data*." His reflection sneezed. "It's a *juniya*."

"A what?"

"*Juniya*. They're like that." It pointed, perhaps less helpfully than might be imaged, at the blue-feathered bird. "About so high. They can work wonders."

Meriwether glanced to the bird, then to his reflection. "It's a *bird*, man. Make *sense*."

The bird hopped along the stone, *cheep*'ing in disdain. His reflection nodded. "I agree."

"You can talk to it?"

"I can."

"What's it saying?"

His reflection spoke in the not-quite-Tebrani language, then frowned. "That's the gist of it, anyway."

Meriwether squinted. "What?"

"She said you're very stupid—"

"I'm not!"

"But also very lost," his reflection continued. "She asked if I could help you. I've inferred she means by doing something other than calling security." Not-Meriwether stroked his chin in a very Meri-wether-like manner. *It's learning from me.* "You've pants already, which limits my options."

"Can I turn the juna—"

"Juniya."

"That thing. Can I turn it into something useful?" Meriwether winced at the storm of *cheep, cheep!* that assaulted him. "Like, to get the lights on here. Actually, cancel that. I need to find the dragonrider."

"Oh, that's easy." Not-Meriwether clapped his hands. "If you get another two *juniya*, you can turn the lights on, then access the map room. It'll show you wherever anyone you want to find is, assuming they have a dragonrider's equipment."

"Ah." Meriwether frowned. "I arrived naked. She'll probably be without her helmet."

"Why naked?"

"Ormeon said everything's broken." Meriwether considered the shaving implements. "Perhaps I should get myself cleaned up. It seems simpler than finding more birds or getting an ancient temple working again."

"That's the spirit," his reflection said. "Have you considered a lighter shade beard? Perhaps a marmalade color."

"Ginger?"

"We can do that too."

"What's the difference? No, don't answer that." Meriwether eyed the bird, who looked cross. "Where can I find another two *juniya?*"

"They're probably all dead."

"Well, obviously."

"But if they weren't all dead, they'd probably be in maintenance. But if everything's broken, I don't like your chances." His reflection looked sad. "They're really quite wonderful."

"And where's maintenance?"

"Oh! It's down about twelve klicks."

Meriwether tugged his ear. "I thought you said *twelve* and then *klicks*, as in twelve kilometers below ground."

"About that, yes."

Meriwether leaned in close, eyeballing the reflection. "Are you trying to be funny?"

The bird *cheep'd*. His reflection nodded. "I agree. Best be on your way."

"What did she say?"

"That you've got a terrible sense of humor." His reflection looked down its nose at Meriwether. "To go with your sense of style."

"She said I have no style?"

"That was all me."

Meriwether felt lost. "How did the ancients put up with magic mirrors that were so sassy?"

"To be fair, it doesn't seem they did. They're all dead." His reflection turned, pointing to the exit. "Go that way, then head right. Down about five hundred meters is a *masead*."

"A what?"

"A big box that goes into the earth." His reflection smiled. "I hope it still works! Twelve klicks is a long way to climb."

THE BIRD RODE HIS SHOULDER AS IF COMMANDING A GIANT TO battle. It *cheep'd* on occasion, but Meriwether had no idea what it said. "You realize I don't speak cheep?"

Cheep, cheep.

"I'm good with languages, but it's all sounding much the same." He resisted the urge to shrug, because his blue-feathered friend had sharp feet that seemed able to pierce hard steel and had no trouble with the fabric of his jacket. "I don't mean to cause offense."

The bird flitted away, hovering in the air before him with a steady thrumming of wings, then returned to his shoulder. It puffed up, as if in a huff, then shook itself smooth again. *Cheep, cheep, cheep.*

"If you're saying you didn't always look this way—"

Cheep!

"Well, I think I understand what it's like to be different than you're meant to be." Meriwether raised a cautious hand, scratching the bird under the chin. After a moment of frozen horror, which turned to mere wide-eyed surprise, the bird leaned into his finger. "No one's given you any attention for a long time, huh?"

Cheep.

They arrived at the *masead*, which turned out to be as described: a small room with a door that opened as he got closer. A skeleton lay within, arm thrown toward Meriwether's feet. The sorcerer nudged the remains with his toe. "I wonder what happened to them?"

The blue-feathered bird flitted from his shoulder to the sad remains, hopping about. She cocked her head, peering into dead eye sockets and looking through the thing's ribcage. *Cheep.*

Meriwether crouched. "You know what bothers me?"

Cheep?

"No, not that at all. I'm concerned this person, whoever they were, managed to get into a…" he frowned the unfamiliar word, "*masead* without clothes on. See, my jacket," he tugged his new coat, "seems to have stood the test of time. I'm imagining the ancients used the same material for many things. Why is this one completely naked?"

The bird eyed him, the skeleton, then him again, as if wondering why she hadn't thought of that. *Cheep, cheep. Cheep.*

"Could be magical, you're right. But I think something else happened here." He stood. "I think this place died because all the people in it were murdered. Something got in here *with* them. Rousted them from their beds. By the Three, it ran them naked into metal boxes that go klicks underground." Meriwether frowned. "No weapons, which suggests not only was this poor soul running for their lives, but they were cut down by someone who didn't care much about murdering the defenseless. Which leads us to an important question."

Cheep?

"Are you still happy to go twelve klicks underground with a man who can't run fast, carries no weapons, and is borderline useless in a fight? Knowing full well that whatever killed this person lurks below."

Cheep!

"We know because I wasn't born lucky, bird. Twelve klicks from the sun's radiance we will find a den of horrors, rife with murderous intent." He stepped into the *masead*, careful to not disturb the remains of his ancient co-passenger. Meriwether glanced down. "Any advice?"

The skeleton didn't respond, which was a plus. Meriwether swiveled to the bird. "How do we make this thing go down?"

The bird flitted to the wall by the door, beating her wings against the smooth metal. Meriwether stepped closer, touching the smooth, cool steel with delicate fingertips. "Nothing's happening."

Cheep.

"My whole hand? Are you sure?"

Cheep.

Meriwether shrugged, then placed his palm against the metal. A thought struck him. "Hmm. I wonder if we should tell Ormeon where we're going, before—"

With a *CLANG!* the *masead's* doors slammed shut. The room lurched, then with a sickening shriek of tortured, ancient metal dropped them into the belly of hell.

Chapter Five

The merchant's name was Mazin, and he never stopped talking. Geneve felt like she might have been better off if she'd let the guard murder him, or at the very least knock a few of his teeth loose. She winced. *What would Meri think?*

Meri would laugh, hold my hand, and kiss me. By the Three, I miss him. I hope he's well.

Mazin took her through the streets of Imshir, head bobbing like a friendly parrot's. His words gained confidence the more he used them, or perhaps it was distance from his assailants. "I thank you again for saving me."

Geneve dodged foot and cart traffic easier than Mazin, the man's bulk both obstacle and ram as he shouldered ahead. "You said the end of the world was coming."

"The Arm are working with the Precept to stop it, but there's little they can do when the moons fall and the old gods and new turn their faces from the world." Mazin shrugged, the motion exaggerated by his bulk. "This heat will kill me sooner than the end of the world." Mazin turned as if lost, then his face lit up. "Ah. Here we are." He squared off as if preparing for combat against a narrow door set in a nondescript wall. He pulled a jingling hoop of keys from the sash at his middle, inserted a silvered key into the lock, and opened it. With a grunt, he turned sideways and forced himself through the gap. "Come in."

Geneve held back. The doorway was lower than the ones at Omrar's store. *How is the old man faring? Did I leave him in a bad situation?* "I should be going."

Mazin peered out from the inviting shade of his house's interior. "And miss the end of the world?" He *tsk'd.* "We have a saying here."

"Here in Tebrani, or here in Imshir?"

"Why, both." Mazin seemed surprised she hadn't come out of the heat yet. He said something in his language. "It means, 'Wherever you'd going will be there when you need it to be.'"

Geneve frowned. "A curious thing to say."

"If you're concerned I will sell you into slavery, don't be. Slaves aren't very profitable anymore." The smile fell from his face. "You're not worried—"

"You must know what I am." Geneve glanced down the busy street, then ducked her head to follow the merchant inside. She found herself in a low-ceilinged room about ten meters aside. Drapes hung, sectioning the space into useful portions, her mind adding labels like *kitchen* and *parlor*. There were no chairs, but stools and cushions huddled beside low tables. The air smelled faintly of spice, both delicious and inedible. The temperature was blessedly cooler than the street outside, the air running a gentle hand down the slick of sweat at her back. "This is ... beautiful."

"I know what you are, Tresward." Mazin held his distance, hands tucked into his sash. "I have seen Or'sen. Once, I watched a demonstration."

"The Tresward do no shows." Geneve's lips pressed into a line.

"All things are shows." Mazin smiled, but there was sadness in it. He turned away, heading for the 'kitchen,' but didn't slow down. "If I take a child to a see a play, that is one type of show. Perhaps happy, maybe sad. Sad ones need treats afterward to make little ones feel better about the lesson. But whether happy or sad, there *is* a lesson. Am I not wrong?"

Geneve frowned. "This feels like a trick question."

"Tricks are another kind of lesson." Mazin emerged with a small tray bearing an embarrassment of food. Geneve saw breads and dates, sliced fruits nestled alongside nuts. A pitcher sweated next to beautifully-crafted glassware. "Come. Sit." He led her to a huddle of cushions next to a table, poured her a glass of water, and handed it over.

Geneve guzzled. *I'm not used to this Three-damned heat. It reminds me of the plaguelands, where everything was death.* "What is the lesson you learned from the Tresward?"

"Your face is unhappy." Mazin eyed the tray between them. "Is the food not to your liking? I can get something else."

"No! This looks fine. Good. Great, even." She looked away. "I miss Meri."

"Who is Meri? Besides, of course, the person you want most in this whole world." Mazin selected a handful of nuts.

"That's it. He's the person I miss most ... not my father, or my sister of blades, but Meri. Two months ago I didn't know him. A month ago he deserved the Three's Judgment. And today, he is a part of my soul." She hugged herself. "I miss him like the sky misses the moons."

"And yet you've not had long to miss him. A night at most." Mazin spread his hands. "The lightning brought you where you're needed."

"He's not ... competent," Geneve tried. "No, that's wrong. He's like an accident waiting to happen. We will go places and meet people who want to kill us. Meri is not good at combat. Surviving, perhaps ... but here, where the language is strange? His gift is words, and he can't use them."

"He sounds like a liability." Mazin shrugged.

Geneve smiled. "I thought that. I wondered how he made it through life without being able to hold a knife right, or dodge the tip of a spear. Then I saw his skill is unlocking hearts. Vertiline was first, I think. Then Sight of Day, and after the Feybrind, Armitage. The Vhemin wanted to kill us all, but—"

"You use 'Vhemin' and 'Feybrind' together like yolk and white in the same shell."

"They are my friends."

Mazin laughed, then the sound dried up as he saw her face. "The Vhemin and the Feybrind can't live together."

"They are also friends with each other." Geneve took a date. It was slightly sticky and very sweet. "That is Meri's gift."

Mazin frowned. "Did you hit your head when you landed in the street last night?"

"It's possible," she admitted. "Meri and I are partners. We face the world together. He is my guide. I'm his shield. And now we're apart."

"How will you save the world without your guide?"

Geneve took another date. "Tell me this lesson you learned from the Tresward."

Mazin pushed a few nuts around, making abstract patterns. His girth suggested he lacked no courage around food, but he didn't eat. "This thing you call from the Three."

"The Storm?"

"That's its name, yes. I saw the Storm perhaps ten years ago, and it taught me about the Tresward. Your shields are what hold the Precept here, rather than crossing the hungry ocean and seizing Or'sen. Oh, I know you would say the queen's armies are strong, or that Vhemin are hard to kill. That conquering a land is difficult. These things are true, but another truth is the Precept is a demon king, and he holds the world in the palm of his hand." Mazin frowned. "Demon... Is that the right word?"

Geneve felt chilled. The food no longer appealed to her, either. "I have seen a demon. Three, actually."

"No man bests three demons. That is their prime number."

"I'm no man." Geneve scowled. "All great things come in threes."

Mazin smiled. "Fair, and my apologies."

"I had a dragon."

He goggled. "There are no dragons."

"Your story, merchant." Geneve brushed red hair aside. "The day grows no cooler."

Mazin offered a heavy sigh by way of apology. "I might ask what happened to your dragon, but I owe you a story first. It was my first merchant sailing. I arrived in Ravenswall, hull full to bursting with wines and silks, as they fetch the best price. My father gave me a ship and cargo as a wedding gift." His eyes showed sadness. "It feels a lifetime ago. We docked, and the unloading began. I was overseeing, while my captain yelled and scowled. We had a good partnership." He chuckled at the memory. "I think I was onto my third cup of wine. The weather in Ravenswall is cold. The wind reaches across the sea, clutching hearts in an icy grip. At first, I wasn't sure I could trust my eyes." He moved a nut about the plate.

"The Storm?"

"You say it like it might be a squall. A young woman ran through the docks. She was a similar age to my wife, but her skin was lighter. Pale, like a clear dawn, and hair to match. Those details came later. What I saw first was the fear." Mazin gulped water. "You see, three Knights followed her. I'd heard stories. Some in Tebrani know the myth of the Tresward. The mountains you climb before breakfast, right before refusing to bend the knee to any but the Three."

"I've climbed mountains and refused to bow." Geneve looked away. "I've hunted those who didn't deserve it, too. So far, your story seems a page pulled from my life."

"And it troubles you?"

"Wouldn't you be troubled by hunting the innocent and delivering them to slaughter?"

"Perhaps." Mazin shrugged, then adjusted his sash. "If my god commanded it, I might not think too hard. If my Clerics willed it, I might not question."

Geneve narrowed her eyes. "You know much for a merchant."

"All merchants are counselors first, and sellers second. Relationships fetch a higher price than anything else." But he looked away. "I mean no offense. You saved my life, and I owe you a debt greater than food or water can pay."

Geneve thought about that. "It is the great honor and privilege of the strong to help those they can. There's no debt."

"That doesn't sound like a Tresward." Mazin leaned back on his cushion, as if to get a better look at her.

"The Tresward ... drift. What happened to the woman?"

"You don't want to know what happened to your fellow Knights?" he countered.

"I think I know both parts of this tale. But you should tell it anyway. It needs to be heard, often, and everywhere." Geneve smoothed her hands against her legs, trying to stop the trembling of her fingers. *By the Three, will I ever make up for the sins I carry?*

"As you say." Mazin looked down as if remembering something unpleasant, or perhaps seeing something unsavory on his shoe. "She died. The woman, I mean. It wasn't a good death, but she made it to my ship before she met her end." He rubbed his face. "She was a good runner. Strong legs, strong heart. Her face was set. Perhaps she thought to make it aboard a ship, convince the captain to cast off, and be on her way. She ran right past me, and I couldn't move. I wanted to, but my feet were stuck to the docks as if they were nailed there. All it took was a touch on my elbow, and I was done."

"Enchantress," Geneve said. "They control the mind."

"And, perhaps, the heart? As I said, she looked like my wife, and I was a young man, foolish, and unwise in the world." He leaned forward, confiding. "Some might say I'm still foolish, but none would argue I'm young."

Geneve snorted. "There are plenty of men older than you. They have a gift you lack."

"Which is?"

"They can finish a fucking story," she hissed.

Mazin burst out laughing, eyes crinkling in mirth. "That's fair. The woman put her feet on the deck of my ship. Her hair twisted in the wind like a dervish from the salt flats. Her eyes still held fear, but also a hint of triumph. She had a *ship*, Tresward! And a crew, skilled in the working of water and sail. My crew scuttled about as if I'd given orders to cast off. Sails unfurled as lines snaked into the water. And I still couldn't move. The only parts of me that moved were my eyes and my hair."

Geneve raised an eyebrow. "You had hair *and* your youth? This tale seems impossibly tall."

Mazin tried for a grin, but it faltered at the last hurdle. "Some of my crew readied weapons. We had all manner of men aboard. Those who knew how the wind lay across the waves, but also those who could tell how a man's insides work and lay it bare for the Three to see. Pirates, you see. They hunger on the dark seas. You'd have missed much of that getting here as you did. Blades came out alongside harpoons and boathooks. Belowdecks, men readied cannon. The three Knights didn't slow. They didn't hurry, either, but not a single helmet looked away."

"They didn't need to hurry," Geneve whispered. "There was nowhere for her to go."

"I know that now, but then? Before my very eyes, my crew were ensorcelled by a wizard! She would get away, and with her, most of my cargo. But I didn't think of that at the time. With the salt spray about me, the ship reaching for the open water, I was afraid for *her*. For all her strong legs and valiant heart, the Knights would have her."

"Her name was Bellany of Redwood." Geneve looked away. "She is a lesson in our archives."

"So." Mazin nodded. "I never knew her name. I guess you know the rest."

"I'd hear it anyway. I know what's written, but not what was felt." Geneve clenched her hands together. "It took someone braver than any Tresward to show me what I'd done."

"Bellany called from my ship to the Knights. She tossed words to them like coins to a beggar. 'I'm free, and the Three damn you all. Steel does not float. The burnished sun anchors you to the docks.' Bellany turned her back as archers on my ship fired at the Knights. The arrows flew true. Faster and more accurate than I'd seen my men do before. It was as if she gave them skills from the Three themselves. Shafts rained on the Tresward, each accurate."

"They blocked with their shields," Geneve remembered. "The pattern was Forgotten Rain."

"Whatever it's called, the shafts burst into flame. They fell against Ravenswall's pier, smoking and hissing, but there was no rain, no matter the name of your pattern. The shields of the Knights *glowed*, Tresward. They held all the colors of the sun. Then the lead Knight—"

"She wasn't the leader. Helene was the junior, but still a Chevalier. I don't know what happened to her. Three went out, but only two came back." Geneve frowned. "The lesson wasn't about her."

"Knight Chevalier Helene died." Mazin's voice was flat. "The Knight behind her ran her through. His sword cut her spine I think, but not before Helene tossed her blade across the choppy sea. I saw it, too, held the colors of the sun. Gold, and red, along with copper and yellow. Dawn and dusk and the midday sky danced on the edge of her steel."

"Glass."

"I'm sorry?"

"Helene held a glass sword. She was a Knight."

Mazin sighed. "A man's memory is a delicate thing. Glass, as you say. Whatever the blade was forged from, it sailed true. It carried the sun like a gift, delivering it to my ship. It hit, shouldering aside planks and cannons. Men screamed, then louder as rice wine from the Fields of Melody caught fire. My ship burned, Tresward. She burned, and on her deck Bellany screamed with the rest. The sound of a person burning to death is a thing you'll never forget. Three masts, and she sank as if she were a child's toy. The fire was so hot the wreck burned and smoldered as the sea dragged her down." He rubbed his face. "My limbs freed, and that's how I knew Bellany was dead. The Tresward Knight who killed Helene sat beside her, cradling his companion's body. But I didn't go to her. I dived in, Tresward. I dived for my wreck."

"For your cargo?"

"For Bellany. When she burned alive, I heard pain, but longing too. A life free of debts and chains. I swam, though I could see nothing. The water was thick with filth. Burned bodies floated like insects in amber. Char settled over everything like ink. But the heat, Knight. I just had to keep going down, you see?"

"What did you find?"

"Death." Mazin rubbed a hand over his scalp. "I wish I could say I found Bellany, or what was left of her. That I was a better man, or a stronger one. One who could bring someone back from the dead. But of the enchantress, nothing remained. Her body, her soul, all belonged to the Three. I swam up. Strangers helped me from the water. I was wet, and cold, and my soul hurt. My men, some my family—distant cousins, but family nonetheless—were gone. The final Knight—"

"Knight Valiant Jerome."

"Jerome gave me a writ. He said, 'Take this to the holdfast in Ravenswall, and they will pay you for your ship.' That's it. Not a sorry, or a tear. Money, for death." Mazin leaned forward. "This is the lesson

I learned. The Tresward stop at nothing, but are fair about it. The Precept can't take Or'sen while your order lives. The Arm guard Heaven's Gate, and the Will hold the shadows, but none can beat the Tresward."

"The Arm? The Will?"

"The Arm are guards. The Will are ... you would call them assassins."

Geneve rubbed her face, finding it wet. "And what do you call them?"

"Believers."

Chapter Six

Blackness, fire, and death.

The air smelled of smoke and ash. Meriwether groaned as conscious returned. It wasn't welcome, as it came back dragging a headache of epic proportions with it. The pain in his skull wasn't enough to make him throw up, but he felt close. A seething nausea roiled in his gut.

The *masead* was a shambles about him. Two of the beautiful metal wall panels had come loose. One lay across him, the other blocking the doorway which was partially open, the doors hissing and grinding as they tried to open or shut. Beyond the doorway, flames licked the walls, and sooty black smoke that smelled acrid rolled up the walls and huddled on the ceiling.

"Help," he rasped.

Cheep! The blue-feathered bird flitted in from the corridor. She trailed smoke like a wedding train of misery, alighting on the floor in an ashy *puff* in front of his face. Which was, he realized, on the ground. He was face-down on the silvered floor. The polished finish did a good job of showcasing just how reflective it was, catching all the orange-bright agony that awaited him through the stuttering doors.

"Other help," Meriwether said. "Bigger. Stronger."

Cheep!

"It's not that I don't appreciate the thought. But you're the size of my hand, and this metal panel is the size of three of me."

Cheep, she allowed.

"Stand back." Meriwether got his palms under him as the bird hopped away. He heaved, the nausea spiking to fever pitch. He lurched upright, the panel sliding off with a *clang*. Meriwether bent over, heaving until there was nothing left inside him, then coughing as he sucked in a lungful of smoke. "Merciful Three, it tastes like death." The smoke was acidic, with carbon and sulfur holding hands up his nose.

Cheep, cheep-cheep. The blue-feathered bird hopped toward the door.

"There's a fire out there."

Cheep, cheep.

"You think there's a safe path through? I can't fly." Meriwether peered through the flames. For all the fire, the corridor was hard to make out, the smoke clutching the light close. "Looks risky."

The *masead* lurched, dropping a handspan in an instant. Meriwether screamed. The blue-feathered bird leaped through the door, flying over the metal panel with ease. He followed but caught his boot on the lip of the panel. He fell on the floor outside.

A *crash* behind him. He glanced back. A ceiling plate had swung into the metal panel blocking the door, by the looks only missing him because he'd fallen. It knocked the panel inside the *masead*. The doors snapped shut like a dragon's jaws, and with a scream of metal that diminished with distance the *masead* went the way of all ancient treasures: to a miserable end.

Meriwether staggered upright. He caught a flash of blue ahead. Dragging his coat over his face to avoid breathing too much smoke, he lurched through the madness about him. Fire laid hands on his person but found no purchase. The ancient's clothing resisted flame, but his body inside sweltered.

He burst free of fire for a moment as the corridor branched. Left was blessedly free of fire; the right held a raging inferno. Meriwether swung left, stumbling on. The bird found him, circling his head. *Cheep cheep!*

"I'm *not* going that way. It's on fire!"

Cheep!

"Look, I don't care," Meriwether said. "This way is not on fire and that works for me."

A door slid open ahead. He picked up his pace, sensing salvation. Through the doorway stepped a horror. It was humanoid, or perhaps once had been an actual breathing human, but those days were long past. Skin sloughed away from rotted meat beneath, showing muscle and sinew only loosely attached to bone. It grinned a death's head rictus, one eyeball bright and wide, the other an empty socket.

It was wearing pants, perhaps a mercy, and held an oblong metal device under one arm. This had a tube along the top. The monster hefted the device, held it to the ruined eye, shook its head, then swapped to the other eye, sighting down the tube.

"Fuck this," Meriwether said. "Fuck *all* of this." He turned, sprinting for the fire. His foot skidded with a squeak on the old stone floor. A *SNAP* sounded, actinic blue-white blinding Meriwether for a moment, but he didn't let that slow him. He scrambled to his feet, and with an arm over his face, plunged into the wall of fire after the blue-feathered bird.

THE LUNGE THROUGH FLAMES WAS BLESSEDLY QUICK; MERIWETHER hit a wall, bounced left, and slid into a white-walled room, the door hissing shut behind him. No smoke, fire, or monsters anywhere in sight. Just a collection of metal tables, which looked uncomfortable, but who was he to tell the ancients how to sleep?

The room was about ten meters aside. At the far end stood glass doors, beyond which was darkness. The blue-feathered bird perched on a metal table, looking a little sooty but slightly smug.

"Okay," Meriwether allowed. "You said not to go that way, and you were right!"

Cheep.

"Yes, there was a horrible monster. What kind of weapon was that?"

Cheep, cheep cheep.

"I've no idea what one of those is." Meriwether poked around the room. The walls were smooth, the surface reminding him of marble but viewed through a layer of water. He touched one, finding it cool and impossibly fine, as if it lined the bottom of a river for hundreds of years, the water softening bedrock to the smoothest of silks. "How did we lose so much?"

The wall, by way of answer, hissed, then *clicked*. A panel a little wider than Meriwether slid wide in silence. It revealed a small coffin-like chamber, inside which was a very dead, but perfectly preserved Feybrind.

Meriwether let out a small scream but recovered quickly. "How long's this been here?" He leaned forward to examine the Feybrind closer. She was naked, but the People didn't mind that state of affairs. Her eyes were closed, whatever jewel-like brilliance she might have gazed at the world through forever cut off from time. He laid a hand on her brow, finding the fur soft, but still without a hint of life. "What's your story? It can't be a good one. You've been left here for so very long."

Cheep.

"Hush. These are the most wonderful people, bird. They make marvelous things, and are gentle, kind, and eternally forgiving. I don't know why they tolerate us at all." With a last smoothing of the Feybrind's forehead, Meriwether pushed the rack back into the wall.

Cheep?

"Because I can't do anything for her. Everyone she knows is dust. There is no city in the forest to take her to. I would make the wrong done to her right, but there's no one here to hold to account." He smoothed his shirt, noticing it didn't smell of smoke. "Except me. I'm here, bird. I'm one of the people who put her in there."

The bird said nothing, but flitted to another metal table, this one closer to the double doors leading to darkness.

"I don't want to go in there." Meriwether held up a hand. "I know. I can't stay here. The monster where we came from might make its way through the flames. There's nothing to eat or drink here. No magic mirrors telling us the way. I'm not sure I'd welcome advice, though. The last time I listened to a barber trapped in a seeing glass, I fell into the earth and arrived in a hellscape made of fire."

Cheep!

"I'm not complaining." Meriwether smoothed his hair back, straightened his coat, and squared his shoulders. "Let's be about it, then."

The bird flitted into the air, hovering by the wall to the left of the glass doors before settling on a table beside it. Meriwether touched the wall, and it slid sideways revealing a cupboard. Within were a hundred things he had no name for, and one he did. A lantern of sorts nestled there. It had smooth sides, a single glass pillar inside, connected to a handle made of golden wire. Meriwether peered at it, trying to work out where the fuel went, then shrugged, lifting it free. He could make light, but the laggard's path was less tiring. If the lantern still worked, he could save his strength.

As his hand touched the golden wire, the glass pillar glowed with a lustrous gold-white light. He held it up, then almost walked into the glass doors. They didn't open as he approached. Meriwether leaned into them, but they didn't budge. With a sigh, he leaned his forehead against the cool glass. As his skin touched the glass, the doors opened, almost dumping him to the floor as he fought for balance. Nothing leaped out at him, but he squared his shoulders anyway, then pushed into the room of no-doubt-more-terror.

Shadows retreated as he walked. This room didn't have metal tables and was large enough his lantern's light couldn't find the walls. Within stood row upon row of vertical glass chambers. Meriwether approached the closest one, holding the lantern high. "Merciful Three," he breathed.

It was a chamber much like the ones at the ancient temple in the plaguelands. A metal base cupped a glass chamber. Unlike the ones at Ormeon's birthplace, this was full. Inside hung a Feybrind man, arms loose at his sides as if he floated in fluid. Meriwether couldn't see any distortion like looking into a lake, but the Feybrind's fine fur lifted as if he were underwater.

Meriwether turned a slow circle. There were easily a hundred chambers in here, and each held one of the People. The blue-feathered bird landed on his shoulder, but stayed silent, her head cocked as she watched the Feybrind.

"He looks asleep." Meriwether touched the glass wall. It felt cool like an ice cellar. He leaned closer, sniffing, but got no odor. Not even the smoke of the corridor outside reached this chamber. "He's not asleep, is he?"

Cheep, she said, perhaps sadly.

Meriwether took a step back. "What did we *do?*"

Cheep, cheep. The bird fluttered atop his hand holding the lantern.

Her weight was tiny, but he was glad of it all the same. It made him feel less alone. "Thank you for saving me. Back there."

Cheep. Perhaps a tiny shrug, if a bird could.

"No, I mean it. Because we'll make this right. This," he swept his free hand at the chamber, "*cannot* stand. My good and faithful friend, Sight of Day, would weep to see it. And you know what? I feel it too." He touched his chest. "Here. The sins of *all* my fathers before me ride on pale horses. They guide my path of what *not* to do. How could we have done this to them?"

Cheep?

"Of course I want to make it right. I don't know how, is all." Meriwether shook his head. "I wish Geneve were here. She'd know what to do."

Cheep. She nodded. *Cheep!* The blue-feathered bird flitted into the darkness.

"Bird?" Meriwether held the lantern high, then headed after her. He hurried through the chamber, seeing more Feybrind. Each of the People hung as if sleeping, their bodies still, all they could have been gone hundreds of years before. *They are so few, and we did this to them. It's no wonder they hide in the forests of our world.*

A *cheep* drew him through the darkness. He found the bird settled atop a glass panel held up by two metal rods. It was beside a raised dais, perhaps a handspan off the floor. Meriwether looked at the bird. "Hell, no."

Cheep?

"Because there was something just like this in an ancient temple in the plaguelands." Meriwether scratched his beard. "I should have shaved this before."

Cheep.

"I wasn't asking your opinion." He walked around the dais, looking for anything that looked like a trap. "Thing is, the last one of these didn't *look* dangerous. But it stole a part of my mind for a while. Geneve got a dragon in exchange, so I guess it wasn't a bad bargain." He remembered how long it took her to wake up from her daze. "These things are dangerous. They can take you away, bird. They don't give you back for a long time."

Cheep-cheep-cheep!

"Of course I don't know how it works." Meriwether sighed. "No one's around to tell me which way you point to the sun, how long to stand on one foot, or whatever else the ancients did. I touched a thing and another thing happened."

A rattle punctuated his sentence. Slowly, so's not to disturb the delicate pool of silence at his feet, Meriwether turned toward the noise. The lantern showed nothing but glass cylinders holding up the ceiling as far as the light reached. "That came from the door, didn't it?"

The bird hopped along the glass panel. *Cheep.*

"It's the monster, right?"

Cheep, cheep.

"More than one? Just my luck." Meriwether sighed. "Are there weapons in here? A place to hide? Help to summon? Even the magic mirror would be useful if he, or I guess it's me, could point a way clear."

Another rattle sounded through the dark. Meriwether took a few paces closer, peering into the gloom. A *crunch* came, then another, followed by the harsh tinkle of broken glass.

Meriwether crouched by the dais, desperate for some cover. He whispered, "Bird, do those monsters have good hearing or eyesight? No, don't answer. You're too loud. I'll just assume they do." He cast about but found nowhere to go. Even the glass cylinders were all full; he couldn't swing inside and hope to weather the storm.

The dais *hummed*. He startled, scuttling back, but managed to keep a hold of the lantern. Meriwether looked at his light. It would bring the monsters to him like moths to a flame, or perhaps like monsters to a terrified sorcerer. His pockets held nothing, because his clothes were new and the transportation device of the ancients stole everything.

He saw movement in the gloom. A figure shuffled forward. It might have been the same as from the corridor before. Meriwether was no expert on identifying decaying corpses. *What would Geneve do? She always knows the right thing. She takes action, rather than mewling in the dark.*

"Ah," he said. "Fuck it." With a swift movement sure to draw even the most rotted eyes he stood, stepped on the platform, and placed a palm on the glass panel. The dais's hum grew, a feeling both through his feet and a sound that made his teeth ache.

A strong male voice, the kind used to telling people what was going on so they didn't scream in panic, spoke in maybe-Tebrani. It would have been better if he said that in a language Meriwether had more than a few words of, but in times like this you took what you could get.

The monster drew closer, in no apparent hurry. Its gait was uneven, as if the bones inside no longer lined up how they should. It held a metal device, same as before, but made no move to raise it. Another drew closer from the gloom, followed by a third. They all wore pants, which was still excellent as far as it went, and one had a coat of sorts draped over its shoulders. The lead one had a missing eyeball—Meriwether tagged that as the one he'd seen before. The last had a scrap of stringy, oily hair covering half its scalp and hanging to its shoulders.

"Hi," Meriwether said.

Lanky Hair spat maybe-Tebrani like it ate a serving of rocks not five minutes earlier and had one or two stuck in what remained of its throat.

A *hiss* came from Meriwether's right. One of the glass cylinders lit from above, illuminating the Feybrind within. The cat's fur matted down as invisible liquid within drained, then gave a brief billow as if air swirled within, but Meriwether heard no wind.

The three monsters swiveled toward the cylinder. Old Coat raised its metal device as the Feybrind's eyes opened, showing the wondrous pink, almost purple of tanzanite. The glass cylinder rose. The monster did something to the device, and brilliant blue-white fire lashed at the Feybrind.

Meriwether shouted, covering his eyes, and staggered off the dais. He realized he still had a mind to call his own, which was a positive step considering what the ancients' temple did to him. He blinked furiously, stars and spots dancing across his vision. He saw nothing but empty space where the Feybrind had been. The air smelled of copper.

It didn't smell of rot, which was curious considering the corpse-like creatures before him, but that was a mystery that could wait until he got out of this pickle. One Eye turned its death's head grin on Meriwether.

The sorcerer shook his head. "You bastards. You've killed one of the People!" He took a step forward, then his feet mired as fear took hold. *Don't be stupid. I can't win against those who channel heaven's might. Geneve probably could, but she's not here. I need to run!*

A wet *crunch* came from Old Coat. The creature staggered, dropping its device. Its chest opened in a shower of wet, rotted meat. A blood and gore-streaked hand emerged, holding what looked like the creature's spine, before it fell to the ground.

Behind it stood the Feybrind, her rose eyes hard as glass, teeth bared and feral. She kicked the back of the monster's leg, spun about it's falling body, and grabbed the device before it could clatter to the ground.

Lanky Hair raised its own device, doing something complicated with the underside. It arced blue-white rage at the Feybrind, but she wasn't there anymore. The cat jumped above the death beam, tumbled through the air, then descended with her device raised like a club. She hit the ground with feline grace, driving the device through Lanky Hair's skull with a wet *pop*. What was probably once brains sprayed like the insides of a dropped watermelon.

One Eye lurched about, bringing its device to bear. The Feybrind danced left, then right as two stabs of blue-white tried to find her heart. The first dodge brought her closer, then second within striking distance. She kicked the front of the monster's knee, then brought her device in a savage arc upward through the thing's jaw.

The skull popped free with a sound much like a head of lettuce would make if you tore it in half.

Meriwether looked at the fallen monsters, then the Feybrind who didn't even look to be breathing hard. He dredged up a smile he suspected was a little on the grisly side. "Hello."

{Command me. I am—}

Meriwether closed on her in a heartbeat. His hands held hers. He felt the soft fur of one and the sticky gore on the other. "No Commands. Thanks, by the way. You saved my life."

Rose eyes searched his face. He saw resignation retreat, replaced by curiosity. *{And you, mine.}*

"That was purely accidental."

She glanced at the glass cylinder she'd sprung from. *{There are no accidents. You aren't here to Command me?}*

"Nope."

{Then why are you here?} Her tail lashed once.

"Not sure." He tugged his ear. "The bird," he pointed to the glass panel, now empty of any birds, "who *was* right there said we should come down here. Or there was a magic mirror. It wanted to give me a haircut. I came here with a dragon. I'm hunting the one true love of my life, because we were separated by lightning after the Three vanished."

She blinked. *{Are you insane?}*

"I don't think so."

{I think you are totally cracked. Shaken as a baby. Dropped on your head, perhaps twice.} A slight half-smile touched her lips. *{But I like you.}*

"Thanks, for at least half of that." Meriwether adjusted his smile, softening it a little. "I'm Meriwether."

She gave a nod, almost a small bow. *{I'm Coming Storm.}*

He glanced at the ruined bodies behind Coming Storm. "That seems a remarkably prescient thing for your parents to have named you."

Coming Storm cocked her head, raising an eyebrow over her crystalline gaze. *{What year is it?}*

"I don't have an answer that'd mean much to either of us." Meriwether hooked his thumbs in his pockets. "But I think it's been eight hundred years since the ancients fell."

Coming Storm didn't ask what he meant by ancients. She nodded, the motion almost sad. *{Eight hundred years is long enough to sleep.}* She padded to the cylinder that birthed her, laying a hand on the smooth glass. *{You said something about a dragon?}*

"No one wants to know about me. It's always Ormeon." He pursed his lips. "Where's the damn bird?"

A flutter of blue entered the lantern's range, the bird landing on his shoulder. *Cheep!*

Rose cat eyes watched the bird, and Coming Storm's tail lashed again. *{That looks delicious.}*

"You can't eat the bird."

Cheep! Cheep! Cheep!

{Is it yours?}

"She. And, not really." He scratched his beard. "I'm not big into owning people."

Cheep!

{Then she's lunch.} Another half-smile.

Cheep cheep cheep cheep, cheep!

"Hold up." Meriwether raised his palm. "You really can't eat the bird."

{That's not a bird.} Coming Storm watched the bird, who watched her right back.

"Everyone keeps saying that. She looks like a bird. Talks like a bird."

{Does she?}

"Uh." Meriwether tried to eye the bird on his shoulder, his neck twinging at his contortion. "Yes? Yes. Definitely."

{Or does she whisper in your dreams, and promise the world?} Coming Storm padded closer. *{Does she seem smarter than your average bird?}*

"I'm not an expert on birds," Meriwether said, a little defensively. Rose eyes held his. "Okay. She doesn't seem like a normal bird. But magic mirrors, dragons, and a graveyard of the People aren't normal either."

Coming Storm raised her eyebrow again. *{The People?}*

"Feybrind." She remained blank. "You."

{Eight hundred years, you said?} She shook her head. *{That makes a surprising amount of sense.}*

"I'm confused." Meriwether felt like the floor was shifting under him in unpredictable ways. "I've met others like you. The Feybrind. You're a wonderful race. You make things. Fine metals. Clothes of remarkable quality. Music. Although you don't sing. You don't say anything at all." He wound down like an old clock.

{Have you ever wondered why we don't say anything? No songs, laughter, or tears?}

"It's crossed my mind."

She raised her hands to the ceiling above. *{Do you know what this place is?}*

"A temple?" he hazarded.

{It's a,} here, her fingers made words he didn't know. She saw his look of incomprehension. *{This is a Fey Branded place.}*

"Fey ... Branded?" Meriwether frowned. "Fey...brind? All those years, crushing the words into one. Like the Vhemin." He held up a hand. "Ormeon says they are Vehement Systems architectures. I don't know what that means."

{It means they are the enemy.} Lash, lash.

"No." He shook his head. "I think it means something worse." Meriwether gazed at the other cylinders, each holding one of the People. "Who were your parents?"

Her hands moved, sharp and hard, cutting the air into manageable chunks. *{Slaves have no parents.}*

Chapter Seven

Geneve glanced out the low-slung windows, gauging the sun. "I should get back."

"Why?" Mazin frowned. "What is out there you need?"

"I don't need anything." Geneve smoothed her borrowed clothes. "A kind man gave me shelter, and when the dogs brayed for my blood I ran. I must fix it."

"So, you're a fixer of things?" The big man rose from his divan, all bulk and majesty like a mighty ship. "Not a Knight, then. A tool, perhaps?"

She narrowed her eyes. "I can tell when someone wants something. Out with it."

"I don't want anything." The merchant stroked his chin, then moved to the window. "Tell me what you see."

Geneve joined him. The day wore on as it always did, the sun unconcerned with the loss of the Three, burning everbright as it circled the world. Its path held it low in the sky, taking some of the heat with it, but leaving its mark. People walked or ran as their needs demanded, but with a wearier air than the morning. "Tired people, as the day nears end."

"Do tired people fear raising their eyes?"

She growled. "Just tell me what you want."

"I've already said I don't want anything. But I owe you, Knight, for saving me from the Arm." Mazin left her at the window, hustling into the rear of his home. She continued to watch the street as his voice came to her, softened a little by distance. "A stranger in Tebrani is unusual. We are a merchant people, sailing the waves to sell things we don't need to people who do. When one comes here, well ... usually they are slaves. Sometimes they are lost, like you. Rarely do they come as fellow merchants."

"I'm not lost," Geneve whispered. *Am I sure about that?*

Mazin continued, unable to hear her words or thoughts. "Regardless of how they arrive, they are always marked by their fair skin and strange tongues. Your skin is passing fair, perhaps showing mixed blood. Unusual but not enough to be remarkable." He returned from the back room carrying a small glass vial holding two or three swallows of dark blue liquid. "What will get you stopped by the Precept's Arm or Will is your speech. You don't speak a lick of Tebrani. You sound like a foreigner's dog."

"Is this the flattery part of the pitch, or does that come later?" Geneve raised an eyebrow. "I'm not sure how merchanting is done."

Mazin laughed. "I'm not trying to sell you something."

"Yes, you are." She put her hands on her hips. "You're trying to sell me what's in that blue vial. You want me to drink it, but you're laying it on a feather bed. *You're* doing *me* a favor, hmm?"

The big man blinked, looked to the vial, then back to her. "You are certain you are a Knight, not a merchant?"

"Last time I checked." Geneve looked at the borrowed clothes she wore. "I'll allow not wearing the burnished sun is confusing for an outsider."

Mazin's eyes twinkled. "And would you like the burnished sun about you again?" He lifted the vial. "This is the key."

"Right there." She stabbed the air with a finger, as if pinning his argument to a board. "Selling me something."

Mazin set the vial on a side table, then rejoined her at the window. "Have you seen anything different since we last spoke?"

"Since two minutes ago, you mean?" At his nod, she grinned. "Nothing but a man trying to ply me with snake oil."

"Snake oil isn't blue." He crossed his arms. "This city is under the grip of the Precept. He holds a ward of each of the five families. Free the wards, and the families will rally to your banner."

"I have no banner or need of vassals." Geneve took a step back. "I hunt demons."

"And who do you think holds the wards?" Mazin raised an eyebrow. "Ah. I see the problem. They don't teach basic Tebrani history in Or'sen." He raised his hands in mock surrender at her scowl. "Mercy, Knight. The Precept's lived a long time. Longer than men, Feybrind, or the dragon you claim to have."

"Ormeon's real! She's—"

"And yet, whatever your dragon is, she's not *here*. The Precept is, and with him, his Arm and Will. They enforce his desires during the day, and all the long hours of the night." He scratched his belly. "The Precept holds Imshir in the palm of his hand. His power is immense. Sorcery unknown since the times of the ancients. The ability to sway a man's mind, as did Bellany of Redwood. Except Bellany was just one woman. She could hold sway against a ship, but not a nation. The Precept's power is insidious. It doesn't *make* you do a thing. He ... makes you *want* to do it. Does that make sense?"

Geneve felt a shiver touch her spine. "He is surely just an enchanter."

"There is nothing just about the man." Mazin looked away. "I've felt the touch of his power. Extended through his Will, when they came calling in the night."

"What happened?"

"I died." Mazin grinned, showing plenty of teeth. "Perhaps that tale can wait for another day."

"You don't smell dead." Geneve shook her head. "I've seen plenty of dead men. The stink is unmistakable. You smell of ginger wine and geranium."

"A fellow botanist! How fortunate a humble merchant I am."

She snorted. "How does a dead man sell spices?"

"Carefully." Mazin smoothed his robes. "Too much cumin, and people think you're trying to hide something."

Geneve pointed to the blue vial without looking. "And how does that raise dead men and protect Or'sen, Tebrani, and the rest of the world? Will it give me back my Meri? Does drinking it return dear Ormeon to my side?"

"No, but it buys you something else." Mazin looked troubled. "Language. If you free a ward, and set your price on his head—"

"So I'm to free people but call it a debt? That's no freedom." Geneve brushed angry red hair from her face.

Mazin paced, holding his words inside until it looked like they would boil over. "But it's the only way! The families will not listen to your words."

"Then my words aren't worth listening to." She shrugged. "I'm not here for them. I'm not here for *you*. I'm here to kill demons, merchant. I'm here to end the threat to the world for all time."

"The demons command everything, Tresward. Sword and shield, yes, but also the stonemason and the baker." At Mazin's words, Geneve thought of Omrar and his humble shop. "They will raise all Imshir against you."

"And will freeing the wards stop that?"

"I—" Mazin floundered. "Do you play chess?"

"I hate games."

"So it would seem." He ambled to the vial, retrieved it, and brought it to her. His fingers, gentle and careful, put it into her hand. Mazin closed her hand over it. "Think on it at least. Knowing our speech can't hurt, can it?"

Geneve shook her head. It was her turn to frown. "Knowing things hurts most of all, merchant."

SHE LEFT MAZIN AND HIS WORDS BEHIND HER. THE STREETS OF Imshir didn't empty as the sun left the sky. Cart traffic dwindled, replaced by a different kind of hawker. Young men and women smelling of honey and cloves took to street corners. Geneve spotted the watchful presence of their masters idling in doorways or up in windows.

Food vendors changed from bread to selling meats that smelled like the tears of heaven. Geneve's mouth watered, and she realized she held no coin of this land. Without Omrar's hospitality, she'd starve. *Or I'd turn to a life of crime. I like my food too much.*

Her feet remembered the way to Omrar's store. She found his door closed, the place shut for the night. There wasn't evidence of violence —no blood spray, smashed boards, or body parts. *What a life I lead, to look for these things wherever I step. Is this what Meri saw when he first laid eyes on me?*

Of course it was. He feared the heavy tread of her boots.

No ... that's not right. He met me in Birdsong Alley. I heard invisible finches. Meri tried to talk to me. She smiled. *He is a romantic fool. I miss him so much.*

Geneve didn't know if she'd be welcome at Omrar's. There was no sign out saying, *All Geneves should go this way!* She strolled to the back of his home, letting herself into the yard. There were no white sheets drying on the line. The gate to the next door's yard was open, gently *clinking* against its latch as a breeze caught it.

Curiosity got the better of her. Food might be inside, but Omrar didn't strike her as the kind of man to leave a gate unlatched. He wasn't as bent with age as the lines on his face suggested he should be. His shoulders looked broad enough to pull a wagon, and if the years took his strength they left a story of a strong man of action.

Men of action do not leave the gate at their back open and unguarded. Geneve wandered into the neighboring yard. It wasn't as well kept as Omrar's, the grass overlong, but still holding the memory of someone who cared for it. Vegetables grew among new weeds. Vines held plump fruit. The back door of the place was open, the door nodding against the frame in time with the hush of wind.

Geneve opened the door with a cautious hand. Inside wasn't black as hell, a light from above showing her the way to a staircase. She wound up to the next level and found Omrar seated on a divan, a lantern laying a blanket of light about his feet.

The old man's eyes were distant, fixed on a memory he'd dredged up for this moment. She knew that look. Israel had stared into their campfire with a face like that often enough. Her father might be remembering the day he'd stolen her memories, or Geneve's mother. Omrar's eyes held that bittersweet yearning she knew so well.

"Hello, Omrar."

The old man turned to her, the lilt of his words questioning.

Geneve sat next to him on the divan, then held out the blue vial. "Mazin says this will let me understand you. I don't know if I should trust him. He says he's died before. Faced the Tresward and an enchantress both. A man with so many tall tales seems fanciful ... but I love a man who tells stranger stories."

Omrar spoke softly, but not unkindly. She wished she knew what he said. Geneve pocketed the vial. "Who's house is this?" She gestured, palms up.

He raised an eyebrow, then nodded as if taking her meaning. "Lily."

"Lily? That is ... not a Tebrani name." He shrugged, face miserable. Geneve tapped the blue vial. "The burnished sun keeps the Tresward safe from many things. We don't ever get sick. None of us will be rolled into the grave by the hands of time." She laughed, short and hard. "Not many of us live long enough to find that out though. We are the shield that guards the heart of the world. But we can't have children, and," she tapped the vial again, "we aren't immune to poison. I don't know why the Three left that out of the plan, but if someone wanted to kill one of us, this would be the way."

Omrar sagged a little as if the weight of her words was a burden it took two men to carry, then stood. He wandered to a wall that looked much like the others, set his shoulder to it, and did something clever with his fingers. A *click* later and the wall slid aside to reveal a small chamber. It held a few knickknacks. Geneve spied a tuft of hair tied with a bow beside a wonderful ceramic vase made so fine she wondered if it would crack if she held it.

Near the back was a handful of books. Not a library like Meri would love, just a few words collected in faded bindings. Omrar teased one free, mindful of the vase, blew dust off it, and carried it to her. He held it out. "Tresward."

She took the book, feeling the age of it. It'd been made before

Israel first squalled free of his mother's belly. The cover was faded with the bleached look of too much sun, but the ink on the pages inside was still vivid black.

It was a child's picture book. Each page held a big squiggle that might be letters of a different tongue, and scratchings beneath in the same language. Beside the text were pictures. Fairies flew in wondrous detail near dragons huge and fierce. Geneve turned each page with care, feeling them crinkle beneath her fingers. The book smelled like a memory she didn't have. She imagined herself tucked into bed with the book held before her, Israel reading to her in his deep voice, his scent about her, a bastion against the cares of the world.

He was a bastion, but not the kind I needed. Perhaps the one I deserved, though.

About half-way through the book she found a picture of three people. They wore full armor, the style a little strange to her eye, but the burnished sun was unmistakable. *Omrar's friend Lily had a children's book of strange and wonderful things. Dragons, fairies, unicorns, and dryads... and us. We're a myth to them. They haven't felt the shield of our faith for so long we're nothing but a fanciful tale.*

Omrar sat beside her, careful to keep a respectful distance. His hand touched the three on the page: a large man, a whip-thin woman, and another woman who was somewhere between them. It didn't take much imagination to see herself standing between Israel and Vertiline. "Tresward," the old man said. "Tresward."

Geneve closed the book, curling over it for a moment, trying to regain the memory she should have had from a father who loved her without compromise. No balancing faith and duty, or turning his face from the Light in case he burned. She felt the old tome's cover rasp on her forehead. "How long has it been since you saw Lily?" Geneve stood, pacing to the window. She pointed to the starry black outside, no moons watching over them. "Was it when the gods fell?"

Omrar nodded as if agreeing.

Geneve padded to the secret cupboard. She found the lock of hair, lifting it to her nose. It smelled of nothing. The person it'd come from wasn't forgotten, but they'd started to fade from the world as all things did. First their presence, the sight and sound of them, but then later their scent diminished from the things they touched, until you couldn't remember who they were, or if they'd been real at all.

Perhaps all you had was a lock of hair and a children's book you shared together. Because there were no Tresward to keep the monsters away.

She snatched the vial from her pocket, tore free the stopper, and swilled the contents back. The liquid within tasted like the hair smelled: of nothing much at all. A slight wetness, more like oil than water, then it was done. Not a drop of blue remained in the vial when she examined it. *If I die, they won't know what killed me.*

Geneve didn't feel sick. She felt strange enough, as if she had bees in her head, speaking a thousand things at once. Each with its own tongue, a word it wanted to give her, a footprint in the sand of her mind. She stumbled, balance lost, and the vial fell from her fingers.

Omrar stood, but he moved as if weights held him down. Geneve wondered what he would be like without his body, the brilliance of what was inside able to shine for all to see. She reached out, fingers stretching, as if a touch might make it so, then her arm shook and fell back to her side.

She didn't remember hitting the ground, but it felt comfortable so she didn't mind. The pink vase fell toward her, perhaps knocked by her. *I haven't lost my balance in fifteen years. I am Tresward, and we don't fall.* Geneve tried to stand, but nothing about her paid any attention to what she wanted.

The bees grew louder, insistent, desperate. There were thousands, then tens of thousands, and before long she thought she could count a million of them. All before the vase hit the ground. It fell as slowly as Omrar moved, the old man not half-way to her by the time the vase reached the floor.

Geneve caught it in one strong hand. She managed to save that one thing for a lost woman, and perhaps that was enough.

Blackness, soft and warm. But there were so many bees.

Chapter Eight

Meriwether felt unsteady, like the world tipped a couple degrees beneath him while it wasn't paying attention.

Coming Storm eyed him warily. *{What is wrong? Are you feeble? Infirm? Sick in the head?}*

"I'm ... not sure," he admitted. "I don't think I'm feeble."

{You look feeble. As a soldier might, if they stopped eating and started reading instead.}

Meriwether took a seat on the ground. "I'm no soldier."

She crossed her arms in a gesture that said, *I could have told you that.* *{Infirm? Sick?}*

"I think not." Meriwether scratched his beard. "I think something else is wrong."

{With what?}

"The world." He took a steadying breath. "With everything." Meriwether clambered back up, the ground once again level. "Explain to me again why we can't wake your friends."

Her beautiful rose eyes rolled. *{Because you have no slave. Because I have no master.}*

"Those feel like the answer to a different question." The blue-feathered bird landed on his shoulder. "Perhaps I should take you to meet Ormeon. But first we need two more birds. So we can get things working again."

Coming Storm eyed the blue-feathered bird. *{It's not a bird.}*

"Merciful Three! Of course it's not a bird. It's a *juniya.*"

The cat glared. *{I know what she is. And you are using the Tebrani word for her, not the Or'sen one.}*

"You could have said," Meriwether huffed. "Wait. There's an Or'sen word for a blue-feathered not-bird?"

Rose eyes hardened. *{I can't speak. You made us mute.}*

"*I* did no such thing." Meriwether brushed his hair back. "Tell me about … how it works, I guess. What do you mean, you're a slave?"

{It's better if I show you.} She turned on her heel, stalking off. Despite Coming Storm's silent padding, Meriwether felt her anger like the hammer clap of thunder.

"Superb," Meriwether said to her retreating back. "Another six ways to die on the way, no doubt."

COMING STORM LED HIM THROUGH THE TEMPLE LIKE SHE KNEW THE way. She said nothing as she stalked on, shoulders stiff and hard like the ancient stone walls around them. Coming Storm muscled through a door that creaked loud as a scream, causing him to glance over his shoulder. *We killed three ancient guardians. There might be more.* He glanced at Coming Storm's lashing tail. *Although she's probably angry enough to kill a hundred.*

The doorway led to a set of stairs going both up and down. She—of course!—went down. The walls here didn't glow, his lantern banishing the dark instead, but the Feybrind paced well ahead of the glow. *She needs less light than me.* He remembered Feybrind could see in near darkness, but the Vhemin could see in pitch black.

"Are there any Vhemin here?"

Coming Storm paused, head cocked, then turned as if confused. *{I don't know that word. The guardians we met before aren't called that.}*

"Vhemin. About this high," Meriwether stabbed his hand at an

Armitage-suitable height above his own head, "and are scaled like a big lizard. Yellow eyes like snakes. Bad teeth. Worse dispositions."

{You call us the People, or slur Fey Branded into sludge. You call Vehement System's creations a different thing too. I can hear how the sounds run together through the treacle of years.} She sagged a little. *{Has so much been lost? Do you know nothing of the eternal war?}*

He came down the steps to meet her. Took one of her hands, fur soft and gentle, in his. "I know nothing much at all. I make no claim to the mantle of the world. *My* people lost everything. But..." He trailed off, looking away. She squeezed his hand, encouraging, offering a little strength. "I think we took everything from everyone else first. The dragons. The Feybrind. And yes, even the Vhemin. I think we put the Three in the sky, banishing them from this world."

Rose eyes, soft as candy, watched him. *{You're mostly right.}*

"I was hoping for better news."

{Only worse, I'm afraid. You didn't put the Three in the sky. That was the demons.}

"Super."

She half-smiled at him. *{You have a gentle heart. How have you survived?}*

I wonder about that too. "I'm a really fast runner."

Coming Storm's lips parted, and he saw the gleam of razor-sharp fangs. *{Your doom is a sprinter, and it's gaining on you.}*

THEIR DESTINATION WAS MANY STEPS DOWN. MERIWETHER LOST count at a thousand, mostly because he didn't want the dispirited burden of knowing how many he'd have to climb back up. Coming Storm took him into a gloom-shrouded room, far wider than the lantern's light would reach. *{We are here.}*

"It's pretty dark. I can't see. My eyes aren't as good as yours."

She nodded, slow and sad. *{That's why you made them so well. We are the brace that holds up your empire.}*

"What?"

Coming Storm turned away, padding into the gloom. He jogged to keep up. They passed more glass cases, but unlike the cylinders above, these were square. Inside were the moldering remains of books, sculptures, and friezes. Meriwether spotted dragons, some like Ormeon, others leaner, longer of body, with whip-like tails. There were Feybrind and Vhemin set in dioramas against each other, snarls of hate shown through bared fangs and locked weapons.

At least, he assumed they were weapons. Swords and axes he knew, but some were devices like the guardians above used. He spotted a pattern. "All the Feybrind and dragons are winning." He held the lantern up as he turned. "In each display, the Vhemin fall."

{This room is for selling dreams.} Her eyes were so sad he wanted to hold her. *{All your dreams are of hate.}*

"I don't understand." Meriwether felt lost. "I dream of my love. I want to see her again."

{And would you burn the world to hold her one more time?} The cat nodded, as if she knew his heart. *{What price would you ask others pay for the sweet smell of her hair? The taste of her lips, or her touch in the dark?}*

"Quite a bit," Meriwether admitted. "I think I already have. She almost killed me."

Coming Storm blinked. *{What?}*

"It's a long story."

{One I'd like to hear. You're a strange human.} She half-smiled. *{Come. We are not here for stale displays and ancient news. You need to see.}*

Coming Storm led him deeper into the maze of artifacts until they arrived at a clear space. There was a familiar enough glass panel set atop two metal pillars, but no dais. "Thank the Three. Every time there's a raised platform, someone's trying to kill me."

Coming Storm held her hand out, palm up to the panel. *{You must turn it on.}*

He pursed his lips. "Why can't you?"

{Slaves give no Commands.}

"Fair enough. Your house, your rules." He sauntered to the panel, laying his palm against the old, cold glass. The glass lit within, a cascade of different colored lights falling from where his palm touched. The light fell from the panel, raining near his feet.

The room hummed, then grew in brightness. He saw they were close to a high wall, perhaps three stories tall. The light at his feet puddled, then trickled toward the wall, climbing like bedazzled rainwater running backward. It stretched against the wall, becoming a man's face.

Old, but kind. An easy smile, no teeth in it. A trimmed mustache went with hair cropped in an unfamiliar style. The man wore clothes like Meriwether's, but a lighter color, more like pale dawn than dusk.

"Merciful Three, he's huge."

Coming Storm smirked. *{He is not real. Not much here is.}*

As if recognizing Meriwether, the old man leaned forward, but his face didn't leap out of the wall. It was like he leaned toward a window, and Meriwether was on the other side, like the barber's mirror above. "Hello. Who are you?"

"It speaks Or'sen."

{This place is not for Tebrani.} She gave a small bow, then backed away. *{It knows you by the color of your blood. Welcome home.}*

"Don't you mean the color of my skin?" Meriwether felt like he was losing grip on the conversation.

"Who are you?" the old man repeated.

"I'm Lord Meriwether du Reeves, servant of her majesty Morgan, ruler of Or'sen and protector of the free peoples of the world." *Not bad on short notice.*

"Greetings, Lord Meriwether. Let me tell you how we're going to change the world together."

Chapter Nine

Omrar didn't know what to do. The woman with red hair fell, eyes lost, locked on his. She still held the vase he'd given Lily when her child was born. She'd locked it away after the little boy met the Arm for the first and last time.

It was like the god warrior knew what was precious and protected those things, right up to the point when the will left her laying barely breathing on Lily's floor.

He knelt by her side, checking for a pulse. Her wrist was warm, solid, *dense*. Geneve was a warrior used to the blade and buckler. She shouldn't have fallen to an invisible foe. Her chest didn't rise and fall, so Omrar put his ear to her lips, hoping for the heat of breath on his face.

There was barely the flutter of a moth's wings. He couldn't leave her here. If the Arm found her, or gods forbid, the Will... Her journey to the Precept's palace would be swift. She was marked and hunted.

Omrar got his arms under her, then manhandled her onto his shoulder. *This was easier when I was younger.* The sky warrior was heavier than any woman he'd known, like her bones were made of steel, forged in the heart of a star. *She is Tresward. Are they somehow different from us?*

Stories from children's books come to life. Next we'll see fairies and dragons. Perhaps a unicorn.

He heaved, struggling upright, almost dropping Geneve. He careened into a wall, found his center, and waited for his breath to even. Down the stairs, one at a time, carefully, *carefully* damn it, he almost knocked her head against the wall, but he made it out the back of Lily's home just as fists hammered on the front door.

Omrar's breath was ragged already, but he needed to get clear. A foot hooked around the door pulled it closed behind him, then he waddled fast as he could through Lily's overgrown garden. The smell of crushed grass followed him, but there was no help for it. The gate creaked as he passed through, a scream of metal he was sure the gods heard, except they were gone. Gone from the sky, forsaking this world, and leaving people to deal with mad kings like the Precept.

Another shriek and the gate closed behind him. He staggered up his own steps, shouldering the back door open. Up the stairs, still one at a time, his heart hammering in his chest. It was old, that heart, and he prayed it wouldn't give out. He'd asked much of it over the years, broken it at least twice, and here he was, asking even more.

Shouting and the crunch of breaking wood carried through the night. *They're in Lily's home. They'll be here soon.* The room he'd laid Geneve in the night before wouldn't do. He had to go higher. Omrar climbed, breath shaking his old chest as if trying to pry ribs free. His back twinged, the sky warrior's weight on one shoulder an uneven load even a fit man would struggle with.

His bedroom. A sanctum from the day's cares. His bed was clean enough. He laid Geneve on it, then tossed a blanket over her. A pillow or three later and she looked like rumpled linen, not a woman the Precept wanted enough to send his Arm into the world.

A hammering came from below. *They're here! They're at my door.* He tore his shirt off, yanking on a nightshirt, then hop-stepped out of his pants as he made the stairs. Down he went, trying to still his breathing. "Hold on! I'm coming!"

The hammering didn't care. Louder, harder, his shop's front door rattling in its frame. Omrar made ground level, hurried to the door, and pulled it open. "Hello—"

An armored man shoved him aside, naked blade catching starlight. "Old man, you were warned."

"What's this about?" Omrar looked behind the Arm officer, seeing five more in the street. Four men, two women. "What brings six of the Precept's best to my humble shop?"

"Treason," the officer hissed. His blade rested at Omrar's throat. "This morning you said there was no woman with you."

"That's because there wasn't." Omrar clutched his hands together. "Please. I make bread. I—"

"You make sin and lies!" The officer smashed an armored fist into Omrar's jaw.

Omrar's vision bloomed and blackened. He slumped back, rump hitting a table, knocking a chair over. A vase fell, flowers and water spreading with shattered ceramic on the floor. "Please. Please don't." But he didn't know what he was asking them not to do. Omrar knew the Arm came and brought the Precept's justice. That's where Lily went. He wanted to see her again, but in this life, not the next.

The soldiers filed in, spreading out to fill the shop. The officer who'd hit him dragged Omrar to his feet, steel once again against his old throat. "Take us."

Omrar raised his hands. "I mean no disrespect, but ... where?" He tugged his nightshirt. "I was asleep, you see—"

"Find her." The officer's eyes never left Omrar's face as his team spread through the shop, a malaise he could never clean away. "You will give me a guided tour. For the Precept, of course. When we find no one here, I will apologize. The Precept will recompense you for the damage to your home. We will clean the floor. A public declaration of your innocence will be made in the market square."

"Uh," offered Omrar.

"Of course, if we find someone, then I will bleed you low and quiet. Our Will saw her enter your home, old man. And our Will knows the night." A smile, nothing of kindness or mercy in it. "How about that tour?"

Omrar swallowed, the blade easing from his throat. "It would be my pleasure." His mind raced ahead and tried to work out where to take these hard-eyed men and women who wanted an old shopkeeper dead and the god warrior he harbored taken to a devil on a golden throne.

Rough hands propelled him forward past unforgiving gazes. Hands were close to blades, and he wondered for a moment if they feared him that much. *No. They fear her. The Precept told these soldiers the heaven's agent brought justice with her.* He almost smiled, but it was too soon for victory. Geneve lay, unblinking, upstairs. She couldn't defend herself.

Up the stairs—*so many stairs tonight! I will die tired*—he showed the officer the living room. "See? There is no one here."

"I see." An approving nod, but the blade held ready never wavered. "Two levels down. Only one to go. Your chances of seeing tomorrow go up with each floor we climb."

On weary feet Omrar led them to his bedroom. His clothes were where he left them, the bed undisturbed. Omrar slipped aside to let the Arm in. "There is nothing but an old man's bad housekeeping to see."

The officer walked into the room, steps measured, slow, deliberate. Two more followed, a bald man and a woman sporting a deep scar that ran from her forehead, past her eye, and down her cheek. The officer turned a slow circle. "Search it."

The other two went to work opening Omrar's cupboards and chests. They were thorough enough, and just as messy, tossing clothes and other items to the floor in their haste. Once everything was done, the woman looked to the officer. Her voice was high and sweet, so at odds with the Precept she represented. "There's nothing here."

"I guess that apology's in order." The officer gave a nasty smile. "Except..." He whirled, grabbed Omrar's sheets, and hauled them clear.

"No!" Omrar took two steps forward, but the bald man had a blade out, whip-fast, razor-sharp, and pressed the point to Omrar's neck. The sky warrior lay on Omrar's bed, eyes still open, face blank. Geneve still held Lily's vase, as if she'd never let the precious thing drop. The Arm officer raised his blade. "Wait."

The officer held his sword still. "What for?"

"Aren't you taking her prisoner?" Omrar wanted to help, to do *something*, but he was old, his body worn out like an battered wagon wheel. Even in his prime, three of the Arm would've been too much.

"The Arm keep no prisoners." The officer brought the blade down.

Chapter Ten

The man's giant image smiled, patient, waiting. Meriwether looked to Coming Storm. The cat knelt, eyes down, forehead pressed to the cold stone floor. *Interesting.* Meriwether smoothed his ancient clothes, squared his shoulders, and cleared his throat. "No."

He heard the cat's indrawn breath. The tiniest of noises, but unmistakable in this ancient room full of dead memories. The visage's smile turned upside down, lips pulling into a moue of distaste, like Meriwether was something on the bottom of his boot. "I don't think you understand how contract negotiations work."

Meriwether nodded. "You're not wrong."

"And furthermore ... what?"

"I don't have much time in my life for contracts or negotiations. You said we'll change the world together, without knowing what the world might need." Meriwether hooked his thumbs into his belt. "Have you looked outside? Belay that. You're a dead man. Of course you haven't looked outside."

"I'm Florian Arsenault, president of—"

"Florian, you're a dead man's memory." Meriwether sighed. "I don't mean to be brusque, but these things are best held up to a good, strong light so we all know where we stand." He held his hand behind him to where he hoped Coming Storm still huddled in fear against a floor trod by masters long dead. "You fucked everything up."

Lips curled into a snarl as Arsenault worked up the memory of anger. "How dare—"

"One of us is in a position to make demands. The other will spend the rest of eternity in a dark room if they don't calm down and take a moment." Meriwether turned his back on the ancient man, strode to Coming Storm, and held his hand out to her.

She raised her eyes, but without confidence. She saw his hand, confusion crossing her face. {What do you want from me?}

"I'd like you to stand by my side. Be my guide. Square your shoulders when you look out under the land the sun touches. Be at peace with your place in the world. Help me build a better tomorrow." He let his hand fall, then dropped to one knee in front of her. "I want you to not be afraid of the dead."

Florian's voice boomed through the chamber. "I will teach you fear!"

Meriwether didn't turn. "I know plenty of fear. Felt its touch in the cold of night. It held me close more than once, more familiar than the touch of a kind father. Fear's dogged my heels for the longest time, always hungry, wanting more of me until there's nothing left." He tossed his words over his shoulder. "You've nothing to teach either of us, dead man." He took Coming Storm's soft hands in his, one still tacky with a dead guardian's ichor. Meriwether stood, pulling her with him, then led her onto the dais. "Let's start again. I'm Lord Meriwether du Reeves, and this is my friend Coming Storm."

"She has no human friends. She is Fey Branded." Florian looked between the two of them, each eye the size of a man's head. "They are *ours*."

Meriwether looked about. "There's no damn chairs in here. I feel this is going to take a long time."

"I can take you on a journey, Meriwether." Florian looked doubtful. "I don't know what's happened while I've slept. My ... mind tells me you're right, that I've been out for an age beyond reckoning. I speak to you in a language not native to this land. All is darkness beyond this room. But I can still show you wonders."

"How would you do that?" Meriwether pursed his lips. "It seems we're both of us stuck here."

"I can show you things in the theater of your mind," Florian promised. "I can share the dream with you."

"Like, asleep?"

"Very much like that, but everything you'll see is real."

"Was."

"Sorry?"

"Was real," Meriwether said.

Florian smiled, a lot of perfect teeth showing. "I promise you, it's all still real. Real as the air you breathe."

Meriwether felt a hand on his arm. Coming Storm's wonderful rose eyes held his. *{I will watch you while you Dream.}*

Florian snorted. "You'd trust a non-Branded Fey? Risky, Meriwether, Lord of nothing, heir to a broken world."

Meriwether ignored Florian. He held his hands between him and Coming Storm. *{I'd be honored.}*

Jewel eyes widened in surprise. *{It is rare one of yours is as elegant with handspeak as us. You don't need to lower yourself to speak in our dirty way.}* She closed her fingers over his, looked away, then squared her shoulders as if remembering what he'd said. *{It will probably hurt.}*

"Wouldn't be the first time." Meriwether tried on a grin he didn't feel. *{It was another honor when one of my best friends taught me the words of the People. He was patient as I made mistakes.}*

{Are you sure this isn't another?} She glanced at Florian, the move furtive, those wondrous eyes fearful of what they might see. *{I don't think you are like them, and that will be your undoing. You shouldn't trust this man. He will take all you are and make it what he needs.}*

"I'll be fine. He needs me to change the world, remember?" Meriwether squared off against Florian. "That's right, isn't it? You need human hands to work the wonders of this temple. Do your thing."

Florian's smile widened, showing more teeth than a man should have. "As you wish. Welcome to the first day of the rest of your life. Let me tell you a story."

MERIWETHER STOOD IN A ROOM FASHIONED LIKE MANY OTHERS IN the ancient's temple. The walls were cluttered with papers and strange writings, perhaps their equivalent of reagents and salt circles for the working of great magics.

Or the summoning of demons.

The room held two men, dressed as Florian was, but each slouched in chairs on opposite sides of a great black table. One had a piece of fabric tied about his throat. It was a bright fuchsia color that reminded Meriwether of Coming Storm's eyes. The other was bald like an old man, but only a few faint wrinkles rested at the corners of his eyes. The table's surface glistened like wet obsidian. Meriwether wondered if they were powerful men. It didn't make much sense, because they both seemed so tired.

Florian's voice was at his ear. "This is how it began."

Fuchsia leaned forward, his stance even seated somehow subservient. *Which makes sense, if that's a slave collar about his neck.* His voice was heavy with confidence and authority. "We're boned."

Young and Bald frowned. "You know I don't like those kinds of terms."

"I'm sorry," Fuchsia said. "What I meant was, we're fucked."

Young and Bald laughed. "That's better. But could you be more specific?"

"The orbital arrays aren't live yet. Vehement Systems got the contract with their unholy monsters."

"It was the Artifices that did it." Young and Bald leaned back further, a feat Meriwether found fascinating as any common chair would have given up by now and tossed him on the floor. "We make better stuff. Why aren't we winning?"

A Feybrind entered, head down to the tray he carried. Meriwether recognized him as one of the People only from what he looked like, because the rest of him was ... *wrong.* Where Sight of Day's shoulders were squared, beautiful eyes up and curious about the world around him, this man hid inside himself. He placed the tray on the table before backing away, eyes down. The tray held steaming cups of coffee, cakes, and fruits. Fuchsia and Young and Bald ignored him, minds elsewhere.

The Feybrind almost made it to the door before Fuchsia took a sip of coffee. He spat the coffee back into the cup. "This is terrible!"

{I'm sorry. We're out of real milk because of the war.} The Feybrind didn't look up, but his fingers moved in perfect handspeak, the language the same ages ago as it was today.

"Don't wave your fingers at me," Fuchsia said.

Young and Bald raised an eyebrow. "They can't talk. That's the whole point. Seen and not heard, remember? We make the servants who never complain because they *can't*."

"They listen fine." Fuchsia stood, cup contents sloshing over his hand. Meriwether winced as the hot liquid scalded Fuchsia. The man hollered, then threw the cup at the Feybrind.

The cat leaned aside as if he'd been waiting for it, eyes still down, and caught the cup as it passed. He held it in both hands, waiting. Meriwether felt something was terribly amiss, that the world was off balance and listing. *They aren't slaves. They're artisans!*

"They make everything for us," Florian agreed, voice a whisper at Meriwether's ear. "Machines, clothes, and coffee. They do it better than we can."

Young and Bald sighed, oblivious to the voice of a man eight hundred years dead. "You want to kick the cat? Fine. But we've got bigger problems. We're *losing*."

Fuchsia looked to the ceiling, as if he could see the Three above. "Fey Branded Command name, please."

The room responded, a soothing female voice used to the demands of angry, impatient people. "Dawn's Gentle Touch and Memory." The Feybrind stiffened as his real name was shared for all in the room. Both men didn't seem to care.

"A poet, huh?" Fuchsia sighed. "Dawn's Gentle Touch and Memory, I'd like you to kill Malcolm Treadwell."

Young and Bald, unfortunately also named Malcolm Treadwell, startled upright, making it half-way out of his chair before the Feybrind was on him, teeth bared and at the man's throat. Blood sprayed, red finding a home on the walls. Fuchsia closed his eyes and turned away as wet ochre coated Malcolm Treadwell from the waist up.

Dawn's Gentle Touch and Memory stood, stepped back, and waited. The Feybrind's eyes held the floor like an island of safety. Meriwether realized the cat's gaze was always down. He hadn't even caught the color of those no-doubt wonderful eyes.

Fuchsia paced to the fallen man. Malcolm wasn't moving. The Feybrind made sure the end of his body's march was certain, not leaving him to bleed out on the ground. Fuchsia wiped his face, smearing spatters of red like warpaint. "It was time for a promotion anyway. Now, to cover up the evidence. Dawn's Gentle Touch and Memory, I would like you to shut your neck in the door. Keep doing that until you're dead."

That's when Meriwether caught sight of the Feybrind's eyes. They were golden, like Sight of Day's, and so very, very afraid.

THE MEMORY, IF THAT'S WHAT IT WAS, SHUDDERED. MERIWETHER stood on a battlefield. A Vhemin host roared toward him, no more than twenty meters away. He screamed, ducked, and covered his head.

A Feybrind leaped over him, landing with perfect grace. Blue light lanced, and the sound of dying gods broke the heavens as an Artifice sheared sky before impacting the ground four hundred meters away. The Vhemin didn't change their run, heading for the lone Feybrind.

Meriwether wondered what her name was, why she protected him, and if she feared death. Florian's voice was in his ear, soft, and urgent. He should've been inaudible with the cacophony about them, but Meriwether heard him just fine. "She doesn't know you. Or care about you. That's what makes them so good at what they do."

"She's one against thirty!"

"The Vhemin should have brought more guys, then." Meriwether heard the smirk in Florian's voice, as if a dead man still liked his odds at cards.

The Feybrind met the Vhemin with bared fangs and twin blades.

Blue lances of light tried to snatch her from the face of the world, but she danced aside as if mere light was too slow for a cat to worry about. The swords she carried weren't glass. She moved like a gymnast, a dancer ready for her greatest performance.

The Feybrind spun past the lead Vhemin, blade taking his head. Meriwether swore he heard Armitage. *Gotta take the head. Only way to be sure.* This Feybrind knew her foe, understood what brought them low, and wasted no strikes.

The Vhemin host's blue-runed armor flared, dazzling Meriwether for a moment. They surged like a wave made of lizards and shark-horror teeth at the cat. Meriwether headed for her. He had to help, to stand with her, to lend his shoulder against the wall of death. It'd be the end of them both, but no one should die alone.

The scene froze. Meriwether saw the Feybrind's bared teeth, her sword caught like a fly in red amber, half-way through a Vhemin's neck. She'd tossed the other blade, and it held its position in the air. When time caught up with it, it'd land in the head of a Vhemin woman bulling forward.

"You can't change what's already happened," Florian said. "She fought well. One against thirty, as you say. This was a proof of concept."

The world started to shudder again. Meriwether shouted, "Wait!"

"For what?" Florian's voice was everywhere, his body nowhere.

"There aren't any ... humans."

"People, you mean."

"I see plenty of people," Meriwether spat. "I see the brave against the fearful. Of humans, there are no sign."

"Why would we fight?" Florian sounded confused. "That comes later. We take the beach, then the land and skies. The castles fall next, and after that the heads of our enemies leave their necks. Only the losing humans will ever lift a blade." He snorted. "Effortless war. That's what we sell."

Meriwether walked to the Feybrind. He circled her, taking in her emerald eyes, her bared teeth, and touched her arm. The fur was soft and warm. Perfect. But those eyes held him and wouldn't let go. For all the anger she clutched close, something else ran deeper. *Fear.* "Does she die?"

"Of course. There were only five of them on this battlefield."

"Against how many?"

"A thousand." Florian sighed. "They *won*, Lord du Reeves."

"Play it." Meriwether made an *after-you* gesture. "Play the whole thing."

"Whatever for?"

"A couple reasons. First, you need me. You need a human hand to turn everything on. To wake from your eternal night, and if you *don't* show me what happens next, it won't be my hand. I can't imagine many people with a dragon about, ready to open up your temple." Meriwether looked around to find where Florian might be. "But secondly, because no one should die alone."

"She's already dead."

"Not yet," Meriwether whispered.

"Fine." Florian's voice was hard. "You want the guts and glory show, who am I to argue?"

The world moved, slowly at first, then all at once. The thrown sword found a home in the skull of a Vhemin. The Feybrind danced and flowed, a hint of Geneve's grace about her, something untouchable in the beauty of her movement.

Vhemin roared and screamed, caught under their own yoke, unable to let go their hate. The woman with the emerald eyes fought them until she lost an arm, a leering Vhemin holding it to the sun's dim rays, before losing his arm and head to the blade in her other hand.

Blood flowed, until it didn't. Silence held council over the dead.

"Seen everything you needed to?" Florian sounded bored.

Meriwether looked at a sky devoid of moons. The Three were absent, turning their faces from this travesty. "I think so. But we should keep going until I'm sure."

"Excellent," Florian said. "I'm so pleased you're on board with our team. Next stop, we'll look at some dragons."

Chapter Eleven

*S*omeone is trying to kill you, Khiton said. *He holds a sword full of your ending. I see it.*

Geneve lay down, his words a blanket for her mind. She couldn't see Khiton, just the edge of a blade bisecting her world. Left from right. Living from dead. She wanted to talk to Khiton, demand answers for why he set her end to be here, *now*, when she was so close to saving...

What? The god's voice was familiar, a soft sound she'd heard her entire life. It was in the last hush of wind that caressed the fields, thunder's final echo as it strolled across the sky, the taste on her lips after Meri's kisses. *Are you saving the world? The universe? Do you know the span of our great works? Would you bear them all on your shoulders?*

This is a test, Geneve realized. *To see if I live or die, whether I'm worthy to carry your Light.*

No, Khiton said. *It's a test to see if you're human. You've carried our Light since you knew how heavy it was.*

Ah. Geneve wanted to sit up, to touch the blade hungering for her, but she couldn't move. The bees weren't done with her, it seemed. *If I answer any way but the right one, I'm damned.*

Just dead, Khiton said. *We can talk about damnation after that.*

Then fuck you, and all your works, she snarled. *I'm not doing this for* you.

He laughed, soft, but happy. *You're right. It's a test, and you passed.*

The blade above Geneve hadn't moved a millimeter. The hand behind it, strong, accomplished in murder, was also frozen in time. *Why can't I move?*

Because we're not done, Ikmae said. They sounded apologetic, as if this was all a terrible mistake. *We're not free.*

Do you deserve to be? Geneve tried to rise again, but still nothing worked. *All the world lives under the yoke of a different master. Peasants to lords, lords to their queen. Knights to the Clerics, Clerics to the Tresward, and the Tresward to you three impossible-to-please gods. You've left us to die, and you complain about freedom?*

I see why she likes you. Ikmae's voice was even, neither hot or cold, dry or oily. Balanced, like the right stance, or the heft of a weapon made by a Tresward Smith. *You remembered what it was like to hold a shield for those who couldn't lift it themselves.*

No one taught me that. I never forgot.

The world did, Ikmae said. *It forgot for such a long time. It's starting to come back to itself, though. Can you feel it? We've waited for you for all these years.*

You did nothing, Geneve said. *You ... watched, like it was a show for your amusement. Even the dragons are dead!*

You say that like it's a bad thing. Ikmae sighed. *Maybe it was. I'm not my brother or sister. I look at the whole of a thing, the structure that holds it steady, makes it strong. I tell you the people who made the dragons were vile, but perhaps their creations weren't.*

Can you help me? Geneve still couldn't move, but the bees were calming down, their hum less insistent. *I need to ... finish.*

You've barely started. Cophine's voice was the ripening of grain, the coming of dawn, warm, soft, glorious. *If you get up from this bed, what will you do?*

Kill this man, Geneve promised. *He's hurt many.*

Perhaps you'll die instead, Cophine suggested. *The swing I started will be hard to avoid.*

Geneve wanted to scowl. *You want me dead?*

I want you to stop wasting time. Find us, the goddess urged. *Find us and set us free. You are part of our Boundless.*

I don't know what that is, Geneve said. *I'm Tresward.*

You're a promise we gave eight hundred years ago. Three were taken, chips removed before the game was played out. Then we … lost. The warmth ebbed from Cophine's voice. *We never lose.*

Or forget a promise, Ikmae said. *We made it to the world, and everyone in it.*

It's time to collect, Khiton snarled. *It's time to end what you were.*

Become what you were meant to be, Ikmae suggested.

Begin again, Cophine whispered. *Find us. Three gods shouldn't be hard to lay your hand on in a world of demons. Now … live.*

Chapter Twelve

Omrar stumbled back as the red-haired warrior swatted the sword blade aside as if it were the poxy swing of a troubled child. The move was done with perfect grace, difficult to achieve when laying on a mattress, swaddled like a baby, but she didn't seem to care.

Geneve flowed to her feet, oiled perfection, the finest machine ever made by the hands of gods. The Arm officer recovered his surprise from the floor, tucked it back in, and squared off against the Knight. He swung overhand, the movement textbook, no wasted movement. Omrar would've been hard placed to avoid that in his prime, and he was a long way past that.

She dodged to the left, taking a half-step as she moved her body aside. The Arm's second swing thirsted for her throat, and she ducked under that like the world moved at a slower speed than her. The Arm's final strike was a thrust to her stomach.

Geneve caught the blade between two hands, twisting. The blade spun across the room, and embedded itself in the wall beside Omrar's head. She kicked the officer in the groin, then punched him in the side of the head as he curled forward. The man hit Omrar's bedroom floor with the crunch of a wagonload of granite.

Merciful gods, is she ... grinning? Geneve glanced his way, teeth bared, savage joy in her eyes. She marked the sword still vibrating beside his head. "Sorry about that." Her voice held no accent, no trace of Or'sen lingering about her vowels. She dusted off her hands, then faced the remaining two Arm soldiers. "You attacked my friend. That was unwise."

The female Arm officer bellowed below. "'Ware! 'Ware! She's here!"

The man looked at his blade, then Geneve. Omrar could tell he didn't really want this fight, heart left somewhere behind after his commanding officer dropped like a body into a mass grave. He'd been trained by the best Trebani had to offer, though, and his blade was sharp as they came. He danced forward, more ballet than fencing, his blade licking for Geneve's throat.

She slapped the blade aside, palm on steel, then slipped forward to kick the man's leading shin. His foot went out from under him. Geneve sidestepped his tumble, torquing her body as she did and bringing a powerful hammerfist into the back of the man's helmet. With a squeal of twisted metal the man dropped in a heap, a leg still twitching.

The remaining Arm soldier held her blade like a holy symbol before her. "Stand back."

Geneve slicked back red hair. "I'm as far back as I can go. It's me, the bed, then the wall. You didn't really think that one through, did you?"

"I mean ... I'm warning you!"

"You're warning me you hold a blade. You've already warned your friends. I hear their boots on the stairs already. What should be bothering you isn't warnings, but consequences. They said you forgot, and I see what they meant."

"They?" The woman goggled.

"Ikmae," Geneve said, as if it were obvious to a halfwit. "They said the world forgot. I'm here to help you remember."

The soldier thought about that for a hot second, then turned on her heel and bolted. Omrar's mouth hung open. *The Arm never run. One mention of a fallen god, and they're done?*

No. It was who mentioned the god.

A clatter from the stairs, some swearing that sounded like a mixture of *fuck me* and *fuck this*, and a cadre of soldiers made Omrar's bedroom. Three of them, as if serendipity rolled the dice all the time, bearing weapons and harsh expressions.

Omrar tore the sword from the wall by his head and tossed it. "Tresward! Here!"

Geneve leaned sideways, because Omrar had thrown it *at* her, then snatched it from the air as it passed by, all without looking at him. She flourished the blade, *swish, swish, swish*, then held the curved blade before her face in a salute. "Do you know what it is to know your purpose? I know mine. It's not to die here, at your feet."

The leading soldier tried to backpedal, was knocked by a comrade, the pair vaulted by a young-looking over-eager man. He wore a patchy mustache perhaps with more pride than it deserved. Omrar remembered when he'd first been able to grow fur on his chin and how he'd marveled at being a real man. He thought about how this youngster was probably no older than Geneve, and unlike her would never see twenty summers.

Patchy Mustache lunged with a blade, a poor choice since his sword was curved, but perhaps he hoped for surprise. Geneve batted it aside, the ring of steel echoing. *This room shouldn't hear that noise. These people brought murder into my life.*

He felt anger, then surprise at the anger, so unused to it after years of keeping his eyes down. Surprise at the surprise, because he wouldn't have taken this excuse for a life when he was younger. Anger at the surprise, because he should've been angry a long time ago, or for a long time, but most recently when Lily was taken.

Geneve lowered her stance, left leg back. She held her sword in a classic fencer's pose, the blade upright, the steel's kiss a promise. *By the Three. She's showing off! This Tresward knows her skill.*

That was unfair. There wasn't pride in the set of her shoulders. Duty, perhaps. But also, justice. Geneve demonstrated to these soldiers what it meant to cross a myth. *Does she hope by showing them before they die, they'll tell their friends? They'll be dead!*

Omrar remembered the woman who'd run down the stairs. *One will live. She'll call the rest, too, and burn my home.* Anxiety should have come, but instead he got more anger. While Geneve held guard against three of the Precept's finest, Omrar kicked a loose board at the foot of his bed. The wood clattered free, revealing a compartment. He pulled free a short chain spear. *It's time for everyone to remember, even me.*

The spear's chain rattled as he wound it about his wrist. "I have your back, Knight."

She half turned her head, acknowledging but not looking. "I know." With that cryptic comment, she surged forward.

Her blade flashed, golden light rippling along the steel. She ignored Patchy Mustache, the man's raised block going to waste as she slipped right past him like he was anchored to the floor. The golden touch of her blade found the man who'd stumbled back, cutting through his armor, flesh, bone, and soul in one strike. The rent in his armor glowed with heat, smoke and steam pouring from the ruined flesh within. He clawed his chest, hands burning as he did, then collapsed.

Omrar tossed the spear, chain rattling and hissing like a mechanical snake. It flashed across the room, right for Patchy Mustache's heart.

Geneve flicked her blade, hitting the spear and knocking it into the third man. It skewered him, cutting off whatever hopes he held for the future. She looped the chain about her free arm, twisting her body and yanking the man toward her. She met his stumble with her blade, kicking the body left as his head rolled right.

Patchy Mustache goggled. His blade didn't seem so steady. "Yield, in the name of the Precept!"

"Now you want to talk?" Geneve cocked her head. "If I yield, what will happen?"

"I, uh."

"You'll take me prisoner, at which point I'll die." She flashed a knowing smile, all feral delight. "If I don't yield, you'll die. Which do you think I'd prefer?"

"It's not kind to toy with those about to die." Omrar blinked as the words came from *his* lips. Still, it was a surprising day. "He's just a boy."

"I'm not going to kill him," Geneve declared. "I'm just going to *scare* him. They'll need the fear in the days ahead." She raised her blade, fast as thought, to rest at the young man's throat. "Do you know why?"

"So we don't come after you?"

She shook her head. "Because I want you to choose. You stand on the bodies of the weak to see a little higher. Perhaps you could be the shoulders they lean on. You *know* what'll happen if you come after me. Following this Precept of yours has but one end. There's another." The Knight lowered the blade. "Go."

Patchy Mustache relaxed about a hair's breadth. "The Precept is an unkind master."

"Do you need a master?" She arched an eyebrow. "You weren't born with one."

The lad thought about that. Omrar watched them talk in fascination. He'd never seen anything like it. *I've never seen anyone so good with a blade either. Fear's left behind when you're above the rest.*

Patchy Mustache reached the wrong decision, swinging for Geneve's neck in a desperate lunge, all fear of the future's death at the hands of a demon. Geneve kicked one of his legs out, the chain-wrapped arm shooting out, fist closed. She struck his blade, knuckle against the edge of his weapon.

The sword cried its submission, shattering into a hail of silver shards. Patchy Mustache looked at the broken end he held. "That's not possible."

Geneve considered that. "And yet, it happened."

Turning on his heel, the officer bolted.

"You blocked a blade with your bare fist," Omrar breathed. "How did they teach you to do that?"

"They didn't." Geneve looked at her fist, still closed, then shook her head. "They taught me to protect the weak, and that boy didn't need killing."

"Boy? He was older than you."

"And no less a boy for it." She tossed her borrowed blade to the ground as if it disgusted her, then unwrapped Omrar's chain, handing it to him. "Your spear."

He took it, coiling chain about his arm. "Where next?"

"We're looking for lost gods. I've a hunch I'll need my armor and blade for that kind of work. Where would the Arm take my things?"

Omrar thought about that. "The Precept's personal stores. They're guarded by vile creatures of shadow and darkness."

"Sounds like quite the party. We should get ourselves an invite," Geneve suggested. "I've killed a demon before."

"There's more than one." Omrar shuddered. "I've seen them. They're unafraid of the light."

Her grin grew wider. "Then we'll teach them fear."

Chapter Thirteen

He didn't look like Ormeon. Meriwether stared at the black dragon, all sleek lines and preening snout. The dragon was slimmer, faster perhaps, and full all the way to the top with being the best.

This dragon is an asshole. The thought hit Meriwether like a bolt from above, a revelation that dragons were like people in many ways. They could be petty, angry, and malicious. This one was ... vain.

While Ormeon wasn't vain, and wouldn't tolerate this fool at all, she shared one characteristic with the creature before Meriwether: they were both large. This one's mouth was more than capable of snapping Meriwether up in a single bite. It helped he was a couple hundred meters away, but distance like that was nothing to a horse, and less to a dragon.

They weren't outside under the open skies. A curved ceiling rose high above them, much like the ancient temple in which they'd found Ormeon. A huge chamber, open and empty, stood to the left, a small-compared-to-a-dragon pool of green liquid near the front. Between the dragon and the chamber stood five people, all wearing white ... cloaks? Coats? Some damnable fashion statement the ancients wanted to make. All held slates of glass, keen expressions, and stared at the dragon with some fascination.

//I AM CHAKES, BRINGER OF DEATH,// the dragon roared. *//KNEEL.//*

None of the people kneeled, but one fussed with his glass slate.

//I AM CHAKES.// Chakes, Bringer of Death, looked a little confused, head drawing back on a long serpentine neck. *//KNEEL?//*

"Not like that." A woman next to the fussing man pointed at something on the glass slate. "There. Encourage, not prevent. It's a dragon, for fuck's sake. We didn't make them for kiddy daycare."

The man nodded, as if appreciating a great understanding, and fussed further with his glass slate. Chakes looked between them. *//WILL SOMEONE PLEASE KNEEL?//*

Fussing Man held up the square of glass. His voice was calm, curious, not at all similar to the overbearing presence of the man who'd murdered his ally by way of Feybrind Command. "Not today. How do you feel about raining death on our enemies?"

Chakes gave that a little thought. He looked to the front of the chamber, which now opened to show a slate-gray sky, heavy with the promise of rain. *//PRETTY GOOD. NOT TOO SURE ABOUT THE RAIN, THOUGH.//*

"Sorry about that. Our thaumaturge got killed last week. We're waiting for another one to come in. Should be blue skies after that." Fussing Man glanced to his four friends. "If you go outside, you'll find an army of monsters waiting to kill us all. If it's not too much trouble, could you sort that out for us?"

The dragon *crunched* toward the door, long slender tail lashing like a Feybrind's. Meriwether wanted to find somewhere to hide. It didn't matter that this wasn't real. Or it'd been real once, and now was the memory of someone long dead, packed into crystal for display at a later time. Chakes looked over his shoulder. *//WILL THEY KNEEL?//*

"Probably not," admitted Fussing Man.

A snort, a puff of smoke. *//I WILL MOTIVATE THEM TO SUBMISSION.//*

A SNAP, AND MERIWETHER WAS OUTSIDE. THE RAIN WAS COLD, sharp and hard with fragments of ice. The open door to Chakes' birthing chamber sat behind him, the dragon in front. A host of perhaps ten thousand Vhemin stood before him, all blue-runed armor and uncertain anger.

"They've never seen a dragon before, have they?" Meriwether almost felt sorry for them. Then wondered why he shouldn't, because they might not be evil. Just on the wrong side of a conflict that everyone lost.

"This is the first. Chakes was an experiment. He wasn't supposed to fight. Try telling him that," Florian smirked.

The dragon roared, and with the noise came an inferno. Blue and white fire rolled in a torrent across the Vhemin. To their credit, none fled. Most ended up as barbecue, but some ducked or rolled aside. They ran toward the dragon, weapons spitting blue lances that burst into a sapphire cascade against the dragon's armored hide.

Or that was what Meriwether thought until one of Chakes' wings almost sheared free, ragged tissue smoldering, the failing pinion trailing smoke and blood. Meriwether shouted, hand outstretched, before remembering this had already happened.

The dragon reared, all long slender power, lean, hungry. Young, an hour old, but with ancient, terrible eyes. He lunged forward, fast as a cobra, snatching a Vhemin from the ground. Powerful jaws crunched on flesh and bone, blood sprayed as the dragon made a meal of his enemy.

Another Vhemin, another meal, the dragon's throat working as he swallowed. More blue light raked his form, shearing a leg away. The dragon fell, twitching.

The Vhemin horde cheered, raising weapons above their heads. Meriwether looked away, but Florian's voice urged him. "The best is yet to come."

Vhemin surged atop the fallen dragon, roaming his body, cheering and leering as they clambered higher. For all Chakes was sleeker than

Ormeon, he was still a dragon, and dragons were massive. A Vhemin woman with slightly more intricate armor than the rest tried to prize one of the dragon's scales free.

The dragon twitched. The Vhemin froze, uncertain. The monsters atop Chakes looked *more* frozen, and Meriwether realized they were *afraid*. "They're your enemy. And they ... heal, don't they? You borrowed that trick from them."

Florian's tone was dismissive. "Their regenerative capability is nothing like ours. Totally different."

"Yours needs the bodies of the dead to work."

"They don't even need to be dead," Florian laughed. "They will become so during the process."

Chakes surged upright, Vhemin flying into the air. The dragon roared, tossing a monster aside, a torrent of flame following. Within moments, very surprised Vhemin were less surprised, because they were dead. Smoldering char was all the memory the ground held of them.

A keening rumble came from Meriwether's right. An Artifice broke through the cloud, spearing toward Chakes. The dragon leaped to the sky, wing whole again, sliding like oil on water between beams of ochre fire as the Artifice hungered for him.

The dragon gained altitude, curling about as the Artifice shot past, then ... grabbed it. Dragon and machine were locked together as they spiraled toward the chamber that created him. *//WE HAVEN'T BEEN INTRODUCED.//* Chakes' voice was the sound of heaven's gate opening. *//I'M THE GUY WHO'S GOING TO END YOUR RIDE.//*

With a bunch of mighty muscles, the dragon tore the Artifice in two. Fragments of metal rained, the dragon curling away.

Meriwether blinked. "Were those ... *men* that fell from the Artifice?"

"One man, one woman," Florian corrected.

"I thought they were devices," admitted Meriwether. "Like a plow."

"Many are. Some have pilots."

Meriwether thought back to the fallen Artifice he and Geneve found, black glass hiding the interior, holding its secrets close through all time. "Vhemin pilots?"

"Unlikely." Florian's tone held a shrug. "I don't see them handing control of their killing machines to their slaves. I wouldn't."

Meriwether nodded. "I think I know a little more, now. I think I know enough."

Florian's voice held a little more low cunning than was palatable. "We've barely started."

Chapter Fourteen

Geneve followed the old man through dark streets. It felt like rain never came here, like the stone thirsted for water so much it'd settle for blood. Omrar's head was lowered, habitual fear keeping his gaze down. "I can't go home again."

"You couldn't go home before. All that's different now is how you feel about it." Geneve stopped short, crossing her arms. "It wasn't a home, Omrar. It was a prison. It sat under the sky but held you in like a cage."

He straightened a fraction. "You don't know what you're saying."

"Perhaps not. What do I know of cages? I was in the service of a great host since the age of five. My memories were bound in crystal, keeping ... *me*, all of myself, all I could *be*, locked inside. The path I walked held me to a standard. I couldn't leave my armor, or my sword. I had duty. Oh, don't misunderstand. I had friends, too. But I was never *free*. I walked the largest cage ever made until a brave man set me free."

Omrar looked away, but in shame, not fear. "I don't mean my pain is the only pain."

"It's the only thing that holds you here."

"That, and an old body."

Geneve offered him a wry smile. "That, too. I just didn't want to say it."

He gave her an answering one. "Come, Tresward. There are demons to kill, and your burial to plan."

He set off, Geneve following. "When I fell from the sky, no one else stopped to help. Just you."

His head bowed again, but this time as if shying away from a remembered blow. "There was someone else who fell when the gods fled, and I didn't help her."

"A neighbor?" Geneve pondered the house she'd followed him to. "A friend?"

He shrugged, then shored up at the corner of a building, peering out. After a moment, he scuttled across the street, beckoning her to follow. "I am no judge of these things."

"More than a friend, then."

He growled. "You twist my words, Tresward."

"Words aren't my thing. That's Meri." She loped in his wake. "Was this Lily?"

"She was taken two weeks past, when the moons fell from the sky." He didn't speak for a hundred meters or so. "You have the same moons in Or'sen?"

"Not anymore." Geneve ruffled some life back into her hair, trying to keep it out of her eyes. "Not since two weeks ago."

"Lily hasn't been seen since then either." A small shrug, loaded under the weight of memory and guilt. "I could have—"

"Died," Geneve said. "If you'd died, I'd have died when I arrived, and then we wouldn't be about to save the city from the clutches of a monster. This Precept of yours is a problem that needs solving."

"About to save..? Don't you think there's a few more steps between the storehouse and burying your blade in a demon's heart?" Omrar looked doubtful.

"Details." Geneve grinned, all harsh angles and hungry teeth. "First, we need good Tresward steel. Let's get it."

Geneve crouched beside Omrar. They were in the shelter of a broken down cart, long since stripped bare of valuables. She hoped they were mere shadows against a greater darkness. *And I wish Meri were here. Not just because he could* make *us shadows ... but because my heart misses his closeness.* They watched a squat building, a smudge against the night sky. No lights bloomed in the windows, which was odd for a storehouse. Geneve expected the glow of a lantern as a night watch kept guard, but there was nothing. Not even a cockroach stirred.

The old man's voice was quiet, husked to a hard-edge with fear. "There. See it?"

She followed the line of his arm. The building's front had a porch with awning, suggesting a previous life as a home until the Precept converted it for his purposes. Beneath the awning a blot of shadow shifted. "I've seen something like that before. Not exactly the same, but..." Geneve trailed off, then made to stand.

His hand on her arm held her firm, surprising strength in the old man's grip. Perhaps fear gave him extra motivation. "There is another way in."

"Demons need killing," she insisted.

"Would it be better with or without your armor?"

Geneve growled. "A fair point. Where is this back door?"

"Who said anything about a door?" Teeth glinted in the dark.

"This is vile," Geneve offered, trying not to retch. Omrar led her to an old sewer, the contents more sludge than water with the lack of rain. There was a small path beside the causeway proper, but lined with... She squinted. "Are those rats?"

"No." Omrar led on. He husbanded a small lantern, hood drawn close, only a sliver of warm yellow leading the way. "Cockroaches. They eat the rats."

The insects were enormous, larger than anything she'd seen before. Geneve's lips pressed into a line. "I *really* need my armor."

"It's fine, Tresward. I don't think they have a taste for human flesh.

Yet." He sidestepped something the size of Armitage's hand that scuttled toward his feet. "Otherwise the city would be overrun."

"The Arm are vermin enough." Geneve hadn't had a sit-down talk with any of the Precept's military force, or their shadowy cousins in the Will. Any conversation would most likely end with bared blades, and she admitted in the quiet of her head she looked forward to those encounters. "This city reeks of fear."

"That's just plain sewer stink." He paused at a junction. "Try breathing through your mouth. Left, I think."

"How do you know about this way?"

"I wasn't always old and weak." Omrar hefted his chain spear, the links clinking their agreement. "Villains of many factions ruled the streets before the Precept crushed all beneath his weight. They used these passages to smuggle or escape. I got used to hunting larger prey in the dark below. Ah. Here we are." He pointed the lantern at a metal ladder set against the wall.

It was old, the rungs rusted through in places. What wasn't rusted was caked in ... well, things it was best not to think about. The ladder led up, darkness waiting at the top. "Is that a hatchway?"

"It's beneath the garderobe," Omrar said. "The demons don't use it."

"The architects put a ladder beneath the jakes?"

"The architects were hired by the Ouzen family. The Ouzens smuggled a great deal, and knew—rightly, I believe—people wouldn't want to poke their head, uh." Omrar glanced up. "You get my meaning."

"This is wonderful." Geneve's gut clenched.

"You speak our language well, but I don't think you're using that word right." Omrar shifted in the gloom, a motion that could be shrug as much as weary resignation. "I'll go first."

Geneve snorted. "Demons are my thing. You hold the light steady and I'll make sure the way is clear." She put a hand on rung. It snapped as she put her weight on it. Dropping the rotted metal, she put hands on the ladder's uprights, pulling herself up the hard way.

She met the closed hatch with her head. *Merciful Three.* Geneve braced her feet against the walls, kicking some of the slickness away with her boots, trying to find a toehold. Her left foot found purchase.

She struggled upward, expecting resistance, but the hatch opened easily enough. Bracing herself with her feet, one hand still on the ladder, she eased the boards above her open. The hinges gave a small cry of complaint but nothing stuck fast.

The room was definitely a garderobe. It was small, with cobweb festooned shelving. Bowls suggested where hands might be washed. No one had used it for a long time. A closed door still offered some privacy from whatever might be outside. Geneve looked below, Omrar's lantern still offering hope. "It's clear. I'll—"

The ladder gave way. Instinct took over, Geneve pushing with her feet to get up, get *up* dammit, hand clawing for purchase. Her feet skidded on the muck coating the shaft's walls, hand clutching desperately for purchase. Two fingers hooked wood, her weight hanging from that tiny clawhold.

She scrabbled, feet struggling for purchase. Metal clanged as the ladder fell below. Geneve hauled herself out, slumping to the cold stone floor of the privy. "Omrar?"

Silence. She peeked into the dark below. The old man's light was gone ... *no*. There it was, his lantern coming back into view. Geneve caught the glint of eyes as he looked up. "What was that, Tresward?"

"The ladder broke."

"Now everyone from here to Im'kalida will have heard you."

"Where's Im'kalida?"

"That's what you want to ask?" he hissed. "Run! There are demons there."

"What about you?" Geneve peered into the dark. "I could find a rope."

"I don't think the Precept is likely to keep rope conveniently about his storage mansion. You'll get us both killed. Find what you came to find, then ... leave." Omrar coughed.

"Will we meet again?"

"Of course." Teeth glinted beside the old man's eyes. "I owe you for showering my best cloak with muck."

She snorted. "If that's your best cloak—"

"You're wasting time, Knight. Be off with you." The lantern vanished as the old man hurried away.

He's not wrong. I need to move. Geneve clambered to her feet, then pressed her ear to the door. *Nothing.* Which was alarming; the amount of noise she'd made would've woken the dead, perhaps even in Im'kalida, wherever that was. Even the laziest of watchmen should have run toward the ruckus.

She eased the door open. She saw a dusty corridor littered with canvas-wrapped bundles that might have been picture frames. Cobwebs lay everywhere, the dust thick. *The good news in this sorry affair is finding my gear will be easy. Look for things that aren't coated in an age's worth of dust.* A soft light emanated from the walls, pale white, almost blue, but good enough to see by.

Geneve slipped from the room, feet taking her slow and easy over a floor made of smooth wooden boards. She set each foot with care, but couldn't avoid the odd creak. She winced with each one, wishing again Meri was here. He'd played the thief to survive, and could have pointed the right places to step.

The corridor led to a corner, around which lay a longer corridor festooned with doors. A stairway leading up hugged the northern wall. The main entrance lay at the end, a door barred with a thick beam. She padded to it, touching the rough wood. *How does one bar their house from the inside when there's no one here?* Questions like that wouldn't lead to good answers, because there were only a few. Could be everyone in here was dead, which made her wonder what killed them, or the things last in here didn't need doors.

I really need my sword. She'd killed a demon with Sway, but it took so much from her. Geneve thought about where to start looking. It made sense the oldest items would be at the bottom level. Feet on the stairs, she climbed. Dust lay everywhere, her boots marking her passage as she went. That was a double-edged sword; she'd be able to find her way out easy enough, but whatever was in here with her would also be able to track her down. *Let them come.* She was hungry for the battle, to seek the hearts of these demons and end their tyranny. She made a landing, more wooden floors and sturdy doors, and bared her teeth. "Come, demons."

Steady. She almost felt Iz's hand on her shoulder, her father's voice in her memory, clear as if he was by her side. *The fight will come to you soon enough. Don't think of winners or losers, where the battle will be fought, or what numbers you'll face. Those are needless details. Worry about your training. Think of your allies, and what they need. Be the strong shield for them, and all the world.*

"Father," she breathed. Her chest ached, Iz's memory chafing worse than any she'd lost. *There will be no more. I won't allow it.* Geneve straightened, heading for the furthest door from the stairs. It opened easily enough, the hinges giving a soft suggestion of a creak without putting their heart into it. Within lay riches: golden cups, open chests of coins, and pouches hinting at a clutch of rubies. All this was shoved against the walls, making way for the real prize: an armor stand.

On it was her Tresward Smithsteel, the burnished sun defying the blueish light, all orange and red greeting her. At the armor's feet was the glass circle of Brilliance, and the worn wooden stock of Tribunal.

Requiem wasn't here. There was no sign of her skymetal sword.

Solve one problem at a time. Geneve hurried to her armor, donning it fast as she could. There was an argument to be made for carrying it out, but she had nothing to carry twenty kilograms of Tresward Smithsteel in. She slipped her breastplate and backplate on, feeling the comforting weight settle about her. The smell of oiled steel made her stand a little taller, a little stronger. *I've missed this. I fell from the sky and lost my way.*

Each piece of armor made her feel lighter despite their weight. Cinching a final strap, she slung Tribunal into its holster over her shoulder, and rescued Brilliance from the ground. Kytto's last gift was heavy with purpose. The glass shield slipped over her left arm, ready to protect her. Or the world, if that was needed.

The doorway behind her creaked. Geneve spun, dropping into a fighting stance. Oily smoke crept in, as if carried by a gentle breeze. The smoke touched a golden chalice, and the metal discolored to a mud-brown before cracking. The cloud flowed across a handful of rubies, their colors dulling, leaving ash-gray hunks that looked like common quartz. *"Tressssward,"* the smoke hissed. Low, sibilant like a snake given voice.

Geneve's fingers grasped for a blade that wasn't there as she raised her shield to guard. "Back, demon."

The smoke roiled, coiling into a human-shaped cloud. "*Sssskymetal sssssword?*"

Geneve bared her teeth. "I don't need Requiem, creature." She whipped Tribunal from behind her, leveling it over the shield's lip. The scattergun roared, its voice bright, hot, and angry. The cloud slipped sideways, the pellet's path tugging at it like it were nothing more than mist.

"*Sssad. No sssssword. No friendssss. Alone, like ussss.*" Its voice held the cadence of someone she was sure she'd known, but couldn't put her finger on with all the hissing. The thing surged toward her, a wave made of black intent. Geneve set Brilliance into a perfect guard, the crystal-clear surface glimmering with golden Light. The smoke hit. She expected it to dissipate on contact with the Three's Light, but instead the impact threw her back like she were a doll from a three-baron merchant. Geneve tumbled through a pile of gold, hit the wall behind it, and passed through in a shower of broken wood.

The hit knocked the wind from her. She tumbled, landed badly, then scrambled upright. The smoke was relentless, surging through the hole in the wall. Geneve spun, stepping back and to the left, stance set and braced, Brilliance glowing with the Three's Light. The demon slid along the shield's glass face with a sound like iron nails on flint. Geneve slid across the floor, wood buckling as her boots tore at the boards.

She glanced about, looking for a weapon as she slid Tribunal into its holster. The room was packed with bric-à-brac, shelves of moldering tomes with once-bright covers vying for place next to decanters and elegant glassware. The oily smoke demon seethed through the shelves, paper curling in its passage, pages blackening at its contact. She wondered what it would feel like if the thing touched her. Would she age a thousand years in a moment? Would her flesh harden to stone?

It's best not to find out. She charged the monster, shield buttressed before her, hitting the smoke thing with everything she had. Light flared, but the creature seeped around Brilliance. It oozed through her hair, caressed her face, and threatened to get in her mouth and nose. Geneve coughed, hand warding it away, but she may as well try to hold back a gust of wind.

The burnished sun on her breastplate flared, and the smoke

recoiled, whirling about her like a shroud. *"Burnssss."* It surged against her, intangible hands grasping with tremendous strength. It tossed her like a salad. Geneve hit the ceiling, fell to the floor, then slammed against the ceiling again. Her armor smoked where invisible hands grabbed her. She felt a rib pop as the roof gave way in a shower of plaster and wood.

She clawed for purchase, one hand on a beam. Geneve was in an attic, dust and cobwebs everywhere. She pulled her legs up, rolled onto her back, and tried to breathe. She managed two breaths before the floor to her right erupted, the smoke demon joining her again. *"Hello again. Thissss isss fun. I never get to play."*

Geneve scissored her legs for momentum and surged to her feet. She screamed at the thing, wound her arm back, and tossed Brilliance. The shield flared with Light, but passed through the smoke monster without resistance. The shield hit the sloping roof, blasting wood and tiles in a shower of burning debris. Night air gusted in, tugging her hair.

The demon turned a lazy coil, peering where the shield went. *"You've losssst your ssshield, Knight. Our gamesss will end."*

Geneve lunged for it. The monster eased aside as she passed, perhaps unwilling to touch her armor again despite its massive strength. She kept going as she parted the smoke, dashing through the hole in the roof and out into cool, calm sky.

I'm two stories above cobbled streets. I'm wearing Tresward Smithsteel. I must make the best landing ever seen. She plummeted, impacting the street with a clang that felt like it vibrated her teeth from their sockets. She caught a glimpse of glass and limped toward her shield. Brilliance was lodged in the wall of a house, broken stone beneath it.

Geneve grabbed it, then spun to the Precept's storehouse. She saw the coiling smoke hiding in the attic, but it didn't follow. It looked like it waved, silver glints where eyes might be watching her. *"Come back."*

She had no snappy comeback, because the thing had beaten her like a child's toy drum. Geneve's hand clutched at her empty scabbard. *I need my sword. I need Requiem.*

Chapter Fifteen

T he world shifted again, dropping Meriwether onto another battlefield. The sky was the color of broken clay, an unhealthy orange that came from nothing natural. He couldn't see the sun, a kind of uniform cloud covering the sky above like a karitane yellow blanket. This particular battlefield was empty of living participants; the party had come, done its thing, and left when the bar closed. Nothing but corpses remained.

"What's odd is the lack of crows." Meriwether scratched at the stubble that followed him into even this dream realm. "At least you invited humans this time." He kicked at an arm by his feet. It wasn't attached to a body, but the hand wasn't furred like Feybrind or scaled like Vhemin.

Florian chuckled. "This can be yours. All of it."

"The bodies?"

"The power," the dead man sighed. "Even the gods turned their faces away when we unleashed the forces of creation and destruction. Your father never touched this kind of potency in all his days. He struggled to be anything more than a mediocre illusionist with nothing to give the world except…" Florian caught himself, settling to silence.

Except me, you mean. Meriwether kept his words inside, resisting the urge to ask *how do you know about my father?* or *how do you know he was an illusionist?* Florian was a ghost that walked the halls of his mind. All it meant was Meriwether had to keep up a charade for a little while longer.

He paced forward, hugging himself. The shattered orange-yellow sky held no warmth. Meriwether couldn't see the Three above but reckoned if he were in their shoes he'd turn his face away too. Glittering caught his eye, and he wound his way through the weary dead to a man wearing what was unmistakably Tresward armor. The style was different, but it was still good Smithsteel emblazoned with the burnished sun.

Walking on, Meriwether found a trail of dead Tresward. Some had shields, others two-handed claymores. One or two carried devices like the ancient dead guardian's he'd faced in the halls above. Some were burned horribly, others dead without an apparent scratch. The farther he trudged, the dead stopped being Feybrind and Vhemin with a scattering of Tresward, to pretty much nothing but fallen Knights.

He followed the trail of dead up a small rise. Arriving at the top, Meriwether looked down into a scalloped crater at least four, maybe five klicks across. There were no more dead here, but a glint drew him on. He marched down the crater's side, heading to the glint. Florian held his peace, which was just as well because Meriwether wouldn't have said anything very nice at this point.

The glint resolved into a lone fallen Knight. Her Tresward armor was brutally charred, left arm and leg gone, helmet missing, but her face was remarkably untouched. He saw red hair and turned away. *No. It's not her. This happened a long time ago.*

But what if it was?

Meriwether spun, refusing Florian's trap, his lies, because this *must* be deceit right to the core. Death on this scale was unheard of. So many corpses, all beneath an ochre sky that couldn't even weep rain. He picked up his pace and headed out of the crater. Cresting the lip, he saw a mound in the middle distance. Meriwether approached it, the hump resolving through battlefield haze into a dead dragon, festooned with fallen Vhemin. The dragon's hide was a dull red, the runes along her face dark and empty. A furrow wide as three ox carts drew a line to a fallen Artifice. The machine had eight legs. The hard shell was cracked like an egg, Feybrind bodies all about it. *It's time to make sure this never happens again. He offered me this power. Taking it could stop this for all time.* "This magic of yours ... there's got to be a catch."

"I'll need your body," Florian admitted. "Just for a while. Oh, don't worry. You'll be there too. In full control. I need to hop in like a passenger. Or you can take me to a Fey Branded host. Come to think of it, just give me Coming Storm. Get her to take you down three levels, and we'll begin."

"You don't need my body at all. You just need my ... permission, because the things here don't work for the Feybrind." Meriwether nodded. "Unlimited power, all for the price of a demon in a slave's head. Seems fair."

"I'm no demon," Florian spat. "We don't know how they came here, but one thing's for sure. Neither us nor the Vehement Systems assholes let them in. It was someone else."

"Unlucky." Meriwether wasn't paying much attention to Florian. He'd come to a two-body huddle. A Feybrind and Vhemin, eyes wide and staring. They lay back to back as if they hadn't attacked each other. Like they'd seen something that made them ally for a moment. A worse horror that overcame the Feybrind's Command or the Vhemin's blue-runed armor of control. There were no other bodies nearby, and no marks on the dead at his feet. "What killed these two?"

"Does it matter?"

"It might." Meriwether shrugged. "You know what? I've got a theory."

"You know what killed them?"

"More. I'll tell you when we get to the transfer point."

"Excellent." Florian's voice was oily with satisfaction. "This might be a little—"

"DISCONCERTING."

Meriwether stumbled. He was back in the ancient room, solid

ground beneath his feet. Coming Storm caught him, fur soft hands on his arm, rose eyes soft and concerned. "Thank you." He wondered if she knew what Florian wanted, and whether she'd pay the price: a dead man back to life, all of her gone to make that happen, but the prize being no more Vhemin.

{What did you see?}

"Nothing good," Meriwether admitted. "Come on, Florian. Where are we going?"

The man's face filled the wall before them. He smiled, a benevolent father, eyes finding Coming Storm. "The Reliquary. Take him."

Coming Storm bowed her head, turning away. Her steps were leaden. *Okay, sure. She knows what's up. But she can't disobey. It wouldn't matter if she tried now. But there's too much at stake. I must know.* "Florian, don't you think it's a bit risky to have her walking and talking?"

"An excellent point," the specter mused. "Her Command name is Sky Full of Promise."

Coming Storm stiffened like someone had slipped a knife into her, back arching, mouth open in a scream she could never make. Then she relaxed, those soft rose eyes empty as she faced Meriwether. *{Command me.}*

"Sky Full of Promise, take me to the Reliquary." Meriwether felt his stomach churn with acid bile. *It shouldn't ever be this way.* "We've got something that needs doing."

THE PATH TO THE RELIQUARY WAS EMPTY OF LOST GUARDIANS, trolls, unicorns, or spare dragons. The only sound accompanying Meriwether, aside from the storm of his thoughts, was the ceaseless haranguing of the blue-feathered bird. She *cheep! cheep! cheep!*'d at him mercilessly, flitting between Coming Storm and him. The bird watched the Feybrind's empty gaze, then flitted back to Meriwether, over and over.

And over.

And over again. "Ease up," Meriwether suggested after a particularly brilliant round of what passed for blue-feathered swearing. "It's got to be this way."

Cheep!

"Suit yourself. You'll just make yourself hoarse." Coming Storm paused before a vaulted door set into the corridor they followed. It was large enough for two to pass abreast but sealed tight and secure. "Could you open that?"

The Feybrind turned her vacant stare on Meriwether. *{It shall be as you Command.}* She bent to a square metal panel, fussed with it for a few moments, then stood back. The door sighed, clanked, then opened. Wind gusted through the widening crack. It trailed fingers through Meriwether's hair as it ran ahead.

"Thank you."

Florian's voice, absent for their journey, beckoned from within. "Welcome back." Light glimmered through the door as Coming Storm walked to her doom.

Meriwether followed. The room was large enough to be impressive, a good twenty meters a side. The walls were lined with what seemed to be tiny lockboxes. Each was about a handspan tall and wide, with small red lights that looked like eyes on the front. At the center of the room was yet another dais, because the ancients seemed to have a thing for elevated pedestals. On the dais was what looked like an uncomfortable bed, with a circlet of metal at one end. The circlet had the look of something a man like Meriwether was supposed to put his head into. Or, perhaps, a wonderful cat like Coming Storm.

At the feet of the bed was a glass pane anchored to the floor with two metal shafts. Coming Storm walked to this. She stood side on, waiting.

Florian's smug face was absent, but his voice was everywhere. "You need only ask her to fetch my phylactery then lie in the Reliquary's transference station. A caution though, friend Meriwether: once the phylactery is removed, I won't be able to talk to you until the end of the procedure."

"What if something goes wrong?" Meriwether looked to the ceiling, as he figured that's what a god-like monster like Florian expected. "And how long will that take?"

"Mere moments," Florian assured him. "Nothing will go wrong. You have Commanded her. We didn't forge her with flaws in the casting."

"As you say." Meriwether faced Coming Storm. "I'm really sorry about this. Sky Full of Promise—"

Cheep! Cheep! Cheep!

"Sky Full of Promise," Meriwether gritted, "fetch Florian's phylactery, then lie in the transference station."

The Feybrind wandered to a wall, her face serene, unconcerned of what was coming. The blue-feathered bird flitted about his head, wings fluttering in panic, but Meriwether brushed her away. "This needs to be done, bird. You'll see."

Coming Storm touched the front of a lockbox. A door opened, and a wedge of crystal eased out without a sound. The Feybrind brought the wedge to him.

The glass before him glimmered with ancient promise. A light glowered at the top right. Meriwether hefted the wedge, eying Coming Storm. "I put it there after you step into the station?"

The Feybrind nodded, then walked to the bed. She lay in it, slipping her head into the silver crown. Meriwether turned the phylactery over, trying to see anything special about it. It was a clear crystal, a thousand fibers like tiny hairs held within. It felt warm, like a human heart but without the slick wetness of the freshly dead. No, Florian had lain dead for hundreds of years. He just needed Meriwether to put the phylactery on the glass, and he'd live again.

Then all the power hidden in this temple would belong to the Lord du Reeves. He could find Geneve, Ormeon, and the rest of their friends. Together they would save the world. All he had to do was put the phylactery on the glass.

Chapter Sixteen

Vertiline watched the black flags behind them. The sea was a little choppy, just enough to add a little spice to what was to come, not enough to make anyone try their breakfast the second time around.

A loud retching made her turn. A wizard, a pity-inducing green, vomited overboard. *Okay, so* most *people won't throw up. There's always one.* She turned back to the vista of a hundred flags, all black, heading in their direction.

"It kinda makes you wonder," Armitage grumbled. The massive man stood to her right, hands on the stern railing. They were on the ship's prominent raised stern. "Where'd they get all those ships?"

"Dead men," Vertiline said. "It's a simple transaction. Blade in, life out, and what they had is yours."

"I've questions, like, which men?" Picotee du Parneer joined her on the left. The once-pirate lord visored her eyes with a hand.

"Probably yours." Armitage sniffed. "No one gives two shits about pirates."

Picotee nodded. "No argument from me."

"A hundred shipfuls of soldiers, though." Vertiline sighed. "That's a lot of Vhemin to murder." She eyed Armitage. "How do you feel about it?"

"I feel great. Killing's killing." The monster rumbled, a low sound of satisfaction. "They should've passed on the job. 'Course, could be they have blue-runed armor of fuckery and aren't in control." He frowned, like the thought caused him a moment's concern, before brightening. "Nah. Word's out. You put on the armor, you know what you're getting in for. We should just toss the anchor over the side and wait for 'em."

"We only have a hundred ships," Picotee said. "A hundred versus a hundred seems like risky odds."

Vertiline fingered the glass blade at her side. "Especially if they have Tresward."

"You see Knights over there?" Armitage squinted. "Where's the damn cat? He'd know for sure."

"Crow's nest, but I think he's sleeping. Says it's sunnier up there." Picotee shrugged. "We've Knights over here, but you couldn't tell. You're not wearing armor." She clapped Vertiline's arm. "Not that I've a problem with that. Armor's a death sentence if you go overboard."

Vertiline held up her metal hand. *I've not tried swimming with this yet. Will it pull me down like Smithsteel plate?* "I want to know how they're gaining on us. You said, 'I've fast ships,' Picotee. We are not faster than a bunch of inbred monsters, and that bothers me."

A soft *thump* made her turn. Sight of Day stood behind her like he'd been there for hours, arms crossed, expression distant as he gazed over the waves separating them from their pursuers. Vertiline looked up, eyes following the rigging to the crow's nest high above before returning to the Feybrind. He offered her a half-smile. *{I couldn't sleep.}*

She grunted. "There any Knights behind us?"

{Let me go ask.} He put hands on the railing. *{Wait. Are they our enemies? Perhaps the monster should go.}*

Armitage frowned. "You better not be talking about me. It's not the end of the journey I care about, mind. That water's cold. Not enough hot rocks in the world to keep me going."

{I don't feel like your heart's in this trip.} Sight of Day shook his head. *{I thought you liked casual killing.}*

"So long as it's not me doing the dying, sure." Armitage grinned shark teeth.

"Humans," gritted Vertiline. "Are there *humans* on those ships?"

Sight of Day blinked. {*Plenty. Some might be Tresward, judging by their posture, and plenty more that have the sickly look of that guy.*} He pointed to the green-gilled mage still retching at the port railing.

"When you say, 'posture,' you mean the armor they wear?" Vertiline frowned.

{*No. Few people walk with the arrogant swagger of Knights. You, for example, stand like you own this ship.*} Sight of Day's golden eyes gleamed.

"I do," Vertiline said. "I own the whole ship. I own the wood beneath our feet and the sails above. It's mine."

"Eh." Picotee waved her hand in the air, *maybe, maybe not.* "Technically you're under royal charter—"

"Anyway, what's wrong with my swagger?" Vertiline raised an arch eyebrow.

{*Nothing, as far as swaggers go. But you look like a Knight.*} Sight of Day shrugged, as if saying, *what can you do? {I think the remaining Tresward are after us. Enough, anyway, and they've brought mages and Vhemin. It's why they're gaining on us.}*

Armitage looked lost. "What?"

Picotee smacked fist into palm. "Of course. A thaumaturge. Wind wizards, teasing more from the air than it wants to give."

"I'll kill that motherfucker first," Armitage offered. "Which one is it?"

Sight of Day sighed, shaking his head. {*I think they'll be within bowshot in a couple hours. Then we'll have to decide what we want to do.*}

"I say we kill them," Vertiline said. "How's that sound to you all?"

"A fair plan." Picotee nodded. "I'd like to add a small addendum. Let's avoid dying ourselves. We're trying to get to Trebani with enough people to be useful. It'll be hard to save the world with a mere handful."

Vertiline looked back over the water. "Geneve could do it. So will we, if it comes to that."

WAITING BEFORE BATTLE'S THE HARDEST THING. VERTILINE RESTED her hands, steel and flesh, on the starboard railing. The enemy's fleet spread across the water, disrupting coordinated defense. Vertiline wasn't an expert at naval warfare but even she could see how the Vhemin horde would attack multiple points simultaneously. There'd be no rallying around a flag or defensive last stand on the high ground.

There's no high ground, and I haven't felt the flutter of a flag in a long, long time. She thought of Iz, how he'd have known what to do or say, but he left her. *He didn't mean to. Stop being maudlin. It doesn't suit me.*

The glass blade at her hip was sharp and ready. Vertiline knew its weight and the color the sunlight made when it refracted through the sword. *I've my balance. The Light answers my call.* She eyed Armitage. He hulked at her side, a wicked-looking cleaver in each hand. Further along the railing Sight of Day stood, relaxed and ready, a thin slip of steel in his hand, bow on his back. She lifted her gaze, taking in all the sailors ready to repel boarders. Even Picotee du Parneer was with them, forgoing the center decks so she could help.

They'd need it. The Vhemin ships were overfull of the enemy. Brutes roared across the waves. Crossbow shafts hissed, some finding targets, others *pinging* from the sailors' shield wall. *If Iz was here, he'd save these people, and if he couldn't, Geneve would. I miss my sister of the blade. I hope the Light listens to her call.* She gritted her teeth. Vertiline visored her eyes with a metal hand, gauging the sun. It slipped lower in the sky, dreary from the day's events, bored of watching. Soon it'd sleep, and if Vertiline was a judge of things, that's when the Vhemin would reach them. *Ah. Now I know why I'm so fucking weepy. I think I'm going to die today.*

It didn't help that the monsters could see at night. Pick out the heat of human bodies. *We're just piles of meat to them.* She eyed Armitage again, then put her flesh-and-blood hand on his arm. His skin was rough and cool, but not unpleasantly so. More like an ale fresh from the cellar on a hot day. "Thank you."

He grunted. "What for?"

"For ... trusting us. Being with us, when it'd be easier being over there."

The monster nodded. "Sure, sure. Most of those guys are assholes anyway."

She let that alone, dropped her hand, and faced the enemy ship closest to them. A couple of humans stood against the railing. Short-cropped hair and sturdy bearing said *Knight* in a language that crossed distance and time. "Most? It seems like all."

"I didn't want to speak for your guys." He sniffed. "But if we're trading truth above a watery grave, those guys are *fucking* assholes."

She laughed. "You're just jealous you can't take them in a fair fight."

Armitage shook his head. "Can't take any of you in any kind of fight. Drunk or sober, hell, you could be most of the way dead." He pressed lips into a line over shark teeth. "You're all so damn good and look so damn pretty at the same time. Not going to stop me trying, though. I reckon there's an odds even chance in the coming ruckus I'll get a souvenir or two."

She turned away, stomach clenched. *I'm not afraid of dying as much as I am of these going with me.* Vertiline looked at her friends: Armitage the Vhemin, and Sight of Day the Feybrind. They'd given everything—family, even children—to be here today. "I don't want you to die."

Armitage looked at her in surprise. Sight of Day peered around the monster's bulk. *{I don't think we want to die either. Did you have another option? And is this something you could have mentioned earlier?}*

"It's a crazy idea." She nodded. "The kind of thing that shouldn't work."

"Sounds great." Armitage rubbed his chin. "What do we need to do?"

"A moment." Vertiline closed her eyes, remembering. "You've said I'm the second-best swordswoman you've ever known. Who was the best?"

Armitage blinked. "Red."

Vertiline nodded. "Geneve is the best with a blade I've ever seen too."

{This is important why?} Sight of Day's wonderful golden eyes held a hint of mirth. *{Fishing for compliments at the end?}*

"I just wanted to make sure it wasn't one of those, uh... What did you call them?"

"Fucking assholes." Armitage grinned.

"Them." Vertiline answered his grin, sparking a half-smile from Sight of Day. "I wouldn't want to go into this unmatched."

{Unmatched for what? What are we doing?}

"*We* need do nothing. *I* need my armor." Vertiline bared her teeth. "If I'm going to die, I'll at least be comfortable. It's time we ... *talked.*"

SHE WASN'T COMFORTABLE AFTER ALL. *THIS IS TERRIFYING. I shouldn't have thought of this. This is something only the sinner would think of, while he was wishing me dead.* Vertiline laid gauntleted hands on the cup below her. *He'd probably laugh, too.*

She was nestled in a catapult's bucket. The device was used to hold hot pitch or solid shot, but at the moment it held a nervous yet armored Tresward Knight, her sword, and a borrowed shield. The shield was strapped to Vertiline's metal arm, the cinching tight enough to cut off blood flow if she still had any there.

Above her the open door of the great hold showed sky with a few cotton wisp clouds. Armitage cranked the catapult's winch, tensioning the spring. "You sure about this?"

"No. Are you sure this will toss me skyward rather than through the wall of the ship?"

"No. The cat said it would though, and he doesn't seem to be the product of inbreeding or incest."

Sight of Day half-smiled. The Feybrind stood, arms crossed, waiting. *{Try not to over tension it. That won't help.}*

"It won't help because I'll go too far across the water, right?" Vertiline eyed the sky again. "Right?"

{Sure. Absolutely.} The cat's tail *swish, swished. {Exactly what I meant.}*

"Will Picotee turn the ship?" Vertiline licked dry lips. "Will this break my spine?"

Armitage bared shark teeth. "You seem strong for a runty human. I give you even odds."

Picotee peered into the hold, hair falling forward but not enough to disguise the delight on her face. "I've never done this before. Spent half my life pirating and this is the first time I've fired someone in a catapult."

"I'm glad you didn't say it's the first time you've dropped anchor to line up pursuers," Vertiline said. "I was nervous."

"No, first for that too. It's a day of firsts!" The captain vanished before Vertiline could ask *why the hell didn't you say that before.* They both know it'd just be more noise, and the day wasn't growing longer.

The plan was simple: drop the heavy sea anchor, slewing and slowing the ship. While the enemy caught up much faster than expected, fire Vertiline using the catapult. Neither party was within bowshot or catapult range, but if they did it fast, Picotee's ship would shoot first.

Except their shot was a human, not a ball of burning pitch or a rock.

Vertiline gripped the bucket hard enough her gauntlets *creaked* on the metal rim. "Sight of Day, you sure you can hit the other ship?"

The Feybrind shrugged. *{Pretty sure.}*

Vertiline made to rise. "You need to be sure. I'm not okay—"

A noise like a giant hissing snake came a moment before a splash as the sea anchor went overboard. The ship listed, Vertiline grabbing the bucket's sides once more. Sight of Day's golden eyes grew wide for a moment. *{We're pitching faster than I thought we might.}*

"So we'll realign," Vertiline offered. "Right?"

The cat half-smiled. *{Wrong.}* He jumped into the hold behind her, sword whispering free, and slashed the catapult's restraining rope. Vertiline had about enough time to scream, but not enough to get out because of her being seated wearing twenty kilos of Tresward Smithsteel.

The catapult arm snapped forward, and Vertiline shot into the sky. Below, Picotee's ship grew smaller. *Is this what it feels like to be aboard a dragon? Would Geneve do this?* Vertiline's launch set her in a lazy tumble, armor catching the last rays of the sun as she turned through the air. Wind caught her pale braid, teasing a few strands by her face. She heard the shout of crew from both sides below, thin through distance, but still tight with excitement and alarm.

She continued the tight arc through the air. Picotee's ship moaned through the waves, trailing the anchor chain like a whale hit by a harpoon, sea foaming and seething below the hull. Vertiline felt sun on her face, smelled the sea without the stench of overcrowded crew or seasick mages. Her heart skipped a beat as water winked a twinkle at her. Her ascent slowed, then stopped for just a moment.

This is what the Three see. The world laid out below, a majestic quilt of tiny people and majestic creation. It's no wonder they stay in the starry sky, looking but not touching.

Then she fell. Down, toward the enemy's lead ship, and a number of surprised-looking Vhemin. Vertiline picked out three humans moving with speed but no hurry, because Knights were always measured. They'd worked out where she'd land—*sweet merciful Three, but the cat got it right, I'll hit amidships*—and were converging on that point.

None wore Smithsteel, but all carried blades that held the sun's light. As if she needed confirmation the Tresward were twisted within, a curved spine holding them back from what they could be, it was glass swords in the hands of her enemy.

Shouts from the enemy ship's captain, hand on the wheel, trying to turn the vessel. Archers, drawing a bead on her. Vhemin readying weapons, making for her landing spot.

It won't be a landing. I'm the second-best swordswoman this world has ever seen. This will be an impact.

Vertiline fell like a star, shield before her, sword hungering from its sheath. The enemy ship came for her, sea and wood and all angry intent, and she screamed her challenge.

She hit, shield first as she entered *Sky's Burning Passage*. The defensive pattern didn't seem to make much sense when she'd learned it, but the Three always had a purpose. It seemed this one was *to land aboard an enemy ship at sea*. Perhaps they hadn't thought of catapults, instead considering dragons or Artifices, but it didn't matter. The patterns worked.

Her shield glimmered, flames kissing the rim right before she hit. Wood exploded beneath her, blazing with the fire of the Three. Vertiline stood, finding herself belowdecks. *I thought my form was imperfect, but my body knows the path.* Dust and smoke swept past her, greeting a Knight dropping from above. He was older than Iz—

Older than Israel was. *Iz died.*

He was nearing fifty summers, a salting of gray like a halo below brown, close-cropped hair. A strong jaw she knew instantly. She raised her glass in salute, then set her stance. *Don't be rude. Luc is honorable, and it's not his fault we find ourselves at crossed swords.* Vertiline offered a tight nod. "Knight Valiant Luc. It's been, what, seven years?"

Luc smiled, as if she'd offered him iced tea on a hot day. "Vertiline. They said, but I didn't believe." He held a bastard sword like Geneve's, except unlike Requiem his was glass. "They said you fell. Now to determine how far."

Another man dropped behind Luc. Where Luc was broad and strong, Martin was lean, smooth, and hard like a river stone. He carried a glass greatsword, belying his slender frame. Vertiline raised an eyebrow, hiding fear behind bravado. *Two Valiants? For me?* "Knight Valiant Martin. I saw you joust for the Three against tides of Vhemin ten years past. You share a hull with them now. What news?"

"Villainy." Martin held his greatsword ready. "A lost Chevalier, stripped of her rank, siding with sinners and demons."

Vertiline blinked, then snorted. "You can't strip me of my rank, Martin."

"Knight Valiant Martin," he corrected.

"See how it feels?" Vertiline countered. "Words are nothing but air teased into shape. You say I'm no Chevalier, but I came aboard your ship with the Three's blessing. Their Light broke your decks and put me here. Do you think you can argue with them? Vhemin are one thing to bandy words with, but gods are different."

"Met one, have you?" A sandy-haired man poked his head through the hole in the deck, then vaulted in. Amaury offered her a smile, but she saw the sadness in it. "Knight Chevalier Vertiline." He drew two slender swords, raising one in salute. He was broader of shoulder than Martin, without Luc's chesty bulk.

"She's no Chevalier," Martin spat.

Vertiline glanced between Martin and Amaury. "Knight Champion Amaury. I am humbled by meeting you. I saw you fight with the twinned blades as a girl, before I took the burnished sun as my own. The sky lit your swords and never left them."

"Knight Chevalier Vertiline," Amaury said again, leaning on her title a little, eyes moving to Martin. "I'd like to hear a story. A tale of one made straight and true, now bent and broken. Where demons come to our world, Knights fall on the field, and you stand on the side wielding the executioner's axe. I've heard of dragons fighting against Artifices resurrected from ages past. All these are confusing to me."

Vertiline took a cautious step back, acknowledging the advance of Luc on her right. The big man's face was blank, nothing but resolve there. *They think me a sinner, or demon-possessed. Only Amaury talks. Martin would see me dead for the righteousness of it. Luc doesn't like the work but sees it must be done. Could I have beaten Iz on his worst day? Two Knight Valiants against my slender Chevalier's blade, and a Champion of the Order as their leader.* Vertiline tossed her pale braid, then wet her lips. "Will there be talking or fighting?"

"Luc," Amaury warned. "Be easy."

"The job must be finished." Luc didn't look happy about it.

"I won't abide," Martin gritted. "She wears the burnished sun! Vertiline mocks us, and all Tresward."

Amaury sighed. "She's doing nothing of the sort. Knight Chevalier Vertiline wears Smithsteel because we gave it to her. Her blade is glass, because that's what her hand knows. She's greeted us with honor, a lone warrior against our host. Where is the mockery?"

"He's got a point." Luc eased back but kept his blade ready.

Vertiline eyed the three Knights. "Israel is dead."

Amaury's smile fell. "I'd heard, but didn't think it possible. He wore the gold bars of a Valiant but walked like a Champion. He could've been my brother."

"He was." Vertiline's smile felt fixed. "He fell because another

Champion cast him down. Nicolette stood against his glass and, and..." Her voice cracked. "She took off my arm."

"It seems fine now," Martin sneered.

Vertiline ignored him. "An Adept took skymetal against her steel and cut her down. She was dead, do you understand? A Champion's husk powered by a monster. The Sway and Storm at the beck and call of a creature we've only heard stories about."

Luc considered this. "It seems convenient the only witnesses to the revenant you claim was Knight Champion Nicolette are dead."

"They're not dead." Vertiline sighed. "Israel's gone, yes. But Knight Chevalier Geneve—"

"Geneve is an Adept," Amaury said.

"Field promotion." Vertiline let a fierce grin show, all teeth. "She commands the Storm and Sway. She speaks with the voice of a dragon."

"And has a sinner as her lover." Martin nodded. "Yes, yes. All of this makes sense. You've allowed yourself to be corrupted by fallacy and lies."

"You've allowed demons to lead you by the balls," Vertiline snapped. "They brought you against us, siding with a host of Vhemin. Which of us is the more likely villain, hmm? I sail with no host of Vhemin at my back."

"Yet one rides on the deck of your ship." Luc's face was resolute.

"He's ... different." Vertiline looked away, guilt and doubt touching her.

That tiny moment was all it took for Martin to lunge, greatsword glimmering with Light, headed for her heart. Martin moved like a prayer on its way to heaven, fast and true, guided by a righteous arm and mastery of all the Three's patterns.

She slipped her blade between her heart and her enemy's greatsword. Sparks of Light bled from the clash to drip molten, burning motes on the floor. *Fuck me, but he's fast. The ancient guardians of a dead city were slugs by comparison.* Her heart doubled its pace, reminding her what raw fear felt like.

I'm going to die alone. There should be three of us, but Iz died and Geneve left.

She tried for *Onslaught of Speed*. A sensible pattern for a dance at an upbeat tempo. Vertiline's blade glimmered, its point seeking Martin's heart, his neck, then his heart again. The Valiant swatted her blade aside like she were an annoying child, inept, unschooled in battling with sharpened sticks let alone glass you could shave a giant's beard with.

"Martin!" Amaury's shout slipped past them both as they came together in a clash of glass, anger, and fear. Anger, because Martin would *have* her, she saw it on his face. Fear, because Vertiline thought he was right. *Who am I to face a Valiant?*

Then, *Geneve fought a Champion.*

She caught Martin's glass on her shield. Rimfire sprayed sparks across the hold. The starboard wall cracked as stray Light hit hard. Water hissed through the breach, a fine misting spray who's cool touch belied the danger waiting outside.

I will never see her again. Sight of Day's warmth won't touch me beyond the grave. The sinner will never know what took me down, and Armitage will wonder if firing me into this ship was a thing he could've stopped.

No, because he knows me. Had my back, when it seemed crazy. Someone believes in me more than I believe in myself.

Vertiline's feet moved like she'd been taught, oiled perfection taking her through *Friend's Betrayal.* The pattern showed her how to bring her shield down like a blade, the blazing edge shearing through Martin's sword, leaving glowing, dripping glass in its wake.

Her blade licked out once, twice, a third time, and Martin was gone, his body slipping into a surprised pile at her feet.

Luc squared off against her. But unless she was sorely mistaken, doubt hid in his eyes, marring some of the certainty he'd worn like a warm winter's cloak moments earlier. "You ... fought well."

"She fought with the Three's Light," Amaury spat. "Put up your blade, Luc. There'll be no more death today."

"Vertiline must pay for her crime." Luc's chin had a stubborn set that put Vertiline's teeth on edge.

"I'm not worried about *her* death." Amaury's words dripped into the silence. "Knight Valiant Vertiline will end you like a bad mistake, Luc."

"She's no Valiant." Luc didn't sound convinced.

Amaury sheathed his blades and stepped closer, but slow and easy. He nudged the parts that used to make Martin into a person. "And yet a Valiant lies dead. I see no greater argument. I would call her Champion, but we've no easy way to test the Sway."

"We are all damned." But Luc slid his sword away and didn't seem sad to see it go. "Why are you here, Vertiline?"

"I come to stop a terrible mistake." She lowered her blade, hands strangely still, none of the post-fight jitters she was used to. "I hoped to stop more Tresward falling on a demon king's orders."

"Do you still drink?" Amaury raised an eyebrow.

"Is Khiton a motherless bastard?" Vertiline raked fingers through her hair, teasing out her braid and letting pale hair fall about her face. "The question should be, 'how much?'"

Luc looked at Martin's remains. "There should be no jesting in a place where our brother fell."

"And yet, here I am, a joke to all." Vertiline gave a mock bow. "Luc! Hear me. The gods left. I'm going to find them."

"How do you know where they'll be?" Amaury scratched his chin, gauntlets rasping as they discovered stubble.

"Because Geneve is across the sea. She's in Trebani. It will take a long time to explain. I feel we need to answer a more important series of questions." Vertiline looked up. "Who captains this ship? How many Tresward walk with you? What are your intentions? Can we stop war between our fleets?" She took a cautious step forward. "We have a hundred ships. We couldn't get the Tresward, but we have brave hearts all the same. Humans sail with us, aye, and a Vhemin and Feybrind. *Both* are my friends and I've no shame admitting it." She lifted her chin at Luc's hooded gaze. "If we cross blades at sea, neither wins. We only make corpses demons don't have to fight later."

Amaury nodded. "Then we'll have to not fight."

The ship canted to the starboard side. A guttural Vhemin voice snarled, "'*WARE!*" The sound of a handful of arbalests thrummed.

Vertiline sighed. "It was never going to be that easy, was it?"

Luc shook his head. "There is always conflict."

"Brothers." Vertiline held out her hand, palm down. "Until we finish this conversation, do we swear to not cross blades?"

Luc hesitated, then put his hand on hers. "Who do we fight for? Who is against us?"

Amaury placed his hand on top. "The Three, as always."

Vertiline showed her teeth. "No, Knight Champion. We fight for *life*, and damn the Three and their demon war. This is *our* world. I aim to save it, or what parts I can."

Two nods, and it was settled. They looked above decks as cannon fire shook the air.

Chapter Seventeen

"I guess it's time to stop lying." Meriwether raised Florian's phylactery, shattering it on the ground at his feet. He stomped on it until only jagged shards remained, breath ragged, rage and disgust filling his mouth with bile. Panting, he rested his hands on the glass panel.

Silence. He looked up to find the blue-feathered bird on the glass between his hands, head cocked, eyes piercing. *Cheep?*

"Because I'm the best liar I know," he admitted. "I just had to lie to myself. It wasn't so hard. Sky Full of Promise, come back to me. I need to..." Meriwether trailed off. "I need you to be you. Be Coming Storm."

The Feybrind shuddered, then spasmed off the bed. Even with her feline grace, she gouged her head on the circlet, leaving a stripe of red across her brow. The Feybrind crouched, backing away from the table, rose gaze full of terror. She crouched by the wall, the red gleaming eyes of dead men watching them both.

Meriwether crouched, lifting a sliver of Florian's phylactery. He touched the point with his finger. It was razor-sharp, pricking a droplet of blood without him feeling much of anything. Pacing to Coming Storm, he held out the shard. "I'm sorry I lied. I had to, or he'd never let us be. Now he's gone." She bared her teeth, but he just nodded in response. "I get it. I put you in a thing that might have made you stop being you. You're young, but that doesn't mean you want to live any less. Here." He offered the shard again.

She snatched it from him, then surged to her feet, edge against his throat. He could smell the fear on her, the sour reek of panic. Her eyes were hard and uncompromising, the same glint in them he'd seen on Vertiline's glass blade the first time he saw her use it.

"I'd like for us to wake up the rest of your family. I think we can then get rid of the ghosts that dog our heels. I need your help for that, and I know you don't need mine." He sighed, suddenly tired. "It's just that they lie to all of us. It's all they've ever done, and they'll keep doing it until we kill each other, or die trying. We don't owe the dead anything. But they keep coming back, trying to take us from ourselves."

Coming Storm stood back, the movement slow, as if she wanted to avoid frightening him. *She thinks I'll take away her will again.* Meriwether reached out a hand as equally slow, taking her free one. He laid her palm over his mouth. *{There. Now I can't Command you. You get to make your choice.}*

She surged forward, teeth bared. The kiss of glass on his skin felt like the rasp of a blunt razor. Meriwether tilted his chin, exposing his neck further, then closed his eyes. *It will be what it'll be. I don't really want to die, but the good news is I don't think Coming Storm is an asshole. Not like Dad, and not like me.*

The blade left his throat, her hand lifting from his mouth. Meriwether opened his eyes. She stood close enough to kiss, rose eyes clouding with confusion. The shard clattered as it hit the cold stone floor. *{What kind of man are you?}*

"The ordinary kind."

Coming Storm shook her head. *{You said you'd stop lying to me.}*

He laughed. "I said nothing of the sort. More like, lying for now."

{I should've cut you while I had the chance.} This with a half-smile, gaze turning away, suddenly shy. *{Weren't you afraid I would?}*

"No. You weren't made that way." He rubbed his chin, as if it'd erase the guilt of his species. "We need to kill the rest of these assholes."

{They are already dead. Florian ... ate them to stay alive. He was also not an ordinary man.} She kicked the shard of glass to spin across the floor. *{Did you mean what you said?}*

Meriwether pursed his lips. "Which particular part?"

{Waking my family. So they can help you win a war.}

"Yes. Well, no. I mean... Wait." Meriwether raked his hair with his fingers, then tugged his shirt straight. "I don't want them to fight a war. I want them to go outside and see the world. It's been waiting for them for eight hundred years. There are plenty of horrors. Vhemin roam the world, eating all. I don't think humans have changed much in all that time. But ... your people have villages at the verges of the world. A friend of mine would call you sister, if you allowed it."

She nodded, stroking her chin. *{Then we need the bird.}*

"You what now?"

{She's not a bird.} Coming Storm shook her head, angry with herself. *{She needs to remember what she was. And for that, she needs you.}*

Meriwether looked to the bird, which had perched on the glass panel, head cocked, beady eye locked on him. "What were you, then?"

Cheep!

"Ah." Meriwether's hand went to the empty space at his hip where the book of High Magic used to sit. "There's a cost to this, isn't there?"

{She used to be more than what she is now.}

Cheep!

Coming Storm half-smiled. *{I misspoke. She used to be* different *than what she is. Holomancers make things that aren't alive. It is forbidden for you to make a living thing. You know this, yes?}*

"Define 'forbidden.' If you mean, I can't do it, sure. Same page, basically." Meriwether frowned. "I'm not sure where you're going with this."

{You can make her what she was. Imagine her old form, and if you get it right, she'll be as she was.} Coming Storm shrugged. *{If you get it wrong, you will be unmade. Holomancers may not make any living thing.}*

"It's just illusions." Meriwether stuffed his hands in the pockets of his long coat. "I don't understand who makes the rules, or why."

{They're not illusions. Who taught you to Holomancer, anyway?} Coming Storm stroked his face. *{You just need to believe. If your heart's in it, it'll be*

real. You can't make living things, raise the dead, or summon the Three. The gods hold license over those domains.} She looked away. *{Until humans broke the covenant and made us.}*

"I can make ... anything?"

She wobbled her hand *so-so. {You guessed right. There is always a price.}*

Meriwether turned to the blue-feathered bird. "You used to be someone, didn't you?"

Cheep.

"Someone important?"

A hop, almost a shrug. *Cheep, cheep.*

"But we need you to wake everyone up?"

Cheep!

"Well, fuck." Meriwether sighed. "I don't get three tries or anything?"

{Just one.}

"Okay. Let's go." He headed for the door.

Coming Storm loped past, turned to face him, and put a hand on his chest. *{Where are we going?}*

Cheep?

"We're going to the one Three-damned person who speaks sense around here. My barber."

THEY MADE THE GROOMING AREA WITHOUT FUSS, MOSTLY BECAUSE there was another on this level. The mirror cleared as Meriwether approached, and he was again faced with the apparition that wanted nothing but good grooming for him. "Hello. Beard or hair?"

Meriwether waved the question away. "Mirror, I need answers."

"I exist to provide excellent advice."

Coming Storm shucked herself onto the bench beside the mirror. *{You aren't even real.}*

"Bah. Spoken like someone with fur the same length all the time." The apparition leaned closer, as if he could step out the mirror. "I could suggest some nice tints for your coat, though."

Cheep. The blue-feathered bird landed on Meriwether's shoulder.

"Exactly." Meriwether pointed to the bird. "I need to know what this is."

"I told you—"

"I need you to *show* me, mirror. Like you showed me my hair of a different length. Give me a picture of what she was." Meriwether crossed his arms. "I know you can do it."

"You know nothing of the sort." His reflection raised an eyebrow.

"You're saying you can't?" Meriwether snorted. "Some magic mirror you turned out to be."

"I didn't say I couldn't," the specter mused. "Maybe I don't want to."

"The fate of the world depends on it." Meriwether sighed. "And if you do this one damn thing, I promise to get whatever haircut you think's most appropriate."

Meriwether's reflection narrowed his eyes. "Promise?"

"I swear by the Three above and all their wonders." Meriwether touched his chest. "I, Lord Meriwether du Reeves, vassal and servant of her majesty Queen Morgan of Or'sen, swear to get whatever haircut you think will make me look the best."

"You should've lead with that. Here's what she looked like." The apparition vanished, replaced with the blue-feathered bird's rightful form.

Meriwether leaned closer. "You're kidding."

The mirror's voice came out nice and clear despite it not being visible. "I have no sense of humor. Not really."

"They've been dead for hundreds of years. All of them."

Cheep!

"That's fair. *Most* of them." Meriwether rubbed his chin. "Look like you?"

Cheep!

Meriwether sighed. "Last chance to stay a bird forever." The bird made no reply, flitting to his other shoulder.

Coming Storm touched his arm. *{Are you sure you want to do this? The mirror is very old. It might have made a mistake.}*

Meriwether shook his head. "I'm not sure of much, but I know it's wrong to have hundreds of Feybrind locked in a cellar away from the sun. You're supposed to feel the wind on your face, not the lash of a human's whip." He held his hand up, and the blue-feathered bird hopped on. He lowered her to sit on the ledge beside Coming Storm. "If I don't make it, can you help Coming Storm set her people free?"

Cheep. Cheep, cheep.

"Good enough." He closed his eyes, imagining the blue-feathered bird as something else. Some*one* else. He reached a cautious hand out, remembering where her beak was. Meriwether touched her.

Nothing happened. He gritted his teeth, reaching deep inside. The tome of High Magic had terms like *inner power* and *expectant force* but was devilishly quiet on the details. His father used magic that was different to Meriwether's. His was a seeming, a set of visions to confuse the mind.

I don't have to do this alone. There are others here.

Meriwether felt about with his thoughts, stubbing his mental toe on Coming Storm's bright force. He touched the blue-feathered bird, felt what she'd been hundreds of years ago. Inside her was a yearning for freedom wings couldn't provide. She'd been caged against her will into a body that was weaker than she deserved. Sure, she'd had wings, but marvelous ones.

Somewhere at the lapping shore of his thoughts meeting hers, gentle sea against hissing sand, he found her name. Not *blue-feathered bird* or some amalgam of *cheep-cheep*, but what her mother's heart named her as she was growing in her womb.

He let his will out, all at once. It sounded to him like the gentle rustle of leaves teased by the northern wind. Summer rain on a windowpane. The intake of breath before a laugh, or the silence before someone said *I love you*. He felt his soul tugging to be free with it, like he'd broken the pact that made the world, and done something wonderful but forbidden. *I'm good at breaking rules. One more step and she'll be good as new... she just needs her name given back to her.* He breathed, "Yasmine Glittercone."

He felt a jerk, like Khiton donkey-kicked him in the chest. It was beyond pain, a clutching agony that held his heart in a vise. The world shuddered, the whisper of creation hissing its denial of what he'd done.

He opened his eyes, and there she was. Bird no more. Then he coughed, hand up, and when he brought it away from his mouth, it was spattered with blood. The mirror specter was gone, a reflection of just himself there. He saw red-stained lips above a corpse's pallor, and then he slid down toward the hard, unforgiving floor.

Chapter Eighteen

Geneve jogged the quiet streets of Imshir, looking for a place to hide. Shore up until all this blew over. *There is a demon I can't kill behind me. I have no sword, and no dragon.*

I miss Meri. He would know what to do.

Her armor was heavy, but for all that the weight was comforting. Familiar, unlike everything else in this city. Omrar was a kind old man, but a stranger. The streets were made of stone like everywhere else, but fit together in strange ways, winding their way to curious destinations. Mazin offered food that nourished as expected, but tasted unfamiliar, the texture odd in her mouth. *Nothing is right. Everything is wrong.*

There were no Tresward in Trebani. Knights didn't call this place home, didn't hunt sinners across the sands, but they'd been here before. A long time ago her kind had carried a shield for these strange people, with their unfamiliar streets and odd food. *Because they're just people. They are different, but we're all the same.*

Still, there was a shortage of Feybrind and Vhemin, which was odd. The cat people didn't offer help here, and the Vhemin didn't show their faces. As scarce as Knights. *Is this what the world looks like without wonderful things? The same, but less for all that?*

Geneve wasn't paying attention, and at another time that would've gotten her killed. When a hand clamped on her arm from the darkness of a doorway, vise-strong against the Smithsteel, she was caught flat-footed. She dropped her helmet to clatter on the cobbles, turned, dragged her elbow back, and slammed her other hand into the wrist that held her. Her assailant's grip broken, she bared her teeth.

"Ow!" Mazin hissed. "That's no way to treat a friend."

Geneve held her empty hands up, half apology, half guard. "Are you?"

"As sure as the night is cooler than the day. I have Omrar." The big merchant's smile gleamed in the dark, not with malice, but welcome.

I'm too used to enemies. I don't know what friends look like. "It's unwise to sneak up on a Knight."

"It's unwise for a Knight to run like a scared child through unfamiliar streets," Mazin countered. "I have food and drink. Coffee, or something stronger."

"Stronger is better." Geneve combed red hair with her fingers. "How do you know about Omrar?"

"I trade in many things. Knowledge is the end of many journeys. Come." He beckoned her inside. She retrieved her helmet and followed. It wasn't the same place he'd hosted her before but was still set below the streets. Inside there were fewer curtains, the benches and cushions less plush, but the smell of toasting bread made her mouth water.

Omrar was on a divan. The old man creaked upright. "Geneve!"

She jogged to him, catching him into a hug. "By the Three. You're okay. I was worried." She tried not to wince as her armor pressed against her broken rib.

"I know these streets." He pulled back. "The Arm and the Will won't find me."

"It's the demons I'm worried about." Geneve turned to Mazin. "You promised something stronger. This tale will take more than ale."

"It's good we've got more than ale," Mazin rumbled. "The end of a good story needs a fine wine."

Geneve unstrapped her shield from her back, then settled on a divan across from Omrar, placing her helmet next to her. Omrar half reached for it, and she nodded. The old man turned it this way and that. "The style is strange."

"It is over eight hundred years old and lets me speak to a dragon with my mind." Geneve sighed. "It wasn't made by Tresward Smiths."

Mazin bustled from the back room, a tray before him. "It was made by the ancestors of your Smiths. It's Smithsteel, but also other things their art's forgotten." He set the tray down. "I'm remembering so many things."

Geneve eyed him sidelong. "If you're about to explode as a flesh-burrowing demon bursts from within, just ... *don't*. I've had enough of demons and their bullshit for one night."

"He's a demon?" Omrar croaked.

"I'm not a demon." Mazin sighed. "I ... died."

"That needs some explaining." Geneve felt tired, the night catching up to her as all hunters did. "You know what? Fuck it. Start with the wine."

Mazin raised an eyebrow but poured her a tall glass. The wine was peach-colored, fragrant, the scent of honey and pear coming to her. She sipped, then guzzled, thirsty. "That was amazing. What was it?"

The merchant frowned. "I'm not sure. This isn't my house. More?"

"Please." Geneve held her glass out while the big man filled it. "I can't kill them."

"Who?" Mazin offered the wine to Omrar. The old man held up his hands. Mazin shook his head. "You'll drink or offend my house."

"I thought this wasn't your house." Omrar took a glass anyway, a cautious sip turning his frown into a smile of delight. "This is quite good."

"All houses are mine, in the end." A frown grew on the merchant's face. "I don't know why I said that."

"Because you're dead." Geneve helped herself to toasted bread and hummus. "Keep up. The thing is, I need Meri. I need him because I love him, but also because he's smart. He'll know what to do."

"About?" Mazin looked into his wineglass. "This is quite fine."

"I need to know why glass won't kill demons. I need Ormeon, and Meri will know how to find her. And I need Requiem."

Omrar sipped wine. "Requiem's your sword?"

"A skymetal blade forged by the greatest Smith who's ever lived." Geneve looked at her glass, remembering her old friend Kytto. "He's probably dead, like most everyone who's served in the Three's name."

"All people die," Omrar said. "It doesn't matter who we serve."

"I know the answer to some of your questions. Glass is made of the wrong stuff to kill demons. It's just sand." Mazin chugged back his wine. "Most normal things won't do it."

"But I killed one before." Geneve leaned back, welcoming the mellow that came with the wine. "I killed a powerful one. I bent the Sway to my will."

"You'll need more than a quick word this time. Skymetal's needed to end the strongest of them. That's why they've hidden Requiem." Mazin's glass was refilled as if by magic, the merchant offering a top up to Geneve. "You should drink some water."

"Are you my mother?" Geneve's words turned bitter.

"No. I'm no one's mother. That's Cophine's job." Mazin's gaze turned distant. "I wonder where she is?"

"Who *are* you?" Geneve's eyes narrowed. *I should leave this alone until morning. I need sleep. My ribs ache and need tending. But this won't wait.* "A priest? You're more than a merchant."

"I'm just a dead man." Mazin sighed. "And not a very good one. I couldn't even *stay* dead."

Omrar settled his glass on the table with exaggerated care. "What happened?"

"Memory's a funny thing. I could tell you about how I saw a group of Arm officers wrestling a woman into a wagon. She had long hair and a frightened expression. If you asked me about the color of her eyes or the clothes she wore, I'd come up empty. That face, though. The fear of death, about a horror you know is certain and unavoidable." Mazin shook his head. "I could tell you about how I followed the wagon, possessed by anger or my own fading strength. I stood in front of them where four roads met. I put my hand up, and they struck me down."

"Who was she?" Geneve whispered.

"I don't know." Mazin shrugged. "But she's all of us, I think. It took me a long time to die. I'm big, Knight. I bled out while a vagabond took my coin purse. Another rolled me over, looking for more the first might have missed. None offered help, and I wondered why I called this city home. I remember seeing the dawn as a bread maker trundled his cart past me, and then I was in the sky."

"Heaven?" Omrar looked down. "It seems so far away."

"Heaven's a place in fanciful tales made up to calm infants and the mentally crippled." Mazin sighed. "The sky held me for a half-second, no more. In that heartbeat I saw all the land. It was more than a vision. It was the world splintered into its factions. Each beating heart struggling to best the other, and beneath all a darkness. Demons seethed, and the worst of them was *here*." He slammed hand into fist. "In Trebani, my home, and my burial ground."

Geneve realized her glass was frozen half-way to her lips, mouth open, breath stilled. *He isn't lying. I don't need Meri to see that. Mazin believes this, like he knows he has five fingers on each hand.* "Then what happened?"

Mazin snorted. "As all things in the sky do, I dropped. It was a long way down. The air burned as I fell. Others came with me. Three of us, I think. I held their hands, but I wasn't strong enough." He held his closed fists up. "Can you believe it? Someone the size of me, but unable to hold something so precious, so essential, as another's life. I couldn't stop the woman being taken, and I couldn't stop my friends..." He trailed off. "I think I knew them better than friends. I landed into my body. I woke in a crypt, other bodies beside me, shrouds covering us all like the last, gentle touch of a world saying goodbye. I was naked. The air hurt my lungs as I dragged it in. It felt like I hadn't ever breathed before, but then I remembered how. I struggled free, barged outside, and saw lightning. The mountainside burned. It took more than a half-second for all that to happen. Perhaps I fell for a lifetime. Perhaps it was only a moment. But I fell all the same."

Omrar blinked. "That's when Geneve came. She came with the storm."

Mazin shook his head. "She brought it, friend. Don't you see? Without her I might have been trapped in the sky forever. Or I might have fallen through the whole world and out the other side. The Tresward ... she's our anchor."

Silence settled between the three of them for a few moments. "That's not the worst thing I've been called," Geneve admitted.

Mazin laughed. "I meant no disrespect."

"But what does it mean?" Omrar shook his head. "That night ... I think you saw Lily. She was my ... neighbor."

"I want to say it seems unlikely, but I died and came back to life." Mazin smoothed his robe. "And I'm not the same. I have visions. My heart yearns for the Precept's palace and the mountain both. The wastes outside the city stop me seeing the scar the lightning wrought, and the Arm and Will stop me going to the palace."

Geneve put her glass down, then creaked to her feet, wincing as her ribs ached. "I need my sword. I need Meri, and I need Ormeon. The sword is for killing demons, and Meri and Ormeon ... together, we're *right*."

"Together, you make three," Mazin suggested. "You will finish what we started. You'll heal the world."

"Who's 'we?'" Geneve growled. "This sounds like someone else's bullshit."

"I might know tomorrow." Mazin gusted air like a bellows. "Or not ever. Perhaps you should ask your dragon to come here. She may know."

"How?"

He pointed to her helmet. "That will call her to you."

Geneve frowned. "It seems a long way from here to the mountain."

Omrar laughed. "You have a magic helmet from ages past. The hands of time gave it to you. They kept it safe for hundreds of years. If the ancients could make a thing last hundreds of years, don't you think they might have solved other problems?"

Geneve bent, winced, then shook angry red curls. "I'm foolish." She straightened, placing her hand on her rib. *//BE WELL.//*

Her hand shook as if in a river current. Mazin and Omrar crawled to motionlessness. The candle flames slowed their hypnotic dance. She couldn't breathe for a moment, then the world surged forward. Geneve probed her ribs, then laughed. "I forgot about the Sway." Her words husked free, throat raw from just two words.

Mazin blinked his awe. "You speak with the voice of dragons."

"Now I'm going to speak *with* dragons." Geneve snared her helmet and slipped it on. The world became clearer through the glass visor as it always did. *Ormeon?*

A heartbeat, two, three, then:

//DRAGONRIDER!// The dragon's laugh gusted to her as if on a strong wind. *//HAVE YOU BEEN SLEEPING? I HEAR YOUTH IS OFTEN LAZY.//*

Geneve laughed, too. *I lost my armor.* She pressed her lips into a line. *How is Meri?*

//ABOUT THAT,// Ormeon growled. *//IT'S COMPLICATED.//*

Chapter Nineteen

"I came here to talk, not fight!" Vertiline took a blow from a saw-toothed Vhemin monster on her shield, stepped around her, then sliced the monster in half. Flesh smoked as superheated glass parted soul from body.

"You are talking." Amaury tossed an easy smile her way as if fighting wasn't a bother. "You're talking right now!"

She caught the smile, then passed it on to Luc. The easygoing giant raised an eyebrow, trying to deny the hint of an answering grin. The three stood on the deck of a strange ship. They'd used rigging lines to cross a flotsam- and body-filled sea as their previous vessel sank beneath the waves. Vertiline thought this one might be called something like the *Seaspray*, which called into question the imagination of its owner.

They didn't stand shoulder to shoulder as if making a last stand. The Knights worked their way across the deck. The stern was their prize, and the small boat lashed there. Vertiline had said *if we get to my ship people will stop trying to kill us*, and Luc agreed that swords down was the best way to talk. Amaury led them, twin blades carving a path. Vertiline took his right side, Luc the left.

The patterns guided them. Step *here* and avoid that arrow. Slip *there* and slice your enemy. Vertiline's shield was slick with gore, her armor awash with the blood of humans and Vhemin. She smelled the copper tang of it, underlaid by the brightness of sea brine and the stink of shit. A sorcerer on the sterncastle threw his arms wide. *He looks like a tool.*

Tool or not, his face lit like he'd found religion, a home in the Three's arms at last. Bright, thin lightning cascaded from the lead-gray clouds. The first strikes lanced the sea, then friendly ships. An arc found a home in a Vhemin near the bow, his body exploding into steaming meat.

Vertiline narrowed her eyes, then ducked behind her shield. Her left foot led forward into *Steelbright Song* as another bolt hungered from the heavens. She caught it on the lip of her shield. It arced to starboard, razing the railing into ash. *I did that wrong. My foot wasn't perfect.* Exhaustion leaned on her like a drunken and unwanted lover, all heavy hands and dead weight. *I'm tired. We've been fighting for what feels like hours.*

Her shield smoked. Another bolt came from the clouds, the enchanter screaming in ecstasy as thunder shattered the air. Vertiline caught this on her shield, her back foot sliding into a semicircle as she tossed the lightning aside.

The shield broke. The straps on her metal hand smoked, the rim bleeding into molten drops at her feet. She shook her arm free. "Amaury!"

The Champion nodded, surging forward, twin swords raised. His blades pointed to the sky, the Three's Storm answering. The sorcerer's lightning was a pale, feeble thing in comparison. Amaury's Storm came as a brilliant pillar of blue-white fury. It rubbed the sorcerer out like a smudge.

It didn't come fast enough. The sorcerer's final cast lanced a vein of electricity at Vertiline. She kept turning from her last movement, but the energy found her anyway, her body a conduit to earth. She took the blast on her arm, hand cast out to ward the blow, and expected to know nothing after that.

She didn't die.

Vertiline opened her eyes. Her Smithsteel gauntlet glowed with heat. Electricity coursed across the armor. She felt no pain, and shook her closed fist. The arm seemed fine.

My metal hand. A tiny bolt of power crackled from her gauntlet, hitting the deck. Her hand vibrated as if holding a stallion's heart at full race, insistent, a pounding that wanted release. *I can't throw my arm away. It's attached to me through dark sorcery and a healthy serving of bullshit.* She took in Amaury's wide-eyed expression and Luc's dour frown. Another bolt of electricity tapped its way along the deck toward Luc.

The big Knight caught it on his blade, tossing it over the railing. Water hissed and snapped. "Perhaps you should do something with that."

"I didn't know it could do that," Vertiline admitted. "Perhaps you should do something with *that*." She leveled her blade at the hole Amaury bored in the deck. The *Seaspray* listed to stern, no doubt because Amaury's Storm carved a hole through all decks and into the sea.

"The launch!" Amaury clattered up the ladder toward the rear, armor gathering what feeble light there was and gleaming despite the setting sun. Luc clambered after.

Vertiline hurried in their wake. Her arm still trembled. She glared at her closed fist. "What do you want?"

The arm said nothing, but it started to hum. *If I put my hand on that wooden ladder, it'll turn to ash.* Her gauntlet now glowed white with heat, causing the air about to shimmer. This close to the rest of her she felt the wash coming off it.

A scream of rage made her turn. A Vhemin stamped toward her. She carried a cudgel the size of a small child. "Human! You killed my ship!"

Vertiline looked at her arm, the Vhemin, then her arm. She pointed her arm at the monster and opened her hand.

A pure stream of brilliant white lanced to the monster, hitting her square in the chest. Chainlink armor flashed to nothing, the flesh beneath cauterized in an instant. The Vhemin tottered for a moment before looking at the hole in her chest. It was about the size of Luc's head, bored all the way through, and right where the creature's heart would be.

The captain clattered to the deck, cudgel rolling free. Vertiline looked at her hand, the white heat now tinged with yellow as it cooled. The palm of her gauntlet was ... *gone*, perfectly cut to show her metal hand within. It didn't glow with heat, smoke, or look any different to how it'd been when she woke this morning.

She slashed the bindings on her gauntlet with glass, the hot metal hissing as it hit the decking. Vertiline flexed her metal hand. "So. You're good for a few party tricks. What else can you do?"

"Vertiline! Stop fucking around!" Amaury beckoned from the stern. She slipped up the ladder, all lithe grace, and joined him and Luc by the launch. "Get over the side."

"I can—"

"You've got a sinner's hand, Tilly." Amaury bit down on whatever he was going to say before measuring his next words like a man counting out gold. "The world's changed. It's different today than yesterday, and yesterday galloped like a frightened stallion from last week. Sinner is just a word for something we were taught to fear by the wicked. The Tresward crumble from within because Clerics fight Knights, trying to work out which pieces to move, where, and why."

A Vhemin scuttled half-way up the ladder, saw who waited for him, and dropped from view. Luc adjusted his breastplate. "I'll make sure we're not interrupted while you have your epic moment."

Amaury watched the big Knight move to the ladder, standing like an angry statue, before turning to Vertiline. "You're the bridge, the proof that both things can be true. Right doesn't have to best wrong. There might not be a wrong." He sagged a micron. If Vertiline hadn't trained her life in the company of Knights she'd have missed it. "You fight with the Three's light but cast sinner's magic. If the Clerics are right, the Three should've cut you down. Erased you like the mistake you are. At the least their Light should be something you can't quite reach anymore."

"For a time, I couldn't." Vertiline looked at her metal hand. "Before I found this."

Amaury snorted. "There's more to the tale than you stumbling across a spare hand in the woods. It'll have to wait until we're clear of this. The story of the hand isn't as important as the very *you* that stands before me. Vertiline, Knight Valiant of the Tresward. Vertiline, wielder of sinner's magics. Vertiline, who fights for sinners and Knights because both are right."

"Vertiline, who is tired of fables and standing in her armor in a raging sea battle."

He snorted. "Vertiline, who I'd like to call sister."

She raised her head sharply, catching his eye. "That has too final a tone, Amaury. We've a way out of this yet."

"There are a hundred ships against you. The odds are low." He gave a lopsided smile. "I've fought a thousand battles in a hundred wars, and today I realized I might have been doing all that wrong."

"Maybe." She watched Luc behead a Vhemin eager for the grave. "Still got a way out of this. It's over the side, in the skiff. Oars in the water, backs into it, and return to my friends. Put enough sail up, and we'll be free."

"There's the small matter of the weather-workers. I admit, hearing the Clerics say we needed sinner's help with one breath and condemning their work with another caused me no small doubt."

"How many are there?"

Amaury looked over the fleet, fires raging, people screaming, bodies in the water, chum for the sharks. "Four, I think." He pointed a metal-clad arm across the sea. "Her, with the red hair. Him, with the scar, and the guy beside him. And the teenager by the bow of that small ship."

Four souls against freedom. Four, standing against her returning to her sister of the blade. *Don't forget that annoying sinner she hangs around with.* "Are they good people?"

Amaury spread his hands. "Good enough. I've no quarrel with them."

"That's a shame, because I do. Come on." Vertiline put a hand on the rail. "Luc! Stop wasting time."

"I'm not—"

"We're leaving!" She vaulted, landing in the skiff. It was time to get to her friends and stop the end of the world.

Half-way to her ship, she realized it wasn't there anymore. Fire still burned to the waterline where the ship *was*. But nothing else remained. She stood, all perfect balance, and ignored Luc's glare. "It was right *there*."

Amaury turned. "You lost a whole ship?"

"I think your assholes set it on fire." She scanned the carnage, looking for a way free. She caught sight of tan fur and gleaming golden eyes. "There. Sight of Day stands on the *Western Frenzy*."

"That's one of our ships," Amaury said.

"Not anymore." Vertiline raised an eyebrow. "You lost a whole ship?"

"Touché." Amaury pointed to the north. A massive ship rode over wreckage of a smaller vessel as it headed their way. It's sails were aflame, but it didn't look to be bothersome for the captain. The ram on the prow would cause problems for any it met, but for the three of them in their tiny skiff the ship just needed to keep going and they'd be lost.

I don't know any patterns for fighting a ship from a rowboat on a churning sea. "We have a problem."

"I know. I just pointed it out." Amaury examined one of his blades. "This feels like a difficult problem to solve."

Vertiline glanced back to Sight of Day, then squared her shoulders. *Please be with me, my friend. Save us.* She cast her voice across the seas. "I bring Tresward Light to stop you! Turn your ship and no harm will come to you!" They might not have heard her, but enough stood on the bow, pointing their skiff out to the helmsman.

Which meant the ship kept coming. The good news, if there was some to be found by grubbing in the dirt of this shitshow, was the *Western Frenzy* looked to be headed their way. *I just need a little time.* Vertiline closed her metal hand in a fist, drawing her other back as if pulling an invisible bow. Sight of Day gave a tight nod. She eyed a sailor on the rigging high above, took aim, and loosed. Unseen by those on the *Western Frenzy*, Sight of Day fired his bow at the same time.

A pause. She thought a woman on the bow sniggered before a scream pierced the air. The man in the rigging pinwheeled over the side, scream cut short as the waves gobbled him whole.

Luc glanced back, then gave her a suspicious glare. "How'd you do that?"

"You row the boat, I'll work my sinner's magic." Vertiline took aim again, this time lining up the sniggering woman. She let fly. Still no one noticed Sight of Day with the real bow and arrow. *Half of warfare is being unexpected. The other half is style.*

The woman screamed, torn from the deck to pinwheel across the waters and then she was gone. The sailors on the bow stopped sniggering and started taking cover. Vertiline aimed, held her breath, then fired again. Another man torn from the ship, blood spray caught on the wind, then he was gone.

"How *are* you doing that?" Amaury looked to her metal hand. "What kind of sorcery do you carry?"

The ship *still* came at them. In place of jeering sailors, an old man stood on the bow. He wore a black robe, perhaps a little moth-eaten, but stood tall enough. He raised his arms, and the sky darkened.

Vertiline drew and fired. The air about the man shivered as it was struck. He stumbled back a pace, eyes widening—they were close enough to see each other clearly now—lips pulling into a snarl. Lightning speared from above.

Vertiline raised her hand, screaming as their skiff was bathed in blue-white. Her gauntlet caught heaven's fury, bound it, and crackled its satisfaction as she closed her fist about the enchanter's power.

The enchanter, not to be outdone by an upstart Knight with a fancy metal hand, brought his fist into his palm. The skies roiled, spitting a sphere of roiling, burning smoke. It roared toward Vertiline like dragonfire. She raised her hand again. *How much can this hand take? Will the ancients stand with me?*

Turned out, not that much.

Lightning hammered from the heavens. Vertiline caught it, fingers up like she was trying to catch a sword blow at her head. Again the enchanter's storm hit, fire blinding her. Amaury yelled, but his voice was lost to the rage of a sorcerer at the height of his power. Vertiline buckled, dropping to one knee in the boat as the sky's rage rained on her.

The storm paused to catch its breath. Amaury gripped the side of the skiff. Luc's hands were frozen on the oars. Both looked at her hand above her. The metal glowed with more than heat, white bleeding from it like a tear in creation leading right to the sun's heart. Lightning crawled over the surface, tiny veins arcing to hiss against the savage sea. Vertiline squinted, unable to bear looking at her arm. It shook, like she held a titan by the scruff, a monster wanting to savage her throat. She croaked, "You should run."

Amaury relaxed his grip. "We've nowhere to go, Chevalier. We're armored on the sea. We leave, we die."

Luc glanced at the enchanter, who's mouth hung open. "We have a few moments—"

Energy blasted from Vertiline's hand. She had no conscious control —it wasn't that she couldn't keep her hand closed through force of will, but that her hand opened like an overwrought escape valve. She screamed as brilliant white blasted the skiff and the boat. Luc and Amaury left ghostly embers on her vision. The skiff incinerated in a moment, and she sank.

Down, like a falling falcon, Tresward Smithsteel holding her in its heavy embrace. A handful of seconds passed as she dropped like an anchor. Sight returned, faster than expected, but she could still see ghostly Amaury and Luc burned on her retinas. *That's all I have left of two brave Knights. I turned them to char.* The water was icy, the shock almost making her gasp, but she held her breath within her teeth.

Vertiline spasmed, struggling to tear the clasps of her armor open. Water boiled as if exposed to magma as her metal arm followed her to the dark below. Smithsteel glowed at the touch of her metal fingers. The clasp beneath her arm fused, the buckle distorting. She tried the other side with her flesh and blood fingers, the cold and dark pressing close. Above, fading light and a trail of effervescence.

Is this the end? I'm not Geneve. I can't swim forever down. The sea will take my bones and crush them. I'll never see the sun again.

Then: *Fuck the sun. I want to see my friends. I want ale with Geneve and to see the smug smile of that sinner she found, made whole, and brought to us. I want to punch Armitage and hug Sight of Day.*

I want to live. By the Three, I want to live!

Eyes still up, she worried at her armor, but the water was merciless as it darkened about her. Above, a dark shape soared like a massive crow overhead, slicing away most of the light, and she almost cried out. Almost, but training kept her air on the right side of her lips.

The water foamed above, something heavy dropped overboard. A trail of brilliant bubbles trailed a huddle of shadow toward her. *The anchor! Less buoyant than me, but will it make it in time?* The dark shape must've been the *Western Frenzy*. She stopped trying to remove her armor and started trying to swim up. It wouldn't work, but it might slow her descent.

The blackness about was almost complete. Her hand stopped glowing, its fury spent against the ocean's impassive calm. The pressure held her like a vise, pressing on her lungs, wanting her to breathe out. Vertiline clenched her teeth, lips pressed in a line. *I've stood against hordes. The ocean's nothing.*

The anchor trailed toward her. She made out a shape against it, a large man, kicking with all his might. *Three's mercy, but that's Armitage. He'll die down here.* The water was too cold for her. It was far too cold for him. But the monster swam down anyway, like he didn't realize this was the last bath he'd take.

She struggled toward him, losing the battle, but he had a sea anchor and a massive length of chain on his side. The Vhemin made it to her as his chain ran out, the *clank* muted by the water. He snared her grasping metal hand, slipped a centimeter, then held like rock. That strong grip reminded her of the living world above, not this angry darkness of ice and cold.

He planted his feet on the sea anchor, hauled her beside him, then fussed with her a moment. Her armor popped free, metal breastplate taking the burnished sun into the depths. He slowed as the cold took away his life by degrees but didn't stop. His hand slipped as he worked by her greaves, and she felt the burn as a poorly aimed knife slit her leg. She imagined his snake eyes squinted in anger, imagined him saying, *Fuck all this.*

The last of her armor fell away, and he sagged. *He's not going to make it.* The anchor jerked as the ship winched it up, but it went too slowly by far. Vertiline snared the monster in her arms. He tried to fight her off, but she slithered behind him, mostly because his movements were clumsy like a child's. She kicked for all she was worth, lungs burning. *I won't trade my life for his. Do you hear me, Khiton? I didn't agree to this bargain.*

Armitage tried to help, but he became dead weight. She kept kicking, their natural buoyancy lifting them faster than the anchor could hope to follow. The Vhemin jerked against her as he tried to suck air, thrashed, and was still. Vertiline wanted to scream, but turned the anger toward the water, legs powerful, long years of Tresward training giving her strength when hope was done.

When her head broke the surface she was almost surprised. She'd focused on her task, not noting the lightening about her, and when she popped into the smoke and screaming felt like an assault after her almost-grave.

A boat hook was offered from above, Sight of Day's golden eyes hard with concentration. Vertiline grabbed it, hooking it under Armitage's arm, then sent him above without her. She grabbed the *Western Frenzy*, metal fingers digging a clawhold into the ship's skin. Vertiline spat saltwater and just ... *breathed.* The boat hook returned, and she used it to shimmy up the ship's side.

She found Picotee marshaling sailors, hot rocks already under Armitage, but the monster was still. Vertiline pushed through, got behind the Vhemin, and drew him against her. She clasped hands below his diaphragm, heaving. He vomited water and bile, struggled weakly, then flopped like a landed fish.

Vertiline stood, slicking back her hair. "Is he going to be okay?"

Sight of Day crouched beside his friend. *{He's not dead. He's Vhemin. Ergo he's probably going to be okay.}*

"Is that a yes or a no?"

{I give you a strong maybe.}

Vertiline offered the cat a grim smile in return. *If he's making jokes, the answer's yes.* She turned to the sea, the fragments of burning ships, and the bobbing bodies. "Where's that fucking enchanter?"

Chapter Twenty

Meriwether opened his eyes, then wished he hadn't. Everything was on fire. The world: yep, lots of fire. Bright, burning fire. Inside: yep, his nerves jangled with it. His teeth *ached*, and his bones itched.

His breath shuddered in his chest. He wanted to throw up, but nothing in his body was working. *If I managed to piss myself it'd be better than this loss of control.*

A face came into view. It blocked out the unholy light a little. Woman, of course. Green eyes. Fawn-colored skin. A pert nose and cherry-red lips. Purple hair with a midnight intensity. In a normally-functioning universe it was an ensemble that would make you look twice, then swing back around for a third try. But something was wrong with the perspective. The face looked ... well, weird. Small. Or, he was large. Meriwether tried to move back, but all he managed was a weak flop of his arm. He heard a wet gurgle and thought it might just have come from him, but with his body upside down he had no real clue.

Coming Storm's face hove into view. She was *massive* compared to the other person next to him. It almost did his head in. Coming

Storm's rose eyes, soft with concern, above teeny tiny green eyes, bright with curiosity.

The Feybrind crouched beside him, gave him a shake, and when he didn't respond, wound back and slapped him across the face. Meriwether's head lolled to the side, and he took in a cool stone floor. The world being on fire? That was just the poor, old, moldering lighting above. He made a noise that sounded like *urrrrgle*.

"Slap him again," suggested the green-eyed woman.

Coming Storm obliged, this time with the other hand. Meriwether's head snapped in the other direction. More stone floor, this a bit grittier than the last. A wall that looked impossibly high up, but perhaps that was because he couldn't use his legs at the moment.

"Maybe one more time for luck?" The green-eyed woman's voice was higher-pitched than Geneve's, but it wasn't the squeak he expected from her size.

"Please," said Meriwether. Coming Storm shrugged, then slapped him again. He *urrrrgled* again, trying to raise his hand. "I meant, please don't."

The green-eyed woman pouted. "I don't get many chances to hit the bigs."

{To be fair, I'm doing all the work.}

"I think I'm doing some of the work," Meriwether said. "I'm the one getting hit."

"Don't be so stupid," said the green-eyed woman. "Even I can see how heavy and ponderous your skull is. You're not doing anything! It's got to be a lot of work to slap the silly out of you."

Meriwether chewed that over for a few heartbeats. He pressed his lips together, moved them around, then said, "I appreciate this might be forward, but have you been told to get fucked today? I only ask because I'm the one who made you what you are, Yasmine."

The green-eyed woman—Yasmine—pouted. "I've always been what I am. It just changed a few hours ago."

"*Hours?*" Meriwether managed to hunch upright. The world swayed, a surprising event in itself since he was seated. After a moment the planet got its shit together and steadied. "I've been laying here for hours?"

{Not just laying. You've been slapped a few times too.}

Meriwether tried to stand, which was harder than he expected. Coming Storm snared his arm, got under his shoulder, and heaved him upright. He gave a small scream as all the nerves in his body lit like a series of tiny fires, all at once. He felt like fainting was the right response, but Coming Storm saw it coming and slapped him.

Again.

"Sweet merciful Three, *stop* that," he hissed.

She braced him against the wall, and when he didn't slide down, stepped back. *{Stop looking like you want to pass out then.}*

He glared. "I think I changed the world. I think I should've died. And you're telling me I'm a, a what, a *pansy?*"

Jasmine Glittercone alighted on Coming Storm's shoulder. She was, of course, a fairy. Yasmine stood perhaps ten centimeters tall, and had wings that sparkled like, well, fairy dust. They were blue at the edges, shot through with gold, and anchored at her back. Yasmine wore a short leather one-piece. *Asking where that came from will probably get me slapped again.* Behind the pair was the magic mirror, faux Meriwether looking on with more concern than the other two showed, but it wasn't a high bar to get over.

Jasmine snapped her fingers, snaring his attention. "Hey. *Hey.* Pansy was a friend of mine."

"Where is she?" Meriwether realized he should've kept his mouth shut, but his brain wasn't firing well, perhaps because he'd changed the world.

"Dead, probably." Yasmine shrugged, but looked away.

"We need to get this place turned on," Meriwether said. "We need to free Coming Storm's people."

"We need a hot bath and a cup of cocoa," Yasmine corrected. "I don't need a big bath, either. Not like you bigs."

Coming Storm shuddered. *{Ugh. Baths.}*

Yasmine jumped to the cat's other shoulder in a flitter of wings. "The bath is a good idea. The fairies will like it."

"Uh." Meriwether frowned. "If they're all birds, I don't know if I've got it in me to do that again. Whatever *that* was." He pushed off from the wall in an experimental foray into balance and found he could more or less do it how he remembered. "I thought the rules were all about not making life, raising the dead, or summoning gods. I didn't make life, or..." He faced the ceiling, as if the Three were listening. "Really! I didn't make anything. I just ... put her back the way she was supposed to be."

Yasmine snapped her fingers again, lassoing his attention in a cute-yet-could-get-annoying-fast way. "First time?"

"You what?"

"First time holomancer." She nodded, as if it were all clear. Yasmine counted on her fingers. "Look, it's quite simple. You *almost* made something that lived, so the universe reminded you of the rules. It's like burning your hand on a stove. Put it there for real, the flesh will peel from your bones, the stench of overcooked pork will fill the air, and—"

"I get it," Meriwether said.

"But if you just put your hand on the stove for a minute, it'll hurt, but eventually you'll get over it. Your hand will remember to avoid fiery things!" She batted her lashes enthusiastically. She raised another finger, still counting. "Second, if you're a first time holomancer, this is really the moment you believed for, well, the first time."

Meriwether looked between then. Coming Storm raised an eyebrow with a lift of her chin, in a *do you see?* motion. Yasmine nodded, encouraging. He frowned. "What?"

"Belief." She shrugged. "You believed you could make something, and you did! Me. Or, remade me, anyway. So here we are, both of us better for it."

Meriwether ambled toward the magic mirror. "I don't feel better."

"You will," the mirror promised. "And until then, you've a promise to keep. Here's your new style." His reflection shimmered, showing an image of a haircut. It was coiffed in an exciting set of curls atop his head, black hair done in ringlets above but cut very short on the sides. "Here we go."

"Uh." Meriwether braced palms against the bench. "How do we do that?"

"That's easy." Yasmine flitted to land beside his right hand. "I can do it. I'm a qualified reactor engineer, information systems specialist, and hair stylist."

Meriwether looked at her, then the mirror, then did a slow turn to Coming Storm. "What the actual fuck is going on?"

{We'll explain while you get your curls on.} The Feybrind half-smiled. *{They'll make you look dashing.}*

"I'm already dashing."

The cat shook her head. *{This is why your incompetent species broke the world. No sense of style.}*

Yasmine laughed, and after a moment Meriwether joined in. He put his hand on the mirror, palm flat. "A promise made is a promise kept. Let's do it."

MERIWETHER STRODE INTO THE MASSIVE AREA HE'D LEFT ORMEON in with a spring in his step and two hundred Feybrind at his back. Yasmine Glittercone rode his shoulder, his hair in her fist, pointing the way like he was a horse she rode to battle.

Ormeon was curled up like a giant cat, tail touched to nose. She opened one lazy ember eye at their approach, lifted her head, stretched, and stood. The clutch of Feybrind behind Meriwether stopped a respectful distance back, leaving him to face a giant, red-scaled dragon. *This takes the right gravitas. I need to impress on the People I found that Ormeon's not to be feared. I need them to understand who's in charge.* He ran a hand through his hair. "Sup?"

The dragon leaned forward, bringing her nose close to his face. She sniffed. *//WHAT HAPPENED TO YOUR HEAD?//*

Meriwether sighed. "I had this whole thing planned out where I'd be all casual in the face of a massive people-eating monster, and my new friends would be awe-struck."

//HOW'S THAT WORKING OUT FOR YOU?//

"Not great." Meriwether turned to the Feybrind. The People watched the exchange, entranced, jewel-colored eyes wide. They all wore the same kind of clothing Meriwether did, because they'd stopped to outfit them on the way. As near as the holomancer could tell not a one of them was older than an hour old, but they walked the world like pros born to it. "She's cool. For a dragon, I mean."

Ormeon chuffed a blast of air that almost knocked Meriwether off his feet. //GENEVE WILL HATE IT.//

"Hate what?" Meriwether tried to find the scattered pieces of his composure on the floor, but they were gone for good.

//YOUR HAIR. IT LOOKS LIKE THE KIND OF THING A BUNCH OF ANCIENT DEAD PEOPLE WOULD COME UP WITH.// She craned her neck, peering at him from different angles. //WHO'S IDEA WAS IT TO SHAVE THE SIDES?//

"Magic mirror's, of course." Meriwether brushed off his long coat. "Look, dragon. It's been a long damn day. We need to ... wait. Did you say Geneve would hate it?"

//ABSOLUTELY.//

"Why?" Meriwether tugged his coat straighter. "I look dashing, don't I?"

//WHAT ABOUT HER ATTRACTION TO YOU MAKES YOU THINK SHE LIKES DASHING MEN?//

Meriwether sucked air through his teeth, wincing. Coming Storm, who was almost by his side, winced more, the Feybrind covering her face with her hand. {That's the kind of blow a man never recovers from.}

Time to move off this conversational track and find a new route. He squared off against the dragon. "I've found friends. With Yasmine's help—"

//YOU REMADE THE FAIRY?// Ormeon leaned closer. Yasmine stuck her chin out. //HELLO, BUILDER.//

"Stop being mean to Meriwether. It's not his fault he's big, dumb, and ugly." The fairy raised her fist at Ormeon. "I'm warning you!"

"Stop helping," Meriwether hissed, sotto voce. "I've got this."

The dragon ignored them, peering at the People behind the sorcerer. //HELLO, CATS.//

The Feybrind eyed each other, hands whispering words too fast to follow. Meriwether caught more than a few swish, swishing tails. He faced Coming Storm. "It's time to kill some demons."

The dragon shook her head. The runes there glimmered a suggestive amber. *//IT'S TIME TO GET TO GENEVE. SHE CONTACTED ME.//*

"Is she okay?" Meriwether took an involuntary step forward. "Is she … tell me she's not dead."

//I JUST SAID SHE CONTACTED ME. IT WOULD BE HARD FOR HER TO DO THAT IF SHE WERE DEAD.// The dragon mused for a moment. *//NOT IMPOSSIBLE, I'LL ALLOW. IT DOESN'T MATTER. SHE'S IN A SHITTY CITY CALLED IMSHIR. IT APPEARS TO BE A STAIN ON THE WORLD LIKE MOST HUMAN HOVELS, BUT SHE LIKES IT FOR SOME REASON I CAN'T FATHOM. SHE WOULD LIKE TO COME HERE TO RESCUE YOU.//*

"I don't need rescuing," blurted Meriwether.

//I KNOW. I TOLD HER THAT, SO SHE'S WAITING FOR US.// The dragon looked at the Feybrind again. *//I DIDN'T EXPECT TO FERRY TWO HUNDRED AND FIFTY-SIX FEYBRIND, THOUGH. THIS WILL CRIMP OUR ETA A LITTLE.//*

"Hol' up a minute." Meriwether frowned. "I've a theory on the whole demon thing. You said we're made of starlight, right?"

//I DIDN'T … OKAY, FINE. I SAID SOMETHING LIKE THAT.//

"I think they're attracted to it. They want us. They want what makes us, *us*. But I can't work out why they're not all over this place. There are a hundred guys in phylacteries below. Feybrind are everywhere. Shake this place upside down and a hundred more would fall out. Plenty of waiting stardust."

Ormeon sighed, the sound impossibly sad. *//OH, LITTLE HUMAN. NO, THAT'S NOT IT AT ALL.//*

"I'm waiting for your wisdom of the ancients, Redeemer. I need to know why they're here. I need to know how we can beat them. What does your manifest say?"

Ormeon chewed that over for a while. *//THE DEMONS AREN'T HERE BECAUSE THERE ARE NO LIVING PEOPLE. NOT UNTIL RECENTLY, ANYWAY. THEY DON'T WANT DEAD MEN. THE CATS WERE UNALIVE UNTIL THE BUILDER WOKE THEM. THEY DON'T WANT THE CRUDE STUFF YOUR BODIES ARE MADE OF. THEY WANT THE BRILLIANT COLORS YOU*

RELEASE WHEN YOU DIE. THEY WANT ALL YOUR STARLIGHT.//

Coming Storm put her hand on Meriwether's arm. *{They want our souls?}*

The dragon looked away for a moment. *//I DON'T THINK THEY KNOW WHAT SOULS ARE. NOT REALLY. THEY LIKE THE JUICE THAT COMES OUT WHEN THEY BREAK THE FRUIT APART.//*

"Okay." Meriwether frowned. "So, is fighting them the best plan? Like, we'll die, and … I guess they'll get what they want."

Coming Storm shook her head. *{We'll die anyway. This way our deaths have meaning. There's no way to starve them out.}*

Meriwether rubbed his chin. "I wish I knew where they came from."

//THEY CAME WHEN WE BROKE THE WORLD. OUR SIDE— DRAGONS AND CATS AND SOME PEOPLE—ROSE AGAINST VEHEMENT SYSTEMS. WE HAD MACHINES IN THE HEAVENS AND SOULS ON THE ROCK BENEATH US. DRAGONRIDERS FLEW, THEIR DRAGONS BREATHED FIRE, AND TOOTH AND FIST AND CLAW MET STEEL AND LIGHT AND SCALE. HATE FESTERED ON BOTH SIDES. VEHEMENT SYSTEMS WERE LOSING, SO THEY … DID WHAT THEY DO BEST.//

Meriwether remembered the lone red-haired Tresward Knight in the middle of a crater larger than imagining allowed. "They used a weapon to kill thousands, didn't they?"

The dragon shook her head. *//RIGHT IDEA, WRONG SCALE. MILLIONS, HOLOMANCER. THEY USED THE WEAPONS BOTH SIDES AGREED WOULD NEVER BE USED. AND AS ALL THAT STARLIGHT LEFT, ALL THE WONDERFUL STUFF THAT MAKES YOU WHO YOU ARE, IT BROKE THE WORLD. THE BOUNDARY BETWEEN OUR WORLD AND THEIRS SHIFTED. A FEW CAME THROUGH, THEN A HORDE. TRESWARD FOUGHT, AND WON. THE DEMONS WERE PUSHED BACK.//*

Coming Storm looked lost. *{Why are they here then, if the Knights defeated them?}*

Meriwether gave a sickly laugh. "Because we're killing each other again. Enough of us are dying that we're blurring the line. Isn't that right, dragon? Vhemin against Feybrind." He remembered the burning village of the People. "Feybrind go first. Such gentle hearts. The Vhemin fight *us*," he slapped his chest, "but we don't retreat. Then just one demon comes over and gets into the head of a black-hearted man. More die. A battle with ancient machines over a city old as sin. Enough Vhemin and humans died to ... what, crack the rift open again?"

//ALMOST.// Ormeon glowered. *//THERE ARE ONLY A FEW HERE. IF THERE WERE MORE, WE'D ALL BE DEAD. IF THEY RAM US TOGETHER UNTIL BLOOD GUSHES OUT ... IF ENOUGH OF US DIE, THEY WILL OPEN THE RIFT AND WE'LL BE UP TO OUR EARS IN ASSHOLES. WE MUST STOP THEM. THERE AREN'T ENOUGH TRESWARD LEFT TO DO WHAT THEY DID LAST TIME.//*

"Those motherfuckers," Meriwether breathed. "They've put the Tresward against sorcerers, weeding out the powerful. Winnowing us down, so we stand no chance."

{Your kind always were kind of stupid,} Coming Storm allowed. *{Did they do anything you wouldn't have got to eventually?}*

Meriwether looked at his feet. "Not all of us are like that."

She touched his chin, bringing his gaze back to hers. She cupped her hands for a moment as if trying to hold her words together. *{It's not about all of you. It's about enough so the world changes, for good or bad.}*

Meriwether clapped his hands together. "Okay then. We've got me. We've got Geneve. Ormeon's probably in. Let's go change it for the better." He swung to face the dragon. "What's Red up to? What's she need?"

The dragon slitted her eyes. *//SHE SAID SOMETHING ABOUT HER SWORD.//*

{The fate of the world and we're wondering about a blade?} Coming Storm's shoulders heaved in a sigh. *{This is how you get the bad outcome. I can feel it.}*

Meriwether rubbed his chin. "It's not just any sword. It's a skymetal blade made of magic and power. It carries the hopes of a legion of dead Tresward. The Three tossed it at the feet of a Smith clever enough to do something with it. That blade will remake the world. Requiem is the final song of our age." He faced the dragon. "What did she say about the sword?"

//SHE LOST IT.//

The sorcerer choked. "She what now?"

//APPARENTLY IT'S HELD BY A DEMON LORD WORSE THAN THE LAST ONE. FOR SOME DAMN REASON SHE THINKS YOU CAN HELP.//

He grinned. "Well, of course."

The dragon rolled her eyes. //GET ON, HOLOMANCER. WE SHOULD MAKE IT IN AN HOUR OR SO.//

"Hold up. What about my army?" The idea of getting to Geneve inside an hour pulled at his heart, but the Feybrind needed him. They'd be alone in this world, and most of them were less than an hour old.

The dragon grinned, orange balefire behind her teeth. //YOUR ARMY?//

{Your army?} Coming Storm padded to stand between the dragon and Meriwether. {You can barely walk up a hundred flights of stairs without fainting. I think someone else should lead the army. Which, by the way, are made of my people.}

"A fair point." Meriwether tapped his foot. "Tell you what. We'll send Ormeon ahead. Geneve could probably use a dragon."

//I'M NOT A TOOL LIKE A WAGON OR CANNON.//

Meriwether ignored her. "We'll go on foot. That way we can talk about which one of you should be in charge after you work out how to tie shoelaces."

"What about me?" Yasmine tugged his hair.

Meriwether pondered that. "Well, what do you want to do?"

"It's not about what I want."

"Sure it is—"

"Don't get me wrong," the fairy stormed on, leaning into his ear for emphasis, which was *quite* loud. "I like the sky. It's awesome! Birds aren't too bad either. But I'm a Builder. I Build things."

"What kind of things?" Meriwether looked at Ormeon. "Like her?"

//AGAIN, I'M NOT A TOOL LIKE A—//

"Yes," the fairy said. "But we need a Skyforge."

"How long does it take to make one of those?"

The fairy gave him a pitying stare. "A long, long time."

Meriwether sighed. "I was hoping we could get some reinforcements."

//I'M A PERSON! I'M NOT A THING—//

"I can make other stuff," Yasmine said. "Like, say, skymetal. All I need is a Build Engine rated to at least thirty-five hundred C, and—"

"A what?" Meriwether felt the conversation sinking, like the sea was replacing the land.

"A. Build. Engine." The fairy flicked her wings, a shower of rainbow motes trickling to Meriwether's shoulder. "Did IQs drop while I was a bird?" She frowned. "I mean, eight hundred years is a long time. There's inbreeding, radiation, starvation, ritual sacrifice, not to mention *selective* breeding, and Three knows what else you lot—"

//HE IS SOMEWHAT SMART,// Ormeon allowed. *//FOR ONE OF HIS KIND. BUILDER, THERE ARE NO MORE ENGINES.//*

"Oh." Yasmine's frown deepened, heading for bedrock, then she brightened. "Well, I can make one of those too. The Fey Branded can—"

"Feybrind," Meriwether corrected, but gently. "Branded are slaves. Feybrind are the People. They are free."

"Cool, cool," the fairy said. "We can talk while we walk."

"*We* walk?"

She waved her hand. "Figure of speech. Onward, steed! We've Engines to make and skymetal to forge. Oh, it will be so much fun!"

MERIWETHER WASN'T SURE WHY THE NIGHT SKY SURPRISED HIM when they emerged from the mountain. The air smelled slightly overcooked, and the sky hazed at the horizon. *Might be a dust storm coming. Or it's passed already. I don't know how many days we were below ground.*

The Feybrind scampered under the stars. Eyes of emerald, gold, agate, and sapphire gazed at stars. The stars watched right back, perhaps twinkling a little brighter. "They look so happy."

Ormeon rumbled her agreement. *//THEY'VE NEVER SEEN THE SKY.//*

"Wait until they get a load of the sun." Meriwether looked to the glimmering point of Imshir. The city waited for them. *Geneve* waited for them. "Best be off, beastie."

The dragon smiled toothily. *//BE WELL, HOLOMANCER. THE WORLD CAN'T DO WITHOUT YOU.//* She crouched, then launched herself off the cliffside. Massive wings snapped, blasting dust and small rocks. Meriwether squinted, but couldn't help his grin. *She's just so damn badass.* Feybrind waved as she flew, wings spread, a glimmer of ruby about her face as the runes there glowed.

"You too," he whispered.

"What was that?" Yasmine yanked his hair.

"Nothing, fairy. It's time to—"

Bright blue-white light lanced from the ground, hammering at Ormeon. The dragon wheeled, tucked her wings, then dove for ground. Light tracked her, brilliant spears thrown from the desert floor. Meriwether couldn't see from what. *Is it Vhemin?*

"Ah," Yasmine said. A lance of light caught Ormeon, and the dragon's bellow came across the distance. She plummeted to earth, landing beyond the mountain's base. "That'll be the defenses."

Meriwether ignored her, breaking into a sprint. He passed a Feybrind with dark brown fur. *You're doing this wrong.* He threw his hand out, imagining a pale disc, and one materialized in front of him. He spoke a Word, giving the disc purpose, then stepped on it. It felt wobbly, less real than he'd hoped, but it served to skate down the mountainside well enough.

Yasmine clutched his ear. "You can't fly! They'll see it!"

As if prompted, blue-white fire kissed the bedrock to Meriwether's right. Rock exploded in a plume of molten fragments. He yelled, tossed from his disc. It stuttered out like a snuffed candle as he rolled down the mountain. Rock bit his shoulder. Branches lashed his face. He scrabbled, trying to find purchase as he approached a cliff edge, but he wasn't going to make it.

Yasmine flitted ahead, gossamer wings trailing motes of fairy dust. She held her palms out to him in a universal gesture to *stop!* If only it were so easy. He slid right under the fairy, hit his face, shoulder, then his face again. Meriwether scrabbled at a root. It came away in his hand. The edge was impossibly close. No *way* was he going to miss it. Meriwether thought about another disc, but there wasn't time, and then...

He was over the edge. Hanging.

Meriwether glanced back. Coming Storm crouched above him at the cliff's edge, hand curled in the collar of his jacket, other braced on the ledge. His legs dangled, and below them there was nothing but air all the way down.

The Feybrind hauled him up, set him on his feet, and brushed him down. *{You don't scream pretty.}*

"There's a pretty way to scream?" Meriwether felt like someone hit him in the head. Sounds were muted as if by distance. The bank above exploded in a shower of fiery rock. His arm was on fire. He patted at it absently, slapping the flames to quiescence. "What happened to Ormeon?"

"Is it safe to land on you? You're not going to fall off a totally obvious mountainside into an endless abyss of death?" Yasmine flitted back to his shoulder. "Endless until you hit the bottom, that is. Anyway! Ormeon was gunned down. The defenses are back online. I guess they woke up at the same time as the Fey Bran... Feybrind."

"Defenses?" Meriwether glanced at the burning mountain above him. "Who's defending what?"

"My guess is Vehement Systems left something here to combat us." Yasmine huffed. "We have to walk."

"My friend's down there." Meriwether ruffled his hair. "She's hurting, and we need to help her."

Yasmine gave him a little side-eye. "The dragon, you mean? They don't have friends."

"Yeah? This one does." Meriwether stuffed his hands into overcoat pockets. "Come on. The walk down's not getting shorter."

Coming Storm touched his arm, then pointed into the dark below.

{Vhemin. They're converging on Ormeon. And there... See? Humans. And Vhemin. And I think I see a Feybrind, but it's a long way off.}

Meriwether stared hard into the dark, but he got nothing back from frail human eyes. "Are you making this up?"

She half-smiled. *{Trust me. People are making for your dragon.}*

"Best we get started then." Meriwether scowled. "The Vhemin are in for a rough time. She's probably hungry about now."

Chapter Twenty-One

Geneve scowled. The expression wasn't just face deep; it went right to her toes. *Meri is in the depths of yet* another *ancient temple. And he's doing it without* me. She clattered through Imshir's night city streets, the almost complete lack of people giving her passing concern.

Omrar tried to keep up. "Tresward, we can't fight the demon."

"Demon's got my sword." Geneve put a little more hurry into her steps. "I'm going to get it back."

Mazin huffed to wheeze at her shoulder. "They say youth is wasted on the young, but I see no evidence of that." She didn't dim her scowl, so he put a hand on her armored arm. "Knight, please. Not all of us are made for this."

She glared at his hand, and he yanked it back like scalded. Still, it had the effect of drawing her up short. "Here's how it is. The love of my life is in a death cave made by ancient assholes. My sword is in the hands of a demon lord. My dragon is in the same mountain, which is over *there*," she stabbed her arm in the general direction of Heaven's Gate, "and hasn't seen Meri for a long time. You," she prodded Mazin's chest with a gauntleted finger, "are a weirdo who used to be a merchant but fell from the sky. He," she jerked a thumb at Omrar, "is a shopkeeper whose neighbor got taken by the Arm, or Will, or whatever name some dark sect of clowns goes under, and *you* just happened to see her before you died. But here you are." She crossed her arms.

Mazin's mouth moved silently as if counting. "Yes, that is right."

"It's bullshit!" she hollered. "I don't care about people falling from the sky. I don't know Lily. I'm sure she's very nice, but I can't do anything about that. What I *can* do is get my damn sword. So, I'm going to do that. Once I have my skymetal blade, I'm going to stare at the sky over there," she jerked an angry arm at Heaven's Gate again, "until a dragon appears on the horizon with Meri on her back. *If* the dragon doesn't come within a day, I will *walk* to Heaven's Gate, sword in hand, and kill whoever keeps them from me."

"As a to-do list, it's got merits." Mazin wiped sweat from his forehead. "What about Lily?"

Geneve felt like her scowl might permanently pucker her face. "What *about* Lily?"

"She's my sister," Mazin said. "We need her."

"*Are you fucking crazy?*" Geneve screamed. A cat *rowled* then screeched in the night. "You didn't even know her before you died."

Mazin nodded, eyes downcast. "I admit, it's perplexing." He lifted his chin. "But it is what it is."

"She's a very nice person," Omrar said. "She's the best person in the world."

Peace, Knight. Two breaths, then two more. It was as if Iz stood at her shoulder, mouth to her ear. She could've been ten again in the Tresward keep she trained in, sweat running down her back, practice sword in hand, bruise forming on her chin from where she'd fumbled the pattern and wore a hit for her inattention. Geneve closed her eyes, remembering the moment. How she'd been ready to knock a friend's skull open for getting one over on her. Her lips twisted in a wry smile. *I might have* tried. *Then I wasn't the equal of any. I was small and confused.* She opened her eyes, looking to the stars for a moment. She took her two breaths, then two more. "It changes nothing." She held up her arm to forestall their comments, Smithsteel catching the glimmering wheel of the heavens for a moment. "I can't help Lily without my sword. All roads lead to Requiem."

"Ah." Mazin gazed toward Heaven's Gate. "And what of that road?" He pointed with his chin.

Geneve swiveled, making out the dark curve of Ormeon's wings on the wind. Her heart skipped a beat, rising with joy, then crumbling as actinic spears of fury reached for the dragon. "*NO!*"

Then she ran. Past Mazin's clutching hand, beyond Omrar's pleading eyes, and into streets unfamiliar and strange. Her boots clattered against the cobbles, the pale stone walls passing the sound between them in her wake. *A horse. I must have a horse.* She found a place that looked like a taverna, set low below the streets. A wooden structure behind it might hold horses. She slammed through a closed door, wood showering as she passed. Inside, darkness. Geneve hissed, blinking as if that would help her eyes catch up or bring back Cophine's pale gaze. She smelled horsey scents and caught a stamp from a surprised beast that was perturbed by the door being knocked aside.

Geneve fumbled along the wall, finding tack and bridle hung there. Her vision adjusted, and she snared a saddle from a stall wall. She clanked through the stable, finding the stall of the unsettled horse.

He was a magnificent stallion, easily the equal of Iz's old steed Chesterfield. The horse *whuffed* at her, then tossed his head. "What's your name?"

Light flared behind her. A man with a lantern in one hand, pitchfork in the other, stood at the stable's door. "His name is Mercurio. He's not for sale."

Geneve took the three steps to the man, disarmed him like taking a rattle from a baby, then put the pitchfork aside. She pushed him against the barn wall, leaned close, and whispered, "I need your horse. I *need* him."

The man gave her a terrified stare. He seemed to take stock of his position, what with a half-crazed armored woman on the wrong side of his weapon. He blurted, "Fifty silver regals."

A snort from the doorway. Geneve glanced to see Mazin there, sweat staining his attire, but he stood with the air of a man about to do the Three's work. "Ten."

"Ten? The horse is worth twice that."

"And so easily do we arrive at twenty." Mazin counted coins from a purse, then held them out. "Here."

Geneve eased her grip. "You didn't have to—"

"Tresward, our world is *on fire*. You need your sword and your dragon. For twenty silver regals I'm buying our salvation. Now *ride*, damn you!"

GENEVE RODE. SHE DIDN'T WANT TO GIVE THE HORSE A NEW NAME, but Mercurio was ... wrong. Every movement he made reminded her of dear Tristan. The old horsey smells tickled her mind.

I don't want to remember Tristan because his death was so bad.

The horse didn't care, and canter by canter his name came to her like a whispered wind that pulled her hair back in red streamers as they ran. *Nightrunner.*

They'd killed Tristan, and they'd used a dragon to do it. Now the dragon was *hers*, her companion, a gift from an ancient time, now used for the benefit of the world. They *dared* to try taking Ormeon from her? Geneve's fingers tightened in the bridle, and she leaned forward over Nightrunner's surging neck. "Run. Run, for the world depends on it. Run like it's what you want to do. It's what you were born for. Don't let them steal your dreams from you."

The horse didn't respond. At their speed he might not have heard her, the thunder of hooves ceaseless ... and yet. She felt him lean forward, urging into it like lions appeared behind them. His canter turned to a gallop, a hammer of shoes on dirt, dust rising like a long cloak behind them. She felt the surge of his blood, her heart answering, and offered the night a fierce grin, all teeth.

Imshir's lights faded behind. Ahead, stars above dark lands. Riding at night on uneven ground was risky, but there was no time for caution. She might fall. Die, even. *But there is no future I accept where Ormeon's dead and I lived for the want of five minutes.*

They rode hard. Distance faded to memory. Nightrunner's mad gallop eased back to a sustainable canter. Geneve rose in the stirrups as a hump rose from the path ahead. Her heart wanted it to be Ormeon, but also not, because it didn't move. She blinked wind and tears from her eyes and saw it for what it was: a small hill.

It'd been thrown into relief by a faint ruddy glow. Behind that hill was firelight. She urged Nightrunning up the slope, then reined him in. The hill ended at a sheer drop off. Geneve slipped from the horse's back, hand trailing absently along his lathered flank as she duck-walked to the edge. She took in the scene, spread out like a diorama a hundred meters below. *How can fate be so cruel?*

Ormeon sprawled on her side. Her red scales were scorched black by one wing. Her mouth was open, the great bellows of her flank still moving, but she seemed uncaring of what was going on. A massive furrow drew a line to where she lay. The dragon had crashed, furrowing up dirt and rock. She'd been staked to the ground, a horde of Vhemin arrayed before her. There were perhaps fifty by the dragon, and another two hundred scattered into the darkness beyond. The monsters had a massive fire tossing cinders at stars. They'd laid great metal poles in the flames. *Do they mean to pierce Ormeon's hide with those?*

She glanced further north. Her heart shuddered, clenched like a stone in her chest. Facing the Vhemin was a man she'd recognize anywhere. His chin lifted in defiance. *He still hasn't shaved, and that prickles.* Hair streaming in the cold desert wind stood Meriwether du Reeves. A tiny mote danced at his elbow. *A fairy! One of the folk's found him.* Behind Meri, Feybrind by the hundred. The People were only crudely armed, but eyes like jewels were hard and cold as they faced their eternal enemy.

Meri's at the front. He's not a fighter. Why is he there? Why doesn't he run?

She felt that hand on her shoulder, Iz's words by her ear. *Ignore the man. See the scene. Your heart will get you killed. Your head will save everyone. Judge, don't feel. Be, don't imagine.*

Geneve closed her eyes, head bowed. *Yes, father.* When she looked again, the little details came to her.

One Feybrind stood closer to Meri than the rest. The cat had rose-colored eyes like star-struck agate. Her tail lashed. *No, not closer. Slightly in front of.* The Feybrind was protecting her man. Geneve would thank her later, once she'd slapped Meri silly for being here in the first place.

Now, Meri: he stood a little taller than she remembered. He crossed his arms, strange clothes about him, a jacket billowing like a cape behind him. Geneve almost laughed. *He's cut his hair. I like it.* He was taller because he stood on a disc. She imagined it glowed, but the bonfire made it hard to see for sure.

The Feybrind, then. They wore simple clothes, similar in style to what Meri had. Shifts and pants, plain whites, blacks, and grays. Such a lack of color was so unlike the People. *Style be damned, the People wouldn't wear such things. They are makers of wonders, not crude sacks.* Prisoners, then? Had Meri freed them? Sought aid? Bought it, perhaps? And with what?

Don't forget the enemy. These Vhemin were like their monstrous kind everywhere. They held weapons ready, wore crude armor, and seemed to have little discipline. They roared and beckoned the Feybrind, but there was something uneasy in the way they moved. Like they were uncertain of the foe they faced but didn't look away from the fight. No blue-runed armor. No strange weapons. Just leather under steel weave to turn a blade, rusty sabers or spears held at the ready. They had numbers, but only just.

Why haven't the Feybrind attacked? Geneve looked again, and saw the same uneasy stances in the People. They weren't ... certain. *I can't count on them for aid. They seem unaware of danger, poorly equipped for this battle. Untrained, perhaps.*

Nightrunner stamped beside her. The horse nosed her, and Geneve gave him an absent pat on the face. Soft breath tickled her cheek as the horse nudged her gaze to the west. She squinted into the dark, trying to make out anything from night-blind eyes. *There!* The delicate scatter of light on clouds. Someone was perhaps a klick away, coming closer. Friend or foe, impossible to tell, but best bet on foe. Luck hadn't been with her since she fell from the sky.

Geneve almost imagined Iz's laugh. *Luck's been with you always. The Three baked it into your soul. No one else but the lucky survive a fall from the sky.*

"No one else but gods," she corrected him, then bit her lip. She was correcting a memory. Not that it mattered, because the memory wasn't wrong. She shook her head, trying to get Israel from her mind.

Another taken from her, and *still* they weren't done. "There's nothing else for it. I'm going to have to save Meri from himself again."

The patterns didn't feel clear here. It was a long way down, and she didn't have her sword. She had *a* sword, borrowed from not-Mazin's house, but the weight wasn't the balance she needed. *Stop complaining. I've trained with mattock, club, and hoe. The Tresward put anything in my hands they could find. A blade made by strange hands is still a blade.*

Something made Meri look up to her crouched location. She was sure he couldn't actually *see* her. It was too dark. Too much firelight stood between them. And yet he lifted his chin, grinned, and raised his hands. *By the Three. He's going to do something stupid.*

Geneve stood, stroked Nightrunner's nose, then gave the horse a soft kiss on the muzzle. "Don't follow me. Find a different way down." She faced the cliff, backed up ten paces, then sprinted for it. At the very edge she jumped, arms windmilling as she ran over the edge into a hundred-meter drop.

Chapter Twenty-Two

This whole land is covered in assholes. Vertiline ran, borrowed armor heavy, burnished sun glinting in the night. They'd landed with a fraction of their force. A hundred sailors turned warriors. Fifty Feybrind, and just ten Vhemin. No horses made it.

And no Tresward. Leastways, not any but me. All fell. Which is why I'm going to kill that fucking enchanter.

The fucking enchanter made shore sooner than Picotee's fleet. They'd scuttled their boats in a blaze of magefire then headed for the hills. When Vertiline leaped from her ship to clatter on the sand, she found nothing but charcoal spars and smoke wind. There were a handful of dead Vhemin by a broken banner, but not enough to show the enchanter's forces encountered any serious resistance.

The dead Vhemin had the look of local boys. Now *there* was an uncomfortable thought, and the principal reason why Vertiline ran, salt in her pale hair, dried sand on her skin. Her scattergun's powder was wet. All she had was her glass blade and devil hand. *I'll make do.*

Sight of Day loped by her right side, the Feybrind making it look trivial. Armitage lumbered to her left, looking like he could do this all day. The brute leered, then confirmed, "I can do this all day. You look tired. Hell, I almost died and here I am."

Vertiline's breath wheezed like a broken bellows. "You still look three days dead, but I look like a stormmaiden of justice."

"You also sound like shit." He hawked, spat something vile, then turned his leer on the darkness ahead. "We're coming to some hills. Might wanna shuck that armor before we—"

"You might want to secure your mouth, monster." But she grinned all the same. "I'll race you to the top."

"You could barely race the cat." Armitage's snake eyes blinked yellow, somehow warm. "Right, cat?"

Sight of Day loped in front, then started running backward, also making that look easy. *{I'll start a fire. Get the kettle on, so you've something to drink when you make the top.}* His hands stilled as he cast a glance over his shoulder. *{Did I say when? I meant if. You're going to hurt yourselves.}* Then he turned, sprinting for the hilltop, tail flat behind him.

Vertiline put a little more curry in her run, turning it just south of a sprint. Armitage tried to keep up, but he raced a Tresward, armor or no.

Despite our reputation, damn that cat is fast.

She reached the hilltop. Sight of Day waited for her, tail lashing, bow held loose and ready. The Feybrind pointed. *{The enchanter, and … friends.}*

The hill sloped on a gentle, sandy slide to a flat plain of desert patched with scrub. A travesty of footprints marred the sand, leading toward a huddle of humans and Vhemin. Clouds gathered overhead, smoke black and quiet. Vertiline marked a familiar black-cloaked figure at the head of their ragged band. *I see you, asshole. And I note you didn't make it with a large force either.* She counted perhaps a hundred and fifty souls with the enchanter, most of them Vhemin in blue-runed armor. The few humans had the slender, thin-armed look of people who made their living casting spells rather than slinging steel. A blessing: there were no Artifices walking by their side. Either they didn't bring their ancient machines or they were at the bottom of the sea.

Armitage grumbled to a halt beside her. "What's all that shit over there?" He pointed in the enchanter's direction.

"The villain himself."

"No, not him. *That* stuff." Armitage jabbed his arm more forcefully, as if it could make her eyes work better.

Sight of Day squinted. *{It could be a large fire. Hard to tell.}*

"It's a huge fucking fire," Armitage said. "It's a fire the size of a castle. I don't know where you'd get the wood for something like that, or what you'd cook on it, but I'm hungry. Let's go look."

Vertiline slicked sweat from her forehead with her metal hand. "You're sure it's a big fire? I see nothing."

"That's because you're puny," Armitage said. "All the parts of you, even the eyeballs. Tasty, but tiny." He paused for a moment in silent, happy memory. "Look, that's not important right now. The cat's eyes see like it's daylight, but it's just … *light*. We," he slapped his chest, "see heat. The juicy inner workings of flesh. And I can tell you that," he pointed again, "isn't flesh. It's a huge fire."

"How far away?"

"Couple klicks." Armitage rubbed his chin. "Easy run."

"With a hundred and fifty mages and assorted mercenaries," Vertiline said. "Don't forget those."

"Wasn't forgetting. Was looking forward to." He sighed, rubbing his arms. "Damn this night air."

She touched the slate stone on his back. "Rocks cooling down?"

Armitage shook her off. "It's fine. There's a fire, remember?"

{We should go around them. Make for the fire, get there first.}

"We might get stuck between two forces." Vertiline shook her head. "I miss Iz, but not enough to see him again today. We could wait." She *hmmm'd*. "Our forces will be here in minutes."

{And yet no one told the enemy to wait for them.} Sight of Day half-smiled. *{Distance grows. Time runs on ragged feet. Fate hurries. All of that.}*

"Fuck it." Vertiline stood, drew her sword, and leveled it at the enchanter at the head of the enemy group. "I'm going to get me a piece of that."

Sight of Day eyed the distance, hefted his bow, nocked an arrow, and loosed. The shaft rose, leveled, then fell. It skewered the enchanter through the calf between one step and the next. The enemy host scattered, scrambled, screamed, bellowed, roared, and generally got under each other's feet. *{I'm tired of running. Now they'll come to us about the same time as our people get here.}*

Armitage blinked. "Did you just steal her kill?"

Sight of Day frowned. *{He yet lives. I made sure.}*

An ebony-skinned woman raised hands to the skies, which crackled with red forks of power. Vertiline gaped. "Did you forget about their sorcerers?"

Sight of Day tapped his chin with his bow. *{Perhaps you should get in there. You can't expect me to do* all *the work.}*

So, Vertiline ran. *Again.* She'd sprinted down the hill, churning sand in her wake, sword held low and ready. Energy blasted the earth beside her, and when it threatened to find her, she caught it on her metal hand. The ancient's gift to her gathered the energy, returning it to the caster tenfold more powerful. She screamed her defiance, for all the good it did. The sound was lost against the crackling thunder of magefury coming down on her.

I'm going to die because a cat poked a hornet's nest.

Which is why the grin on her face made no sense. *I'm going to die. Why am I happy?* Vhemin charged her, pillars of flames erupting from the hands of an enchanter behind their line. Her sword felt heavy, *hungry* for blood. A Vhemin made to shield-barge Vertiline. She saw the ugly planks, the grain of the wood, and where blood had soaked in from another battle. Vertiline jumped, body corkscrewing as she spun over the top. She saw disbelieving wide eyes as she sailed over the monster, sword arcing in fury, Light glimmering down the blade.

She cut through the creature's head and shield, burnt skull and meat splashing to the sand. The Three's force guided her arm, her *will*, and when she hit the ground Vertiline was already spinning to take her next opponent. She barely registered *male, human, bad teeth, worse hair* and then she was past him, steaming blood seeping into thirsty sand in her wake. A Vhemin screamed her rage at Vertiline, then stopped mid-cry as her head left her shoulders. Blood staggered to the sky in great heart-pumped gouts before the monster fell.

Spin. Cut. Block. She took two more on her blade without looking, the patterns guiding her steps. Vertiline caught an attack from behind without thinking about it, her will guiding arm, then blade, a perfect matrimony delivering heaven's fury.

And then she was through. Before her, six Vhemin, behind them, the enchanter who'd dropped lightning on her boat like an anvil. *He killed my brothers.* A Vhemin lunged for her, all jagged shark teeth and fury. She took his mace on her blade, the steel head crying like birdsong as the metal gave. Vertiline swept past the monster, steps moving into a pirouette that would make a dancer weep. Her blade arced at neck height and left the monster in two pieces.

The second gave a massive overhand swing, which she solved by not being there. She felt her heart hammering its urgency, driving her faster, *faster*, because there was a man who took the lives of two Knights and he was just over *there*, by the Three. Vertiline lunged, point of her sword tearing through the heart of a Vhemin with a single braid down her otherwise smooth head. Vertiline's sword glimmered with Light, the monster turning incandescent, eyes blazing, head burning, skin on *fire* as the Three held her arm swift and sure, guiding her toward the sinner.

The enchanter, clearly no moron, raised his arms. Vertiline wasn't in the mood to stand and take it, dropping her stance and sidling behind the third now surprised Vhemin. She slipped her arm through his, then turned the monster to face the enchanter as lightning blazed. The Vhemin shield crisped, and Vertiline screamed her defiance. She screwed her eyes shut at the cascade of power that tore the Vhemin's soul from his body, the skin from his bones, and the fury from his heart.

Vertiline stood, Smithsteel armor smoking, and flicked blood from her blade. She felt a fierce joy, because the enchanter was there, dammit, right *there* and there were only three Vhemin left. She clenched her metal hand, slightly surprised to see it glimmering with blue-white rimlight. "The gods will have their justice for what you've done!"

The enchanter pursed his lips, frowned, then ran.

She raced after him, rolling over a Vhemin whose bare midriff encouraged swordplay. Vertiline was happy to oblige, leaving screams and entrails in her wake. The last two tried to take her at the same time. One went low, the other high, and it wasn't a crazy idea, but Vertiline had a pattern for this. She'd trained in the halls of the Three, and she *knew* the steps of this dance. She wasn't born to it, not like Iz, but damn it, she'd done the *work*. Vertiline dived above the swing of a greatsword destined for her legs and below the dashing crescent leer of a scimitar hungering for her throat. She clattered to the sand, armor still smoking, then struck twice. The tip of her blade spilled blood on the thirsty sand as Light glimmered along it.

Vertiline snarled, white locks flying, then sprinted after the enchanter. She heard Armitage bellow behind her, but then his voice was lost in the chaos of battle. The enemy brought their sorcerers and witches against men and women of Or'sen. Vhemin roared, and humans screamed. Vertiline ignored it all, eyes locked on the back of the enchanter who'd killed Amaury and Luc. Hours of Three's Bastard kept her body hard, and the long days of drills kept her strikes true. "Don't run!" she yelled. "You're only going to die tired!"

The enchanter glanced back at her, saw a madwoman, and slowed his roll. He faced her. "I've done nothing in defiance of the Three! You call us sinners. You give us no place to stand. And you wonder why we fight?"

Vertiline licked someone else's blood from her lips. She circled the enchanter, eying the electricity coursing over his clawed hands. This close Vertiline saw how scorched and burned his skin was, the terrible price he'd paid to bring her low. "I know you've been sent against *me*. You caused *mine* to die. This isn't between you and the Tresward. It's not even between you and the Three." She felt her snarl tighten another notch. "It's between you and me."

He pointed his chin at her glowing hand, not releasing his caught storm's fury yet. "You're one of *us*, Knight. Join us. Your friends fell, and for that I'm sorry. But would they have asked questions before putting a blade through my heart? We seek to stop a dragon, a Knight, and her cursed lover. They twist us about. Nothing is clear while they live."

Vertiline raised her sword in cross guard. "It's clear to me, sinner. I don't name you that because you call the forces of nature to heel like a whipped dog. I call you sinner because you treat with demons before your own kind. You name my friends, my sister true as if she were my blood, your enemy. You speak, and the rains part. The sky clears. I can see everything like never before. And I bring *justice*."

"I'll see your justice and raise you the *true* meaning of family." The enchanter's shoulders gave a tiny slump, resignation showing for a moment before they straightened. He pushed his palms toward her. Vertiline raised her metal hand, energy coursing from him to her, tangling around her fingers, writhing her arm. He banished night, bringing searing, arcing day. Beyond him, a sorceress raised her arms, bringing more of the storm onto Vertiline. Next to her, a man barely out of his teens joined in, then another, and another still.

The sky rumbled and roared. Lightning slammed Vertiline, pushing her to the dirt. She held her metal hand above her. Heat blasted from it like a furnace, yet still the enchanters hammered ruin on her. She wanted to say *stop, you'll die!* or *hold, Three's Mercy just hold!* but the lightning's rage was too loud, to urgent.

Too final.

I must stop them before this kills everyone. Sight of Day and Armitage are at my back. If my arm casts their magic back, everyone will die. Everyone but me. Vertiline felt bowed under the onslaught of the sky. *I must stand. I must stand.* She pushed against the hammering force of enchanters as if holding up the blows of a Smith's hammer. Centimeter by centimeter she rose as the air about her ignited from the heat. Vertiline could smell her hair burning. Or perhaps that was her skin blistering. She gritted her teeth, giving a last triumphant surge, and stood with fingers curled around the lightning.

Vertiline held the sky tethered by a bridle of actinic power.

She clenched her fist, her arm shaking with the fury in the palm of her hand. Then she brought her arm down, *down* toward the earth, and brought the sky with it.

Lightning blasted from her hammerfist. It fed back to the

enchanter before her, turning his body to ash and motes in the blink of an eye. Behind him, the sorceress raised a shield that flared a brilliant vermillion for a heartbeat before snapping out, her along with it. Her teenage friend, gone as lightning raced across the sand, hungering, wanting its own vengeance for being held captive.

On it ran, the Vhemin forces turning into pyres, witches burning alive, mages lost in the relentless cascade.

Then, silence. Her breath, harsh in her chest as if she'd run a hundred klicks. Blackness, even the stars absent as the world took a breath. From her left, a scream, and behind her, sobbing. The charnel stench of barbecue too long on the grill. Her metal hand glowed a vicious white, the sand under her feet bubbling glass. Smoke curled about her arm, a silken glove to remind her of what happened.

Vertiline raised her eyes. Nothing stood before her. Not a man or woman. No monsters or sinners. No horses, no scrub, just ... gone. She tasted ash. "What have I done?"

"Come on now." Strong arms gathered her up. She smelled Armitage, his sweat and strength, heard his rough name in her mind, but felt the gentle heart that kept a killer bear by his side. "It's okay. Come away."

She let herself be lifted, led away, eyes refusing to see. So much death. So much gone. Sight of Day padded to her. *{Are you okay?}*

"Don't ask me that," she said. "Don't you see what I've done?"

Armitage growled low and deep. "Saved us, it looks like."

{He's not wrong. Well, not about this. He's wrong about other stuff.} The cat gestured; of the enemy, there was no sign.

"How did I do that?" Vertiline demanded. "I called the sky down. How did the sky know to save you?"

{Perhaps the sky knows your heart like we do.} Sight of Day shrugged. *{Perhaps the sky is fickle.}*

Armitage nodded, considering. "Not bad. Maybe you're not the second-best swordswoman after all."

Chapter Twenty-Three

Meriwether had been wrong a few times in his life. There was that time he'd thought Geneve was going to kill him —*okay, not wrong at the time, but people can change*—and the other time he thought his father might love him—*also wrong at the time, because some people can't change.*

There were a few times he *thought* he'd been wrong, but found out he was wrong about being wrong, but spending too much time on those issues made his head hurt. Sometimes he wanted to be wrong, because being in love with a Knight was *stupid*, but he couldn't be wrong about something that felt so right.

Today—or, more accurately, this night—was a time he was both wrong and right at the same time. Coming Storm asked, *What do you mean about Ormeon being hungry, she just got shot down*, and he'd said, *That dragon's going to tear every Vhemin she sees a new asshole.* Then they'd arrived, with his fancy floating disc and handful of newborn Feybrind drifting along behind him, and found Ormeon trussed up like a bird for roasting.

It wasn't a great thing to be wrong about. It sucked, mostly because he really liked Ormeon and it hurt to see her like that. It hurt more because there were like five hundred Vhemin scattered around in various states of anger, outrage, and hunger. *That* was a story that wouldn't end well. He wanted Geneve to save him. She was good at saving him from the world, monsters, and himself, and it was about time for her to show up and do it all over again. But mostly he'd believed she was alive, and he *was* right about that. No one knew it yet, though, so he needed to buy a little time.

Ormeon shifted but didn't wake. The dragon looked three-days-drunk, assuming there was enough liquor in the world to make that happen, but it was too early to see if she suffered hangovers. Meriwether urged his disc closer to the biggest, meanest-looking Vhemin here. He crossed his arms, making sure to not be *too* close, and called out, "You! Asshole!"

Coming Storm tugged his sleeve. {*What are you doing?*}

Her handspeak was echoed by Yasmine as the fairy hissed into his ear, "What are you doing?"

Meriwether blinked in surprise. "I'm picking a fight with the biggest one. Establishing dominance."

{*Why would you do that?*}

The Vhemin sneered. He was about two hundred, maybe two-twenty centimeters tall. Big bastard, too, broad in the shoulder like an ox. Had the kind of seasoned look that came from a lot of outside work like murdering innocents. His skin was lightly scarred in places, but not as many as might be expected, which suggested the monster was good at fighting, healing, or both. "Hello, twig. We were after dessert, and here you are, just in time." The blazing fire shot a round of sparks skyward. "Irons are nice and hot. We've never had dragon kebab, but we know the sweetness of human flesh."

"A moment." Meriwether held up his hand, turning slightly toward Coming Storm. "I'm doing this because if we beat this guy, we'll gain the respect of the tribe. Then we can avoid fighting the rest of them."

Coming Storm's brow furrowed. {*Who told you that would work?*}

"Uh," Meriwether said. "It's obvious, isn't it?"

{*And what's this mythical we? You're picking a fight with five hundred Vhemin. They're good at killing. There are only a handful of us.*} She shrugged. {*We're not involved. Your funeral. Would you prefer burial or cremation?*}

"Wait, what?" Meriwether blinked. "You've got my back, right? Please tell me you're joking."

The cat sighed, turned, and walked back a few paces. The fairy flitted from his shoulder to hover before him. "Can I go with the cat? I don't want to die because you're an imbecile."

Meriwether swallowed, then turned back to the Vhemin. "Where were we?"

"Running away." But Yasmine returned to his shoulder.

"Dessert," the monster prompted.

"Ah." Meriwether smoothed his stubble. "Were you offering some?"

The Vhemin bellowed a laugh, then drew his sword. "You've got pluck, twig. Let's be about it, then." He grabbed a shield from the ground, then held his arms wide. "Come on. I haven't got all night. There's good eating to be done."

"Perhaps we should wager."

The Vhemin raised an eyebrow. "You've got nothing. We've got a dragon."

"I assure you, you most definitely do *not* have a dragon. Your burning poles will do little but annoy Ormeon, and a pissed off dragon is a thing to behold." He held up a placating hand. "But I have two hundred Feybrind."

Coming Storm tugged his sleeve again. {*What are you doing?*}

"Involving you." Meriwether didn't take his eyes off the Vhemin. "We beat you, you come with us. You beat us—"

"And we'll eat you. I get it." The monster nodded. "Let's get on with it."

Meriwether caught a flash of movement from the cliffs behind the monster. A gleam of starlight on metal so brief it could've been a trick of the universe. He suppressed a grin, because an unlucky night might turn out all right after all. "Or you could just ... join us anyway."

The creature frowned. "Why would we do that?"

Geneve landed between the Vhemin commander and Meriwether. She dropped like a meteor, Light trailing like a cape, sand blasting away from the crater she made. The Knight stood, flourished her blade, and faced the monster. "Because I will carve the soul from your body if you don't."

The commander had the look of a man who thought two and two coins made four but found only a single copper baron in his palm. "Who the fuck are you?"

Yasmine took flight again. "Who the fuck is that?"

"Vengeance. Justice." Geneve didn't move, shoulders squared, blade ready.

"Seems like that's two names that mean nothing out here on the sands." The monster grinned shark teeth, then spat.

Meriwether coasted closer on his disc. "I tried all that. The stupid thing won't listen. He's not like Armitage at all."

Geneve didn't take her eyes from the monster. "What held you up? More trouble like this?"

He stepped from his disc, and it dissolved into mist. "I've walked the skies and marched inside a mountain. I found ancient mysteries and the living dead. I freed these Feybrind and promised them an end to slavery. And gave a fairy back her form. Which I'll admit might have been a mistake—"

"Hey!"

"But nothing could keep me from you." He found himself grinning like a fool.

Geneve blinked, then gave him a little sidelong smile. "You say the nicest things."

"I also woke up the things that caused the dragon to crash."

"You say the stupidest things, too." Geneve kept smiling though.

"I want to kiss you, but it doesn't feel like the time."

"Bookmark that," she suggested. "Let me deal with this guy first."

"'Deal with?'" spluttered the commander. "I've five hundred strong fists to hammer on your shield!"

"I also learned," Geneve continued in a conversational tone, "this land's been without Tresward for hundreds of years."

The commander looked blank, like an angry rock. Meriwether whistled. "That explains why everyone's so stupid."

"Hey," warned the Vhemin.

Yasmine flitted on glittering wings. "To be fair, I've been a bird for eight hundred years. I couldn't warn anyone."

"You couldn't wear pants," Meriwether said. "Let's give you a pass on that."

"Hey!" the commander barked. "What's a Tresward?"

"Come find out," the fairy suggested. She frowned, then eyed Meriwether. "You sure this one's up for it? She seems very young. Adepts against an army ... it's risky."

"What's a Tresward?" The commander's voice rose.

"I dunno." Meriwether rubbed his chin. "I'd wager my coat she's up for it."

"Your coat wouldn't fit me," Yasmine said. "And the color is terrible."

"*What's a Tresward?*" roared the commander.

//SILENCE,// Geneve barked. The commander's face mottled, throat bulging as he tried to form words, but nothing came. She faced the dragon. *//ORMEON, RISE.//* Geneve coughed, rubbing her throat. "Please. We need you."

The dragon shifted, flexed, then opened an angry red eye. It found the commander, and she gave a toothy smile. *//YOU BROUGHT ME BREAKFAST, DRAGONRIDER. YOU SHOULDN'T HAVE.//*

The commander froze, then turned—very slowly—to face the dragon. She rose, the cords lashing her to the earth snapping like guy wires in a gale, each a twang that promised a power of hurt to whoever lashed her down. The Vhemin commander, still without the power of speech, tried for a war cry. All that came out was a squeak. He wrestled with his voice for a moment longer, seemed to sag, then ran at the dragon, waving his sword.

Meriwether goggled. *Of all the people here, he goes for the* dragon? *He's got spine, I'll grant.* Ormeon snatched the monster on the hoof, squeezed her hand, and pulped him. A leg splattered on the ground. The dragon crunched, chewed, and swallowed.

The Vhemin before them charged. Geneve charged right back, but where the creatures yelled rage and death threats, she was silent. Red hair flowed behind her. Ormeon breathed deep, stretched her wings wide, then blasted enemy ranks with dragonfire.

Meriwether looked away. *It doesn't matter that they're the enemy. It matters that they die for someone else.* It was the looking-away part that drew his attention to the night sky behind them. Lightning shot to the earth in signature magelike pillars. The arcs hit the same place over and over, a ceaseless tide of fury. *What would cause that? What are they trying to kill? And how are there so many mages?* "Geneve!"

He may as well have called to the sky. The Knight danced among Vhemin, dragon by her side. Ormeon flame-grilled monsters by the score, and those that made it through Geneve took on the blade. The noise of the battle drowned out Meriwether's voice. If he had a signal fire, maybe, but—

Three's mercy, I'm a holomancer. I'm made *of signal fires.* He slapped his forehead. Yasmine flitted before him. "You do something stupid again?"

He pointed with his chin. "Over there."

The fairy squinted. "Looks like mages being mages."

{But what are they being mages to?} Coming Storm sidled up. Meriwether had no idea where she came from. Her left side was blood-spattered, but it didn't look like hers. The cat pointed at Geneve as a massive pillar of Light and fire smote the earth in response to Tresward skill. *{She who you get all moon-eyed over?}*

"I'm not moon-eyed!"

{I don't blame you.} The cat half-smiled. *{I think you're reaching, though. She's an easy ten any way you measure, but you... More like a six.}*

Yasmine scowled. "He's at least a seven."

"I hate you both," Meriwether said. "But what's going on—"

The ground in the distance erupted. Even at this distance Meriwether blinked away stars as his night vision left on blue-white wings. Dark turned into day for two seconds. The ground gave a small heave, like the earth hiccupped. Lightning coursed along the clouds above, followed by a massive *BOOM!* Meriwether glanced behind him, then jabbed his arm. "Red!"

The Vhemin horde stilled. Cats stopped fighting reptiles. Yasmine forgot to call Meriwether names. Ormeon's slow, insistent breathing was the only noise.

A monster to Meriwether's right coughed and spat. She had a fantastic headdress of red feathers from a type of bird Meriwether didn't know. The creature growled, "What the fuck was that?"

"Meri." Geneve's voice was low but insistent. He turned. She stood, gleaming blade lowered, eyes wide. Her armor was slick and red from blood spray, glinting in the firelight. "Can you see what's coming?"

"This reminds me of that time I died," Yasmine said to no one in particular. "It sucked."

"I can see," boomed a man. Meriwether looked up to the small cliff Geneve jumped from. *By the Three, she really dived off a hundred-meter drop. She's incredible.* The man was large, but in a too-much-food or too-much-exercise way impossible to tell at this distance. He had robes sashed about his barrel-like frame. "There is a Storm coming. This squall has white hair and a heavy heart." He spoke in the language of the ancients, which Meriwether knew because he once held a book of magic written in that language. He thought of mentioning it offhand, because it seemed important, but:

"Vertiline," breathed Geneve. "It's Tilly."

"Hold up," Meriwether said. *This guy speaks in the language of the ancients, he knows Geneve, and he looks like a merchant. These things don't add up.* "Who are you?" He rewound a few moments, then eyed Yasmine. "What do you mean, you died?"

{*How can he see that?*} Coming Storm glared at the man atop the cliff. {*He's only human. Even I can't see that far.*}

"What of a Vhemin and a cat?" Meriwether called. "We are together."

The stranger peered into the darkness. "There are others with her, but none burn so brightly."

"Mazin!" Geneve strode toward Ormeon. "Find my horse!"

"It's not your horse, Tresward. I paid for it." The man on the cliffs —Mazin—laughed. "But you can borrow him a few more moments."

Geneve laid her hand on Ormeon's flank. "Can you get them?"

//THERE ARE WEAPONS HERE.// The dragon shook her head. //I CANNOT FLY.//

"Oh," Meriwether said. "Maybe I can help. You stay here and beat the monsters to a pulp. I'll get Vertiline." He focused his will for a moment, the disc snapping into shape by his feet. He stepped on, turning to where Mazin claimed Vertiline was. "No, this isn't right."

Geneve looked at him, really *looked* at him. "What's not right?"

He nudged the disc toward her, stepped off, and pulled her into a kiss. Her eyes widened, then she leaned into him. He lingered a moment. "I wanted to do that the first moment I saw you."

"Liar." But she smiled.

"I would walk another hundred deserts to be with you." He returned to his disc, hand lingering in hers. "I'm going because there's—"

"I know," she said. "Try not to die. You're not good at staying alive."

"I've managed it so far." He didn't want to let her go. "You stay alive too. I'll admit it's more in your wheelhouse, but there are a lot of Vhemin here."

"Meri." Her voice took on urgency, hard and brittle at the same time. "Be careful. Come *back* to me. Come back to *me*."

"I will. Always and forever." He turned, because Vertiline might be dying, not because he wanted to go.

Yasmine flitted to his shoulder. "Why are you risking your life by going toward a Knight?"

"Because I owe this Knight more than I can explain in a moment. Are you ready to face your doom, fairy? We ride."

"Float," she corrected. "You're standing on a disc of light and memory. It floats."

Meriwether gritted his teeth. "One day you're going to tell me how you died."

"One day you'll explain to me what you owe a Knight. When that happens, I'll tell you how I died." She pointed with a tiny arm. "Charge!"

Chapter Twenty-Four

I don't want him to go. Three's mercy, but I want Meri here. Geneve scowled at Ormeon. "I thought you were armored and could do anything."

The dragon eyed the Vhemin, making sure none were about to rush them, then lowered her head to Geneve's level. *//I THOUGHT YOU WERE SMART. I GUESS WE WERE BOTH WRONG.//*

The strange Feybrind who'd been with Meri sidled closer. *{I am Coming Storm. I'm a friend to your lover-for-life.}*

Geneve felt herself blush. "I, uh."

{This is where you tell me your name. It will perhaps be the last thing I learn before the Vhemin horde rise and kill us all.}

Geneve touched her breastplate over the burnished sun. "I'm Geneve, Knight Chevalier of the Tresward."

The cat eyed Geneve, brilliant rose eyes glinting in the firelight. *{The land slept a long time waiting for you. You have two tasks, Knight.}* Her fingers flicked *two, two* insistently. *{You need to stop these Vhemin from trying to kill us. And you need to ask that guy up there how he spoke our language.}*

Geneve blinked. "He's a merchant."

Ormeon chuffed. *//HE IS NO SUCH THING. NOT ANYMORE.//*

{Is it common for merchants to speak a language eight hundred years dead?} The cat's tail lashed. *{We've only just awoken, but even I can tell something funny's going on. It wasn't common when our time was the now.}*

//THE CAT ISN'T WRONG.// The dragon sniffed. //YET.//

Geneve rewound the conversation in her head back to Mazin's arrival. She hadn't thought anything of his words, understanding them perfectly, and so had Meri ... *but Meri studied the ancient's language.* "Mazin!"

{Don't forget about the monsters.} Coming Storm sidled behind Geneve as a contingent of Vhemin stormed closer.

Geneve rounded on them, sword held low but ready. "Who wants to die first?"

The group held five monsters. One had the weathered, old look of a wind-blasted tree. By his side stood a woman missing shark teeth from her upper jaw, which gave her a demented appearance. Next to her, a young man, barely a teenager by how Geneve reckoned their span. Behind the youth stood an older woman, perhaps his mother, and beside her a hulking brute with bloodshot eyes.

The brute spoke. "We don't want to die. We want to get the fuck out of here. That asshole," he pointed at the Vhemin commander's legs, all that remained of their previous leader, "said we needed to get here, so here we went. Back then *that* asshole," he shifted his point to Ormeon, who snarled ruddy-lit teeth, "was asleep. Then you," the arm moved to Geneve, "arrived, bringing a power of hurt. I'm going to be honest. We thought we'd settle in for some barbecue." He spread his hands. "Night's not gone how I expected."

"Me neither," agreed the weathered man, who worked a tooth loose, spitting it to the sand. "I didn't sign up to fight a woken dragon. It's not right, and I don't mind admitting it."

Coming Storm stepped from behind Geneve, like a smooth ripple on a pond. *{Is it not right because it's no longer unfair in your favor?}*

"What's the cat doing with its hands?" The kid squinted. "Anyway. It's not a fair fight. Not anymore."

Geneve glanced past them at the horde. She saw hulking brutes, monsters, creatures that ate the flesh of civilized peoples, murderers, savages, and villains. Her eyes wandered over to the fallen body of a

Feybrind, his fur blood-matted, emerald eyes sightless and staring. Geneve tightened her grip on her sword. *I should end them. They are a scourge.*

A sniff drew her eye. Mazin stood a respectful distance from Ormeon, staring up at the dragon. The merchant beamed like a fool, eyes glinting with pleasure. "I never thought it would work. I never thought ... oh, *my.* A *dragon.*"

"We were just talking about that," the red-eyed monster said. "Ain't right."

"Oh, it's right." Mazin stepped forward, placing a hand on one of Ormeon's legs. The dragon sniffed him, as if trying to decide if he were tasty. "Eight hundred years ago the world lost its dragons, and it's not been right since. Cracked to the core, spinning on a broken axis. We abandoned the Skyforges, or killed the Builders who knew how they worked. But they were so beautiful. A dragon in flight is—"

"Fucking terrifying," suggested the kid. "I ain't seen it, and I don't want to."

Geneve looked to the kid. *Not a teenager. Younger. Big, as humans see things, but starved and skinny as Vhemin measure. I wish Meri hadn't left. He would tell me if I should kill them or ... what? Let murderers live?* "Ormeon is the Redeemer of our world."

//LET'S NOT PUT TOO MUCH PRESSURE ON A SINGLE DRAGON,// Ormeon suggested. *//I WILL GET PERFORMANCE ANXIETY.//*

Mazin sighed the contented sound of a man who's had a full meal, then walked to Geneve. He passed by the Vhemin, raising an eyebrow in their direction, before arriving before her. "You're struggling with something. A heavy weight, a boulder that would take five people to lift, and it's yours alone."

"Who *are* you?" Geneve said. "How do you speak the language of the ancients?"

"Those aren't the questions you want to ask." Mazin pursed his lips. "They're not bad questions, but they're not the best for the moment."

"Tell me why you should live." Geneve rounded on the monsters. The tension knotted her shoulders, made her jaw clench, and her fist tighten on her borrowed blade. "Explain why I shouldn't strike you from this world like the mistake you are."

The five shuffled like nervous children. The probably-mother-of-the-kid stepped forward. "Would you at least let my son go? He's young, and..." She trailed off, avoiding the snake-eyed glare of the weathered man. "I know it's not our way, but he's my only remaining boy. The world's taken the others. Taken, and given nothing back."

Mazin put a hand on Geneve's arm, the weight on her armor so light she almost didn't notice. He faced the monsters, but she thought the words were for her. "This is how the dragons died. We put blade, fire, and tooth and claw to the test. The price of failure was the death of a wonder."

//FINALLY,// Ormeon growled. //SOME RESPECT.//

Geneve snorted, then tried to stop herself because this was a dire situation, then she gave up and laughed. Long, and loud, hands on her knees. She let it out, nervous energy and pent-up ridiculousness all at once. When she looked up, the five monsters were staring, slack-jawed and wide-eyed. Ormeon examined her like she'd turned into a fish. Coming Storm backed up a pace, like she might have something contagious.

But Mazin? He smiled like they shared the same damn secret. Geneve felt her hand unclench from its death-grip on her sword. She felt release in her gut, in the hold of her shoulders, and how she held her head high. *I needed that.*

Geneve straightened, brushed back red hair, and calmed herself. "Monsters, here is how it is. We can beat on each other for hours. You will lose."

"There's like a hundred of us," interjected the kid.

//FIVE HUNDRED AND NINE REMAIN.// Ormeon looked away, as if embarrassed for the youth. //IT PROBABLY ONLY FEELS LIKE A HUNDRED BECAUSE YOU ARE VERY SMALL.//

The red-eyed monster puffed up his already impressive chest. "Who are you calling small?"

Ormeon leaned down, reaching out a scaled talon. The monster watched it nervously. The dragon poked him in the chest. //YOU,

TINY ONE.// Then she flicked her claw, sending the Vhemin tumbling back head over heels.

Coming Storm watched the Vhemin tumble, then faced Geneve when the monster came to rest. *{Did anyone forget the battle between us? We might not lose, but we are diminished.}*

//TWENTY-FOUR OF THE PEOPLE LIE DEAD. ONE HUNDRED AND NINETY-EIGHT VHEMIN LIE, COLD AND LIFELESS.// The dragon sighed. *//IT IS A GOOD RATIO.//*

"Hey," said the Vhemin mother, clutching her kid. "We're doing all the dying."

"As you always do," Mazin said. "It's why you were made."

Geneve scowled. *More mystic bullshit.* "Mazin, be still." She ignored his goggling eyes. "As I was saying, we can fight each other, and you will lose. The People are better fighters gram for gram than Vhemin. No, don't interrupt. You face a dragon and a Tresward Knight. We are allied." Geneve hoped it was true; the Feybrind arrived with Meri, but they hadn't had a chance to talk through what that meant. "There is another path." She looked at her sword, then lowered it. "Join us."

"Fuck off," said the weathered monster conversationally. "We just want to get out of here."

{And kill anyone you find?} Coming Storm's tail lashed. *{I will not allow it.}*

Mazin eyed the cat speculatively. "Ah. He gave you back yourself."

"What did the cat say?" the weathered monster said.

"She said she will kill you where you stand and leave your body cooling on the sand," Mazin said. "She was quite specific."

{I what now?}

"That is, if you don't join us." Geneve glared first at Mazin, then the cat. "But it's not the right way."

The red-eyed monster limped back to them. "Why not?"

"Because a promise coerced isn't worth its weight in breath." Geneve shrugged. "It's not how your kind work. You follow only strength and coin."

"They'll follow me," said a familiar voice. Geneve turned, and there was Armitage, the hulking brute beside Meri on a floating disc. Behind the pair were Tilly and Sight of Day. At the back, Picotee and another lad who looked broadly terrified. Geneve almost sagged with release. "And I'm going to tell you why."

Chapter Twenty-Five

Vertiline knew Armitage lied to her. It wasn't anything about the tone of his voice or how his arm felt across her shoulders. The monster was a good liar, almost as good as the sinner. *Meriwether's less a sinner than me.*

She knew Armitage lied because of the smell.

Monster and cat led her from the battlefield. There were no calls from allies, and few screams of the dying. All about was smoke, rich and delicious, the scent of fine barbecue. She almost gagged, because the smell came from people.

Her armored boot *crunched* through a pile of char at her feet. Puffs of ash wafted on the heated breeze. Vertiline's foot snagged on something brittle, and a piece of bone followed the boot from the carcass she'd stood in.

"I killed them," she breathed. "I killed them all."

"Kind of a team effort," Armitage suggested, still leading her on, directing her travel, husbanding her from the battlefield.

{The sorcerers did all the hard work.} Sight of Day's hands moved as if sticky, imprecise, as if his heart wasn't in the lie. *{You just stood there like a post.}*

Vertiline gave a half sob. Armitage led her from a crater, all that remained of the land, and people she'd stood next to upon it. Above the rim, a blasted sandscape, sticks of burnt wood and cremated people scattered for a half-klick in every direction. The night sky above was still the color of coal, sullen and unforgiving. She tried to speak, but nothing came out.

"Yeah, it's pretty shit," Armitage said. "Come along."

{You should only own your own crimes.} Sight of Day stopped them both, golden eyes hard and sad. *{This was not yours, pale sister.}*

"But what of my sins?" Vertiline shouldered off Armitage's arm. "I carry plenty."

{It is not a game of scales.} The Feybrind touched a fur soft hand to her cheek. *{You didn't do,}* he slashed an angry arm down, *{this.}*

"Cat's not wrong. C'mon. There are a few survivors." Armitage trudged off, scratching behind his ear. "We got a couple out."

"How?"

"Saw you in trouble. Didn't think we could fix it. Not sure you could've, either." Armitage paused, stretching. Vertiline saw an angry red-stained rent in his shirt. "So, we ran. Cat ran faster, but that was because he wasn't carrying two people."

Vertiline quickened her pace. "What survivors?"

"The angry one who hates the runt." Armitage frowned. "It's a P-word, I'm sure of it."

"Picotee du Parneer?" Vertiline asked. "She doesn't hate him. Picotee loves him."

"Yeah?" Armitage frowned. "She's got a funny way of showing it. Say. Do you think her loving him will be a problem? What with Red and all."

Sight of Day shook his head, padding past the monster. *{You're slow in all the ways.}*

Vertiline tugged a hand through once-pale hair. Brittle charred strands broke off in her fingers. "Who else?"

"I dunno. You lot all look the same." He trudged into the ash-shrouded gloom.

Who else turned out to be a young man with frightened eyes. His hair was cut short by someone with no skill at the job. Like Picotee, he looked terrified, but also covered in a fine layer of ash. It was like seeing a couple ghosts with eyeballs.

Picotee wobbled to her feet. "What *was* that?"

"It was my fault," Vertiline said. "I—"

"Bullshit." Armitage shook his head. "You got that hand because the runt's father set up a deathtrap showcase in his castle. There were like fifty dead, and you would've made fifty-one. 'Cept you're human, and the ancient's tech worked just fine. If you didn't have that hand, you'd be dead *today*. The fault's with those vile sorcerers who—"

"I got it," Picotee said. "Vertiline, are you going to kill us?"

She didn't mean *on purpose*. How do you tell someone *I don't know?* What words would assure the admiral of the queen's navy? "Are you a sorcerer?"

"No."

"Then probably not." Vertiline's mouth tasted like ash and regret.

{There's good and bad news.} Sight of Day looked to the west. *{The bad news is our army's mostly gone.}*

"You call this 'mostly?'" Picotee snorted. "Feels like the whole damn thing."

{We're still here.} The cat half-smiled. *{The good news is another sinner is coming. You'll like this one, because he's learned some style.}*

Vertiline spun, hand on an empty scabbard. *Where is my sword? No Tresward should lose their blade.* She squinted, trying to break the darkness. Across the sand, a glimmer of light. It was a gentle ochre, low to the ground, and approaching fast. "I need a sword."

"Ease up," Armitage growled. "It's the runt."

Vertiline's fingers relaxed. "Meriwether? How ... you know what? Never mind."

The ochre light resolved into a floating disc, above which stood the sinner. He'd got a new wardrobe since they'd last seen each other, and Vertiline admitted he didn't look half bad. *Although it's possible that's because he's not covered in ash.* "Ho, sinner."

He halted his disc before her. "Ho, Vertiline." Meriwether stepped from his disc smooth as you please, stepped four paces across the baked sand, and swept her into a hug. She stiffened, then grabbed him back. "Hey. Easy. Easy!"

"It's really good to see you," she admitted in a whisper, then released him.

Meriwether nodded. Sight of Day eased forward on the sinner's left, Armitage coming on the right, and both grabbed him into a hug. He laughed. "Easy already!" After a moment he extricated himself from the semi-violent man-hug, then walked to Picotee. "My Lady du Parneer."

Picotee gave a tiny nod. "Meriwether."

"Rough day?"

"The worst," the admiral admitted. "This is Felix."

Meriwether offered his hand to the ash-covered youth. "Hello, Felix. How'd she sucker you into this mess?"

"I tried to steal her horse," Felix said. "It was a good horse."

"Great." Meriwether clapped his hands. "Look, I hate to rush this along, but Geneve's got a problem—"

"Geneve's alive?" Vertiline grabbed Meriwether's shoulders, spinning him to face her. "How is she? What's happened? *Where* is she?"

"Easy," Meriwether said again. "I feel like I've said that a hundred times, but it bears repeating. She's good. Might not be soon, though. There's five hundred and nine Vhemin—"

"That seems a suspiciously specific number," Armitage rumbled.

"And also, a dragon," Meriwether continued, as if that answered everything. "And some weird guy who can see better than a Feybrind at night and speaks in the language of the ancients. Anyway, it's complicated, and I'd like to get back to her before it gets more so."

"You forgot about the fairy," said a small voice. From beneath Meriwether's hair flitted a tiny woman. "Everyone forgets about the fairy. I'm Yasmine Glitterconc, and I Build things."

And why not? It'd been a day of surprises, and seeing a fairy felt like the least of them. Vertiline stepped on the ochre disc. "I hope you can make this bigger, because I'm not walking."

BEFORE THEY LEFT, VERTILINE FOUND HER BLADE AND RETURNED IT to her sheath. It was unmarked, waiting on ground turned to glass by heat. *I should be less careless with things. The Smiths made it well, but all forging has limits.*

The race across the sands was exhilarating. Vertiline had never been on a ride so smooth. Horses had a living, breathing urgency. You could be in touch with one, feel the beat of its heart, and share its joy. A wagon rattled and swayed and could carry a Cage of Judgment, among other things.

The disc, though. It was smooth as an eel in water, slick like rain on glass. Meriwether urged them faster, but she couldn't see how he did it. "Is this a trick of the ancients? Another thing like an Artifice?"

"What? No." He faced ahead, focusing on what looked like a big fire in the distance. "It's light and memory."

"*You're* doing this?"

"If you're going to sin, do it right." He gave a fierce grin. "I've learned a few new tricks."

"So I see. What happened to your hair?"

"What's wrong with it?" He sounded a shade defensive.

"She'll hate it," Vertiline guessed. "I don't know why you changed it."

Meriwether turned to Sight of Day. "What do you think?"

{I think you look like a show pony, and not in a good way.} The cat's tail lashed. *{Who convinced you to do something so bad?}*

The sinner looked to the front. "I hate you all."

"It might have been my fault," Yasmine admitted, climbing Meriwether's head like a boulder and sitting on top. "*I* think it's nice."

"You would. You shit sparkles," Armitage rumbled. "Ain't no kind of haircut for an honest man."

Meriwether sighed. "Okay. Here we are."

The disc slowed. Sure enough, Geneve stood by Ormeon, a large man, and five Vhemin, all in conversation. Geneve held a naked blade, a fact that caused Vertiline's tension to rise. A fire burned a little further to the west. Armitage sniffed. "I got this."

"Hell, no," Vertiline said. "You'll make it worse."

Geneve hadn't noticed them yet, no doubt because of the noiselessness of the ochre disc. "Because a promise coerced isn't worth its weight in breath." Vertiline's sister of the blade shrugged. "It's not how your kind work. You follow strength and coin."

Armitage shouldered to the front. "They'll follow me. And I'm going to tell you why." He stepped from the disc, hulked toward a enormous red-eyed Vhemin, and hit the man so hard in the head *everyone* winced. The Vhemin dropped. "I invoke the right of Confab."

Silence fell, interrupted by the pop of the bonfire. Ormeon leaned forward, muzzle above Armitage. *//CONWHAT?//*

"Confab," the monster repeated. "If I win, I get to be the boss."

The weathered Vhemin opened his mouth to speak, closed it, then tried again. "There are five-hundred of us."

"Better get started, then." Armitage stripped off his shirt, revealing his truly epic physique. He had muscles on muscles, and those muscles were breeding more muscles. Tossing his shirt to the ground, he flexed, clapped his hands, then said, "Unless you'd like to quit now."

Vertiline stepped from the disc, hurrying to Armitage's side. Something was *wrong*, and she didn't know what. "Monster. What's Confab?"

He gave her a tight, small grin, a few shark teeth showing for good measure. "When Vhemin loose a leader, there are three things that usually happen, assuming everyone's still alive. First, hereditary claim. Son or daughter takes charge, usual thing. Second, a lot of talking and hand-waving. We don't usually do that one because it's slow, dumb, and boring."

Vertiline took a step closer. She could smell his musk, the animalness of him. "And the third?"

"Confab." Armitage let his grin widen. "If I fight the tribe and win, I get to be the boss."

"Like, fight the tribe's champion?" She blinked.

"No, the whole tribe. Wouldn't be fair, otherwise."

Ormeon looked over the gathered Vhemin. *//FIVE-HUNDRED AND NINE, MONSTER. ARE YOU INSANE?//*

"I'm talented, is what I am." Armitage stalked to the fire, pulling out an iron. It turned out to be a two-meter pole with a blade at one end. He offered the point to Geneve. "Red, if you would. Take the blade off."

Geneve looked between Vertiline and Armitage. "Why?"

"I can't kill 'em. Confab rules."

Meriwether seemed to come online all at once. "Confab means talking."

"We have a different conversational style," Armitage admitted. He waved the spear toward Geneve again. "If you would."

"You're going to die," Geneve said. "*I can do this.*"

"You would kill at least one. It'd be an accident, but they'd be dead anyway. And you," he swiveled to Vertiline as she was about to say *Are you totally mad*, "no. Just, no. None of you can do this."

{I can.} Sight of Day stamped closer, tail lashing like a pissed off snake. *{My brother, you will die. I won't.}*

"The confidence is overwhelming." Armitage's voice softened. "There are a couple of problems. First, you're not good enough to fight five-hundred of my kind. No, don't go waving your hands at me. You know it, I know it. You'd tire out. Cats are good in short bursts. They made us for ... fights that last." He eyed Meriwether. "Ain't that right, runt?"

"I think so." Meriwether nodded. "I think that's exactly what they did. You heal from wounds that would kill anyone else, because you might be needed tomorrow."

Lash, lash. *{What was the other thing?}*

"I've already started the Confab." Armitage nudged the red-eyed monster with his boot. "Can't be undone. So, let's get on with it."

ARMITAGE STOOD BASKING IN FIRELIGHT. VERTILINE WATCHED FROM sidelines of their makeshift ring. The fighting circle was ringed by spears drawn from the fire. Ormeon presided above, runes glowing an angry vermillion, but she kept her words to herself.

Across from Vertiline stood Geneve. Her sister of the blade's eyes were hooded, hand on the now-sheathed hilt of her borrowed blade. Meriwether stood by her, fairy on his shoulder. The sinner's eyes were soft and sad, like he could see the future and it promised hell. Beside him, the fat merchant, who was as much a seller of pots as Vertiline was a cobbler. Mazin's eyes held no expression, the man's mouth in a dry line.

Sight of Day stood by Vertiline. *We share a love of monsters, it seems.* The cat's golden eyes were hard, unbreakable, resolute. *{If they kill him, I will...}* Swish, swish. *{I will end them all.}*

Vertiline looked away. "This isn't right. We don't fight alone. We're—"

Armitage bellowed, "Who's second?"

A monster stepped between the poles. He carried a blood-stained rusty mattock. Like Armitage, he wore no shirt, but had a gladiator's manica and pauldron armor combination. "Don't you mean first?"

"Nah." Armitage twirled the now-bladeless metal staff like it weighed no more than a toothpick. "That was the other asshole I decked. Go for the biggest one first."

The other Vhemin charged, swinging overhand with his mattock. Armitage stepped aside, sand spraying underfoot, and clubbed the other man in the side of the head. Mattock, armor, and Vhemin clattered to the ground together. Armitage offered the crowd, and growing queue, a shark-toothed grin. "Five-hundred and seven to go."

{He is already tired.} Sight of Day's fingers slashed air like brittle steel. *{I don't know what to do.}*

Vertiline touched his elbow. "Pray."

Another monster entered the ring. She had slightly darker scaled skin, wearing a sneer like a promise. Armitage met her charge without shifting from his position, grabbed the arms trying to grapple him, heaved, and slammed her to the sand. She groaned, clawing weakly, so he kicked her in the ribs. "Five-hundred and six. C'mon. We haven't got all night."

{The gods fell. They don't watch us anymore.} Swish, swish. *{Besides, I never had much time for them anyway.}*

Another monster entered. He held two blades and wore a breastplate. Vertiline frowned. "Is armor against the rules?"

{Why are you asking me? My people don't do this kind of thing.} Sight of Day looked at the moonless sky. *{Maybe I'll start on my prayer skills.}*

Two blades flashing, the challenger swung at Armitage's head and torso. Armitage slipped aside, so very quick despite his size, and poked his stick into the gut of his opponent. A soft sigh of air, then Armitage finished him off with a massive uppercut that made Vertiline wince. "He *is* good at this."

{Fighting monsters, or protecting his friends?} Sight of Day looked down. *{If we were better at either, he wouldn't be there.}*

So it went. Geneve and Vertiline stood across from each other, both staring at their friend as he fought for them. Tresward, made to hold the shield of the world, standing like statues. *Some Knights we are. We are powerless when we're most needed.* Vertiline's fingers itched to hold steel, to get beside Armitage, to...

I want to have his back. He's had mine, like no one else.

He needed it at the seventy-third fight. A thin Vhemin, tall like Armitage but far faster, came at him with a chisel. She got close enough to kiss, because Armitage was tired, and wouldn't have been fast enough even when fresh. The chisel slipped between the monster's ribs, gouging up, *up*, toward his heart. Vertiline wanted to scream, *STOP!* but there wasn't time. Oh, there was time aplenty for her mind's eye to see how the tip of a rusty weapon could find Armitage's heart, to take his life, to spill all he was upon the thirsty sand. She'd fought enough people, over more years than she was comfortable admitting, to see a killing blow. Vertiline sucked air, readying for a scream, for *something*.

Armitage curled over the blow, his big frame folding like a low quality tent in a gale. A hush fell, the savage silence of bright eyes and hungry shark-toothed grins. Armitage coughed red, then straightened, tearing the chisel free. He held his attacker's hand in a vice grip, her arm up and away, controlling the weapon with his massive strength.

He kicked her in the crotch, then head-butted her. There was the *crunch* of bone, but Vertiline only saw the gush of red onto the sand. Armitage held his opponent, fingers held on the back of her head, other still controlling the chisel, and head-butted her again. The chisel fell from nerveless fingers to the sand beside his blood. Armitage lifted her body, both arms above, and dropped her back first onto his bent knee.

Then he tossed her like trash out of the ring. Coughed a little more blood. Scratched his side where the chisel entered. The flow was crawling toward a trickle, then to nothing at all. He leered. "Who's fucking next?"

Sight of Day looked on, wide-eyed. *{He should not be alive.}*

"The head," she breathed. "It's the only way."

{Perhaps it's more a question of style.} The cat's fingers were hesitant, like someone new at finger painting. *{I would've dropped him.}*

"I ... don't doubt that." Vertiline hid her fear behind tight lips and a dry mouth. "We have to do something."

{Could you fight five hundred and nine Vhemin?} Swish, swish. *{I admit while it would be fun to try, the big stupid creature is right. I would run out of puff.}*

"Maybe." She looked at her metal hand. "I don't think I could do it. Geneve, perhaps. She's..."

{Younger?}

"No. Well, she is, but not that."

{Better looking? More fit?}

"You're not helping." Vertiline ran trembling hands through ice-colored hair. "She's the best swordswoman I've ever seen."

{Perhaps that's because you've never seen yourself.} The Feybrind shrugged. *{I think you should think about that, because soon Armitage will fall, and five hundred and nine Vhemin will try to kill you.}*

"What about you?"

The cat half-smiled. *{I will be long gone. I don't have to outrun them, just you.}*

Armitage struggled on. His movements came slower, his opponents no less vicious. They were all snake-eyed, hard, *hungry* for his blood. Monsters in deed, not just form. He lost a finger in his hundred and ninety-ninth fight ... or was that the two-hundredth? Vertiline lost count, heart hammering as if she were in the ring.

Across from her, Geneve looked to their friend fighting on the sand, then met her eyes. She tilted her head, offered a tiny shrug, and a raised eyebrow. Vertiline knew what she meant. Geneve was saying, *I have your back. I will honor your play, even if we die.*

Vertiline touched Sight of Day's arm. "I'm going to do something stupid."

{How is this different from the other things you do?}

She gave a hard smile. "I'm telling you so you can run, cat. You have two hundred newborn babes to save."

Golden eyes met hers. *{I find myself overtired.}* He gave an exaggerated yawn. *{I'm in no state to run.}* He looked to his hands for a moment, then touched a soft hand to her face. *{He wants this. Don't take it from him.}*

Aye, Armitage's chosen his fate. Now, I join mine with his. Vertiline's smile softened. "Thank you." She spun on her heel, storming to the queue forming to spill more of Armitage's blood. Vhemin watched her come, all hard stares and hungry, hungry teeth. She stopped at the front of the line, staring up at a monster who towered above her by two handspans. "Hold, creature."

"Fuck off." His voice sounded smoke broken, ragged and coarse. He fingered a jagged blade, the edges notched and broken with misuse, time, or both. "I'm next in line."

"No." She shook her head. "*I'm* next."

"Wait your turn," he responded, voice thickening with anger.

Vertiline's hand found the pommel of her sheathed sword as if by accident. She straightened, the burnished sun on her breastplate catching firelight. She lowered her voice, put weight into it, teased the words out long and slow. "Has it been so long since the Tresward taught your kind to heel, cur?"

The monster roared, lunging for her. She moved like the Light itself, sword leaving scabbard, cutting once with a sound like meat searing on a grill, golden luminance flashing before returning home in less than a heartbeat. The Vhemin staggered three paces past her, then stumbled to a halt, swaying. Vertiline didn't have to look, waiting for the slick, wet slop as the monster's torso slid sideways onto the ever thirsty sand.

Silence. The flicker of torchlight.

//THAT DOESN'T LOOK LIKE A THING YOU WALK AWAY FROM,// Ormeon growled.

Vertiline held her pose, eyes searching the line of Vhemin stretching three hundred strong, all waiting to carve a souvenir from Armitage's hide. She raised her voice, holding it clear and bright. "I am Knight Chevalier Vertiline of the Tresward. I fight for the three gods Cophine, Ikmae, and Khiton." A flicker of wings as that damned fairy Yasmine flitted to hang from a pole to her left. "I fight for this world, and all its people. But I fight for," her arm jerked behind her, stabbing at where she hoped Armitage stood, "this man. I won't stand in the way of your custom. You want to bloody yourself on the sand, that's up to you. But *I* will wait. I watch. And if Armitage falls, I will be his second."

She turned, entering the ring and offering a curt nod to Armitage. The monster looked dumbfounded, but stood straighter, the moment giving him time to rest, to catch his breath. "So ... you don't want to fight me?" He looked hopeful, wary, and tired at the same time. "I'm confused."

"No, monster." She shook her head, pale braid lashing like a tail. "I fight *with* you." Vertiline walked past him to the edge of the fighting circle, turned, and kneeled. She put gauntleted hands flat on her thighs, watching. Waiting. Eyes past Armitage, and on the line behind.

"Uh." The next monster in line kicked sand. She was squat, like an oversized barrel made of anger and muscle. "What's that mean?"

Vertiline tipped her head. "It means you will fight *me* if Armitage falls. I'm happy to start at one and go right to five hundred and eight, or pick up where he leaves off. But I will carve you from the world for taking the life of one for whom *I* fight."

"I'd prefer it if you fought beside me," admitted Armitage. "When you said 'with,' that's kinda what I was hoping for."

"Take what you can get." She offered a small smile. "Now, get on with it. We don't have all night."

The crisping of sand made her look. Sight of Day padded behind her, Coming Storm by his side. The two Feybrind knelt behind Vertiline. The golden-eyed cat sighed. *{Is this where the queue for free ale starts?}*

Coming Storm half-smiled. *{This is where we wait to die.}*

Sight of Day shrugged. *{Close enough.}*

Vertiline watched as Geneve strode over, standing behind the cats. She eyed Armitage, and the legion of Vhemin behind him, then very carefully kneeled as Vertline had. Meriwether hustled to her side, sitting cross-legged. After a quiet moment, Ormeon crunched over, massive form bulking out the sky. Geneve cleared her throat. "I'm up for an ass-kicking."

"I'm not." Meriwether gave a nervous laugh, quietening as Ormeon looked down on him. "But I'll watch you give one."

//I WOULD BE HAPPY WITH FREE ALE.//

Feybrind padded from the shadows, forming line beyond line behind each other. A pyramid of people trailed behind Vertiline, all holding vigil for a single man who fought for them.

Armitage squared his shoulders, facing the line of Vhemin. Vertiline let her smile broaden, because not only did their companion stand taller, straighter, as if the flickering firelight held him up, the line of opponents looked ... *nervous*.

When the fighting started again, she looked on. Relaxed. Ready to do what must be done, if Armitage fell. But she knew he wouldn't.

Chapter Twenty-Six

Meriwether hunted shadows while dawn's light tried to banish them. He was weary, like he hadn't slept for a hundred years, but they all were. Geneve was tired, and Vertiline more so. Armitage was past exhausted and into dead-on-his-feet, but he'd felled five hundred and eight Vhemin before passing out, so maybe that was fair.

He'd wanted time with Geneve, the taste of her lips and the touch of her skin, but Meriwether knew they needed to solve a problem first. A mystery, dragged on the heels of fate. And fate wasn't to be found, nor the mystery. He scowled. "Where's that damn fairy?"

Meriwether worked his way through the Vhemin encampment. The tents were crude but serviceable. The stench wasn't too bad, no worse than humans would've made, and perhaps a little better. The Feybrind waited a little to the east, but Yasmine wasn't with them. Oh, for a certainty she was small, but she also sparkled and couldn't keep her mouth shut, so he didn't figure she was hiding anywhere.

He approached a small circle of tents beside a burned-out fire and beheld the mystery and fate at once. Mazin sat on a rock, Yasmine on his knee. They watched each other in silence. A wineskin sat beside Mazin, forgotten.

Meriwether clapped his hands. "There you are."

They both turned, startled, perhaps bashful. Yasmine's wings fluttered. "Who are you after? The merchant or the magnificent fairy?"

"Both," Meriwether said. "I am also after the story of how you died. Or, more precisely, the when of it."

Mazin blinked. "The when?"

Meriwether counted on his fingers. "Geneve said you died, merchant. Told a gripping tale of murder in city streets at the hands of guards. She stopped kissing me to tell it, because she knew it was important, and let me tell you I've missed her kisses, so I feel this needs resolution. But the fairy," a second finger joined the first, "also said she died."

"I did." Yasmine looked to turn sulky.

"Out with it." Meriwether crossed his arms. "I've got all day."

Yasmine fluttered from Mazin's knee, scuffing her toe against imaginary dirt. "I was a bird."

"I remember. I made you not a bird." Meriwether waved a hand. "Perhaps leave out the eight hundred years of being a bird and cut to the moment you died."

"I was in the desert—"

"This whole land is a desert," Meriwether scoffed. "Could you be more specific?"

"Over there." Yasmine pointed at the massive mountain fortress of the ancients. "On the other side, where we met. Only, I was a bird. You remember that?"

"Blue feathers and all," Meriwether confirmed.

"I've stayed by the mountain a long time," the fairy said. "I wanted to go back inside, because I'm a Builder. But I couldn't get in without a big. They put me in that body for not doing what I was told, then they all died, and I was stuck." She flitted sideways a handspan, as if dodging memory itself. "For eight hundred years."

Mazin picked up his wineskin, took a pull, and offered it to Meriwether. "At least you still had wings."

Meriwether took the wine. It was fruity, red and rich, and quite delicious. "This is excellent wine. Maybe wine for breakfast is a thing that'll catch on."

"I'm a wine merchant." Mazin shrugged.

"I'm not sure about that, but we'll get to it." Meriwether handed the wineskin back, then looked to Yasmine. "What killed you?"

"A cat," the fairy said. "Not a Fey Branded, but a—"

"Feybrind," Meriwether said. "Or the People. Fey Branded isn't ... right. It is their slave name."

"Right. Sorry." Yasmine nodded, glittergold dust falling to the sand. "It was a cat about the size of a small dog. Weird-looking ears. Sharp teeth. It bit me here." She touched her side. "Shook me about, and I thought I was going to die."

"And you did."

"And I ... well." She looked at the sky. "I fell. It was a long way down. I was in the sky for I don't know how long, and I don't know how I got there, but then I was *leaving*, and it was bad. The air burned as I fell, because I was going really fast, but it still took a long time to hit the ground."

"What happened to the cat?" Mazin scratched his chin.

"I landed on the cat. The cat's dead. Forget the cat." Yasmine zoomed closer to Meriwether. "Then I found you. The very next day."

"That's what I thought you'd say." Meriwether sighed, suddenly wanting to sit. "Were there moons in the sky before you died?" Yasmine looked to Mazin, and they both nodded at the same time. "Ah."

"What does, 'Ah,' mean?" Mazin offered the wineskin again.

Meriwether took it. "It means we need to find the third one. I think it means we're in worse trouble than I thought. And I'm pretty sure we're all going to die as a result, but let's not get ahead of ourselves."

THE COMMAND TENT WAS PALATIAL. MERIWETHER HAD BEEN IN A few in his time. Some were crowded affairs, mere field promotions of what should've been pup tents, but the Vhemin looted this one from someone important. It had divans, a refreshments table laid with desert fruits, and someone had scared up a carafe of wine or three. *Definitely breakfast wine.* His stomach didn't care, and his heart was onboard, so he poured himself a goblet while watching everyone watch him right back.

Geneve, first, and always. His love stood by the fruit bowl, absently munching. Her face was dirty, a sooty smudge on her nose, but her eyes were bright. Beside her, Vertiline, metal hand free from gauntlet, but the Chevalier's expression was guarded. *No, that's not right. Tilly's haunted.*

Sight of Day curled on a divan beside Armitage. The Vhemin toyed with fruit but looked too tired to get into something that wasn't made of an animal. Sight of Day looked relaxed, golden eyes alert and ready, the cat ever curious. Armitage was two heartbeats from a coma.

Mazin still held his wineskin, hands clutching like it was a child's toy and he was near tears. His face was a roadmap to uncertainty, population two, because Yasmine flitted by his ear, her tiny face also confused.

Meriwether cleared his throat. "Thank you for coming. You're probably wondering why I called you here."

"Breakfast?" Geneve took another slice of fruit, this one purple-skinned. Meriwether had no idea what it was called.

"That's not breakfast," Armitage growled. "That's an insult."

{He's not wrong, for once. It is not made of meat.}

"They're *your* people," Vertiline said. "Get out there and lead them to a decent hearty meal."

"Later." Armitage closed his eyes, head lolling. "I need about forty hours' sleep."

"You'll get one or two." Meriwether sighed. "Both Yasmine and Mazin died, came back to life, and arrived with us. I'm not a big fan of coincidences. What's more pressing, though, is—"

"Where my sword is?" Geneve's hand clutched the hilt of her borrowed blade.

{I think we should talk more about the benefits of a proper breakfast.}
Swish, swish.

"What's more pressing," Meriwether gritted, "is where the third dead person is."

Silence. Blinks. Even Armitage looked up to scowl. The monster scratched an armpit. "We left a pile of dead assholes about two klicks that way." He pointed, arm swinging like a damaged compass. "Plenty there."

"It will be one specific person." Meriwether took another sip of wine. "It will be the third person the Three sent to help us before they disappeared."

Mazin nodded, nice and slow. "Three gods. Three helpers."

"I understand how Building is very important," glittered Yasmine, "but what purpose does a wine merchant serve? No offense."

"Wine." Meriwether raised his goblet. "I'll allow it's not a very compelling argument, but I propose an alternative theory. You are both *guides*. Yasmine, you helped me in the ancient's mountain."

"Heaven's Gate," Mazin said.

"Heaven's Death Rock, more like," Meriwether said. "There were living ... *dead* people in there. And an everliving lich, and other unpleasantries."

"Did you destroy the phylactery?" Geneve tensed like a bowstring.

"All the way dead, now," the sorcerer confirmed. "He's not getting up from that. Yasmine helped me through that, even as a damn bird—"

"Hey! I was fabulous!"

"And has continued to be my guide." Meriwether gave a tiny bow. "Thank you, Yasmine. You saved my life."

"Well, okay then," she huffed. "You're welcome." Her voice didn't sound like Meriwether was very welcome at all.

"Mazin guided Geneve through Imshir. He helped her evade capture, gave her a tonic to teach her Tebrani, and bought a horse so she could be here again." Meriwether frowned at his empty cup. "And brought some excellent wine. Let's not forget that."

Geneve selected a slice of what looked like dried apricot. "He has also kept me from death's door. I agree, his food and wine are top-shelf. Thank you."

"She eats like three people," Mazin complained. "You're welcome."

"Cophine, Ikmae, and Khiton." Meriwether counted on his fingers. "Three last gifts to this world: dead people resurrected, not like liches with their phylacteries and death magic, but living, breathing, their souls returned."

"That's forbidden, just like making a real person," Yasmine said. "We aren't allowed to Build that."

"If you make the rules, you can do what you want." Mazin toyed with his wineskin.

"Who has the third ... guide?" Vertiline frowned. "No one on our ship died and came back to life. I'd remember."

"No, they just died." Armitage winced at Vertiline's face. "Sorry."

{One step forward, two back. You are terrible with words.} Sight of Day rose, pacing. *{We are all here. Who else needs a guide?}*

"Requiem," Geneve breathed. "My sword."

"Sword's not a person," Armitage grumbled. "Unlikely to follow directions any better than you, Red."

Geneve's eyes flashed, then she grinned. "I've missed you, monster." She scanned the room, eyes lingering on Meriwether. "I've missed you all."

Meriwether felt warm, like the Light itself touched him for a moment. "Can we bookmark that?"

"Count on it," she said.

"Speaking of bookmarks." Mazin stroked his chin. "Perhaps the third is to ... guide us in? A stake in the sand. A beacon to follow. The north star. Like a moon, but glittering. A marker—"

"I think we have it." Vertiline nodded. "I'm sure we've got it."

"Sorry." Mazin frowned at his wineskin. "Something's off. This feels incomplete, a cake made without flour."

"Stop talking about real food, or I'll eat your horse," Armitage warned.

Mazin's lips quirked in a grin. "This feels like stone without mortar." At Armitage's approving nod, his grin widened. "I didn't come back to life to bring Geneve to a place she could see by herself. Lightning blasted Heaven's Gate. A dragon fell. These are not things a guide needs to show."

"You bought her a horse at the right time. You showed her back to Omrar." Meriwether shrugged. "I don't have all the pieces, but I fear the Precept has the third and the sword. Until we get them, we can't complete our quest."

"To save the world." Geneve nodded. "I really *need* my sword."

"Skymetal or glass, what does it matter?" Vertiline frowned. "You carry the Light like its master. I've never seen the like. You could use a broom handle and defeat the horde."

"Because of the smoke demon," Meriwether said. "Geneve used a shield of glass and couldn't cut it. She needs her damn sword, and she needs it now."

"How do you know this?" Yasmine's wings buzzed, confusion or anger bringing her closer.

"Hunch," Meriwether said. "The book I read? It spoke of the Boundless. It told of dragonriders, and yay verily, dragons too. A devilishly handsome sorcerer accompanied them to make three. There was one missing piece."

Yasmine glared. "Out with it, devilishly handsome sorcerer."

"We spend so much time looking at what is, rather than what isn't. Tresward use swords of glass. They encase themselves in good Smithsteel. We assume these things even when we're not told to ... who ever heard of Tresward marching with broom handles? If such a thing happened, we'd surely hear of it."

"Broom handles." Yasmine squinted at him from the safety of an arm's lengths, wings humming to iridescence. "You've lost me."

Meriwether doffed an imaginary cap to Vertiline. "Tilly's idea."

"I had no such idea!"

"Anyway," Meriwether charged on, "at no point in the book did it tell of glass swords. Smithsteel. They fought with none of that ... or found it not worth mentioning." He shrugged.

"That's it?" Armitage guffawed. "You think we should run into hell itself to get a sword because it *wasn't* on the page?"

"I think you should run into hell because you'll find it fun," admitted Meriwether. "The rest of us are doing it because it wasn't on the page."

"Madness," Yasmine breathed. "A kind I like."

{I'm with the insect. I always liked that sword.}

"I'm *not* an insect!"

"It makes a weird sense," Vertiline allowed. "Skymetal came from the heavens. A final gift, perhaps, against the darkness. Sent to the one Smith..." Her voice cracked like old clay. "Sent to a Smith with the skill and vision to forge it anew. Dropped by the Three just when we needed it. Given to one who could use it. The best swordswoman of all." She looked away.

Geneve grabbed her arm. "Tilly."

"Enough." Vertiline pulled her arm away, but without rancor. "I didn't have all my memories taken from me. I didn't have to do the work to make up for the Light's lack. When I lost," she waved her metal arm, "my balance, it was like I'd lost myself. I don't know how you did it."

"Orneriness," Armitage said.

{Mule headedness.} Sight of Day nodded.

"Perhaps it was the result of a head injury," Meriwether murmured.

Geneve glared, arms crossed. Her voice turned ominous. "Does anyone want to *get* a head injury?"

Vertiline smiled, tired and wan. "I could've said, Geneve. Iz and I carried a secret between us. To keep you safe, aye, that's how we justified it. You can justify any crime if you tell yourself it's for another's benefit. Especially if you don't ask them first."

Geneve looked sideways at Vertiline. "It is in the past. Sometimes family do stupid things. But they're always doing it because they care."

"Charming." Armitage shifted, scratching his belly. "Anyway. We've got zero skymetal swords. The enemy have all the damn swords. Which is still only one, but it's more than we've got."

"So we get the sword," Tilly snapped. "How hard can it be?"

{Depends if we have to fight a demon of smoke.}

Geneve squared her shoulders. Meriwether thought she looked like she prepared to face a bigger, stronger opponent, someone who would knock her to the dirt, but she was going to do it anyway. "It doesn't matter how hard it is. We need to do it."

Meriwether's heart went out to her. *We are the same. Not yet twenty summers but we shoulder the broken world handed down to us by those who walked before.* "No one told you to do this."

Her fist hammered the burnished sun on her breastplate. "The Three gave me this task. I'll see it done."

"They gave *us* this task." Vertiline stood by Geneve. Haunted or no, her chin jutted just the same. "*We'll* see it done."

"The Three didn't give me anything except shit for three squares a day." Armitage stood, rolling his shoulders. "But I'll see it done anyway."

"It's not your fight," Geneve said.

{We're making it our fight.} The cat slipped upright like water flowing backward. *{Sword, then the demon, then we go home. I can handle that.}*

Meriwether dredged up a lopsided smile. "Then we have an accord. Let's see if the dragon's finished sleeping." As he reached for a piece of dried fruit, a clanging came from outside. A poor man's alarm, ringing a warning.

Ormeon's voice shook the ground. *//YOU WILL STAND DOWN, OR BECOME ASH.//*

Geneve shared a look with him, then bolted from the tent. Meriwether sighed. *This shit never ends.*

Chapter Twenty-Seven

Geneve made weak daylight, head on a swivel. She spotted Ormeon's bulk to the east, wings spread in angry challenge. She pivoted, dust and sand spraying from her heels, and ran. The sun was still struggling to rise as she burst from a line of tents and into the open desert beyond the Vhemin encampment.

She saw Ormeon, runes on her face blazing brighter than the sun, wearing a dragon-red smile. A handful of Vhemin, rude weapons raised, but standing *behind* the dragon. A clutch of Feybrind beat Geneve here too, most unarmed, still wearing the smocks they arrived in. Beyond this scattering of defenders: the threat.

Geneve skidded to a halt, not comprehending. *Is this a trick?* Two hundred meters from Ormeon was a line of men and women wearing armor of the Tresward. Among them, more stood wearing the robes of Clerics. Geneve counted perhaps fifty Knights, and a little more than twenty Clerics. The Knights stood in three perfect rows, weapons sheathed. At their head, a lone elderly woman in Justiciar's garb, a slender staff of shod oak in her hand. Geneve blinked, rubbed her eyes, and blinked again, then called to the woman. "Eleni?"

The old woman nodded. "Knight Champion Geneve. We have much to discuss."

Geneve blinked—*again*—and swallowed. "What?"

//YOU KNOW THIS WOMAN?// Ormeon's gaze didn't leave the Knights and Clerics opposite. *//LAST TIME WE MET THE TRESWARD, WE ALSO MET THEIR STEEL. OR THEIR COWARDICE AS THEY LEFT US TO DO ALL THE WORK.//*

Eleni winced. "The dragon speaks true. But ... I'd borrow a moment of time anyway, sister."

Geneve wanted to turn away, to say she was no *sister* of the Tresward. She remembered Eleni's first words. *Knight Champion Geneve.* "I'm no Champion."

Eleni's smile was visible even from here. "And I'm no Justiciar, and yet here we stand. Shall we walk?"

They shared silence as much as steps. Eleni used her oaken staff to poke her way through the sand and scrub, while Geneve glowered at her side. The camp was far behind them, Knights still waiting, Clerics holding their peace. Geneve wanted to demand answers, to yell at the Justiciar, but she also remembered Eleni putting her back together, sharing kind words, and not judging her for her lack of skill with the Light. So, she contented herself with glowering and waiting. *I am good at only one of these.*

Eleni stopped, squinted back at their footsteps in the sand, then put both hands on her staff as she leaned on it. "I'm sorry."

Geneve pressed her lips into a line. "For what?"

"For everything the Tresward did, and also failed to do. We have wronged you, sister. And the price we payed was this." She spread a hand at their footsteps. "This is all we have left. Bought and sold against the armies of this world while demons battled for our realm."

"You..." Geneve shook her head. *It was me too.* "*We* killed sorcerers, Eleni. We hunted them, burning the life from them with steel and flame. They were our best hope against the darkness."

Eleni shook her head. "No. That's you. And," she chuckled, "the sorcerer who follows you."

Geneve turned away. "Don't forget the dragon."

"How could I? She is very impressive."

"Why are you here, Eleni?" Geneve rounded on the older woman. "Have you come for Meri? To use the cage on him, to Judge him? I won't allow it!" Fingers clutched for missing Requiem and touched the pommel of a borrowed blade.

Eleni marked her hand. "They say you speak with the voice of dragons."

Geneve simmered, then came off the boil. "It hurts my throat."

"No one in eight hundred years has done that." Eleni looked at her hands on the staff before her. "All we are is a shadow of what we were."

"No." Geneve shook her head, angry red hair lashing. "We are the purest heart of what they were. They gave us hope almost a thousand years ago. They burned their world to ash to do it, yet here we stand. A few of us, together, are ready to face our enemy again. I will not ask again, Eleni. Why are you here?" She felt her heart strain in her chest. *If they've come for Meri, I will kill them!*

Eleni bowed her head. "Fifty-seven Knights and twenty-seven Clerics stand at my back. Tilly came for aid, and when she left with not even a handful ... well. When I took over the Tresward, there was ... conflict. Some said you were a slave of dark masters. I called you Champion, not just of the Tresward, but the world." She gave a tiny shrug. "We are all that remains. And we're here to march against what you face, with you, and save this world from damnation."

"And of the rest?" Geneve put hands on hips, chest out, chin jutting. "Will more Tresward come to end us?"

Eleni bowed her head. "Perhaps I was unclear. There are no more Tresward. We are the last. Fifty-seven Knights. Twenty-seven Clerics. Vertiline. You. And me. That is all."

Geneve blinked. "Three's mercy."

"There was no time for mercy, only survival. You speak of ancient hope? I give you the purest distillation of that. Eighty-six. Eighty-nine, if you count us stragglers." This with a wry smile, vanished too quickly.

"You expect me to believe bygones are buried? That you're here to help?" Geneve felt her mouth turn down, teeth clenched.

"No." Eleni shook her head. "We're here to *win*, Knight Champion Geneve. There is no other option."

Geneve turned away from the old Cleric. *Her words ring true. She's not used Sway against me. If it's a ruse, I can't work out its meaning.* "And of Meri?"

A long pause. Ages past in those seconds. Eleni shuffled to Geneve's side. "There is no more Judgment. Not for your lover or any other sorcerer."

"What if we don't want your help?" Geneve scratched her hair, feeling as if the sand and dirt were getting under her skin.

Eleni laughed, short and tight. "Then we fight alone. We won't win without you, but we can't stand by."

"Why can't you win? You are the High Justiciar. You can make men hate their brothers or love a stranger. Your word changes the world. You could walk to Imshir," Geneve absently waved toward where the city waited, "and command the Precept to give you my sword."

Eleni nodded as if agreeing, but her shoulders tightened like a bowstring. "The Sway is the Three's word. A different weapon than the Storm, but just as effective. Tales say you've Swayed a man's soul back into his body." She tucked her hands into her sleeves, a small conceit for the desert's cold wind. "The Precept is no man. He is a demon of smoke and memory. The Sway holds no power over him. For that, we need the Storm."

Geneve rounded on Eleni. "How do you know I fought a demon of smoke?"

The Cleric took a step back, eyes wide. "I didn't."

"Then how—"

"Here." Eleni pulled a small book from her sleeve. It wasn't bound with leather, some ancient fabric holding the leaves together. "Your wizard might make sense of this. We've pored over it and got fragments. Half the truth or less, when weighed against the world." She offered the little tome.

Geneve took it, almost dropping it. For all it was no larger than her hand's span, it felt ... *heavy.* What had Eleni said? *When weighed against the world.* Geneve turned the small book in her hands, fingers running against the fabric binding. It was almost worn smooth, time and memory wearing it away. She lifted it to her face, breathing in the scent of ancient paper, and something sweet. Opening it she found a dried flower pressed between cover and first page. The breeze tried to steal it, but Geneve put her finger on the ancient stem. A purple head adorned the stalk. "A flower?"

"An eight-hundred-year-old flower, unless I miss my guess." Eleni shrugged. "That book was in the Justiciar's library. The *other* Justiciar, that is." She paused. "The dead one."

"I got it." Geneve flipped to a random page, but carefully, like she was turning a moth's wings. The text inside was written by hand. The person who'd written it shared Geneve's general distrust of pens, the writing a little cramped, but it held a firm structure for all that. She knew none of the letters, could speak no words of the ancient language. "What does it say?"

Eleni returned her hands to her sleeves. "I think it's a diary."

"A what now?"

"A small keepsake. A person would write their thoughts, hopes, loves, and fears onto the page."

Geneve raised an eyebrow. "Who would have time for such a thing?"

"Someone with many thoughts, hopes, loves, and fears." The High Justiciar showed a few teeth in her smile. "They say the writing of a thing lessens its burden. And, perhaps, gives the weight over. You feel it, don't you? The heaviness of the book. The worry in the pages. The things she could tell none other, because to share those fears would unman her comrades."

"Wait. She?"

Eleni nodded. "I think you hold the personal diary of Knight Champion Mireille. We don't have your sinner's..." She trailed off, biting her lip. "I'm sorry. Your sorcerer's gift of the ancients' tongue. A few words, scraps from a feast is all. Dates and times that remove all doubt from when it was written."

"Who was Mireille?"

"The first of the Boundless." Eleni's grin widened. "The last until now, if you'll forgive an old woman's whimsy."

"I'm no—"

"She rode a dragon and spoke with her voice." Eleni counted on her fingers. "Used the Storm. Counted one of the three holomancers who walked the world in her time as friend."

"There were other dragonriders. Other holomancers." Geneve wound down like an old clock, feeling tired, as if the book was a weight she'd carried too long, despite it being only minutes. *I'm tired. I've run without stopping for what seems an age. I want just ten minutes with my Meri. Five, if it pleases the Three, would do.* "There's just *me*, Eleni."

"No, child." Eleni toucher her jaw. "There's you. Vertiline. Eighty-six Knights and Clerics. Two hundred Feybrind, and five hundred Vhemin. A holomancer who can make imaginary worlds real. And a worn-out old crone."

Geneve snapped the book closed, clutching it in both hands. "What happened to her? What happened when she fought the Precept?"

"She died." Eleni sighed. "Or she retired. There are no more pages left. Mireille talks of fighting the forever foe of our world, her trust in her friends, and then nothing. The world broke. But we remain."

"Are you saying if I fight the Precept, I'll die? That Meri will die? Vertiline, too? Sight of Day will not make more swords, and Armitage won't get in more fights?" Geneve's voice felt small and tight, like over-wound clockwork.

"I'm saying what happened is in that book. Read it. Learn from Mireille. She trusted her worries to paper, so the next Boundless would find them and know what to do."

"And what do you think I should do?" Geneve searched the old woman's face. "I feel off course. Sailing against the wind."

Eleni turned toward the camp, setting off at a slow shuffle. "I think you should read the book. You should *definitely* let eighty-six Knights and Clerics help. More than anything, you should have a bath. After that, who knows?" She tossed a grin over her shoulder, showing a glimpse of a much younger woman for a heartbeat. "Perhaps prioritize that bath, though."

A bath, thought Geneve. *No, that's not the most important thing.* She faced the sky. "Ormeon!"

//YOUR PURPOSE, MY WORLD.// The dragon leaped from the camp in the distance, a speck resolving to majesty in a handful of heartbeats. She soared over a wide-eyed Eleni to *crump* before Geneve. *//WHERE ARE WE GOING?//*

Geneve vaulted into the saddle, running a hand against the dragon's warm scales. "We're going where we're most needed."

Chapter Twenty-Eight

I f there was one thing that would see them undone faster than facing impossible odds, it was getting shivved in the spine. Vertiline stalked the camp, looking for dissent.

The sands heated as the sun kissed them, the day going from cool to *quite nice thank you* in minutes. In an hour, it would be unbearable. She didn't want to get sunburn and chapped lips again. *I'm pale like snow, and like it I can't stand the sun's light for long.*

The Tresward she left behind. If the Knights turned on them, the fight would be bloody but quick. She might be good with a blade—*or a broom handle, aye?*—but Vertiline didn't like her odds against fifty or more of the Tresward's best. Add in a salting of Clerics, and that wasn't a fight she wanted.

She wandered off the camp's main thoroughfare, heading between tents and leather awnings. Vertiline spotted another's bootsteps in the sand before her and squatted to examine them closer. *I'm no tracker but I've marched enough. Those are Smithsteel treads.* She creaked upright, praying for a break in the fighting so she could get some sleep. Her back gave an unpleasant twinge, reminding her she'd been fired from a catapult before dropping her armor into the hungry deep, then worn twenty kilos of borrowed Smithsteel for days. Blade against sorcery, and then her hand...

My hand is either blessing or curse. It was made by ancient men and women who thought they knew best. They broke the world but made dragons. Do I carry one of their greatest works, or worst mistakes?

The clash of steel brought her out of her reverie. Back forgotten, she charged forward, bursting into a huddle of tents. A Knight stood, a tall blond man with a jaw you could break rocks against. His helmet lay on the sands, and he faced a giant Vhemin woman whose jaw was even more impressive. They stood, blade on blade, as the sun crept through the lines of tents to dapple shadows on the ground.

Vertiline's sword was in her hand before her brain found its footing ... then she held. *Do I fight the Tresward? Do I stand with him? Is the monster a monster? Does she need help?*

Both combatants froze, staring at her. Then the Knight smiled, clear and bright, like he hadn't just spent days marching across a blasted wasteland. "Well met, Knight Valiant Vertiline."

"I, uh." She scrambled for better words. "Who are you?" Vertiline winced. *Better words, nonce. Better!* "Uh. How do you know my name?" The wince sharpened.

"Knight Adept Adrien, at your service." Adrien's smile didn't falter. "Your deeds are legendary in a time without hope. You travel with Knight Champion Geneve to save our world. How could we not know your name? The earth rings with the sound of it."

The Vhemin woman sniffed. "I didn't know her name. I like her hair, though."

Save ... our world? I just killed our armada! Vertiline flailed for something that wouldn't make her sound like a child. "Uh." Another wince. *Stop stammering. By the Three, you're a Knight of the Tresward. Act like it.* "I thought you two were fighting. For real."

The Vhemin sniffed again, then spat something vile onto the sand. "For someone good with a blade you seem to know precious little about how fighting works. There's usually blood. A lot of it. Maybe some steaming guts in a pile. Be some screaming too, I reckon." She nodded sagely. "You see blood, guts, or hear screaming?"

"No." Vertiline sheathed her blade, then scrounged around for a lopsided smile. "In fairness, if I were in the fight you wouldn't have time to scream." She held up both hands, metal and flesh side by side. "But I agree, there's no guts in a pile, nor any blood. Your point stands."

Armitage bulled in from nowhere, slamming into the female monster. They scudded sideways, and Armitage pounded a fist into her head, one, two, and on the third, a crunch of teeth. He hefted her skyward, then dropped her onto the sand.

Adrien winced. "Hold a moment."

Armitage panted, scanning about. "I thought I beat you fuckers so you wouldn't start some unnecessary shit."

Vertiline examined her still-raised hands, then lowered them. "A baron late and a regal short, monster. There was no brawl."

"I was teaching Mallet how to deal with the three-point reaching strike from Cophine's first stanza, *It Begins*." Adrien sidled around Armitage, helping the woman to her feet.

"Do you see blood? Hear screaming? See guts in a pile?" Vertiline gestured to the sand at their feet. "No? Then there's no fight."

Armitage blinked. "I thought—"

"You thought to white knight in here and save the damsel." Vertiline clenched her teeth to stop screaming. *I don't know why I'm so angry.* "Do you see any damsels among the invisible blood, guts, and silent screaming?"

"Uh—"

"That's my line!" she yelled.

"Uh," Adrien offered. "I feel as if this morning's taken a sharp turn into the bad part of town."

Vertiline shouldered past Armitage, her much smaller frame be damned, because fury rode her like the Storm. She grabbed Mallet's arm, hauling the woman about. Vertiline had no fixed destination in mind, except *anywhere but here*. She charged between the tents.

After a handful of meters, safely past earshot, Mallet shook her arm free, spat another tooth onto the sand, and tilted her neck to the left it made a loud *crack*. "That's better."

Her words sounded like she was speaking through a sock, but

Vertiline expected having lost a bunch of teeth would do that. "Are you okay?"

"See any guts—"

"Aye, aye, I remember. No guts, nor do I hear screaming. There's a mote or two of blood, though." Vertiline swept back her pale hair. "It looked rough."

Mallet hitched her pants up. "I could use a drink."

"It's barely breakfast time."

"The ale won't mind." The monster turned about a full circle, oriented herself with the rising sun, then set off in a westerly direction. After trudging in silence for a few minutes they arrived at a wider circle between tents. Blazing in the middle was a bonfire, around which cold-blooded monsters huddled for warmth. A large pavilion sagged to the north. Mallet headed toward it.

Inside were benches and tables, more rude planks set to a new purpose than thoughtful construction. On the benches: Vhemin. On the tables: tankards, cups, and Vertiline even spied a mug made out of a skull. The northern wall held a more impressive table bearing large vats. It was too early for the flies to have shown much interest. Braziers burned, making the interior uncomfortably warm, but the Vhemin needed the heat.

Mallet shoved through the throng, heading for the vats. She rummaged on the ground beneath the table, found two mugs of questionable provenance, and scooped to the brim from the vats. Mallet handed one to Vertiline, then pushed her way toward a table with a couple spare seats at one end.

They sat. Vertiline stared into her cup. "What's this?"

"An alcohol."

"No, I understand that. What kind of alcohol?"

"Dunno." Mallet sniffed her cup, then took a swallow. "The good kind, I reckon."

Vertiline tested her own brew. It smelled of honey and spices, but if it was ale it was much stronger than she was used to. "It's quite," she coughed, "strong."

"Kinda bland, I think." Mallet took another swig. "Gets the blood going, though. So. You're Tresward too?"

Vertiline thought about that. "I was, once."

"I didn't think you fuckers quit."

"We don't." She scratched angry fingers through her hair. "But ... things happened."

Mallet grunted. "You fell in with a bad crowd. Monsters, all."

"I..." Vertiline thought about Armitage. How the monster tried to save her—*her!*—from his own. How he'd dived off a ship into water sure to kill him, for *her*. The countless, myriad times he'd stood against his doom so they could live. "There are no monsters, Mallet. Only the ones we carry inside. I spent my life fighting for the Light. Carrying the Three's word. Turned out, it was a lie. Oh, don't look so surprised. The gods are real. Cophine, Ikmae, and Khiton are as real as this." She took another swig. It wasn't half-bad on the third try. "But they're ... *missing*. Their word is misremembered. Repeated with the creative embellishments humans use to tell the stories they want to hear. Over time, we stopped being a shield. Tresward turned into a weapon. Agents of darkness pointed us at their foes, and we blindly followed. We never questioned. Didn't look up at the moons and wonder why."

"Another?" Mallet gestured to Vertiline's empty cup.

"Oh, my." Vertiline blinked at her cup. "How did I talk and drink at the same time?"

"It's a kind of magic." The monster stood, elbowing toward the 'bar.' Vertiline watched her go.

Another Vhemin sat before her. Tall and meaty, like a boulder made of muscle. Yellow snake eyes. Sharp shark's teeth. "You got a fucking problem?"

Quiet spread out from the question. The people at their bench stopped talking, turning those snake eyes to watch. Behind her, tables stilled. The ripple of silence washed to the pavilion's entrance, and out into the morning sun beyond.

"Aye," Vertiline said. "But it's not you."

The Vhemin loomed forward, hands pressed to the table. His weight made it creak. "What if *my* problem's *you?*"

Vertiline felt no fear. For all she was flat-footed, sword awkwardly tangled by her legs under the table, she had a pattern for this. The patterns were never the problem. Tresward knew all the clever ways to shear a man's soul from his skin. *I could kill this brute with a wet sponge.* She took a breath. *But I don't want to. I don't want what makes him unique to stop.* "Then I'll go. I offer my apology for offense. I … didn't know I wasn't welcome."

She stood, swaying with the ale inside her, found her balance, and faced the pavilion's entrance. Daylight and a half a thousand Vhemin waited beyond.

The monster surged from the table, slapping a mug aside. It sprayed ale, clattering to the sandy floor. He vaulted the table, hulking before her. "Who said you could go?"

Vertiline peered around him. Ten more steps and she'd be free. *But what do I deserve of freedom?* She drew her sword whisper-quiet, cobra fast, the blade finding its rest against the monster's neck. His eyes bugled in alarm, but she didn't cut. Vertiline held the moment for three of her calm heartbeats and what was no doubt thirty of his, then lowered her blade and offered him the hilt. "Take it."

He blinked, then snatched it from her. Good Smith-forged glass it was, holding the light beyond the pavilion's entrance. He didn't know how to use it, but it'd stand a single slice against her neck before it broke. She took his hand, gently like he was a child, and raised it so the blade rested against her throat. "Like this, see? A moment's thought, and you can end it all. End the monster that's killed so many." Vertiline closed her eyes and breathed, just *breathed*, and waited for it.

The kiss of glass left her neck. She opened her eyes, saw the monster drop the blade to the sand. "You're crazy."

"Aye." She scooped a toe under the sword, flicking it to her shoulder height and snatching it from the air. *I'm not going to die this morning. Maybe later today. Could I do something good before then?* "But I'm a good enough teacher, too. Would you like to learn how to respond to the three-point reaching strike from Cophine's first stanza, *It Begins?*"

Chapter Twenty-Nine

When Meriwether reached the dragon, she was already fast asleep, without any evidence of a dragonrider in residence. He'd seen Ormeon wing the short hop from where Geneve spoke with the head of her order, *crump* to the earth, and then ... nothing. No Knight with red hair. No harsh words, either. Just ... a missing piece of his heart.

What *was* with the dragon was a boy. Meriwether was no great judge of Vhemin ages, but if the lad were human he'd count ten summers his own. Ormeon was a curl of red scale, nose nestled under tail like a giant puddle of armored cat. The great bellows of her flank rose and fell like the seas, the depth of her breathing a calming balm to Meriwether's scattered nerves.

The boy didn't look up when Meriwether approached. He squatted on his haunches, peering into the dragon's face from a not entirely safe distance of five meters. The urchin had the same scaled look as the rest of his people, perhaps with a lighter shade of skin. *Three's Mercy, the lad's broader of shoulder than I am and he's not half-grown.* Meriwether thought about walking away, then thought about all the trouble he might have got into with a dragon at the age of ten, and anchored his feet in the sand. "Ho, lad."

The lad cocked his head a fraction but didn't turn. "Aye?"

"Seen a dragon around here?"

That got a turn of the head. "He's right here!" A fling of the arm, and a snort of derision even Vertiline would envy.

"She," Meriwether corrected. "The dragon's a girl."

"How can you tell?" The lad went back to staring at the creature before him. His voice didn't have the gravel of a Vhemin full-grown, but wasn't the high-pitch a human child would have. Somewhere middle of the road, and an incautious man might think him older than his years.

"That's a surprisingly good question I'm in no frame of mind to answer." Meriwether pulled his jacket closer about his shoulders. The sun was climbing higher, shedding heat like a molting dog flung hair, and for all it defied reason his ancient's jacket kept the temperature at bay. "Did you stumble here by accident? Get lost?"

The boy swiveled again, pity for Meriwether etched on his monster's face. "The camp is tiny. Only an imbecile would get lost."

"Aye, I didn't want to say, is all."

The boy thought about turning pity to a glare, then laughed. "You're a dragonrider?"

"More a dragonpassenger." Meriwether tugged his ear. "Red does all the flying." He lowered his voice. "Just between us, I'm not sure that's true. I'm pretty sure Ormeon does the flying and puts up with her."

"The dragon has a name?"

"The dragon does." Meriwether nodded. "She's quite smart too, for a dragon." He checked Ormeon's closed eyes. *Still asleep. Good.*

"I want to be a dragonrider." The boy went back to gazing at the dragon before him. He'd fit in one of Ormeon's massive scaled, clawed hands with room to spare but there was no fear in him. Just ... wonder. "They say I'll hold a spear for the tribe, but how can I do that when I know about dragons?"

"Can you hold a spear?"

"Can you?"

"Not well," Meriwether admitted. "There are fighters in this world. Strong men and women ready to stand shoulder to shoulder against any odds. I'm more of a screaming and running kind of guy."

The lad raised an eyebrow. "You ride a dragon. I saw you at the fight, standing with your people behind King Armitage."

"Oh, 'King Armitage' is it?" Meriwether made a mental note to put a fork in that one later. "Armitage is a friend of mine. He's one of the strong fighters. I'm more like a, a..." He mentally clutched for the right word.

"A mascot?"

"Not quite," Meriwether gritted. "Perhaps a jester, though." He ambled closer to the lad, squatting beside him. "Everyone needs to laugh. I'm Meriwether. The best of my friends call me Meri."

The boy looked up. "Hi. I'm, uh."

"Uh, aye? A good, strong Vhemin name."

"Most people call me Van."

Meriwether pondered on that, then decided not to kick over the stones hiding what else the boy was called. "Van, did you see Ormeon land?"

"Yeah. Hard to miss. Big dragon. Wings! Then she fell asleep." Van put his chin on crossed arms.

"Speaking of things hard to miss, where did the red-haired Knight go? The *actual* dragonrider."

A shrug. "I was watching the dragon."

"Fair enough." Meriwether eased himself into a cross-legged position. "Are there many Vhemin children here?"

Van sighed. "Only two. There were five more last week, but they got eaten by sand sharks."

Meriwether wound that sentence through his mental fingers. He softened his voice. "And how many the week before that?"

The boy shrugged. "I can only count to ten."

Three's mercy. Meriwether craned about, taking in the sand, the sun, and the rickety Vhemin encampment. "So much blood is spilled against the sand."

"It's what the sand's for." Van scratched an armpit. "Don't they teach you anything?"

"Not enough, it seems." Meriwether's attention was drawn by a glimmer as Yasmine flitted from the tent line to whizz about his head.

She backed away, then perched on Ormeon's nose. The dragon didn't stir.

Van's eyes opened wide as plates. "A fairy!"

"I like this one," Yasmine said. "Notices the important things."

"Apparently they're tasty." Van smacked his lips. "You roast 'em, see, and—"

"I no longer like this one," the fairy said.

"Why would you bother eating a fairy?" Meriwether glanced between the two. "Hardly any meat on one."

"I don't like you either," Yasmine said.

Meriwether laughed. "Ho, Yasmine. This is my friend Van. Van, this is Yasmine Glittercone. She saved my life. Barely taller than my hand, but her heart is as big as the world."

Yasmine crossed her arms. "Okay. I like you a little bit."

Van leaned forward. "Yasmine. I like the sound of that name. Vhemin names are ... so practical. Rough. Ugly." He looked away, staring at the open desert.

Yasmine's glare softened, and she flitted to hover before Van. "Vhemin names are like Vhemin people. Strong, like the pillars of the world. Heavy, like an anvil. If you drop a Vhemin name on stone, it rings like a steel hammer." She sighed. "In days gone, you were the crutch on which we all leaned. We've all forgotten the way back. There's no map. But your names remember what you were, Van."

Van blinked. "What?"

"Good talk." Meriwether clapped his hands. "Have you seen Geneve?"

The fairy mock-slapped her forehead. "Oh! That's right. I came here to find you."

"Because of Geneve?"

"Aye." The fairy glimmered for a moment. "She needs your help."

MERIWETHER GOT HIS FIRST CLUE NOT ALL WAS RIGHT WHEN THE Vhemin population thinned out. The camp wasn't huge, holding just five hundred monsters, but they came of a certain size and weight and left an impact. A single Vhemin was bothersome, a noisy hulking mound of meat that damaged anvils like normal folk broke eggs. A clutch was worthy of concern even for the stoutest of hearts, and it was told in tavern corners that even the Tresward thought twice about facing them in numbers greater than ten.

Geneve showed no such fear, even at the start. Before she carried the Light, she stood between me and the horrors of this world. Of course, back then she was carrying me to execution, but let's not allow a trifle like that to spoil a happy memory.

The creatures normally huddled in fours and fives, but twenty meters into the thick of the camp he only saw the odd brute shambling about. When they caught sight of him, the reaction was always similar: a widening of the eyes, a duck of the head, and then a swift about-turn to walk *away* from Meriwether. He checked himself, patting his ancient's garb with quick hands. No, no blood spatters or giblets—not that they'd concern Vhemin. No stray illusions dogged his heels. Just Meriwether, following a glitterbug fairy.

He cleared his throat. "What's going on?"

"Stuff," Yasmine said, in a tone that was neither helpful nor clarifying.

"Is Geneve okay?"

"She will be, if you pick up your feet." The fairy spun about, clapping tiny hands. "Chop chop."

"You what?"

"Oh. Right. You might not know that one." She *hmmm'd*. "*Ándele.*" At Meriwether's blank stare, she gave a tiny-yet-somehow-massive sigh. "Hurry up."

"I'm hurrying." Meriwether picked up his pace, following glowing dust Yasmine left in her wake. She rounded a corner of tents, flitted over a still-bubbling pot above a cookfire, and took a sharp right. Meriwether lost sight of her for a moment, panic touching him for a hot second. He broke into a jog, foot slipping on loose sand, rounding the corner to see...

Nothing. No fairy, no Vhemin, not even blood or tousled sand to mark an encounter. A wall of tents led a short ten-meter path to a larger one. Canvas gave a tired flutter in the desert wind. Meriwether looked into the dark maw of the large tent, raked hair back, squared his shoulders, and marched forward.

He burst into the tent's interior, hand raised and ready to cast a spear of light. Meriwether's eyes took a moment to adjust to the lower light. He spied a clutch of candles atop a rickety table. Beside them, a selection of fruits and bread. A pitcher stood, clutching cold moisture to its side, next to two battered metal cups. Meriwether lowered his hand as he turned. Geneve's armor glinted on the sand to the side, the burnished sun smirking from beneath a tossed pile of gauntlets, greaves, chain, padding, and other death-defying accoutrements. A pile of furs and pillows held their peace in an inviting pile.

The floor had been laid with tired rugs, but the sand was beaten from them. The rugs laid a clean path toward a massive washtub, bubbles aplenty in the water, a fire smoldering below. The washtub looked to have been repurposed into a bath, and bobbing like the world's happiest cork in the water was Geneve. Her face split into a grin like the sun coming over the horizon after a night of lapping the world, and Meriwether felt the same on his lips. He took a stumbling step forward, then caught himself. "How?"

"That's the question you want to ask?" She moved to the water's edge, ripples slopping suds over the side.

"I don't really *want* to ask questions, but my dumb brain just works that way."

"Yasmine's a Builder. She ... helped." Geneve brushed damp red hair aside. "Now, come here."

THIS CAN'T LAST. MERIWETHER STARED AT THE TENT'S CEILING, HIS mind making patterns with the rippling canvas and the markings left on it by time and memory. His fingers drew lazy circles on Geneve's shoulder. She lay sprawled atop him, red hair hiding half her face. Geneve's lips were slightly open, her eyes closed, and her entire body held the boneless weight of exhaustion mixed with contentment. His hand stilled for a moment, and she growled. "Who said you could stop?"

Meriwether's hand picked up the pace again. *This can't last, because I'm happy, and I'm never happy for long. The love of my life is here. She didn't run off to slay demons or save worlds. She stole my fairy to make a wonderland, if but for a moment. And thus, it's doomed.* Despite this he smiled to himself, because he was damned if he wasn't going to enjoy it. He moved his hand to the back of her neck. She groaned but didn't move a muscle. *Geneve is exhausted. She has been running and fighting, but more, she's carried all the world for a spell. It's heavy.*

He shifted, glancing at the scattered clothes on the rugs. His ancient's coat, black as purpose. Her borrowed sword resting beside her armor. Something dug into his back, and he wriggled for a moment, fishing with his free hand. Geneve growled, but there wasn't any fight in it, so he continued fishing until his fingers found the offending object. It was a book, the cover a hand's span tall. Ancient like his clothes, but weathered in a way they would never be. He opened the cover, spying a flattened purple flower, pressed ages ago, perhaps just for him. Meriwether propped the book on his chest, careful not to knock Geneve with it, and began to read.

It took a little effort. Aye, aye, he knew the language, he'd learned enough of it not long ago, and this was easier than the High Magic. It was how the ancients spoke, and he understood that well enough. The author had no love of the pen, dueling with the page as if it were a sacred duty. "This person writes worse than you do."

Geneve opened one eye. "How did you get that?"

"It was stabbing me in the spine."

"That's odd." She wriggled into him, closing her eyes. "It was with my armor. I don't know how it flew here."

"Sometimes things are where they need to be."

"Oh indeed, wise sage?" She raised an eyebrow, eyes still closed.

"No, really. That's the first line."

She raised her head, suddenly awake. "You can read it?" He gave her a withering eyebrow raise, which she ignored. "What does it say?"

"Besides, 'Sometimes things are where they need to be?'" She dug a knuckle into his ribs, which he felt was unfair, but laughed. "Aye, okay. Settle."

"Tell me to settle again. I dare you."

"Fair." Meriwether shouldered his way into the furs. "Let's see now."

SOMETIMES THINGS ARE WHERE THEY NEED TO BE.
This diary. This pen.

"OH!" GENEVE BRUSHED BACK HER HAIR. "I KNOW WHAT A DIARY IS. It's a book for people with too much time to tell people who don't care about things that aren't important."

"Hush," Meriwether said. "This might be important."

She *hmph'd* onto his chest. "If you say so."

THIS PEN. THIS WORLD. IT SPINS ON THE FINGERTIPS OF ANGELS, A SHINY *bauble for demons beyond the gate. And me.*

I'm the last to stand against the demons. It hasn't happened yet, of course. My holomancer sees it coming. My dragon feels it. The Three's Wardens stand ready, and all will die.

"THREE'S WARDENS. MUST BE TRESWARD," MERIWETHER MUSED.

"You think? Keep reading."

Meriwether thumbed further through the diary, looking for an interesting passage. "Ah."

THE BATTLES ARE ENDLESS. WE STAND, AND THEY BREAK AGAINST OUR shields. Demons are hard to kill. The Light and Sway work, but only against the smaller ones. The archdemons seem impervious. Renly fought their leader yesterday. I remember his touch, his kisses, but I'm already forgetting the shape of his face. We had to leave his body on the battlefield. It was twisted and broken, like the butcher's boy from my village. After the wagon hit him, there wasn't much left of the lad that made him look different from the wares he sold.

Weapons of cold iron do almost nothing. Actinic lances make them angry. Pure dragonfire does the same, but the dragons are almost all gone. Our Skyforges run dry, and there are few Three's Wardens with enough soul left to power them. Battlements are overrun, villages lost, and the endless hordes of Vehement System's monstrous creations surge like the sea against our sandy shores.

Our Fey Branded die, and I cannot bear to look. They tell me they're slaves, without will or purpose, but I have killed more monsters wearing the skins of men than demons. I feel the shape of the lie the Justiciars tell because it is a brittle sort of half-truth that binds us like a bloody bandage. The Fey are people, brave, and scared. So I turn my face away and hope they don't see my tears. As Knight Champion, I'm their strength. As Boundless, I cannot fail.

If we stop dying, the demon gate closes. Our world remains ours. But we can't stop dying.

"THAT'S ... GRIM." MERIWETHER FELT THE DRYNESS OF HIS MOUTH.

Geneve's eyes were hard, the green of stony emerald. "Keep reading."

"I don't know—"

"Keep reading," she hissed. "She won. We must know how. Tomorrow, we may need her armor."

WE PUT THE MOONS ABOVE TO WATCH US. THE LAST OF OUR BUILDERS made them, and if they don't work, we can't make more. The moons are our last weapon. They were Cophine's idea. Ikmae urged her on. But it was Khiton who gave us the know-how to finish it. He told me—

"WHAT?" GENEVE STARTLED UPRIGHT. "SHE SPEAKS MADNESS, THIS woman. You cannot speak to a god."

"Do you want me to keep reading or not?" Meriwether snapped the diary closed. "You seem agitated."

She surged from the furs, stalking to the pitcher of wine. Geneve poured two glasses, then snatched a heel of bread and chewed like a feral. Meriwether marveled at her grace, the smoothness of her skin. He pulled the furs up to cover his body, and the thousands of scars across his skin, the memory of what seemed an endless past of beatings.

Geneve caught the movement. She hurried back, tugging the furs free. "Don't hide from me, love. Don't ever hide."

"I ... made mistakes," he said.

Her fingers touched his chest, tangled briefly in the strands of hair, then walked down to his stomach. "You—"

Meriwether clutched her hand. "You are what this world needs." Her eyes widened. "You were built by an ancient order, a gift handed down through the ages to be the shield we need, just when we need it. I am a broken, useless thing. I have no purpose. No, don't interrupt. I'm not proud. I don't need to stand in the Three's Light. I just ... don't understand why you're with me."

She enfolded his hands in hers. "Because you are what this world needs, too. You say you made mistakes, and that you're broken. Kytto told me the best steel is folded a hundred, nay, thousand times. It's continually broken, over and over, ash and coal hammered into its length, to make a thing that is bright and sharp and strong and true." Geneve's eyes were wet, perhaps at the memory of her old friend and teacher. "There is nothing in this world with strength that wasn't broken. Your father was a monster. Aye, I know villains and demons. I've bared steel and fought the worst. And none of the bad ones *look* bad, Meri. They all wear silken smiles and profess kindness to your face."

"That feels true."

"It's as true as the sun above. You have a thousand kisses of the lash on your skin. You know what that tells me?" She waited him out, and when he shook his head Geneve bared her teeth. "It tells me you didn't ever kneel inside." Her finger touched his heart. "If you did what was asked, expected, you'd have unblemished skin and a broken soul. When I look at you, I see what we," she touched her chest, "should be. Valiant. True. Bright and sharp. Strong."

"Uh," Meriwether said.

"Wine?"

"Please."

She left him to his thoughts while she shouldered her way into a shirt. Geneve brought wine back to the furs, and the tray of fruits and bread. She put the tray on his lap, then fetched the diary from the floor. "Read it. I need to know how it ends."

Meriwether took the diary, then flipped to the very end. He took a breath, not sure if he wanted to know, then dived into a dead woman's world for the last time.

TOMORROW, I DIE.

My dragon Rulbenen believes we will win, but I've not told her about the moons, and our last, desperate chance. I will do my part, but I can't bear to see the last of the Wardens die. If we fail, there must be some to remember, and carry on the fight.

Rulbenen told me of a last Skyforge. It's in the fertile lands across the seas. Our grain supplies run low. Perhaps the ships sink. Or the lands are no longer fertile. We've sanded the world dry with our weapons, and there's so little left. Rulbenen told me I was being melodramatic when I said this to her. She asked whether one more dragon would make a difference. Tip the scales. Perhaps it was a dragon joke.

I told her no. I don't want another dragon to die, even if it's the greatest one ever made. We have no more souls to power them, anyway. We'll let the dragon sleep. Rulbenen said it's a female, and I said I didn't care. I shouted at Rulbenen, and she shouted back. This is how the world ends, reader. Not because the enemy carves our hearts from our chests, but because we do their work for them.

After this entry, I will find my dragon and tell her I'm sorry. I'll tell her I love her, and ask her to stay here when we go to fight. She won't, but I have to try. If you've shared time with a dragon, you would understand. They, like all the things we make, are so much better than us.

We drop the weapon on the Precept tomorrow. It will—

GENEVE SNATCHED THE BOOK FROM HIM, PEERING AT THE PAGE AS IF she could make sense of it. "Precept?"

"Aye. This word." Meriwether tapped the page with his finger.

"Oh, no," Geneve breathed. "She didn't win."

IT WILL BREAK THE EARTH WHERE IT LANDS. THE WEAPON IS STRONG enough to boil the oceans and burn the land. We will rape our world so the demons die. This is the cost of winning.

I will be at the front. Blade against blade, distracting the monster. Holding him steady, right there, so the weapon will end him. The Builders think if we kill enough of us all at once, it will be like starving a fire of air. The fire goes out and can't be rekindled until the air comes back.

We are the air. They are the fire.

Cophine, Ikmae, and Khiton will be with me. They promised their aid. They've anointed my sword and tell me it will cut true. All had sad eyes as they handed it back to me.

I don't want their sadness. I know I go to save millions. The cost of my life is nothing.

If you're reading this, remember us. We fought so you wouldn't have to. Remember our mistakes. And remember what it costs when we hate each other so much it hurts.

"WHAT'S NEXT?" GENEVE SIPPED WINE.

"A blank page." Meriwether turned the diary to face her.

"She died?" This in a small voice, face down, red hair draping like a curtain. "So be it."

"Aye, I think she died. But the manner of it is … not expected." Meriwether frowned, tapping a word on the page. "The gods anointed her blade. What do you think that's about?"

"Not expected?" Geneve brushed red hair aside. "What's *expected* about facing an army of demons?"

He raised his hands in surrender. "No, love. That's not what I mean. I think I saw her. There was a lich."

"Aye, you've said as much, but not dredged the depths of the tale." She looked away. "Which I thought was unusual, with you being so generous with words."

"Hey!"

"Truth is truth."

"I'll grant you that." Meriwether ambled toward his clothes, slinging his arm through a sleeve. *This fabric's a marvel. So fine a weave, so smooth on the skin.* "Florian Arsenault was the risen master of a dead kingdom. His people brought the Feybrind into this world. Aye, wonders, but wrought by villains. He gave no thought to the cost to us or his creations." Meriwether paced. "He showed me battles. We walked fields of corpses. Or, I did the walking, and he did the talking."

"Was your mouth bound?"

"Hush, now." Meriwether slipped into his pants, then fossicked for a boot. "I saw the first dragon, I think. He was marvelous, of course, but died like a perfect sunset. Feybrind fighting Vhemin, claw against steel, fear against rage. Humans, watching for a time, then dying just the same. At the end, a mighty battle. A land, blasted back to stone. Nothing grew, Red. Everything was dead. Great furrows lay on the skin of the earth, carved there by the weapons of gods."

"Not gods, Meri." Geneve shook her head. "Just people."

"There was nothing just about it. It was wicked. The demons didn't have to fight us. They urged us on, sure, but we did all the heavy lifting." He fell silent, remembering the blasted world he'd seen, Florian's silky voice at his ear, comforting, sure, and utterly evil.

Geneve took his hands. Looked into his eyes, her green to his brown. "And then you saw her?"

"Aye." Meriwether pulled away. "I thought it was you. A cruel joke pulled from my memory. A valiant Knight, fallen on the battlefield. I couldn't see her face, but the red of her hair was the same as yours. The armor was different, but not so much. Sleeker, perhaps, or more finely crafted, like this." He held up his ancients' sleeve. "She fell like a broken toy."

Geneve's voice was a whisper. "What killed her?"

"Heartbreak, perhaps. I saw no sign of Rulbenen. But no, that's too trite." He sniffed. "Here's the way of it. Her body lay at the bottom of a vast crater. It was two klicks I walked to reach her. There were plenty of Knights dead on the field behind her, but none about where she fell. I think she..." Meriwether shook his head. "I know little of the Light and its masteries, save what I've seen you practice. I know Cophine's the start, and Ikmae guides you through the dark middle chapter. Khiton waits with a steady hand to end things. I see beauty in how you move. The cry of larks when you swing your sword perfectly, or the flight of butterflies when you block a killing blow. I've seen it all, including heaven's wrath when the Storm fights with you. There was nothing like that where she lay, Red. There was nothing at all. I like to think she shielded her fellows. Took the blow of the gods' weapon on her shield and carried the power of it to her grave. But..."

Geneve looked down. "But life's not that easy."

"Life's not *fair*, is the problem." Meriwether shrugged. "I think she did all that I said, but one thing more. I think she starved the killing strike of power, and that's why the Precept lives on. She made a bad call by saving her friends, her *family*, but the worst of demons survived. Bided his time, built his army, and now eight hundred years past her death, we must fight them again. Except this time we have no gods in the sky above. The moons broke when we fought the last archdemon. They sent us guides, but they're confused fools. No, don't interrupt. I call Yasmine a friend, good and true. It's clear Mazin is like a brother to you. But they offer us nothing, Geneve. Less than half a story, and not even the good part." He shook his head. "We don't have their actinic lances. The Artifices lay silent, machines as dead as their masters. The mountain of Heaven's Gate used to be a bulwark against the dark, but it's full of weeping ghosts and a broken magic mirror. All the beautiful dragons but Ormeon are gone. We have but a single Builder, bless her heart. Less than one hundred Tresward remain. We have five hundred Vhemin and two hundred Feybrind with no reason to fight our battles. We stand here, on the raggedy edge of our fate, and I see nothing but darkness before us."

"Good pep talk." Geneve tried for a smile, but it crumbled like badly made caulking.

"At least our wine merchant has good stock." Meriwether's lips quirked.

"Your wine merchant has excellent stock." Mazin's voice brought him round whippet quick. The fat man grinned. "Oh, don't be so surprised to see me here. When things are darkest, they can only get brighter. And for that, I have a fine Tebrani red."

Geneve gave the merchant a grateful smile. "Wine we could use, no mistake. But more than that brings you here, no?"

"I bring much-needed good news, it seems." He let the tent flap fall closed behind him and counted on his fingers. "The Feybrind killed a clutch of sand sharks, so we have meat for lunch. The Vhemin and the cats are sharing recipes, and neither party is talking of barbecued human. The best of my winter stores remain—fifty fine bottles of red to share with all our friends, and if that doesn't give people fire in their bellies I don't know what will. Oh. And Omrar's here. He brings more much-needed good news."

Geneve waited, and when Mazin's smile only grew wider, she boiled over. "What is it?"

Mazin steepled his fingers, an orator delivering his best and final line. "He knows where your Requiem sings her final song."

Geneve turned to Meriwether, her face broken in a savage grin. "My *sword*. You spoke many truths, holomancer, but one thing rang false."

"Aye?" Meriwether cocked his head. "I've been known to trade a lie or three in my time, but never with you. Or, uh, not recently."

"Recently?" She shook her head. "Doesn't matter. You said she made a bad call by saving her friends. Yet here's one of ours, with a gift we don't deserve. It's never a bad call to save those you love." She strode from the tent, tugging her sash tight, the ends of it trailing a dance.

Meriwether stood alone for a quiet moment. "I hope you're right. And curse me, I'd make the same call, too. Perhaps that's why we failed last time. We're too weak to do what's needed." He bowed his head. *My father wouldn't have been too weak. But he sided with monsters. Is this our fate—to be monsters or their food?* Squaring his shoulders, he marched in Geneve's footsteps, but without the same sureness of tread.

Chapter Thirty

Geneve found Omrar waiting astride a horse a respectful distance from a clutch of rough-looking Vhemin scouts. She rode out on Nightrunner, Meri at her back, looking for the old man.

He hadn't made it to the camp proper, and had the manner of a man with no desire to. Omrar's eyes moved from his escort to the camp in the distance and back again. His fingers never strayed far from the chain spear dangling from his horse's saddle.

The horse also looked like it had places it'd rather be. She stamped hooves wrapped against the shifting sand, tossed her head, and showing a lot of eye-white. The horse was a beauty, young and full of the same kind of prance Tristan had. Geneve's heart twisted for a moment in memory. *Another taken by this war. I don't know why I'm so upset about a horse.*

Perhaps aware of their effect on the skittish horse and the chain spear's owner, the clutch of Vhemin didn't try to hulk and menace any less. Five in number, armored in rag-tag leather, chain, and plate. One squatted, but the other four stood, weapons ready, arms crossed, or scowling, no doubt trying to one-up each other on most intimidating halfwit.

Omrar's head was wrapped against the sun's promise. His eyes sparkled at her approach, but she could see the right side of his face was mottled with a fist's indelicate touch. *That eye will swell shut before the day's done.* Geneve stopped Nightrunner right behind the Vhemin, waiting for Meri to swing to the sand. She followed him, then pushed through the brutes to her new friend. "Ho, Omrar."

"Ho, Tresward." His eyes moved from her to the Vhemin. "What news?"

"Safe tidings," she assured him. "We are allies, more or less."

"I'm worried about the less part of that," he admitted.

"What's he saying?" growled a squat Vhemin with an eyepatch.

Geneve and Meri both turned to the creature. "You can't understand him?"

"Bits and pieces," the creature said. "Different dialect, see? The Vhemin over there," he swung an arm past Imshir and the blasted sands beyond, "are more his local boys. We're from the south. Better hunting, fewer assholes."

"Different language," Meri mused. "Why am I able to understand him?"

"Heaven's Gate," Geneve guessed. "The lich must have touched your mind. Much like Mazin's gift of language in a bottle."

"I've been meaning to talk to him about how a humble wine merchant lays his hands on a thing like that." Meri kicked sand. "It'll keep."

Omrar slid from his horse, giving the beast's flank an affectionate pat, then unwrapped his scarf. He creaked about, wincing. "My old bones aren't used to the ride anymore."

Geneve walked to him, eying his face. "I don't think it's the ride so much as the klicks before. You've traveled a hard road."

He nodded, eyes shifting to Meri. "This must be your sorcerer friend."

Meri brightened. "I'm famous!"

"You are, in both your lover's heart and the mind of the Precept." Omrar gritted his teeth, a flash of pain crossing his face. "I could use a seat, if it's all the same. I've news of a stolen blade, a captured friend, and a demon king."

THEY SAT IN WHAT GENEVE THOUGHT OF AS THEIR COMMAND TENT. Armitage and Sight of Day perched on a divan with Tilly between them. Coming Storm stood a little before them, rose eyes missing nothing. She claimed to understand the Tebrani tongue and did a fair job of translating with handspeak for those who weren't up to speed with it.

Mazin bustled about with a tray laden with food and wine. Yasmine shimmered by his shoulder, offering help with a held cup or a steadying hand on the tray. Geneve marveled at how close they'd become so soon. Yasmine no doubt thought people were people, but Mazin had never seen a fairy, or dragon for that matter, before the week started. He was taking it all in stride, and if anything, looked heartier and more alive for it.

Meri held his peace behind Geneve. Quiet, alert. *He has my back. Happy for me to lead wherever we go. What did I do to deserve that? When we met I was taking him to his death.* The pair stood by the pavilion's entrance. A contrast to Meri's stillness, Geneve paced. She could almost hear her father counsel patience. Iz's pale memory laid hands on her shoulders. *Wait, daughter. A story rushed is a story poorly made. The caulking won't hold. Let it chart its own course.*

Omrar held his wine like a drowning man holds rope but didn't drink. "They found me right after you left."

Geneve wanted to ask *who?* Or *how did they know you were with me?* But she knew the answer. The Precept knew, because his smoke demon bested her. She ran with tail between her legs, and one of the monster's spies must have seen her. Perhaps his Arm, or the insidious Will she'd heard so much about but never seen. "I'm sorry this happened to you."

He blinked. "I'm not. I didn't come here to wail like a spoiled child." Bruised lips parted in a grin, teeth white despite his years. "I saw Lily, Tresward. I *saw* her. She's alive!"

"The captured friend," Meri murmured. "And what of the demon king and the stolen blade?"

Geneve could almost feel Israel's memory roll his eyes. "Don't rush the story, sorcerer. You of all people should know the value of a few well-chosen words."

"Aye, aye, but often told at a higher pace, so we don't find our graves before the telling's done." Meri's eyes glittered with mirth.

"He's not wrong." Omrar turned his goblet, staring into the ruby-red liquid. "This isn't a long story, or hard to tell. They found me on the streets after you made your escape. Soldiers, if I can dishonor the label. They dragged me to the Precept's palace for an audience."

"You saw the Precept?" Mazin stopped his fussing with drinks for a moment. Yasmine flitted to stand atop his head, hands on hips as she watched Omrar. "What is he like?"

Omrar shook his head. "I didn't see the man himself. Only his consigliere. She was a hard woman, able to make you feel exposed with a handshake. Scared me without speaking a word." He sighed. "She took me deep within his palace. Up stairs, through empty corridors, and to a tower right at the back. I saw no guards apart from the two who minded me. Not a soul stirred in the whole place. I heard no one, either. There were no cookfires or the scent of roasted meats. It was deserted, except for my two guards, the consigliere, and me."

"And the Precept," Meri said.

"Maybe." Omrar shrugged. "I saw many things that made little sense. The consigliere took me through a torchlit chamber bare of any furniture. The windows were barred with steel plates and had claw marks in their surface. Curls of metal lay on the ground beneath them. Can you imagine what might cause something like that?"

Geneve looked to the northern wall of the tent as if she could see where Ormeon rested, baking like a cat on hot sand. "Nothing that would fit into a room."

The older man nodded. "It defies reason. Another room without barred windows, cold as the steppes of Al Mar, but without snow or ice. Dry, like the sand we stand on. A painted circle sat in the middle, strange glowing runes about, and smears of what looked like blood."

"What kind of circle? What kind of runes?" Meri straightened, professional interest radiating from him.

"I'm no cunning man." Omrar shook his head. "It wouldn't matter if I was. I tried to look at them, but my mind skittered away from the letters. I could see one for a moment, and it made me cry. Another, and I was barking with laughter like a sick hyena. I stopped after the third made me sick."

Meri looked troubled, eyes hooded, but shook his head and said nothing. Geneve raised an eyebrow. "And what did the consigliere do?"

"Nothing." Omrar pursed his lips. "Other than walk a shade faster, perhaps. That's when I saw the sword."

"Requiem," Geneve sighed.

"Aye. It could be nothing but a sword for a Knight. They had the blade in a small chamber. A portcullis blocked the way. The sword was naked, no sign of a scabbard. It rested point-first on a stone plinth."

"Without a sword rack?" Meri rubbed his chin. "How was it held up?"

"No idea." The old man crossed his arms. "I've never seen anything like it."

"I have." Meri tossed a little side-eye in Geneve's direction. "Only, the last time I saw something like that it couldn't last."

"Because only gods can balance a blade for eternity," she breathed. "Only one of the Three."

"It was a short walk to Lily's cell. The interior was plush. Carpets, good furniture. Food and drink of every kind imaginable. A window with a view of the wide north. But a cell all the same. The window was barred, the door locked. Inside..." He trailed off.

"Oh, come on!" Meri clapped his hands. "There's taking the right time with a story, and there's stretching it on a rack."

"Well." Omrar nodded, slow and thoughtful. "That's what came next. Lily was there. Paler than I remember, more distant than I thought we were. They tortured me before her. Fist and brand both. The guards were workmanlike about it. Almost professional, except they asked no questions of either of us. Then the consigliere showed me out. Or her guards dragged me. She said one thing as I groaned on the steps of the Precept's palace. 'Now you have seen, tell her.'"

"Tell ... *me?*" Geneve blinked. "They took you inside, tortured you in front of a woman you knew, showed you my sword, and then tossed you out like a drunk at closing?"

"It's a trap," Meri mused. "They want you for something."

"And they shall have me!" Geneve turned on him. "I will get my blade. And I will end this monster."

"Oh, aye." He nodded, taking no offense. "It's the manner of it that could use some thought. Tell me, old man." Omrar winced, but Meri plowed on. "Did Lily say anything? Do anything?" Omrar shook his head. "Right. Third guide." Meri clapped his hand. "The Precept has the final Mazin. Or Yasmine, whatever." He waved off the fairy's shocked expression. "It's more than your sword, love. He's got the missing piece of the puzzle. But no first and second pieces. The Precept's more in the dark than we are."

Geneve turned to the tent flap. "Ormeon!"

"Hold a moment." Meri held her arm and firmed his grip when she tried to tug free. *He's never done that before.* She stilled under his touch. "The very worst thing would be to do what he expects, which is to hop on a dragon, fly over there, and set the place ablaze. He's emptied it of people in readiness. They'll close on you like the jaws of a shark when you land. I've a better idea." He kicked over a rug, exposing sand, and beckoned Omrar. "Come. Draw me a map. Then we will work out how we break in." The magician grinned. "We know his defenses. This will be easy."

GENEVE PASSED TIME BY STALKING THE CAMP. THE VHEMIN SEEMED more relaxed when she was about. *Perhaps it's because I'm more relaxed around their kind? They look like monsters from our worst nightmares, but they know love and loss all the same.* Yasmine followed her for a spell but gave up when all she could get from Geneve was a grunt or growl.

The sun rose, blasting all beneath it. The day wore on, hot and tired, and she was glad she'd not put on armor. The burnished sun might challenge her foes, but she could do without one above *and* one on her chest for a moment.

The camp wasn't large. She could walk across it in minutes. The Tresward's extension was more orderly, but smaller. Geneve watched her brothers and sisters for a moment, resisting the urge to join them.

That path is closed to me. I believe in the Three, but I can't be certain of an order run by people. We are too brittle to be trusted with eternal vigilance. Eyes on her feet, she turned away, melting back into the Vhemin's world. *The kingdom of monsters. Reviled and best forgotten.*

The clash of steel drew her like a magnet. This was the clanging, methodical sound of practice. The ringing brought no urgency to her. She found a training square setup to the south. Vhemin lifted large rocks, tossing them to each other. *They are so very strong.* The Feybrind might be better fighters. More urgent under Command. But the monsters were savage, all raw might and endurance. If you wanted a fighting force and didn't mind losing a few, Vhemin were the ones to have.

Geneve eyed the sky, as if her ancestors looked down. "And that's what you did, wasn't it? You made the Feybrind perfect, and the Vhemin to die."

No one answered, but a few monsters gave her a quizzical look. She glared at them until they looked away. Her glaring softened as she saw past them to the southern lonely edge of the training space. Puffing and sweating under the hot sand was Mazin. The portly merchant held a sword, but not well. Geneve charted a course around the edge of the training ground toward him. "Mazin! What news?"

"Nothing promising." The merchant lowered the blade, wheezing. "There was a time I spent a night at a wonderful restaurant. It wasn't the kind of place I usually went, as I guard my barons like I guard my wares." He loosened his shirt, which immediately re-stuck to his sweaty body. "Still. There was an important client. We drank. We laughed! I got an immense order for fine sweet red. It's best served after chilling in a cold cellar."

"I'm sure I'll need that knowledge later in life."

He polished up a wink. "Always attend to the small things. Toward the end of the night a group of troubadours played. Their songs were marvelous. One in particular caught my ear. I learned it by rote before the night was done, left feeling warm, full, and drunk, and when I awoke I could remember only one word in three."

Geneve crossed her arms. "We've all had nights like that."

"Aye, true enough, but imagine for a moment you woke up knowing one word in three of a song you've never heard." He hefted the sword. "I'm no swordsman, and yet something urges me to swing this sword in a certain way."

Geneve raised an eyebrow. *Meri speaks of guides. This can be no coincidence.* "What kind of way?"

Mazin twirled the blade, almost severing his arm in the process. "My feet go this way." He stood planted in a classic ready stance, weight even-ishly balanced between both feet. "I hold the sword high." Mazin hefted the steel to a classic high guard, pommel higher than the blade's tip.

Well, 'classic' if your fencing master was drunk. Geneve couldn't take it. "No, not like that." She touched his elbow, bringing it closer to his ribs, then lifted the pommel about a centimeter. "Like this."

"What's the difference?"

"Certain death versus a fifty-fifty chance of survival." Geneve shrugged. "It's your call."

"You moved my arm a fraction and the pommel even less." He lowered the blade—for all his arms had mass, they lacked the rigor of hefting a blade for hours, or even minutes, on end. "Can such tiny movements make a difference?"

Geneve gestured to a couple Vhemin who'd drawn close to watch. "If you're them and fighting, say, *you?* Not really. They're strong enough to bull their way through most defenses."

"Thanks." Mazin looked at his feet.

"Warfare isn't about making you feel good," she snapped. "It's about being alive. It's about saving those you love more than your own life. We are the shield that stands for the world!"

Silence. The two Vhemin glanced at each other, shifting their feet. Mazin nodded, head bowed. "Aye. I'd forgotten."

Geneve unclenched her fists, surprised at herself. *Iz would have brought me to task for throwing a shit fit.* "No. I'd forgotten. You're a good friend, Mazin. I'm just .. I've got a lot on my mind."

"Being one shield for the whole world could do that to a person." He tried for a small smile. "But I truly mean I've forgotten. There's something here," he slapped the flat of his hand against the back of his head, "that I *knew*. It was in my blood and bones, but it's gone. I don't know if it's the dying that did it, or the coming back to life. It could be as simple a problem as drinking too little wine, and I aim to remedy that before the day's done, because swinging steel is thirsty work. The grapes may stir memories."

"Not how *you* swing it. That won't make anyone thirsty," growled one of the Vhemin. "You're like a maid singing to the birds and bees about the beauty of life. There's no will behind your steel."

"It's my first day on the job," Mazin protested. "Cut me some slack."

"Your enemies will cut you all the slack you need," the other Vhemin muttered. "Then they'll cut you down to size."

Mazin looked at his belly. "What are you trying to say?"

"The thing is," Geneve gritted, "you stood in Spring's Stance. It's one of Cophine's starting poses. You held the blade in Catching Winter. Ikmae gifted that to us. Aye, aye, I know your form was poor, and I mean no criticism. The opposite—because I recognized the stances and saw the pattern beneath. I spent ten hours each day for over ten years learning the stanzas. It's right I should know them, but it's a mystery how you do."

"What's more of a mystery is that I know more." Mazin set his stance again, lifted the blade—this time, with elbow close—and stepped forward. His movements were halting, his form worse than the lowest Novice, but behind them was the borrowed will of the Tresward.

Mazin stumbled and hesitated across the sand, brow furrowed, teeth clenched. Geneve could *feel* him trying to remember. He walked through a part of Cophine's earlier patterns, stepped into fragments of Ikmae's, and finished with a handful of Khiton's, then ... stopped.

Geneve crossed her arms. "That was terrible. Where did you learn them?"

Mazin rubbed his face. "I said I can't remember. Wait. What do you mean 'them?'"

"You used pieces of fourteen patterns in your steps." Geneve pointed to the ground three paces from where he started. "Mare's Run. Here, see? Wings of Dawn. This piece here was where you tried—and failed, I'll note—to recreate one of Khiton's masterworks. It's called

Fury's Rest, but I call it the end of all things. It is the last stanza he ever made." She turned a circle. "Fourteen, Mazin. Fragments all, but pieces nonetheless."

"What's weird is I feel like I shouldn't have stopped." He moved back to his starting point. "I feel like... can I try something?"

"It's your baron. Spend it how you please." Geneve took a step back. She'd learned early enough that more injuries came from the wild swings of Novices than any practice bout with a Champion.

Mazin began. This time, his steps were more certain, but still a hodgepodge of a double fistful of patterns. He shuffled about the sand, wheezing, then extended his arm, tossing the blade. "There!"

It tumbled through the air, landing point first in the sand. It didn't vibrate or give a hefty thrum. It just stood there for a handful of heartbeats, then sagged to the ground as the sand gave way. Geneve laughed. "What was that about?"

"The finishing move! So I can start again." Mazin flexed his now-empty sword hand as if reaching for the blade. "I think it's supposed to come to me."

"Swords can't fly." Geneve retrieved his steel. "Oh, aye. There's parts of patterns that call for the throwing of one. I've done it myself—Tilly would tell you, too many times. But they never come back. You'd better be sure you've another weapon handy."

"Throwing a sword is the kind of thing an imbecile would do," the first Vhemin said.

"One that'd been dropped on their head as a child," the other offered. "From a great height. And the ground would be stone, not this half-assed sandy shit."

"Right," the first growled. "You give up your weapon when you give up your life."

"The problem with Vhemin is you don't believe," Geneve sighed. "I mean no disrespect. I *see* you. I call one of *yours* one of *mine*. A friend. A brother. Family. But the world has pushed on you for so long, everything but what's before you is gone. Let me show you a tiny piece of wonder, so you can think about whether your sword is better in your hand or not." She moved to Mazin's starting point. "Imagine here," she pointed to the sand, "is a man with a knife. I've a sword, and I could end him."

"So, stab him already." The first Vhemin looked smug.

"Aye, that's one solution. But over there," Geneve pointed fifty meters distant, "is a horde of your enemies. The man before you is a single threat, but the rest will kill your village." She beckoned the first closer. "Stand where the knife-wielder would be."

"No problem." The Vhemin drew a curved blade a little longer than his hand. "I've even got a knife handy."

His friend stood at Geneve's back. "And here's me waiting to finish what he starts."

"Perfect." She smiled.

"That doesn't look perfect," Mazin offered. "That looks like a rough time. He's but a pace behind you. Both are armed. You've seen the knife, but—"

"Don't tell me his weapon." Geneve closed her eyes, feeling the sun's heat above her. "Now I will show you the power of belief. You may attack me at any time."

"You're not going to count down or nothing?" The monster behind her sounded hesitant.

"No." Geneve kept her eyes shut. "When you're ready."

The barest intake of breath was her warning. She felt the weight of Mazin's steel in her hand. It'd been forged by a poorer smith than the Tresward used, but the weapon was serviceable enough, albeit the balance off. Geneve stood lighter on her feet because she wore no Smithsteel. The Vhemin before her was past the point of no return on his strike, blade moving to her heart. She knew by his motion what the man behind her was doing. A thousand patterns a thousand times over in a thousand different places made her move to the left. Her blade came up, edge glimmering with Light, and knocked the knife into the sky. She kept moving, shifting into a turn, and sweeping the other knife from the Vhemin behind her into the sky too.

Geneve completed her spin, tossing Mazin's blade end over end. It flew an impossible fifty meters at a speed even a Feybrind arrow couldn't match. The air burned as it passed. A flock of tiny finches made of fire took wing along its path. It hit the ground, blasting sand skyward. She caught the knives as they fell and stopped moving with the blades against the necks of the Vhemin.

She waited five heartbeats, opened her eyes, then spun the knives about their balance and offered them hilt-first to the monsters. "Here. You might need these."

Mazin gave a slow clap. "Impressive."

"You'll note I don't have the sword in my hand, though." Geneve shrugged. "They can be thrown, but they never come back."

"But what if they could?" the merchant mused.

Geneve snorted. "Let's focus on what's real." She eyed the blasted sand. "Maybe when you can do one of Cophine's first patterns without hurting yourself, we can talk about flying swords."

Chapter Thirty-One

Vertiline walked the empty sand outside the camp like it owed her something. The command briefing, if you could call it that, was the sinner telling them a plan that'd get them all dead. Sure as rain was wet, it was suicide. The reason she was so damn angry was no better idea came up. Not from her, or the monster, or the damn cat, or even Geneve. Meriwether said *We go in the front door* and Vertiline laughed, but no one joined in.

Oh, he'd done right by the planning. Yasmine built him a tiny model replica of the Precept's palace, right down to faux runes on the cold-ass floor Omrar wheezed about. Meriwether said *That's where we kill him*, like getting into a keep fortified by about thirty walls, moats, portcullises, and no doubt at least an armed guard or two was going to be easy.

But the sorcerer wasn't done. No, he said they had to split up. Vertiline would lead the charge, the Knights, Clerics, Feybrind, and Vhemin under her command. Sight of Day and Armitage would go with Ormeon to steal the sword. Meriwether and Geneve would face the Precept.

Vertiline had asked, *Why do you need a dragon to steal a sword?* And Meriwether had sighed, like she was five and asking why the sky was blue. *Because it's the most important thing. It will be well guarded, and besides, Ormeon can't fit into the summoning chamber.*

She decided not to ask why he'd called it a summoning chamber, or even how he knew that's what it was. He'd read a book, no doubt.

"Still angry with yourself?"

Vertiline startled, one hand drifting to her sword before she recognized the speaker. "Hail, Eleni, and well met." The Justiciar leaned on a staff, standing in the barren wasteland like she'd been waiting her whole life for this moment. Vertiline took in her slumped shoulders, her lined face, but also bright, twinkling eyes. "Wait. What do you mean, *still* angry?" She did a slow turn. "How'd you get out here? I see no footsteps but mine." True enough, they were a couple klicks from the encampment. Vertiline chose this direction because it looked flat, barren, and devoid of people she knew. And yet here was Eleni, High Justiciar of the Tresward, *waiting* for her?

"So many questions." Eleni fell in beside Vertiline. "There's one yet unasked."

Vertiline gritted her teeth. "Why did you come?"

"Because the final war is here."

"Not here, as in this desert, but *here*, to disturb the quiet peace of my morning walk?" Vertiline was too damn angry to clip her words to a softer shape.

Eleni eyed the sun. "Some might argue it's no longer morning."

"Some might walk back to camp if they're going to be dicks."

"Fair enough." Eleni plodded along for a handful of paces, using her staff to steady herself. To Vertiline's eye it looked more prop than requirement. "We don't have a lot of time, so I'm going to give you years of counseling in mere moments. You are angry with yourself because you feel you killed innocents."

"I *did* kill—"

"And you are more angry because you want to reclaim the sword. You know as I do that getting the skymetal blade is the cornerstone of this plan. It will have the most guards. Demons will cluster about it like flies on honey. It is the very place someone wracked with guilt would go to find her grave."

"I'm not—"

"Still, it poses an interesting question, does it not? You're curious as to why you lead the frontal assault. The second-best swordswoman in all the world, but separated from your comrades. Is it because they don't trust you at their backs? Is it because Meriwether, a holomancer of such power only the ancients saw its like, fears what your hand might do to him? Or to his love, the Knight Champion who felled an Artifice from mid-air, after jumping from a dragon?" Eleni frowned. "These are confusing times, but one thing I'm sure of is Meriwether wants you in the place you will do your best."

"He knows nothing of—"

"What Meriwether knows is your skill with a blade. Geneve must face the monster with him at her side. They face a foe of impossible power. That is as true as the sky. What he also knows is your strength of heart. He needs a Knight who will not fall when the forces of darkness break like a wave against the failing Light. Meriwether wants that woman holding strong." Eleni stopped, leaning on her staff. "Child, he knows we all go to die. He has tiny pieces to move about the board. You are one of his best, in the place you were made to be."

Vertiline flexed her metal hand. "But this—"

"It is a gift, Knight Valiant Vertiline." Eleni faced the horizon. "You will need it at the end."

"Then take it!" Vertiline spat. "Take the cursed thing. Put it on someone who can control it, who won't kill friend and foe alike!"

Eleni didn't face her. "There it is. We got here faster than I hoped. You think you are less valuable. You always have. Vertiline, who followed Israel. Vertiline, who kept his secret at the cost of her sister's power. Vertiline, who lost a love, then another, because she wasn't worthy of their regard." Vertiline's fist closed on air, wanting a blade. Eleni cocked her head, eying Vertiline's hand. "You *are* worthy, Tilly. The only one who doubts is you. I've no Knights I could give your arm to, even if I knew how. They are all more brittle. They would break."

Vertiline sagged, all her tension leaving at once, a sadness replacing it, deep as the ocean, still as the grave. "I won't fall, Justiciar. It's everyone else around me that will."

"The Feybrind and Vhemin?" Eleni resumed walking. "The Feybrind worship Meriwether because he set them free. They'll do as asked, without question. But the Vhemin? They follow only strength. And not a one of them missed how you stood behind a monster, called him comrade, and offered to face them if he fell. That's the kind of thing that leaves an impression on them. You've only yourself to blame, really."

Vertiline scrounged for more words to throw at the old woman but came up empty. She spent a few moments watching her verbal sparring partner. Eleni walked like a crone, shoulders hunched, neck bent. There was a fire in her, but it was banked against great need. "What happened?"

"When we Tresward squabbled among ourselves?" Eleni gave a dry chuckle, leaves on stone. "We won. We lost, too."

"Aye, I see that, but I meant to you." Vertiline dragged hair from her eyes. "You're my elder by a span of years but walk as someone twice my age." She hugged herself. "Was necromancy involved? When we fought a fallen Champion at Ravenswall, she was the risen dead."

"I didn't think I looked that bad."

Vertiline snorted, flexing her metal hand. "At least you've still got all your limbs."

"Fair." Eleni plodded for another handful of meters. "How much do you know of the Sway?"

"That it can turn a mind. Make real what's not." Vertiline shrugged. "This is what all Novices know."

"The Sway can do those things, and others. It is the Three's will, Tilly. It is their last breath left in our air. The Sway achieves all things forbidden and otherwise. It can raise the dead, as Geneve demanded of it at Ravenswall. Not necromancy, creating a reanimated corpse, but true life." Eleni gave a small smile. "It is harder the longer dead someone is. Oh, I see it on your face! You find even the smallest Sways difficult. You believe it another of your failings." Eleni sighed. "It's not that simple."

"Sum it up," Vertiline snapped. "We go to die tomorrow, and you're most of the way there already."

"Geneve raised her holomancer because he was barely dead. The cost was ... tiny."

"Cost?" Vertiline blinked. "What cost?"

"Sway and Storm are gifts of the Three, but the levies are different. Storm needs years of dedication. Perfection of the blade." Eleni growled. "Shit I just never had time for."

"I've seen you with steel. You're not horrible." Vertiline grinned. "Not amazing, either."

"Ignoring all my many faults for a moment." Eleni halted, wrapping both hands about her staff. "I need a breather. My, what a beautiful country this is."

Vertiline looked at the same patch of desert Eleni stared at. "It's sand and more sand. I've got it in places sand shouldn't go. There are sand *sharks*, Justiciar. Creatures swim under the surface of the Three-cursed ground."

"And yet, it's still beautiful. Beauty cares nothing for comfort." Eleni rested her head against her staff. "I've not much time, Chevalier. No, don't fret. I'm not sick like dear Kytto. But I borrowed against a ledger I can't hope to repay."

"The Sway costs more than years of practice," Vertiline hazarded.

"Aye. It still costs years, just as the Storm does, but they leave all at once, as soon as the debt's accrued. If you heal a scratch, it may cost a minute of your allotted span. A severed limb, years. What Kytto had would've cost more life than was left in all of us. Bringing the dead back..." She trailed off, looking at the desert again. "It really is very pretty."

Vertiline put herself in Eleni's eyeline, lowering her voice. "What did you do?"

"I dug deep. We fought Storm against Storm, Sway against Sway. We blasted the walls of Ravenswall to rubble in our anger. The queen called us there, you see. She wanted to help but didn't know who the real enemy was." Eleni shrugged. "When I found her body, she was truly dead. I tore the souls from the two Knights who did it, then put Morgan's back in her body." The Justiciar sagged. "Vertiline ... the weight of a soul is a terrible thing. It's heavier than the world. Morgan was dead for minutes, and it cost me twenty years."

"And yet, she's not here."

"We broke her city." Eleni tapped a finger against her staff. "She wasn't happy about that."

Vertiline laughed. "I like Morgan. She's a good person."

"Aye. And a good leader. Better than her father." Eleni turned back toward the camp. "She won't come, because she can't. There aren't enough people in Ravenswall after a siege and a battle between Tresward to rebuild. I didn't bring her back because I wanted more ships. I did it because it was the right thing to do."

"They sent a few with me already. Under Picotee's command." Vertiline looked at the desert, not moving. "The Tresward who didn't join me came for us."

"More rogues," Eleni agreed. "Dealt with, but like at Ravenswall, at terrible cost."

"There are so few of us left." Vertiline hugged herself.

"It's one of the reasons we can't mope about, worrying about whether we've got a cursed arm attached to us." Eleni grabbed Vertiline's metal hand. "This isn't your fault. It was never your fault."

Vertiline closed metal fingers around Eleni's human ones. "You say it like it's true."

"I could make it true." Eleni freed her hand then wiggled her fingers. "Speak Sway, and change the world."

"When we fight the demons, the Clerics will die." Vertiline hunched. "They will Sway the land, and piece by piece they will fall apart."

"When we fight the demons, we'll all die." Eleni looked at her feet. "The Knights will stand to the front in their beautiful armor, glittering like silver suns. They'll fall first. The Clerics behind will raise hands to the Three and ... change the world. The Three's cost to Sway is a reminder that they made everything perfect already. If we dare change it, we must be sure of our conviction." Eleni raised her head. "The Feybrind will leap to defend us, because they are wonderful. They will die. The Vhemin will be enraged, and die all the same. Their deaths will be bloodier because they are so very hard to kill. They don't go quietly, and it hurts them more." She shrugged. "You will stand by the last. Vertiline of the Tresward. Blade in hand, standing at a demon gate, holding fast, because Meriwether du Reeves believes you can. You will still die, but if we're very lucky, you will die after the Precept is dead."

"Oh," Vertiline said.

"Don't listen to an old woman," Eleni said. "I can't see the future. But I can guess it as well as any."

"What will be left after we're all dead?"

Eleni grinned. "Finally. The question you were going to ask at the start."

"Well?" Vertiline growled. "What's the point of it all?"

"Why does there have to be a point?" Eleni walked toward the camp. "Perhaps it's that we've done it wrong, and it's someone else's turn. Or perhaps it's that we've done it right, and this is the end to an uncomfortable song."

"But a beautiful one."

"Now you're getting it." Eleni stamped through sand. "Come on, Valiant. Help an old woman to her doom."

Vertiline held for a moment. She eyed the sand, dared a glance at the sun, then laid hand on the hilt of her glass. She felt the honest heft of the sword, and the promise it held. *I have made many mistakes. But I've never run. And I won't today.* Despite her imminent demise, she gave a small smile that cracked into a grazed grin. She cackled, laughter breaking out. "We're all going to die!"

Eleni laughed too. "Isn't it wonderful?"

Chapter Thirty-Two

The day finished with sorcery. Meriwether sweated in the setting sun as he beheld all the weapons of their army. The Vhemin and their misbegotten scraps, booty from a hundred clashes with a technically superior but less brutal foe. The Feybrind, with weapons borrowed from anywhere, or made from desert flint lashed to scavenged sticks, but beautifully made all the same.

And, of course, glass. His fingers trailed over the Knight's blades, glittering like jewels in the sun.

"We're waiting, sinner." Vertiline brushed pale hair from her brow and wiggled her fingers. "Do something epic."

Five hundred pairs of Vhemin eyes watched. Two hundred Feybrind, and just shy of a hundred Tresward. He gave a strangled laugh. "No pressure."

"Maybe he can't get it up," Armitage offered.

"You're not helping," Meriwether countered.

"I'm not trying to help. I want my sword, and I want to kill someone." The monster shrugged. "Is this going to help?"

Meriwether tapped a glass blade with a fingernail. "All these weapons are insufficient."

A Knight shifted on the sand, her brown eyes hard as stone. "These are made by Smiths. Held by the right hands they can kill any man," her gaze shifted to a Vhemin ten steps away, "or monster."

"Yeah, but you're not holding one now, so let's have at it," the monster replied, turning.

"Hold a moment," Meriwether urged, raising his hand. "Before we murder each other, that is. I mean no disrespect to any here. This blade," he walked down the line of swords, selecting a length of glass, "is yours?"

The Knight did a double take. "How did you know?"

"Because it looks like it would fit your hand." Meriwether lifted the blade from the collection. Like all glass swords the edge was sharper than human cruelty. You could shave a beard coarse as steel wool and have a face smooth as a newborn babe's skin after. The Knight's chosen weapon was a standard broadsword, nothing fancy, but held by a Tresward it brought the Three's Light to those needing justice, or just a good killing. Meriwether handled it with care, laying the flat of the blade across his arm to display it to the crowd. "It's a fine sword, made with care by the best in the world. When I say this blade is insufficient, I don't disrespect its maker, or the one who holds it, or the order behind them. We fight demons, and they will not stay dead."

"Like us," Armitage chuckled. "Outstanding. Finally, a worthy foe."

"Worse," Meriwether said. "If the stories are true, some decapitated demons turn into two. Slicing off an arm makes a matched pair. Running them through just makes anger course in whatever excuse for veins they have."

"Okay, that sounds a rough time." Armitage rubbed a scaly hand against his chin. "How do we kill them?"

"With a little magic." Meriwether eyed the Knight who wanted to pick a fight with Vhemin. *Or maybe it's the other way around? We're so used to murdering each other at someone else's command.* He spun the sword, but carefully, because he didn't want to lose an arm. Then he closed his eyes, imagining all the things that would hurt a demon, and pressed his fingertips to the glass blade.

It is a bright summer's day. I can hear children play in the distance. Their laughter's what happy rain sounds like. I smell water, deep and cool. There's a

267

lake just down the hill. Geneve sits by me, hand on mine. The bottle of wine between us is half-empty. It's a good Tebrani red, one of the best, the last in the crate Mazin gave us, and tastes of berries and chocolate. A lark cuts the sky, a bright chirp boasting how fast, how high before it speeds away. I feel her green eyes on me. "You went somewhere."

"No, love." I kiss her. "I've been here all along."

"Good." She scoots closer, shoulder to shoulder. I feel the heat of her body, the soft/hard of her skin and the muscle beneath. "What should we do today?"

I breathe the air. It feels like a promise of things to come, a hint of ripening fruit, fresh-cut hay, and woodsmoke from the village. "Whatever we want."

He opened his eyes. The blade under his fingers glimmered, light playing hide and seek with the sun's rays. Cool blue marched to a husky orange before glowing bright and clear like the yellow sun above.

He felt Geneve's eyes on him. She took a step forward. "What was that?"

"All the things that are good in the world." He looked at his feet. "I didn't think you could see."

"How could I not?" She stepped to him, touching the hands that held the blade. "Tomorrow, it will be true."

He nodded, tying a little bravado to the motion. "That's the idea. Now, if you'll excuse me for just a moment." Meriwether walked around the tables of weapons toward the Knight. He handed the blade to her. "Here."

She took it, uncertainty making her look to her fellows. "This isn't the Three's Light. It's—"

"Sinner's magic. I know all about it, trust me." Meriwether shrugged. "If it makes you feel any better, it's not real. It's a dream. Or, I don't know..." He trailed off. "Think of it as all the things that could be true. The ones you want. The toy you didn't have as a child—"

"Tresward have no toys."

"Exactly my point. It could be the sun you remember when it's raining. A good horse beneath you, tireless, running for the dawn when nothing but night's in your wake. Friends, comrades, family, who argue over dinner but fight at your side."

He waited for her nod. When she gave it, the motion was sure. "I know what you mean. Is it a trick?"

"Kind of." Meriwether looked down. *No, I owe her truth. Meet her gaze.* He looked into the Knight's dark brown eyes. "It's us, don't you see? It's all of us, and what we want. Not the petty squabbles of which fields we plow first or whether red or white wine is best. It's the very heart of us, and it is what the demons want most of all. But it's a thing they can't touch until we're dead. Like this," he tapped the blade she held, "it is fire and acid in an edge. They can't stand it."

"You're sure?"

"Well, no. I read it in a book. High Magic, they called it. I don't know if that's correct. The Right Magic, maybe." He closed his fingers around hers holding the sword and lifted her hand to her ear. Her eyes widened, but she didn't pull away. "Listen." He let her hand go.

She leaned toward the sword, eyes widening further, then a smile lit her face. She closed her eyes. "It's … singing! It sounds like angels." The Knight quietened for a handful of seconds, smile widening. "It's my mother. I remember her. She sang this song at hearth. There's a smell of fresh-baked bread. It's a sourdough." Her nose wrinkled in the memory. "Father liked it best, but I didn't. I can hear outside our small house. There's a horse. It's ours, I think, but given by my uncle after the storms took most of our crop. He only had two, and neither was spare, but gave us one." Her eyes opened. "This is a wondrous gift!" She held the blade at arm's length, eyes large as saucers. "How did you do that?"

"I don't really know." He tugged his ear. "It's like … can you tell me how you see? It happens. It's a part of you. It's like that."

The Knight set her brown eyes on Geneve. "Thank you, sister."

Geneve blinked. "For not killing him?"

"That, but what lies beneath. For your courage to do the right thing."

"It was a team effort," Meriwether said. "We both agreed the killing part was bad." He walked back to the piles of weapons. He selected a guisarme, this one a little dented, a little rusted. *But aren't we all?* As he lifted it, he felt light-headed, swaying a little on his feet.

Geneve was at his side faster than thought, hands under his elbow. "Are you okay?"

"I'm amazing," he lied. "One down, about eight hundred more to go."

"Rest," she said.

"If I rest, we die." He uncurled her fingers from his arm. "The battle will start tonight. You know that."

She nodded. "I feel it. But like the river runs to the sea, it's a part of a greater journey. We meet the Precept tomorrow, after midnight's bell tolls."

"Then I'd best get to work." He placed the guisarme's butt against the sand. "This can only be yours." His eyes found a Vhemin, scars crisscrossing his broad chest. "Right?"

The monster nodded. "Don't break it."

"Hah! No fear, I can barely lift it. Come closer and let me tell your wonderful story."

WHEN YOU'VE NO IDEA WHAT YOU'RE DOING, DON'T TELL ANYONE. THIS rule guided Meriwether's life, taking him between tavern brawls, heists, throne rooms, and blasted wastelands. He liked to think he moved between those environments like a fish between different colored water, his north star the relative confidence that no one could hear the terrified screaming inside his head.

When Yasmine made the perfect replica of Imshir, he'd nodded sagely, and proposed putting forces in various places. Inside, he was plagued with questions like, *what can a dragon actually do?* Or, *why me?* Asking these aloud would help no one, and more than likely harm the fragile furnace of bravado he stoked in his friends.

He was slightly hurt none had seen through the veneer, though. Time on the road, and all that.

After setting things in motion, he felt there'd be time to reflect, but that wasn't happening. He was here, on a borrowed horse, riding at night, while Ormeon crunched along a respectful distance away. Nightrunner was a brave enough beast, but a dragon was a thing that defied the eyes and mind. The horse didn't like the dragon, whereas the dragon probably viewed the horse as an *hors d'oeuvre*. Geneve sat atop the dragon, magnificent as always. Meriwether clutched his ancient's clothing to him, as if he could borrow some of their forgotten splendor. *I'm a sham. She's the real deal.* Exhaustion rolled over him like waves on a beach, and he took a moment to steady himself. *You don't see her asking for a nice cup of a tea and a lie-down.*

"A baron for your thoughts, sinner?" Vertiline walked by his side, not seeming to mind the wear on her feet. Tireless. Strong. All the things she was made to be. She wore motley scraps of armor, having given her borrowed Smithsteel plate to those she'd said needed it more. The Tresward were fresh out of forges to make more, and had no Smiths standing by. With her straight-shouldered stride she looked like a very angry, very pale gladiator, a longsword at hip, pieces of battered steel clutching her leading shoulder, arm, and chest.

"We talking royalty or a shitty coin?"

"A shitty coin is worth more out here." She spat on the night-kissed sand. "No offense."

"I'm no baron. I'm the Lord du Reeves, scion of a fallen house. Also, I can make pretty pictures with my mind."

She snorted. "Why are you here?"

"Aside from comic relief? I'm here because the world needs saving."

"Liar."

Meriwether laughed. "I'm here because the love of my life," he jabbed a hand in Geneve's general direction, "is fixing to fight an ancient evil. No way there's a position for a spectator in that."

Vertiline squinted. "We talking the dragon or the woman?"

He ignored that, eying the city's smudge ahead. "You'd expect more lights."

"It's near midnight."

"How about just one light?" Meriwether stood in the stirrups, trying to glean something from the greedy dark. "I see a big wall. Something that might be buildings. And if I didn't know better, I'd say the walls are moving. Ho! Ormeon!"

The dragon gave him a baleful stare. *//YOU'VE JUST NOTICED THE DEFENDERS, HAVEN'T YOU?//*

Meriwether mentally rifled through a few responses before settling on, "You didn't think to mention anything?"

//YOU'D ONLY WORRY.// The dragon swung back to the city, her heavy feet shaking the earth with each step.

Geneve laughed, then removed her ancient's helmet. "There is a sparse force of soldiers outside the walls. I've fought the Precept's Arm before. We've little to worry about."

At mention of the villain's elite fighting force, Omrar hustled forward on his nag. "Do you think it's usual to put a handful of men and woman *outside* your gates?"

"The old man has a point," Meriwether mused.

Vertiline blinked. "What'd he say?"

"Ah. He said the Precept is a moron for putting forces outside the gates." Meriwether stroked his let's-call-it-a-short-beard. "He's got a point. Where's Sight of Day? And that layabout Armitage?"

Vertiline looked away. "Readying themselves."

"Well, let's ready them faster. It's showtime. And get that dragon out of here!"

At least it wasn't hot. The downside was it was damn cold. Meriwether welcomed his ancient's garb. Geneve was at his right, Tilly on his left. They walked toward a clutch of men and women under a probably-white flag a klick from Imshir's closed gates. Both sides left their respective fighting forces amassed at their respective backs.

A man who looked about ten summers Meriwether's senior stepped forward. "Who's in charge?"

Meriwether glanced at Geneve, and when she didn't step forward, he frowned. "It's more of a group effort."

The older man scowled. "You're doomed, of course. Only a fool runs an army by committee."

"Not much of an army, if we're trading truth." Meriwether tugged his ear. "Here's where it's at. I've got about five hundred Vhemin, a couple hundred Feybrind, and—"

"Feywhat?"

"Feybrind. You'll love them. They're cats." The sorcerer smoothed his coat. "And about a hundred Tresward."

The bannerman laughed, and not in a pretty way. "You bring fairy-tales to a sword fight."

A glimmer came from beneath Meriwether's coat for a moment, then Yasmine burst forth, hummed about the startled officer's head, then settled on Meriwether's shoulder. "We brought fairies to a sword fight!"

The officer had the good grace to look shocked for two long seconds. "I suppose you've a dragon at your backs too."

"What? No. We sent her somewhere else." Meriwether grinned. "I guess you've got about a thousand troops out here, and more inside. You've probably given pikes to children, because that's what evil overlords do. You figure, fairytales or not, you've got us outnumbered ten to one. How hard can it be? Flex a little muscle. Wave a sword or two. We'll turn about and be on our way." He gave an encouraging nod.

The officer frowned. "That's the size of it."

"Well, there's a problem. Our ships sank. We're out of provisions. The Vhemin want to kill everything, the cats don't like eating sand shark, and the Tresward think you're sheltering a demon." He leaned forward, offering a conspiratorial whisper. "They don't like demons."

"And I don't like fools, but here we are."

"A good ripost, but I felt it was a little rushed." Meriwether scanned the clear night sky. "Look, we're coming in. We need food and shelter. One way or another we'll get it. The shortest path is by way of killing your Precept and us all sharing ale after. What say you?"

"I say I see no cats."

Meriwether scanned the sky again. "They're fixing something. It should be fixed already, though." He frowned.

"Troubles?" The captain asked, not unkindly.

"You could say," Meriwether admitted. "I sent them off to take out a giant weapon of the ancients. It was put here to protect the land against attack by Artifice, or so I think, but was turned against our dragon because nothing works right anymore."

"So," mused the officer, "not only are we talking invisible dragons and cats, but magic weapons of ancient times—also invisible, I add—designed to destroy the invisible things backing up your army?"

"I'll agree, it doesn't strike quite the ring of terror I was aiming at," Meriwether admitted.

"Hurry this along," Geneve muttered. "We don't have all night."

"Eh." Meriwether adjusted his belt. "Anyway. Our invisible friends will be along momentarily, and at that point you're really fucked."

"You're remarkably direct, so I'll give the same courtesy. Our lord will give all safe harbor in exchange for the heads of your leaders." The officer crossed his arms. "Which I'm guessing is you three."

"A mere subcommittee," Meriwether assured him, risking a glance at the sky again. *How to buy more time?* "How do you fancy a quick bout, one on one, to settle this?"

The man snorted. "With you? You wouldn't last a second."

"Not with me, you imbecile. Her." Meriwether jerked a thumb at Geneve. "Or her." He swung the thumb toward Tilly. "Dealer's choice."

The Arm officer stroked his chin, thinking. "Look, all joking aside, I admire your courage. I also admire your integrity. But we both know this isn't how it ends. Out of curiosity, would you honor a weary soldier and tell me why you keep looking at the sky?"

"No reason," Meriwether lied. "If you want to change teams at any point, just sing out." He turned away.

"Hold a moment." The officer squinted at the sky. "What *is* that?"

"The coming of salvation," Meriwether assured him. "I wouldn't go into the city for a while though."

What appeared first as a speck birthed from the side of Heaven's Gate grew in size. The naked eye was first drawn to wings, the mind trying to fit natural form to it. A gull, perhaps, although with a more ponderous wing sweep—and of course, this was klicks from the shoreline. A gull wouldn't be this far inland. An osprey? Again, the sea was far away, and so an osprey, pelican, or other mighty bird of the ocean wouldn't fit.

When the bird thing was the size of a large man's thumb against the skyline, it gouted red fire. The officer took a step back. "Precept's Gaze, what *is* that?"

"A very angry dragon." Meriwether grinned. "Last chance, sir."

The captain glanced at Meriwether, did a quick round-the-room of Geneve and Tilly, turned, and ran. He was joined by his retinue, who wasted no time in dumping everything they carried, including their flag of truce, onto the cold sand.

Ormeon grew in size seemingly all at once as she approached at high speed. Meriwether thought he could make out two forms clutched to her back. One muscled, monstrous, with snake eyes, the other sleek and supple, eyes golden like the sun. The runes on the side of Ormeon's face glowed an angry orange, her eyes red as forge coals. The dragon flashed overhead, wind and sand blasting in her passage. She sent another massive torrent of flame at Imshir's walls. Stone exploded in the heat and fire wash. Arm soldiers unlucky enough to be there were incinerated to ash in a heartbeat.

Sand swirled in her passage. The dragon was gone, sweeping her way across the night sky to the Precept's palace. Silence, just for a moment. The cool kiss of the desert's wind.

Then an answering roar to Ormeon's rage, made from five hundred throats, fists beating against makeshift shields, feet stamping the ground. Sword on sword. The thunder of running feet.

The Vhemin horde surged past Meriwether for Imshir's breached gates. Their eyes were front, on the enemy, on the prize of a city clutched by an overreaching demon. Interspersed in their ranks was the glimmer of Smithsteel or the fluttering of cloth as Knight and Cleric joined the final rush to save the world. Snake eyes and shark teeth joined glass and steel, as fury frothed through the broken wall and into the city beyond.

Chapter Thirty-Three

This is not a good fight. Geneve walked the gritty streets of Imshir looking for warriors, but all she found were monsters wearing humans as cloaks. Three blocks past the wall's breach found her in a market square. It was two klicks east to west, one north to south, worn cobbles holding the memory of a million deals, arguments, and bargains. She found a skeleton force of Arm soldiers holding a line ahead of a mass of citizens. She saw a woman with a baker's apron next to a man covered by butcher's leather. A blacksmith held a hammer beside a seamstress with hair the blue-black of the night sky.

There were thousands of them, all different except for their eyes. Where people looked on the world with irises of black to blue, these all had mirrored lenses. Tiny flecks of silver showed the world what they saw.

She lifted her gaze beyond them to the Precept's palace. It crouched, dark against the sky, not a torch or lantern to be seen. Geneve knew it was walled in stone, girded with iron gates. *To reach it, I must go through these people.*

A handful of the People were with her, intermingled with a clutch of Vhemin. All stopped as they saw their foe. Geneve took point,

Vertiline guarding her right, Meri on the left. The Chevalier's mismatched armor did the bare minimum job, a gladiator's pauldron and metal plates leading to a gauntlet. *That's no gauntlet. That's her forearm. A metal promise made by the ancients.* Tilly's almost total lack of protection spoke of a woman with a surfeit of zeal, confidence, or a will to die. She carried a glass blade in a grip so relaxed the casual observer might have thought it careless. She held a small lopsided smile with the same regard, easily, but carefully too, lest someone take it from her.

Geneve glanced to the sorcerer. Meri stood with his feet shoulder-width apart, the ancient's clothing he wore fluttering in a breeze that only touched him. He poured blue-white light from one hand to the other, brows furrowed, eyes searching their foe. "They really know how to throw a party."

She snorted, then clamped down on it. "They're Imshir's people. We can't just kill them." She looked to Vertiline for support. "Can we?"

Tilly shrugged, the motion more relaxed than Geneve ever remembered seeing her. *Oh, sister, I wish we had time to talk. I want to know what's going on for you. After the battle there will be time.* "I'm not fond of killing clothiers in the name of justice." A quick glance to Meri, then back to the force ahead. "On balance, I've killed more than my fair share of innocents at another's bidding."

"Then ... how?" Geneve glanced about the square. They *could* take a side exit, but the mob would hound them. Their march to the palace would be a panicked dash.

Meri took a tentative step forward. The mass of enemy didn't move. If you weren't prone to nightmares you could look at them as if they were the night sky, a patterned darkness holding glittering silver orbs. He lifted his left hand, the blue-white light turning a lazy lap about his wrist, closed his eyes, and pushed. The light jumped as if startled, then loped toward the enemy line. It spread wide as it ran, a fisher's net cast into the sea. It grew to two klicks wide in a handful of heartbeats, a wave that broke over the rocks of Imshir's people.

It did no damage. Nothing burned, no one screamed. But where the light touched, an echo remained. Behind the blacksmith, Geneve saw the hulking shadow of a thing with three heads. The seamstress's shoulders held two crooked imps. The baker was ridden by a slip of shadow suggesting a woman's proportions but starved to a stick. A crown of thornlings stabbed the butcher's skull, but no blood escaped. On and on it went, monsters clutching their thralls like sock puppets.

Meri raised an eyebrow. "I don't think they're people. Not anymore."

Geneve shook her head. "Still ... we can't."

He didn't argue, eyes everywhere, looking for another way. "Makes you wonder, though. Why all the fuss? The demons need our deaths to open a gate, but it looks like they're all pretty much through already. How'd they get here? And what are they waiting for?"

She watched the line but saw no clues. "It doesn't feel right."

His hand found hers for the briefest of moments. "We could slip to the shadows."

"There is not enough time." Omrar pushed forward, his chain spear ready. "Let me speak with them. In my soul," he touched his chest, "I heard the Precept's call. I didn't listen. Others might heed my tale."

"We'll go with you." Geneve stepped forward.

"No, brave heart." The old man smiled. "When was the last time you listened when a blade stood ready for when the talk was done?" He considered his chain spear, then offered it to Meri. "Keep this safe for me."

The sorcerer took it like he held an asp. He *almost* managed to put his eye out in the first two seconds. "How the hell do you use this thing anyway?"

"Give it here." Tilly held her hand out, securing the chain spear to her belt. "You'll hurt yourself."

"Omrar." Geneve felt her chest tightened. "You be *careful*. Keep your distance. If the monsters come for you—"

"Don't you worry! I will run like I'm your age." The old man plodded toward the line of demon-ridden people. The shiftless mass made no noise as he approached. *Nothing* made noise. Geneve could hear no night birds, nor the sound of battle from other parts of the city. She watched Omrar walk a couple hundred meters to the enemy line, stopping twenty meters out. *He's too close!* Geneve shifted from foot to foot as the old man spoke to Imshir.

Geneve stilled. She couldn't hear what Omrar said, or if it made a difference. There were no sounds of argument or assent, just mirrored eyes watching, waiting. *Which begs a question. What are they waiting for?*

As Omrar talked, he moved with passion, arms waving, hands coming together only to separate. He reached out to the back of the crowd, then turned his attention to the front again. Geneve's fingers didn't stray from the hilt of her blade, but she wondered, *This man used to lead people with his heart. Is this how we turn the tide?* The rippling host of demons seemed agitated, scuttling over the bodies of their hosts, circling with predatory hunger.

No one moved. Omrar nodded, then turned to Geneve with a small smile. "I think it's safe to come forward."

The thornlings about the butcher's skull shivered into high action. As the man twitched, Geneve broke into a run, armor clattering, sword clearing its sheath in a heartbeat. Attention locked on the butcher, she ignored Tilly's cry, and Meri's tossed *Wait!*

Her attention was caught by the blacksmith. His three-headed shadow reached into his back. The man arched, a silent scream turning his face to a rictus of pain, then he lurched, tossing his hammer. It tumbled end over end, hit Omrar on the back of the head, and split his skull like overripe fruit. The hammer kept going with its own momentum, Omrar's body knocked over with the force of the blow, and just like that, a good man died for a demon king.

Geneve screamed, "*NO!*" but she was too late. Omrar was gone. *His death will not go unanswered!*

Tilly streaked past her, all long limbs and slender speed. Her pale skin carried the starlight. She made it to the enemy line like a tossed stone into a breaking wave. The people ridden by monsters groaned, then surged over her. The whole crowd wanted a piece of the Valiant. Ten, twenty, no *fifty* at least tried for her blood with grasping hands and ghoulish mouths.

I'm not going to make it! I'll lose two friends today. Her heart strained with her sprint, but the realization Tilly might die pushed her harder. *Wait. Is Vertiline ... smiling?* Her sister of the blade met a host too great to take on the blade with a soft smile and an iron stance. She didn't run. Brighter than a flash of the Three's Light, fifty meters from her friend, Geneve realized Vertiline wanted to die.

//VERTILINE!// Tilly's head snapped about at Geneve's roar. Geneve turned her sprint into a spin, arms pinwheeling, and tossed her blade into the surging demons. It turned end over end, brilliant with Light, electricity from the heavens marking its path across the square with a staccato of thunderbolts. She saw Tilly's eyes widen, her metal hand outstretched, fingers spread, then the blade...

Hit.

Chapter Thirty-Four

When the old fool stumbled toward the enemy line, Vertiline hadn't thought, *That's brave*. She'd fingered her sword hilt, thinking, *I should've done that*. It wasn't a question of bravery, but of results. She gave the sinner a sideways glance. *Actually, he should be up there. He's got a silver tongue and the confidence of the gods*. But Meriwether looked three-weeks-on-the-run tired, perhaps a little stupid around the edges, so it was Omrar wading into shark-infested waters.

It all went downhill from there.

Vertiline saw how the demons agitated and started her sprint a half-beat before Geneve reacted. She held a glass promise and wore a welcoming smile because she was probably going to die, but she was also going to extract a price for her death. It seemed only fair. She'd felt the impact in her gut when Omrar died. She'd crossed steel and glass with enough to know the weight of a hammer, and how you never got back up from a blow like that.

Night wind kissed her face as she ran. The starlight laid a clear path at her feet. Smooth cobbles rang under her boots, her breath singing in her chest, heart pounding like the drums of war. She caught the scent of night blossoms rather than the stink of sweat and fear. *If this is how I die, then it's enough.*

When she hit the enemy line it wasn't with a crash. Vertiline was slender, light on her feet, slipping between blow and under grasping hand. Her feet found the six-star pattern of Ikmae's *Battle's Memory*, blade up through a woman's arm, Light and blood spilling. The demon riding her gave a silent shriek, hopping to another body to the left, a shop boy now with two masters. Her sword remembered the way, slicing horizontally to take the lad's head, but Vertiline couldn't watch. If there was an after, she might lie to herself about what she did. *I needed to keep my flanks clear from attacks.* But as her sword killed a boy of no more than twelve summers because demons held him thrall, her heart knew the truth.

I'm a monster.

Vertiline pushed herself, using her speed and grace against fifteen, twenty, *fifty* foes. A mighty wave of humanity and its demon corruption washed over her. *I welcome it. I* welcome *it!* She grinned, feet still moving, stepping from Ikmae into Khiton, taking a head, cutting a body in half. Without armor she was speed. She was wind, and movement itself. Death would find her, aye, *aye*, but it would have to work for a change.

//VERTILINE!/// Tilly spun, saw Geneve's tossed blade, the weapon a staggering brilliance of Three's Light against the night. Vertiline saw the intent, how she could step into Cophine's *Friend's Gift*, take the sword and the power it held, and deliver it to the enemy.

And yet.

Death is here. An old friend, long seen beside me, always patient. I've sent him so many, and now it's my turn. I'm tired of the killing, and would welcome the rest. She threw her cursed metal hand out, because if she was dying, the damned arm would go first, rather than linger on as a relic to poison the land. She spread her fingers, reaching, *urging*, demons about her frozen in time's cruel embrace.

Geneve's eyes were wide, horror and a sick fear on her face. *She is so bright and true. I could have been like her, but I chose to kill her family and be complicit in the cloistering of her earliest memories. And now she will think she's killed me, without knowing how much I welcome her justice.*

Geneve's blade was no longer shaped like a sword. It was a brilliant whirling golden arc. Lightning hammered the cobbles on its way to Vertiline, and when it hit her outstretched hand...

Darkness.

Vertiline opened eyes she hadn't realized she'd screwed shut. Her metal hand shook like she held an earthquake, black fingers leaking brilliant gold. Light dripped like syrup between her fingers, the cobbles sizzling into red-yellow magma where it fell. She tried to keep her fingers clenched, remembering her hand's unleashed rage that killed her allies. She thought of Geneve and her sinner, and the Vhemin and Feybrind at their back. She could only imagine what would happen if she let go.

And *yet*.

Geneve was stumbling forward, weaponless. Vertiline screamed, "Get back! Please, Geneve, *run!*" Her voice cracked at the end, because Geneve would die like all the rest, and Vertiline the monster would live on. A courtesan stumbled toward her, the demon at her back goading with needle-sharp nails. Vertiline swung her clenched metal hand about, liquid Light splattering the ground. "You fucking want some? Is that it?"

The courtesan lurched back, hissing at a droplet of Light that scorched the stone at her feet. The demon host groaned, a sound of yearning and dread rolled together. Vertiline's hand shook harder, the Three's clenched will in her fist wanting release.

And yet.

Vertiline saw the dead at her feet, the boy, a woman, a man, a crone, people she hadn't remembered killing. Her hand swayed through the air, seeking release. It hit her all at once, like a bolt from the heavens.

It doesn't want release. It wants a target. She swung her arm toward the demon host and just ... let go.

The sound of gods and thunder, angels and monsters, a dragon's roar, a night storm. Red and white, gold and blue. Cobbles cracked. At the far end of the square warehouses vanished into ash, a channel furrowed in the ground between Vertiline's outstretched arm and five klicks of cursed hate into Imshir. Everything along that line vanished in the blink of an eye, a swirling, choking ash rising into the sky. Buildings. The people inside them. Cobbles, mortar, wagons, and chickens were simply not there anymore. The blast line was like a tunnel of air, a perfect circle carved through the walls of buildings and into the street's bedrock. Where her hand's recast of Light touched, a glowing, molten memory remained on the stone.

Every demon in that line was gone. Not on another body, but ... absent, like a memory you never had.

She sucked air, breathing ragged, then coughed. *The ash is people. I'm breathing people.*

The folk she faced took a step back, then another, as the demons riding them struggled for control. *Or are they afraid? Have I given what we feel to the enemy?* Vertiline straightened, holding her blade in cross guard. The glass was dark and heavy, waiting for purpose.

"Tilly! You're alive!" Geneve clattered to her side. "Are you ... well? Are you hurt?" Her armored hands grabbed Vertiline's arms, her shoulder, touched her jaw.

Vertiline shook herself free. A sound bubbled from her chest, parchment-thin, brittle like old bones. It sounded like laughter, but she didn't feel like laughing. "I just killed ... everyone, Geneve." She stabbed a finger at the glowing furrow in the earth, voice rising to a shriek. "*Everyone!*"

Her legs didn't want to do the work of holding a monster upright, so they gave up. Vertiline sank to her knees, wheezing, glass blade resting on her thighs. Geneve stared at her, but where Vertiline expected the hate she deserved or fear she earned, she saw...

Pity? *No, that's not it.* Geneve crouched, gauntleted fingertip under Vertiline's chin, raising her face so their eyes met. "Sister. Dearest heart. Rest a while." Geneve reached for Vertiline's belt, and with a *clink*, pulled Omrar's chain spear free.

What must she think of me? Weak and broken, a cruel killer of thousands. She turns her back on me, not daring to see. Was that disgust I saw in her eyes?

Geneve stood, facing the horde, chain playing through her left hand to tickle the ground, end clutched in her right as she set the spear to spin with an angry thrum. *One woman against five thousand. She's good, but she's not that good. None of us are.*

A growl drew Vertiline's eye. A Vhemin lad of maybe ten or twelve summers arrived at Geneve's left. He held a crude spear, but the sinner's gift touched the tip, a hint of gold and blue about the crude metal. Then the sinner himself stood by the lad, hand on his shoulder. Meriwether's gentle voice reached them all. "All right, Van?"

The lad nodded. "I'm all right." He brandished the spear as an older, far more grizzled Vhemin joined them.

This one wore scavenged scraps of leather. *He may as well be wearing pantaloons for all the protection they provide.* His voice held the rumble of old thunder. "Run along, Van. Run along now."

Van didn't take his eyes off the enemies they faced. "I'm going to be a dragonrider. You don't get to ride dragons by running away."

Meriwether sighed, then pulled a slip of steel from within his jacket. It was no more use against the foe they faced than a butterknife, but he stood there all the same, magic spent, but still using the one coin he had left to pay: his life.

Geneve stepped forward, chain spear a blur. Her feet found Cophine's *Vigil of the Seasons* as Light licked the chain, turning the blur golden. More Vhemin clustered behind her, brandishing their shitty weapons while shitty Vertiline sat on the cold cobbles. *I need to get up. I need to help, but when I try everyone dies.*

A man with a green top hat lurched forward. Geneve let the spear fly, holding the chain firm. The spear hit the man in the chest, the force of the blow knocking him into the air, feet flying up as his momentum warred with the impact. Before his body fell to the stones, she yanked the chain. Blood and bone gouted from his ribcage, the demon on his back flitting into the night sky to find another.

She set the spear to spin again, turning to face a demon sidling to her left. From the Precept's palace a bell tolled, deep and clear. Purple light glimmered from the windows, sickly and sweet. Geneve glanced at it, then turned back to their foes. "Meri?"

"Hell if I know." The sinner looked at his knife, as if wondering why he held it. "If I had to guess, I'd say that was a portal opening into a demon realm."

"A *what?*"

"It's just a guess." He turned and examined the host they faced.

"You stopped to wonder why they're not hammering us to the dirt? I think they—and by 'they' I mean those demons puppeting them—want their hosts to die. If enough of us fall, the gate opens. That's how it works. These ones are just the remnants from the last war. Maybe they want to go home." He shrugged. "I doubt it, though. I think they've been vacationing in Trebani for hundreds of years after throwing out the one thing they feared, and are now summoning their friends."

"What did they fear?" Vertiline's voice was a croak.

The sinner seemed surprised, eyebrows hunting his hairline. "You, of course." He turned a slow circle, arm sweeping to include the Vhemin, Geneve, and then the demon-ridden host. "All of us, really, but you most of all. There's one force that holds the Three's Light despite the gods going gods-knows-where, and that's the Tresward."

"There's only two of us here," Vertiline said.

Geneve spun to face another demon, the person it rode fighting for control and falling back. "We can't kill all these people."

"I don't think it matters anymore." Meri looked to the night sky as a cluster of bats took flight from the Precept's palace. "I think we're proper fucked."

"Because of a few bats?" Geneve never let her perfect form slow, the whirring promise of the chain spear keeping a circle of calm about them. Her wet eyes were the only sign she felt the death of Omrar deeper than a sword cut. *That, and the spinning web of steel she's holding.* Vertiline saw grief in Geneve, but anger too.

"Those aren't bats. We're just a little too late, is all." His voice was sad. "Those are reinforcements."

A scream came from somewhere in the night, then another. Not of panic, but of pain and loss. Still another, as the demons bursting free from the Precept's palace descended on the city of Imshir and the delicious people within.

The cobbles beneath Vertiline vibrated. She touched them with her metal hand, trying to work out what was coming. "You should go. Get to the palace and close the gate."

Through the wound Vertiline burrowed through the city, people emerged, all ridden by demons. Men, women, and their children bolstered the demon host's ranks, filling the square. Geneve glanced at the palace. "We'll never make it."

The vibration beneath Vertiline grew, a noise joining it from the east. She swiveled to the line of buildings there but saw nothing. The demon host also turned, a few at first then a mob. *Get up. You can't let them do the dying part.* Vertiline dragged herself upright, glancing east as ripples spread through the small army before them.

Geneve grinned. "Do you hear that, Tilly?"

"Aye." Vertiline squinted. "What is it?"

"Can't you tell?" The chain spear never stopped turning. "That's hope."

Vhemin burst from the easternmost street. Monsters built for an ancient war no one remembered anymore roared their defiance. Feybrind were amid them, fangs barred, weapons ready.

Vertiline might have allowed that hope a home in her heart if it wasn't for the dragon's scream that broke the sky. Ormeon's roar of terrible agony spun Geneve to face the Precept's palace. A thousand demons stood between her and the last of the dragons.

Meriwether put a hand on her shoulder. "I'll go."

"You can't—"

He kissed her, then pulled a disc of light from the air. It flickered before guttering out. The sinner frowned, brows furrowed in concentration, then pulled another one from starlight to reality. He stepped on it, then rode it into the sky above the army below.

An archer took aim at him, then died as a spear went through his skull. Vertiline glanced at Van, now weaponless, as the lad watched the sinner fly away. She looked to Geneve as she watched Meriwether leave, the look on her face similar to the way she looked at Vertiline.

Ah. That's what that look is. It's love.

Vertiline stared at her glass blade she held, then gently pushed in front of Van. "Stay behind me."

"But—"

"Kid, stay the *fuck* behind me. We're going to get your spear back." Knight Valiant Vertiline, facing an impossible force with no armor and a single glass blade? No problem. Friends and companions were with her. "To me!" She pointed with her sword toward the Precept's palace, the *make a path* motion unmistakable. *I will get Geneve to her lover, then I'll rest.*

It wouldn't be such a bad way to die.

Chapter Thirty-Five

Dragons were bullshit.

Armitage clutched Ormeon's armored hide with a Three-driven fear deep in his heart. *I'm not afraid of dying. Not really. But fuck falling all that way first.* The dragon soared over the meager army outside Imshir. Wind hauled on Armitage, trying to drag him from the dragon's back. He wanted to yell, or maybe scream, but knew the cat wouldn't let him live it down.

Sight of Day was astride the dragon in front of Armitage, ears back, that damned half-smile almost splitting his face in two. Golden eyes were bright with wonder. Armitage held Sight of Day close, because while he might be a *little* afraid, he'd never had a real brother before and didn't want to fall alone.

The cats, now. They were something. They'd stormed some ancient pile of shitty stones in the desert, dismantled it like they had the sand sharks, and now Ormeon could fly again. Nothing would bring the dragon down, and here the two of them were, flying toward a castle with a real-life demon in residence.

These were the reasons why Armitage drank.

As they approached the walls of Imshir, Feybrind way the fuck behind them and certain doom right the fuck in front, Armitage squinted snake eyes against wind tearing. He didn't see at night like the cat. Armitage's people saw heat, like the hunters they were. Faces became indistinct, replaced with form and intent. It was better this way. For instance, at this distance he could easily see what was going on, who was involved, and know things were going according to the runt's slipshod plan only an unschooled Vhemin tactician could be proud of.

Speaking of: there was the runt, talking the good talk with the fascists at the gate. And Red, too—it didn't matter that her hair was hidden by her helmet, or he couldn't see the color at night anyway. No one else stood on the ground quite the same way, like she owned it but would give you a piece if you had the decency to ask.

On her other side was Tilly. The skinny waif with those haunting blue eyes didn't have the common courtesy to wear steel. *She's fighting like a Vhemin, burning the coins of bravery instead of shoring up common sense.* He wanted to get off the dragon right there, hop on down for a talk, or...

Or, what? I'm a hideous monster with jagged teeth and eyes that make humans look away. I've killed people, all kinds, not fussy, and eaten some if I was hungry enough. She's got, wossit ... poise, *that's it. Probably never ate anything that could've spoken back to her. Holds a blade like the dawn holds light. She's pining for two dead men, no room in her heart for a third.*

Even if I was a man.

Which was why he was happy to be with the dragon and the cat. All three knew everyone was dying today, but it was a race to see who was first into the casket.

The dragon blasted the ground with fire, blowing the walls right *off* the city, and then they were inside. Armitage glanced back, but the horde was lost in the night. *My horde. People I purchased, and now I'm selling. It's what monsters do.*

They flew over a market square, the kind of place humans bought and sold useless shit to make themselves feel better. It was full of humans, packed in like cows for slaughter. They were all just standing there. Not milling, nor pushing and shoving. Bedded like stones in a river. Not a one looked up near as Armitage could tell. It's not like the dragon was invisible, what with the glowing grin, bright runes, and shiny red scales.

The Precept's palace lay ahead, the dragon approaching at what felt like death speed. Their approach wasn't the main gate, because it was too long a trip to the back room where the sword lay. No, the dragon was fixing to go in the side entrance like an oversized servant, but bringing fire and death instead of victuals.

The palace was set atop a small hill, walls and shit all about it. The side entrance had road snaking down the north side, and Ormeon headed for that. The dragon spread her wings at what was well past the too-late mark, but Armitage didn't scream because he thought she was trying for that. Ormeon landed on cobbles with a *crunch* that went right into Armitage's spine.

Sight of Day leaped down like a Three-damned spring, bow in hand, golden eyes watching the walls. Armitage winced, easing a leg over. Ormeon glanced back at him with a red leer. *//PROBLEM?//*

"Yeah." He slipped to the ground, landed in a crouch, winced, then unslung a hammer he'd stolen from some asshole back at the camp. "You can't fly for shit."

The leer turned to a smile and made it to the dragon's ruby eyes. *//I LIKE YOU. IT'S NOT OFTEN I MAKE AN EMOTIONAL BOND WITH MY LUNCH.//*

The side entrance presented a sheer wall about four dragons high, if Armitage was a judge. A portcullis type affair was in evidence, but it was up, which wasn't the usual configuration for a siege. The monster sniffed. "They forget to shut the back door?"

{Perhaps they know one of us is simple, and are leveling the playing field?} Sight of Day stilled, raised his bow, then loosed a shaft. It lanced into a slit window about two dragon heights up. No scream, though.

"Miss?"

He got a golden, withering stare. *{Like I said. Simple.}*

Armitage sniffed. "This feels like a trap." He spun his hammer by the haft in one hand. "It's a kill box. We go in there and we don't come out."

The cat nodded. *{We don't have to come out. Only the sword does.}* He stroked his chin. *{On balance I'd prefer to come out too, though.}*

The dragon ambled forward, each footfall shaking the ground. *//PERHAPS I SHOULD GO FIRST? I HAVE GLAMOROUS ARMOR.//*

"You're also a huge target."

//DID YOU HEAR THE ARMOR PART?//

"Wait. Where's the cat?" Armitage saw Sight of Day was already most of the way to the side entrance. He broke into a run, trying to keep up, but it was like trying to catch a hare, while carrying an anchor, a boat, and the whole damn ocean.

Sight of Day made it inside the portcullis, then crouched, examining something on the ground. Armitage joined him, Ormeon waiting outside. *{See?}*

The monster squinted. The cat was fingering something at ankle height, but the temperature was the same as the surrounding ground. "No?"

{Trap. The tripline goes there,} Sight of Day pointed to the north wall, *{and up through the roof. There's another there, there, and there. See the holes in the walls? Three platinum solars says arbalests wait behind.}* He stood, dusting off his hands. *{Should be simple to avoid.}*

Armitage blinked. "I can't see them."

{You what?} The cat snapped his fingers in front of Armitage's face. *{How can you not? Are you blind as well as simple?}*

"They're not warm, I guess."

The cat looked to the ceiling as if seeking divine aid. *{Why did I get partnered with the useless ones?}*

//WE SHOULD PRESS ON,// Ormeon rumbled. *//IF NO ONE'S COME OUT AT OUR APPROACH, LANDING, AND OH SO QUIET CONVERSATION, NO ONE'S GOING TO.//*

{Speak for yourself. My conversation is quiet.} Sight of Day flicked an ear. *{We should run in screaming? Well, for those of us who can.}*

//YES.//

"I'm not so sure." Armitage crouched, reaching out as carefully as he knew how. Yes, *there* it was. The wire felt like steel, thin but strong, the kind he'd made a garrote from about ten years back. "You don't set a trap without a step two."

Sight of Day narrowed his eyes. *{Step two?}*

"Yeah. If you're snaring stoats, you don't sit by with a grab bag. The stoats are wise to that kind of shit. Cunning little buggers can smell you, maybe even what you had for breakfast, that kind of thing. So they steer clear. No smart trapper waits by their snare."

//I'M NO TRAPPER. NOT MY STYLE.//

{Nor me. Take it on the bow or not at all.}

"You're missing the point." Armitage followed the line by touch to the wall, then up to a hole. He delicately felt around the circumference of the hole. "Ain't smooth. Newly cut. This isn't a usual gig for these guys."

{What would a smart trapper do? Come back later?}

"Maybe. Do we think demons like stoat?" Armitage brushed off his hands. "Our local boys set a trap. They'll let us spring it, then come in at their own sweet time."

//SO... WE CAN SPRING IT AND WORK A WAY OUT?//

Sight of Day shook his head, then rested his forehead on his palm. *{Stoats don't spring snares.}*

"Lemme see an arrow." Armitage took a shaft from Sight of Day, snapped it in three, then carefully placed it near the hole in the wall. He held the wire in his other hand, keeping the tension on. "Cut it." Sight of Day slipped a thin blade through the wire, severing it with a *snick*. Armitage felt the steel snap at his skin, dropped a muttered *fuckit*, then bound the wire tight around the shaft, nestling it against the wall. "There. Safe as houses."

//HOUSES ARE NOT SAFE FROM ME.// Ormeon craned her neck through the portcullis, sniffing. *//IT SMELLS LIKE FEAR IN HERE.//*

"Not helpful," Armitage argued. Working with Sight of Day, he secured the other wires in moments, squared his shoulders, and headed into the inner courtyard. It was regular enough as keep courtyards went, with a small stable annex for courier's horses, a shed that could punch its way up to a guardhouse if it tried, and another massive door leading presumably inside. This door was closed, but it didn't look like it'd been built to withstand a dragon.

The courtyard had walls of stone, with some fancy Tebrani-style interlocking construction method that looked both difficult to do and mortarless, which was probably the point. High on each side of the portcullis was a massive rust-spackled iron ball connected to a chain. Armitage could see how a soldier up there could, with the right motivation, unleash the ball at anything coming through the gate, like a dragon, except a dragon would probably just fly inside, and not many people built for dragon defense these days.

The walls of the room held spikes about a meter long. They looked new enough, but completely useless as they were higher up even than Ormeon.

The courtyard was about a hundred meters long, with a vaulted roof above. The roof was done in more fancy interlocking wood, with stylish skylights to let sun and rain in, depending on the weather, which seemed stupid but it probably cut down on the candle bill.

Sight of Day padded further in, head on a swivel. The cat held his bow ready, but there didn't appear to be any guards presenting themselves as targets. Armitage scratched his chin. "Something ain't right."

Ormeon shouldered through the portcullis, glancing about. //IT'S A BIG EMPTY ROOM. IS IT USUAL TO BE THIS WASTEFUL OF SPACE?//

"No." Armitage scanned the inner courtyard again. "Three wires seems a small number. Send in ten guys and you've barely made a dent, and if they're Vhemin, you're just wasting your time. We'd walk it off." He glared at the far door. "No guards. A prize inside by all accounts. What's going on?"

That particular question was answered as Ormeon entered the courtyard, crunching forward after the cat. She made it ten meters in, then the floor beneath her sank a handspan under the dragon's massive weight. Both balls on the walls released with a *clank*. Ormeon roared, moving with as much speed as something the size of a house could. She got out of the way of one ball but the other hit her in the flank, knocking her into the air. Ormeon impacted against the wall, impaled on the spikes, and screamed.

She clawed the wall, struggling to get free, blasting fire. Sight of Day rolled, leaped, and sprinted clear. Armitage took a half-step toward Ormeon's pain, but the cat put a hand on his shoulder. *{You will die.}*

The dragon writhed, trying to pull herself free of the spikes.

Molten orange liquid seeped down the wall from where the spears pierced her hide. *I will die, but I was always going to.* "Yeah, but you know that a dead Vhemin isn't here or there. Plenty more of us. There's only one dragon." He shook himself free.

Sight of Day bounded in front of Armitage, putting both hands on his massive chest. *{Brother, there is but one of you. If you die, or the dragon dies ... the world weeps either way.}*

Armitage bared shark teeth. "Out of my way, cat." He bulled the Feybrind aside, trying not to think, to feel, because all that was bullshit getting in the way of the problem. When he made it to below Ormeon he could see the damage. Her side where the iron ball hit was concave, which looked like broken ribs for sure. Not all the spikes had made it through—a bunch were bent flat like an angry carpenter had a go with Khiton's hammer. One pierced her shoulder, another her neck, and a third below her front foreleg. That was where the orange shit was coming from. "Ormeon! I'm going to get you down!"

//IT'S YOUR KIND TO BLAME! YOU! ALWAYS SCHEMING! INSECTS!// The dragon was mad with pain, teeth snapping air. She tried to breath fire again, but what few flames came out were mixed with the shitty orange goo that was leaking from her side.

"I hear you." Armitage put his hands on hips. Getting her down was going to be an ass, because she was higher than him. "Cat!"

Sight of Day arrived like smoke on wind. He looked at Ormeon, ears flat. *{She is dying.}*

The closed gate at the far side of the courtyard opened. The darkness within was broken by the glint of steel as first a handful, then a phalanx of guards came forth. Long spears. Big shields. Like the fuckers planned on hunting big game, the biggest around. Some were mounted, pennants fluttering at the tips of steel-tipped lances. "Here's what we'll do. Throw me up there," he pointed between the wall and the dragon, "and I'll push her down. We hop on and get clear."

Sight of Day shook his head. *{There is only one of us getting clear. The dragon is doomed.}*

//I WILL KILL YOU ALL!//

{There might be some fight left in her,} the cat allowed, *{but not for long. The force of men and women were sent to finish her. And us, too. They have*

horses. *We can't outrun them. But one of us can get free.}* The cat stroked Armitage's cheek. *{You.}*

"No." The Vhemin shook his head.

{It is the only way.} The cat stood close, hands between them. *{I give you my heart. I give you my soul. I'm sorry it took me this long to trust you with them.}* His fingers were hesitant.

Armitage enfolded them in his big hands. "No, cat. There's another way. There's always another way."

The forces drew closer. No hurry rode them. They had plenty of time to get in, kill a wounded dragon and her two sucker friends, and finish off with a nice hot cup of gloating. *{Roars.}* The Feybrind glanced back. *{Like.}* Armitage could make out the pennant's details. They were blank, just scraps of faceless white cloth. *{The Singing.}* Sight of Day closed his eyes. *{Sun.}*

Armitage sighed. "Roars Like the Singing Sun, huh?" The cat stiffened, the animus of Sight of Day leaving in a moment, replaced by something blank and ready. "Hang on. I didn't mean it! I ... ah, fuckit."

//YOU'LL DOOM US BOTH TO SAVE YOUR HIDE? WORTHLESS SCUM!// Another gout of fire and orange ichor, but more ichor now, far less fire. Ormeon's struggles weakened, her throes slackening against the spears that held her.

Armitage looked to the dragon, then to Sight of Day ... or what had been his friend, but was now nothing but a tool from a forgotten time. He leaned closer, shark teeth next to Sight of Day's ear. He held the cat's head with a hand, stroking the soft fur. "Hear me. We will see each other again, in the next life." *I feel sick. My brother made himself a slave to my will. This isn't right.* The enemy grew closer, patient, merciless. Their horses didn't even have the grace to look panicked in the face of a dragon's dying light. "Here is what I want you to do. Throw me up there like I asked, then buy me time."

The cat moved like the light, sweeping Armitage up by the waist and tossing him like a feather-down pillow. The Vhemin shot into the air, arms pinwheeling. He flailed, grabbed a spear. Held it, grip tightening against the slickness of Ormeon's blood, or whatever it was. Armitage's skin scalded against it, smoke peeling off. It burned like fire, or acid, or ... well, dragon blood, probably. He roared, grabbing the spear with his other hand. *That's it. The pain won't be here much longer, because I'll be dead soon.* He got into the gap between the dragon and the wall, braced his back against the stone, feet on the dragon, and *pushed. Ikmae's sometime balls, but she's heavy.* "Work with me, you useless bitch!"

Ormeon screamed, claws tearing stone from the wall. Scales fell like rain. Her bucking smashed Armitage against the wall. He felt his shoulder pop, then his knee. He also screamed but didn't think anyone would notice what with the dragon making a ruckus. The Vhemin braced his good shoulder and leg and heaved. He thought of the cat below, fighting a hundred men and women with a bow and a slip of steel, and heaved again. He thought about his red-headed friend, and yeah, the runt too, and put his back into it. Something grated, gave, but he ignored it, because he imagined a blue-eyed woman, skin like the pale right after dawn, and gave one final push.

The dragon slid from the spikes, landing on the ground with a thunderous *crunch.* Armitage fell with her, hands worthless, useless, just used-up smoking Vhemin muscle and sinew. Good for nothing now. Sight of Day fought like a dervish, so fast and fluid the wind itself couldn't touch him. But the wind was just one thing, and the Feybrind faced a hundred hardened soldiers. They'd been kept back for just one purpose: kill the dragon. *This whole fucken thing is a well-laid dragon snare. Get up. You're not done.*

He dragged himself to his feet, wheezing, crippled, broken. The dragon struggled weakly, one red eye finding him, red grin all but gone. *//MONSTER. YOU'VE COME TO FINISH ME?//*

"I ain't good for much." Armitage winced as a spear found the Feybrind's side. The cat didn't even pause as red flowed, taking the head from his opponent, shoving an arrow in the eye socket of another. "But I remember stuff. Like, how when they made you, they made you to hunt people like me. Made it so you couldn't heal except when you ate us. They built you of their fear and hate, but I got no hate for you, dragon. You're my sister, my tribe, my friend. That cat's the only brother I've known. So. One last thing. Time to chow down." He stood in front of the dragon's massive maw. "Just ... make it quick."

//YOU WEREN'T RUNNING?// Ormeon lifted her massive head,

the movement slow, weak. She stared at Armitage for a long second. *//YOU WOULD SACRIFICE YOURSELF FOR ME?//*

Armitage shrugged. "For all of you, sure. You got a better option? The cat's worth five of me. You're worth at least two of him." He got a weak dragony chuckle at that, followed by a cough filled with orange. "I've never been who you needed. Built wrong, I guess. Put here for one reason, and that reason's now."

//I CAN'T DO THIS.//

Sight of Day took a sword slash in the back. Red sprayed. Another human died, but even Armitage could see the Commanded Feybrind slowing. *No, he ain't slowing. He's* dying. *Move this shit along.* Armitage grinned shark teeth as he moved down Ormeon's neck to the gaping wound there. "You were right about one thing. I *am* a monster."

And he rammed his hand into her wound with all his broken strength.

Chapter Thirty-Six

The night air was cool. No moons meant no moths to get in Meriwether's teeth as he flew. The freedom of it was exciting, exhilarating, a wind beneath virtual wings he'd waited his whole life to feel.

Or I'm terrified. It's probably that.

The Precept's palace was ahead. Echoes of dragonfire came from a portcullis in the side, red light stretching ruddy fingers across a cobbled road. He headed toward it, but he didn't need fire to draw him in. Ormeon was in tremendous pain, screaming all kinds of nonsense about traitors and monsters.

Meriwether tipped his disc, aiming for more speed. Wind pulled its strong fingers through his hair. Tears bled from his eyes. None of that was bad, not like what was going on down there, so he tried for even more speed. The disc beneath him flickered with his waning strength, because he was tired, so damn *tired*, and keeping the image of it in his mind dragged at him like an anchor.

If I let it go, I'll fall to my death, and then Geneve will be really, really pissed off with me.

Thinking of his love brought a tight grin to his face. She faced a horde of Three-damned demons, true monsters from another plane.

She was tired too, but marched like a tide made of iron. *Can I do any less?*

He made the Precept's palace, swooping through the portcullis. The disc flickered again, so he let it fade, hitting the ground at a run then halting, wide-eyed. "What the hell happened here?"

There were fifty, maybe a hundred charred bodies near a large entranceway to the south. Humans by the look, toasted to coal inside their melted, twisted armor. The room was lined with spikes. Below some was a pool of smoking, bubbling orange. The cobbles beneath the fluid looked *soft*, sagging and hissing as the liquid melted its way into the earth. A huge metal ball hung from a chain, like it'd served its purpose and was on an ale break.

The entranceway had seen better days. A ruin of kindling showed what might have been doors. Stone and mortar lay in crumbled heaps. Smoke curled from wood and stone alike.

There was no sign of Ormeon, Sight of Day, or Armitage. Meriwether could root through the bodies for Sight of Day and Armitage in case he'd missed them on first pass, but he was sure he'd have noticed a dragon corpse. No, the massive damage to the door showed where his friends had gone. Ormeon didn't seem to need rescuing anymore, and if Meriwether was honest, he didn't really want to be around a pissed off dragon.

He stuffed his hands in ancient pockets, taking a moment to brood. *I could follow them, but there's bound to be all manner of accidents in that direction. A better use of my time would be finding what they were supposed to be here for.* Because sure as shingles, Ormeon was no longer heading for Requiem. The dragon was coring her way to the meaty, chewy center of the keep, which left an important job undone.

Meriwether squared his shoulders, found a sword that didn't look like a total loss, and went looking for the damn stairs.

Meriwether wheezed to a halt at the top of the stairs. *The Precept's a man of principle, I'll give him that. This is a proper-ass tower.* He was on a short landing, perhaps ten meters long. A closed door lay at the far end. Half way down the passage was a doorway sealed by steel bars. If the model Omrar and Jasmine built was true, that was where Requiem was.

He winced. *And Lily. She'll be at the end. Don't forget Omrar's friend. Oh, my. What am I going to tell her about him? 'Sorry, your sometime man-friend-thing is dead?' Or, 'He died a hero.' Nothing there is a good story.*

He swiped sweat-slick hair from his forehead. *One problem at a time, sorcerer.* He headed for the door holding Requiem, because the edge of steel he'd stolen below felt cheap, and he'd be happier with Geneve's blade. He'd held the skymetal in anger before, guarding her body as an undead Champion of the Tresward came for him. *I like that sword. It hasn't let anybody down, ever. Also, that was incredibly stupid. I should never stand against a Knight. It was dumb then, and it's dumb now.*

The steel barred doorway was a simple enough affair. Criss-crossed metal struts the thickness of his thumb blocked his way. A simple lock of metal sat in an imposing fashion at his belt height. Behind the door, metal gleamed in the gloom. *Requiem.* He'd recognize the damn thing anywhere. He knew it almost as well as Geneve. Where she was, so was the blade.

Omrar hadn't lied. The blade was on a low plinth, perfectly balanced on its tip. Geneve had done that for him once before. What had she said? Something about how she couldn't balance the sword forever, because she wasn't a god. Well, *someone* had put this thing here and it'd balanced this way presumably for the better part of a week or two. Was there *another* Champion cruising about in the Precept's employ? That didn't bode well for anyone involved.

Meriwether put his hand on the lock, gave it a tickle, and ... nothing happened. He stared at his fingers, then the lock, and finally gave the door a kick for good measure. *Clang.* He winced. "If that didn't summon every guard on this floor, nothing will."

When did I start talking to myself so much? He cocked his head, listening. *Nothing.* He pressed fingertips to the metal lock, closed his eyes, and looked inside. It was harder than he remembered. Perhaps switching away from a life of crime left his lock-tickling skills rusty, but c'mon! This was a simple gaoler's device. He took a deep breath and pushed his will into the mechanism.

Click. He opened his eyes as the door swung open. "That's more like it." He stepped inside Requiem's chamber, sparing an idle thought for why a sane person would imprison a sword. *It's not like it'll get up and walk away.* Meriwether walked to Requiem, placing his feet carefully, quietly, but the sword didn't budge. It stood on its tip, as if daring him to touch it.

This has got to be a trap. He walked a circle around the sword's plinth, pausing as the ground trembled. No doubt Ormeon was doing her best to level the castle. But why didn't the sword fall? He reached a hand toward it.

"You're probably wondering why the sword didn't fall."

Meriwether jerked like he'd been stabbed in the kidneys. Standing at the door was a woman who looked a little older than Tilly would if the Knight had the decency to show her years. Her hair was probably black in the right light, only a few grays nesting there. The lines on her face told of joy and sadness being regular companions. Thin, like summers were lean and winters harder still. *Still has all her teeth, though.* "Hi."

"Hi, yourself." The woman walked inside, crossed her arms, and leaned against the old stone wall. "It's not magic, if that's what you're wondering."

"I know." Meriwether tapped his head. "Bit of a sorcerer myself. Doesn't smell like magic. More like..." He trailed off.

"Practice," she said. "I'm Lily." Her brows furrowed. "No, that's not right. Lily died."

"Out*standing*," Meriwether breathed. "The third guide. I'm Meriwether. My friends call me Meri." He stamped his foot, leaving it to her to work out if she was a friend or not. "You're right, though. It's weird the sword doesn't fall."

"Meri, it's because the person who put it here imagined all the things that would come after that moment. They knew when people would walk outside. Also, when a dragonfly would settle on the pommel, or when a breeze walked uninvited inside. They heard the call of battle below before the first arrow flew. All of this they held in hand when they placed Requiem there."

"You know the sword's name?"

"Of course." She sighed. "I used to live next to a sweet man. They took me away, killed me, and then I fell. On the way down I saw so many things. Kingdoms falling, a dragon's fire, my brother and sister dying. I saw a red-haired warrior with skin the color of amber honey, and a man of questionable character at her back."

"Hey!"

"I felt myself hold that sword. I knew its name, and which part of the sky it fell from. I knew who first put it in the heavens, and why. And when I hit the ground, I forgot almost all of that." She walked to Requiem, grasping the hilt, and lifting it as easily as if it were a feather. "They brought me here and killed me again. It was after that I remembered how to balance the blade." She flourished the sword, then laid it flat against her arm. "Here."

He took it from her. It wasn't a trick. He remembered the weight of the weapon, how his red-haired love looked when she stood against the dark with nothing but this between her and death. "You put the sword here? Are you Tresward?"

She gave a sly smile. "No. And you don't believe I'm one either, do you?"

"Not really." He tapped the sword against the stone floor, stopping at Lily's wince. "If you died twice, does that mean you're immortal?"

"Not in the way you think." She shook her head. "And neither are Jasmine and Mazin. We can die. It's just ... there's one particular way of dying that'll be better for everyone." She got a far-off look in her eye. "Guides, hmm? I think I like that. It's better than what they used to call us."

"And what was that?"

"Gods." She spat, turned, and left the cell. Meriwether stared at Requiem for a hot second, then ran after her.

Chapter Thirty-Seven

Geneve tried not to think of Meri. About how he smiled, or how tired he was when he left. She couldn't think of wonderful Ormeon, beautiful Sight of Day, or brave Armitage. She was up to her armpits in demons.

She and Tilly fought back to back, demons and people coming at them in a tireless wave. The enemy didn't falter. What they lacked in skill they made up with numbers. The Vhemin and Feybrind with them were a speck of blood dropped into an ocean of sharks. The monsters used their strength as a shield. The cats darted between them, their teeth bared.

It's not enough.

Geneve stepped into *Four Cities Falling*, her chain spear hungering. She spun it in a whirl of steel perfection, keeping space about her and Tilly with the blade, then sending it out to snare an enemy to kill or drag closer. Tilly stepped beneath the spinning chain, her blade an edge of Light and purpose.

"We can do this all day!" Geneve tried for a grin, but the darkness hid it.

"I'd prefer not to." Vertiline took the head from a bald man. They swapped positions, the steps of the pattern guiding them, each trusting the other. Gods-given perfection, slightly lopsided because there were only two of them.

That's not fair. There are *three of us.* She lunged into a forward-leaning stance, chain spear snaking in a line, bluebells falling in its path, as she sent her weapon into the heart of man attempting Van's murder. The Vhemin lad fought with the pride and courage of his people, but he was young. It wasn't his fault he lacked the summers behind him to know how the spear worked best.

Geneve felt the air harden, heard the rumble of a storm, and stepped to Van's side, holding her chain spear in high guard over his head. Lightning pillared to the blade, found Light's defense, and spat in blue-white rage to the ground. *Where did that come from?* She scanned the horde. "There! A sorcerer!"

A woman stood on a warehouse roof, hands raised to the dark skies. Tilly snarled as another bolt of blue-white arced for her. She raised her metal hand, grabbing the lightning like the bridle of a horse. Bolts twined through her fingers, and she *pulled*.

Golden Light leaped up the snarling, snaking bolt, found the sky, and hammered back down on top of the sorcerer. She vanished in a roiling ball of fire, as did much of the warehouse. Stone, wood, and mortar rained across the square. Geneve shielded her eyes in the crook of her elbow. When she raised her face, Tilly stood with blade in one hand, a crackling whip of sorcerous power still tangled about her fingers. She lashed out, carving a line through the horde. Bodies charred.

That arm is something else. How did the ancients lose when they could make themselves gods? Geneve stood in front of Van, shielding him from the horde, but the lad skirted about to stand at her left, spear ready.

Ormeon's scream rang out from the palace again, somehow more desperate, ragged, filled with the despair of the lost. Geneve took a step forward, heart lurching. *Meri. Ormeon. All my friends. I must be with them.* "Vertiline!"

"I hear it." The Knight Chevalier stood in a patch of calm, demon-ridden humans clotted about. "We must help them, but..." She sucked air, chest heaving with exertion.

"But there are too many." Van gripped his spear. "I will draw them off." He pointed to a bookseller's store. "Give me time enough to get there. I'll set a fire. Then you draw them in and slip out the back."

Geneve didn't know whether to laugh or cry. Van would die, and for what? "That's not the way."

"It's the only way. I'm not good enough to do anything but get underfoot." The spear shook in his hands. "This is the Vhemin way. For the tribe."

Geneve shook her head. *There's no way this child dies as a trade for the life of another. I will not allow it.* "Vertiline! We carve a path."

//BACK!// Commotion tugged at the crowd. Demons and people parted, drawing a line to the edge of the square. There: Eleni leaned on her staff, robe tucked close. She strode toward Geneve. A man in fool's livery twitched closer, and the Justiciar spared him half a glance. *//STAND THERE UNTIL THE WORLD DIES.//* The fool jerked, but stopped moving, feet still as if mortared to the stones.

Geneve took off her helmet, slicked back her hair, then put it back on. "Hail, Justiciar."

The crowd seethed. Eleni raised her hand. *//ALL WILL..//* Her voice cracked. *//ALL WILL HOLD.//* Three words, but each one seemed to lay a massive weight on her, bowing the Justiciar's shoulders. She gave Geneve a half-mad smile. "It's not as easy as it looks."

Weary Vhemin and Feybrind backed away from foes. The odd Vhemin gave a last punch or slice, but they drew back to form a ring about Geneve, Vertiline, Van, and Eleni.

Geneve scanned the crowd, that impossible gulf of people sent to stop them. *We need to move faster, cut the head from the snake.* "Eleni, we need to get to the palace."

"To save the world?"

Geneve eyed her chain spear as Vertiline backed toward them. *I should say yes, but that's not what this is about.* "To save those I love."

"Good." The old cleric eyed the crowd. "Did you have a plan?"

Vertiline snorted. "This is Geneve we're talking about."

Van looked at the pale-haired woman. "You said she was smart."

"I say a lot of things I don't mean." Vertiline held ready, waiting for the crowd to come for them, but none did. "What did you do? I've never seen its like."

"The Sway." Eleni tried for a shrug but the weight of all those people held her shoulders still. She raised a shaking hand to the skies where demons circled, not yet daring to swoop into the reach of her Sway. "Soon enough the demons will find their courage. You may want to run."

Geneve stared at the old woman. *You healed me when I was hurt. You never used Sway to take power, but you are born to it.* "How did I not know you better?"

"Because you're young. And, as Tilly said, not very smart."

Vertiline bridled. "I didn't—"

"Despite that," the old woman steamed on, "I have one card left to play. It is a hand we've husbanded to this moment. We can only play it once. Are you ready?"

Geneve nodded, glad her helmet hid her fear. "I will not fail."

"Oh, child." Eleni shook her head. "That's not something in your power to control. But all of us, together, might tip the scales just enough."

"This is my burden."

Eleni's face turned grim. "If you say so. Here it comes."

"What comes?" Tilly cocked her head. "No, I can hear it."

Geneve turned to the south. Rumbling grew until it thudded the cobbles. Chained people and demons struggled against the Sway, but stuck fast. A building against the southern edge of the market shook, then with a flash of Light exploded. *Tresward!*

Their Smithsteel armor gave silvery challenge to the night. Every Knight and Cleric Eleni brought with her came to share their final stand. Light from a half a hundred swords whirled, a clockwork army of heavenly perfection throwing down against the blight on the world.

Geneve gaped. Vertiline grabbed her arm. "Remember what Eleni said? Run!"

She nodded. *We've little time and much to do.* Geneve whirled the chain spear, links of metal wrapping her arms, put her head down, and ran. Not toward the enemy, but to the bookseller's store Van had pointed out. They passed Tresward, three souls hurrying against the tide of a hundred. They didn't knock into anyone, because Knights saw the pattern before it was needed. They slipped between armored ranks like pebbles through a grate. Vertiline was in the lead, but slowed, turned, and ran back. Geneve watched, trusting her friend would tell her if she needed aid.

The Knight Valiant went back for Van. The Vhemin lad's shorter legs starved his speed. Tilly husbanded him along, metal hand on cold-blooded shoulders, blade held ready, but no attack came.

Geneve reached the bookseller and launched herself through the front window. Glass broke as she tumbled, hard rain cascading to old wooden floors like droplets from a waterfall. She took the fall on the blade of her hand, curled, and rolled to a standing position. She spun, chain spear rattling from her hand to hang ready. Vertiline was ten meters back when she grabbed a surprised Van, tossing him through the window headfirst. Geneve slipped between the lad's spear and body, snatching him from the air, and set him on the ground in time to spin as Vertiline rolled through the window as she had.

They stood, panting, waiting. *Watching*. The Vhemin lad trembled at Geneve's side, spear shaking, a bamboo reed in a hurricane. She put an armored hand on his shoulder. "Easy."

"I don't want to die," he blurted. "I don't want to die. I don't want to die."

The Tresward outside formed a hair-thin line against the mass of humans and demons. A hundred souls, spent all at once. Geneve removed her helmet, crouching before Van. He tried to look around, but she tipped his chin toward her. "Van, I will tell you something my..." She trailed off, glanced away for a moment, certain she felt Israel's hand on her shoulder for a moment. She could almost smell him, the strong man sweat and metal oil that came from a life in service to the Three. Strength like an anvil, and yet not quite strong enough. "My father told me no one wants to die. But we don't get to choose that. We only get to choose *how* we die."

"What do you mean?" The boy's voice quavered.

She brushed hair back from his forehead. "We can go on our knees or feet. Take a knife in the back or face it head-on."

"Good pep talk." Vertiline turned away, lips hammered to a bitter line.

"Don't look at her," Geneve urged. "She's worried she hasn't chosen right. That she followed the wrong people—"

"Wrong men," Vertiline murmured.

"The wrong people for the wrong reasons." Geneve sighed. "What do you think?"

Van considered that, the night beyond the window silent, still, waiting for the first blade to fall. "That's bullshit. She's strong and brave." Vertiline's head jerked at that, but Van wasn't looking at her, eyes on Geneve's. "I've never seen anyone fight like her. I want to be a dragonrider, but I also want to be like her."

"See?" Geneve stood. "And thus, she chooses how she dies. Not whether she dies *here* with a blade in her gut, but in your mind and heart. Leaving you a little piece of herself to remember. Not the mistakes or fear, but the courage, action, and heart. This is what my father meant. We must make the next best choice we can, and the next after that. A lifetime will wear your will to the nub. You'll feel tired before your span is done, want to take the easy path, to let your guard down. To *not* stand for what you feel is right. And that is the wrong choice." She rattled her chain, the spear shivering in sympathy. "It's not whether we live or die, only that we stand or fall for the right reasons."

Van looked at his spear. "I still don't want to die." He sniffed. "But I can't choose that."

Geneve brushed red hair aside, shaking her head, voice sad. "No. And I can't choose it either. I could promise to protect you, but it would be empty. I will do my best, but the world is dangerous. And there are thousands of demons who want the starlight inside you." She touched his small chest right above his heart. "I don't know if I will live until tomorrow. A woman much like me died with the might of all the ancients behind her. But I won't stop trying, because everyone I love is in this world, and if they're not safe there is no life here I want."

"I want to be a dragonrider," the boy whispered.

"Then let's go find the last dragon," Geneve suggested.

"Always one more thing." Vertiline sagged for a moment as she watched Van scamper through a back door. "Israel never said those things."

Geneve stilled, glad the darkness hid her cheeks. "I always wanted him to."

"I thought you were going to tell him to run." Vertiline pointed after Van.

"Would you have said that to me?"

"Would you have listened?"

"Exactly." Geneve put her helmet on. "One last push, Knight Valiant Vertiline."

"Aye, one last, Knight Champion Geneve." Vertiline looked to her metal hand, but only for a moment. "I'm so glad you're here. There are so many things I want to say, to—"

"Tomorrow," Geneve said. "There will be time enough."

Vertiline's eyes were wet, but she nodded along with the lie. "Tomorrow, then."

THEY DASHED THROUGH IMSHIR'S STREETS. GENEVE SAW DARKNESS and blades, and fell into *Fearless Pursuit*. Her feet knew the way, the chain spear in her hand whirring. A flash of Light from Vertiline's blade threw back the heavy shroud of night. Van was at her side, spear ready, heart strong.

That was not the most amazing thing Geneve saw on the mad run to the Precept's palace.

A VHEMIN FELL, SPINE SEVERED BY A BLACK BLADE. A FEYBRIND STOOD above him, fangs bared, her blade cutting a bright rebuke. It wasn't enough, and she fell atop the Vhemin she tried to save.

The demon above them both came in for a killing stroke. The Vhemin heaved the Feybrind aside, taking the blade in his chest. With strong arms he pulled himself up the blade, grabbed the demon attacker's hands, and bit with shark teeth, severing hands at wrist. Blood, dark as sin, and all three quietened.

A FEYBRIND, STRONG AND PROUD, BARRING A DOORWAY. BEHIND HIM, injured humans. A glance inside showed a Vhemin tending as best she knew how, but these brittle people didn't heal like hers did. She tried to press a rag against wounds, but there was too much blood and bone bared to air. Red wet seeped through cloth, coating scaly skin.

Wailing, and weeping, with three dead already.

"They are done," she said.

{But we're not.} The Feybrind half-turned, words curt.

"Aye." The monster staggered upright. "We hold, for as long as we can. Did I ever tell you I'm allergic to cats?"

{Did I ever tell you I'm allergic to stupid?}

A KNIGHT HELD THE LINE BEFORE A CART PACKED WITH REFUGEES. SHE held a sword Geneve recognized. This was the first weapon Meri blessed at their rag tag camp. A Cleric stood in the wagon's rear, hands raised, bloodstained robes showing the evidence of too little time at drill and too much in the library.

The Knight nodded to Geneve as she ran past but didn't leave her guard. She readied for a surging breakwater of demons, black wings, and obsidian teeth. She stepped forward into a Dawn's Brace *so perfect it made Geneve's heart ache. Light ran golden fingers across her blade as she cut the first demon from shoulder to crotch.*

Geneve smelled sun-kissed grass, and felt a warm breeze touch her face. She thought of her mother calling her to hearth, fresh-baked bread ready after a morning's play. Meri's enchantment, paid forward for this very moment.

The demon screamed, vile black and foul ichor spraying from its back. The Knight stepped into the pattern's second step, blade moving up, then a third step taking the weapon across. A demon's entrails spilled to the cobbles, and another lost its head.

"You must run!" the Knight called to the Cleric. She pointed with her blade to the refugees in the cart. "Take them to safety!"

"*Where to?*" *The three silver bars on the Cleric's sash made him a Lucent.* "*Nowhere in the world is safe.*"

A KNIGHT, THREE SPEARS THROUGH HIS CHEST AFFIXING HIM TO A DOOR. *By his feet, twelve dead demons, smoke and ash, char of the Light's justice. His blood, tacky on the wooden door, a line that couldn't be crossed.*

Behind the door, a lantern's glimmer, and scared faces. A room of wounded and fearful. A field triage center for those near death's cold fingers, still alive because one man didn't run.

They didn't know each other's names. It didn't matter.

GENEVE PASSED A CLOTTED MAT OF FUR. SIGHTLESS ROSE EYES STARED AT *the skies.*

FOUR CHILDREN CLUSTERED AROUND A WOMAN'S BODY. WINGED DEMONS *circled, their jeers echoing from the buildings.*

"*This stops now,*" *Vertiline hissed.*

"*The palace.*" *Geneve knew the palace was perhaps two blocks ahead. They were so close. But she felt it too. All fights were important. The Precept had to die, but surely not at the cost of innocents.*

"*And yet, it stops now.*" *Vertiline closed weary eyes, then jerked them open as Van scampered past. The boy spun, back to the children, spear pointed skyward. Cold, hard snake eyes above a bared shark-toothed grin. The mana of his people not yet tempered by the weary world rooted his feet as he stood guard.*

Geneve gave a war cry, joining Vertiline to stand with Van. The demons circled still. One dropped, a comet of black teeth. Geneve turned away, knowing Tilly had that one, stepping into Seconds Count *at her friend's back. She spun the chain spear as she moved, then loosed. It impaled a winged horror with two heads. Light shimmered along the chain, the monster's four eyes glowing incandescent as the Three's justice boiled from its body.*

She yanked, pulling it to the ground, where Van ran it through with his spear. Geneve put her foot on the corpse, tearing the spear free. She turned about the Vhemin lad, ichor splashing from the chain spear's tip as she set it whirring again. Vertiline knew the pattern well, ducking as Geneve spun it at head height. The blade carved a path through three monsters swooping low. She squeezed her eyes shut.

Lightning reached from the heavens to earth through their bodies, a blinding brilliance that shook the world. Geneve stilled, waiting, watching, and listening. Leathery wings flapped away, seeking easier prey.

Van put up his spear, reaching to a boy. "You're safe now."

The child backed away, shrieking, "Monster!"

The Vhemin lad reared back as if he'd been kicked by a horse. His chin jutted, fighting a wobble. Vertiline's hand found his shoulder. She leaned close to his ear. "Hear me. It is a word like any other. You determine the weight, not them."

Geneve looked down, stomach churning, hurting for the lad. Just months ago I was the same. When I saw Vhemin, I saw creatures made to end us all. Now I count them among my closest friends, family not of my blood, but of my heart. What has made us this way? *"And yet." She struggled for the words. "And yet you can take the weight for others, I think. Only the strongest can, but I think a dragonrider might do it."*

Van straightened, nodded once as if settling an argument with himself, then crouched before the terrified human child. "I'm sorry I frighten you. I didn't choose how I was made ... but someone told me I get to choose how I die. I think I like being a monster. Do you know why?" The human lad shook his head, confusion and fear fighting a war with his face as a battlefield. Van pointed to the sky. "Because those things need something to fear." He bared shark teeth. "I will be the thing that hides under their bed. They will have nightmares until I take back my world. Me, and my dragon."

He stood, hefted his spear, and eyed Vertiline. The Valiant smoothed his hair, touched his face, and straightened his shirt. "We humans are ... adaptable. The Feybrind are perfect at everything they do. But the Vhemin have the courage of ages."

"We also have big sticks," the lad said.

She laughed. "Then let us find a demon worthy of your weapons, and your courage."

AND SO, THE PALACE. THE STEPS LEADING TO THE MAIN DOORS WERE almost two hundred meters wide at the base, tapering toward the top to less than fifty. Each step was a meter deep, smoothed by the passage of a million hurrying feet. Imshir was an ancient city, the old steps marking just how long people had served a single master.

The gate at the top stood open, double doors fit for a giant standing wide and empty. No guards waited. The palace itself was a massive affair, crenelated towers and spires springing up from the crazed architecture of a mad mind. The central spire was perhaps a klick high, made of stones fit perfectly against each other without mortar.

Vertiline nudged Geneve's elbow. "I think someone's compensating for something."

She snorted, but the uneasy feeling in her gut remained. "Let's find out what."

"Hold a moment." Vertiline faced her. "There is a true monster within those walls. He's bided for eight hundred years."

"Then we've no time to waste." Geneve spun the spear, wrapping her forearm in chain. "The world's not rebroken, but it will be soon. We can still fix it."

Van cleared his throat. "What are they doing here?"

Geneve jerked her gaze away from Vertiline to the top of the steps. Mazin stood before the open doors, sparkling Yasmine riding his head, fists twined in his locks. Beside them stood Eleni, leaning on her staff. Geneve spun to the city, then back to Eleni. "How did you—"

"Get here so fast?" The Justiciar smiled. "It's more you were slow."

"Quite slow," Mazin agreed. "Also, you left these at the camp." He lifted a canvas-wrapped bundle. "By the Three, this is heavy."

Geneve bounded up the steps. *Are they my friends, or illusions? I wish Meri were here.* "I don't see how you could have beat us."

"And yet we did, huge one." Yasmine flitted free from Mazin's hair, settling on the bundle he carried. "You should open this. You'll need it."

Vertiline joined her, Van close behind. The Valiant held naked glass, but the blade nosed the ground as if uncertain. "If I didn't know better, I'd say this was a sinner's trick." She looked away. "But there aren't any sinners. Not in the way we thought."

Mazin hefted the bundle, causing Yasmine to flit away with a tiny *harrumph*. "Please take it, Tresward."

"Because you want me to take a trap?"

"Because it's heavy." He sighed. "Not everything is what it seems, unless it is."

"That sounds like Mazin." Vertiline looked away.

"Open the damned bundle, Knight Champion Geneve." Eleni took a step forward. "We didn't bring it up these steps, standing theatrically above you with the most epic of entrances, for you to fret at the last step." When Geneve made no move, Eleni rolled her eyes. "Three grant me strength." She flicked the canvas wrap aside.

Glass sparkled within, nestled next to worn wood and metal. Geneve sighed, shoulders easing with relief. "This is no trick." She took the bundle, handling the curve of glass carefully. As the canvas fell free, she held up her prizes. Kytto's last gift, the glass shield Brilliance, and her old scattergun Tribunal. She turned the weapon over. "I thought it lost."

"It's lucky you have someone who knows how to find things," Eleni murmured.

Geneve strapped Brilliance to her arm. She didn't find it heavy like Mazin had, but rather comforting—the weight of an old friend leaning against you. Then she belted the scattergun at her hip, before drawing it to check the action. It gave a well-oiled *click*. Yasmine drifted closer on a night eddy. "It took me a little while to get it working right. You need to care for your things better." She sniffed. "Also, I made some modifications."

"What kind of modifications?" Geneve sighted down Tribunal before holstering it. "Will it explode?"

"Probably not." Yasmine tapped her chin. "You know, I could make it do that if you want."

The floor shook as a dragon's roar came from within the palace. Geneve squared her shoulders. "It's time to finish this." Eleni nodded, ambling toward the entrance. "Wait! Where are you going?"

Mazin joined the Justiciar. "Finishing this."

Yasmine flitted before them, her glow lighting the darkness ahead. "Together."

Van joined them, spear ready. "We only fall when we're divided."

Geneve felt a hand on her shoulder as Vertiline drifted past, offering a tired smile. The Chevalier's eyes were bright blue though, full of life Geneve hadn't seen there for what seemed a lifetime. "This is not a fight you have to do alone."

"I..." Geneve swallowed the lump in her throat. "I started all this—"

"And we'll finish it with you," Eleni nodded.

"That's not what I mean." Geneve readied her chain spear, links jangling by her side. "I started this by trying to kill the man destined to be my love. I followed a liar who stole my power, but I loved him all the same, because he was my father. I met a dragon who killed my horse and became my friend. Monsters joined my family. We saved Feybrind and were saved in kind. Don't forget how we rescued Ravenswall, and the Raven Queen who rules there. We've fought ancient machines brought back to life and watched the Three leave the sky. The ancient tyranny of demons against so-called sinners was dragged into the burning Light by us. All of us." She looked over their heads and into the dark entrance beyond. "I am honored and humbled to have you with me. Thank you all."

Vertiline's smile grew. "You talk too much."

"Did she say anything about fairies?" Yasmine gave an anxious glitter. "I didn't hear anything about fairies."

"Nor wine merchants, and yet I still feel included." Mazin extended a finger, letting Yasmine settle on it. "Come, little one. Let's be the guides they need and light their way." He turned and charged into the palace.

Geneve bared her teeth. *It's time.*

Chapter Thirty-Eight

"I need to know more about this god thing." Meriwether hurried to keep up with Lily. *The old woman puts on a decent pace! She should start a club with that witch Eleni.* "Like, real gods, or ancient gods, or... what?"

"Gods are gods." Lily paused at an intersection.

North looked much the same as south to Meriwether, but the guide-slash-god looked wracked with indecision. "Need help guiding the way?"

She gave him a withering glare. "It's all about timing." Lily had rescued Requiem from him lest he do himself injury. She tapped skymetal on the old stone floor, then cocked her head to listen. "Does the echo sound longer from the south to you?"

"The echo?" Meriwether glanced down the southern passage. Aside from some tasteful armoires and some tasteless artwork it looked much like the north route. North had tasteless everything, too.

"The echo."

"Now I hear it!"

The withering stare didn't lighten even a degree. "I don't know why we bothered." Lily put Requiem tip-first onto the floor then let the sword go. It stood upright, just as it had when Geneve did the same trick. "South it is."

"How can you tell?" Meriwether crouched before the blade.

"See how it vibrates?" She pointed to the edge. "It's subtle, but the skymetal yearns for its next encounter."

Meriwether glanced at Lily, the blade between them. "You're a weird person, you know that?"

She snatched the blade up, shouldering it. "We're all weird, Lord Meriwether du Reeves. Some of us are weird because we crave pickles with our candied sweets. Others have dark wants, seeking to hurt or enslave. Those of us who guide see it all. It's as clear as the marks on your skin."

He self-consciously raised a hand, meaning to touch his shoulder blade where the first whip blow landed, but let it fall. "How can you see these things?"

"The same way I hear the echo." She shrugged, Requiem glinting with the motion. "It's plain for anyone with eyes to see or the wit to listen."

"I'll try not to take that like a criticism." Meriwether pushed himself upright. "Can you use that sword?"

"For what? The killing of demons?" At Meriwether's nod, her eyes turned sad. "Aye, young Meri. Called that because you made her heart sing, you know that, yes?" She waited for his eyes to find the floor then back up to hers. "I can kill many demons with this blade. But I can't kill *the* demon. That job falls to another."

"Why not?" Meriwether put his hands on his hips. "If you're here to kill a monster, then be about it."

"Oh." Lily tapped her chin with an old finger. "I see what's wrong. You mistake why I've got this blade. You think we head south to help Geneve fight the Precept." At his nod, she gave a soft smile, full of summer wine and the smell of fresh-cut grass. Then the smile turned knowing, the aged grace of one who'd worn a groove into the world. "That's not why we're here. *You* must fight the demon."

"Me?"

"Not *you* you, but you as a people." Lily huffed. "We're here for something else."

Meriwether scuffed the old stone floor. "What could be more important than killing the Precept? He's been a blight on this world for eight hundred years."

Lily raised her hand as if lifting the air. "Eight hundred? No. Think of a much bigger number."

"A thousand?"

"More."

"Merciful Three." Meriwether scowled. "How? Why?"

"Does it matter?" She stroked the side of his cheek. "You'll understand soon, I think. We've all sacrifices to make. Not one of us will make it clear without hurt. You will have it hardest. But like all of your wonderful kind, you'll think it the easiest step of all."

"Okay." Meriwether faced the southern passage. "Are you going to tell me what's more important than killing the Precept?"

Lily led the way. "Dying, of course."

Chapter Thirty-Nine

Geneve followed Yasmine's glimmer. The fairy flitted into the darkness, fearless as a mountain ogre. They'd left the entranceway far behind. If they wanted to run, it'd be a long way back.

I didn't come here to run.

They entered a massive room. The ceiling was glass and stone, a beauty and wonder melded together. Geneve could see how a person here would have an unimpeded view of the three moons when the gods still watched over them. No city lights would distract the view of the heavens.

All that weight was vaulted by beams thicker than the keel of a deep-sea merchant ship. Ten pillars stood proud and tall along the room's length, holding their share of the weight. The room was fed by six doorways. They'd entered through the southern one, and its opposite lay north. Two each lay east and west. Toward the northern end a dark purple glow shone. It wasn't the color of lilacs, but a bruise. Above it the ceiling was shattered, the stonework sagging in against broken spars.

"Bet you that's where the demons came from." Vertiline pointed with her sword at the purple glow.

"I'm not taking that bet." Geneve stalked forward. The room's two hundred meter length held many shadows that could hide demons, but she had a dead friend's chain spear and needed no excuse to use it. Nothing leaped at her. She got about fifty meters from the purple glow until she could make it out: runes writ in purple fire about a glowing circle on the stone floor. The stone was intact, which suggested this demon door—for that's what it had to be—was closed. She glanced up at the broken ceiling. "That's the kind of thing a dragon could fly through. How many demons came to our world?"

"*Thoussssandssss.*" The hissed whisper came from the east, where a smokey form crept under a door. It resolved itself into a humanoid shape. The hint of glowing eyes watched Geneve from the gloom.

She felt her heart sink. "The smoke demon? *You're* the Precept?"

"*Yessss.*" A ghostly hand rubbed a suggestion of lips. It had that damnably familiar pattern of speech she couldn't quite put her finger on. "*You tasted so sweet.*"

Vertiline stood shoulder to shoulder with Geneve. "Is now where we get to the killing part?"

"*Hold a moment.*" It slipped around a pillar, drawing closer on a mockery of legs. "*Do you not want to ssssave thiss world? You and I, Geneve of the Sssstorm. We sssshare a throne and bring jusssticccce and Light wherever we walk.*"

She laughed. "You and I, to hold hands and sing songs while we rule the world?" Geneve sobered. "You mean it, don't you?"

"It is a trick, child." Eleni joined them. "He does not lie, but his form of justice is ... singular."

"*Asssss wasss yoursss, Tresssward. You cassst your legion to the four cornersss of a compasssss, seeeking sssssinnersss.*" The demon slipped to another pillar, sliding through the distance in the blink of an eye. *It has no form*, she realized. *No weight, no substance, but it hits like a mule.* "*Your Three are falsssse!*"

"I think I speak for all of us when I say, 'Eat a dick,'" Yasmine chimed. "Anyway. What's with the hissing? Cat got your tongue? Or maybe your whole mouth?"

The creature's eyes flashed brighter in the gloom. Mist formed to a hint of substance, and a man stepped forward. His outline was ... hesitant, almost, as if it didn't want to be here. Strong jaw as such things went. Blond hair, broad shoulders. A cape, because why not, draped over finery fit for a king. When the Precept spoke, this time his voice held no hint of the serpent. Geneve goggled. She knew that face, his cruel smile, the constant better-than-you smirk. "Is this better, tiny fool?"

"No. You're huge and ugly. But whatever." Yasmine flitted to crown Mazin's head. "Should we beat on this clown?"

"By we, you mean the Tresward?" Mazin frowned. "It seems hardly fair. A Justiciar, Knight Champion, Chevalier, two Guides, and a Vhemin boy with an urge to kill."

"You should've brought more people." The Precept smiled. Full lips that were kind, soft, full of compassion. "The last time your kind fought mine on a battlefield like this, you lost."

"And yet we're still here." Geneve stepped forward. "She *beat* you. And so did I, at your Trial, fallen Knight Wincuf." Because that's who stood before her: Wincuf, trained in the ways of Knights and their Light. A boy grown to a devil.

He inclined his chin. "And yet, here I am. With my demon army, humans as slaves, and no gods marking time in the sky above. You've got less than one hundred Tresward. When they last came for me there were a hundred thousand Knights. Your numbers dwarfed my forces. You dropped the *sky* on me! And here I stand." Wincuf smoothed his doublet. "You still had dragons, and mages were your allies. I left none to remember the shape of my face"

"Mages are still our allies. We still have dragons." Geneve's chin jutted. She couldn't help it.

"You have a failed illusionist and a crippled red lizard." He shrugged. "I'll take those odds. I spent *years* learning your Light's tricks. Holding the cursed pattern so tight it burned. I'm everything I was before, and so much more. I sacrificed foes, watching at Ravenswall to learn all about you, soon-to-be-forgotten Knight Champion Geneve."

The door to the north clicked, creaking open. Geneve whirled, the chain spear's links singing their metal warsong. An old woman stepped through, a blade Geneve would recognize even mostly dead leaning on her shoulder. She was followed by... "*Meri?!*"

The holomancer looked behind him, double-checked himself, and nodded. "I found the third guide. It's Omrar's neighbor, Lily. *And* she's got your sword. She's got Requiem."

"Finally," Geneve breathed, holding out her hand.

Lily smiled, unlimbered the sword, and flung it. It sailed above Geneve, glittering in the darkness as it flew. It passed over Eleni, the Justiciar's mouth half-open in surprise. It swung past a startled Yasmine, arm raised and pointing, and Mazin's wide-eyed astonishment. Geneve kept her eye on it but couldn't help but notice Vertiline's mouthed, *well, fuck*. Geneve kept her arm raised even though Requiem passed high above her fingertips, because she couldn't believe what was happening.

The blade tumbled end over end, all star bright promise, right into the outstretched hand of Precept Wincuf. The demon smiled like ten cats. "And *now* we finish this." He flourished Requiem, and Light glimmered on the skymetal's length.

Chapter Forty

Well, *that's fucked everything up.* Meriwether was tempted to dust off his hands, turn around, and walk away. His anchor was Geneve's expression of horror and betrayal, such utter loss his heart almost broke.

Meriwether swiveled to Lily. "You ... *bitch!*" Then he ran toward Geneve.

He made it maybe half a step before Lily's punch knocked him to the ground. She hadn't pulled it for old time's sake either, all pointy knuckles. He felt something *crick* in his neck as she hit him, then *pop* the other way as the floor flattened his face. "Not so fast, holomancer. Good things take time."

From Meriwether's position on the ground he got a fine view of Lily's feet, then the rest of her, running toward the Precept. Vertiline made the monster first, her lithe athleticism not weighed down by Smithsteel. The demon flourished Requiem once, twice, three times, each blow landing against Tilly's glass. Each hit flared with Light, the Valiant moving like sunlight racing the dawn to catch Requiem against her edge.

She wasn't fast enough. The Precept swung past her, feet moving like the finest clockwork. He swung Requiem like a club, catching Vertiline on the back of the head. The *crunch* was sickening, dropping the Knight like a sack of unwanted kittens over a bridge.

That's not right. Meriwether was no expert in the Storm, couldn't use the Sway, and barely understood which end of a sword to hold. But he'd watched Geneve countless times, knew the sway of her body in and out of armor, how she held her head, the set of her shoulders, and what a sword looked like when held by a true master. Her steps wound through intricate patterns without seeming thought, a blend of movement so pure it was art.

It unlocked the Storm, channeling the Three's Light, and made any Tresward worth a hundred normal soldiers.

The Precept used no patterns Meriwether could see. Oh, *aye*, he moved like silk on water, but his body didn't follow the damn rules. His elbows bent at odd angles. The demon's neck could turn a full one-eighty without any discernible discomfort. He was fast because there was no weight, no *substance*, to his body.

He'd dispatched Vertiline like a drillmaster faced with a two-year-old child. Took the rattle from the baby, tossed it into a hedgerow, and made off with the candy.

What's more was the Precept using Light. The thing was a demon, a monster from another world. It and Geneve seemed to share a connection, but he was *certain* no Tresward would be so stupid as to train a demon at their holdfasts. Yet, patternless, Light found Requiem in the demon's hand. And dispatched the second-best swordswoman in all the world in three strikes.

All these thoughts arrived in a heartbeat. A single moment of perfect clarity, followed closely by, *I think we're truly, deeply fucked.*

"Vertiline!" Geneve screamed, running toward the demon. Her chain spear rattled free. She was slower, armor weighing her feet, but not by much.

Eleni raised her hands, but the Precept was faster. *//SILENCE!//* he roared, and Eleni croaked, then crumpled to the ground, hands about her throat.

I see. He can use the Sway too. That's ... really, really bad.

Meriwether tried to move, tried to get his damn worthless body *up*, by the Three, just *stand*, man, but no, nothing happened. Lily suckered him good. It made sense. If she knew how to stand a sword on point for a couple weeks, knocking out a wayward sinner was no effort at all.

Geneve was going to die, and all he could do was lay here watching.

Chapter Forty-One

Geneve felt sick and broken when Vertiline fell. She saw Meriwether hitting the floor face-first, wondered if she should kill the bitch with him, then faced the demon Wincuf. *Iz would've said the Precept was the most important thing to kill, and he would be right. He'd also tell me the creature's watched and learned everything about me for this one moment, and he'd be twice right.*

She charged, but stumbled to a stop as a sound like a hurricane came from above. Van was at her side, snake eyes up, mouth showing shark teeth. She followed his gaze to the broken roof as darkness blotted out the stars. A swirling swarm of wings and teeth, a horror host from another world, and Geneve realized: *the demons are here*.

They burst through the broken ceiling, loose glass and stone following their descent. The boy at her side took a step back, but there was nowhere to go.

She raised Brilliance, the clear edge flashing with crystalline Light as the demons reached them. Geneve set her shoulder into the block, the host of demons pounding against her ward like the very ocean itself. A surging tide trying to sweep her into the sea.

She screamed as lightning arced from the skies to the rim of her shield. A brilliant pillar of blue-white fury found Brilliance. The demons hitting the shield were ash and dust in a moment. Electricity reached its clawed fingers out, leaping from foe to foe, killing ten, a hundred, a *thousand* with that one block.

But there were more. Always, always more.

Geneve set her spear spinning, the chain rattling over Van's head. The blade whipped in a circle, and everywhere it touched a demon a lance of blue-white reached from above to take another away. Her stance was perfect. Shield never held better. Chain spear in hand, she battled a horde of demons alone.

But the chain spear was no Requiem. It hadn't been forged by the best Smith in all the lands. It certainly hadn't been forged for *her*, a promise of love from one gruff man who believed in her more than her own father.

The chain snapped, the spear tip tumbling into the darkness. The demon host fluttered higher, a swirling tornado ready to thunder down and swallow her. *I'm so tired. I misstepped, and the Light left the chain. We will die because I didn't walk the perfect pattern.*

Van nudged against her, his spear raised. The boy trembled, but his eyes were clear. His voice held no tremor of fear, because the Vhemin were many things, but not cowards. "Stand behind me."

Her heart went out to him. *I should protect him. This is wrong.*

Above the demon host, red glimmered. The swirling horde of teeth and claws eddied, uncertain, then a blaze ignited the top of the room. Glass and stone thundered free, and through the falling fragments dragonfire led Ormeon the Redeemer into the room.

Geneve wanted to shout with joy, but the cry died on her lips. Ormeon held only one rider, a single hunched Feybrind with golden eyes. *Where is Armitage?* And she was horribly injured, her side scales battered, once proud flank concave. Orange stained her armor, but the dragon gave a red grin anyway. *//I SEE YOU ARE IN TROUBLE. AGAIN.//*

"Dragonfire cannot hurt a demon," the Precept said. "You stirred them to anger, nothing more."

Ormeon swung her massive head toward the demon king, then reared up, snatching a winged horror from the air with a clawed hand. She breathed deep as the thing struggled in her grip, then blasted concentrated flame at the demon she held. The fire was hot, white hot, so bright Geneve squinted and held her hand against the glare.

The fire snapped out, and Ormeon dropped half a smoking demon to the stone floor. *//CITATION NEEDED.//*

Sight of Day landed with catlike grace, then stumbled and clenched his teeth in pain. He was covered in makeshift bandages, the cloth stained red, but his eyes burned like molten metal. The Feybrind eyed the length of chain she held, then glanced to the Precept. *{That's the guy?}*

"That's the demon," Geneve agreed. "I ... know him. He dies today."

"Ho, child," the Precept said. "I have a thousand thousand demons hungering for blood. Your Justiciar is out, your holomancer down by one of your own." He pointed to Lily, who stood with Mazin and Yasmine. "Your guard is a child of a fallen race. You've an injured dragon and a slave cat, and I have your sword. The last time we ... fought, our blades never met. You've no idea what you face. What is it you think to accomplish?"

{I thought he'd be taller.} Sight of Day looked down at his hands for a moment as if considering the blood matting his fur, sighed, then blurred into motion. Six arrows left his bow faster than quicksilver minnows. The Precept dodged the first, then slapped the second and third aside with Requiem. The sword's Light ignited the arrows as they passed. The fourth, fifth, and sixth arrows hit Wincuf ... almost. They passed through his body to shatter on the wall behind the demon. Sight of Day looked at his bow, then the Precept, then to Geneve. *{Maybe you should take this one.}*

She held out her hand. "Sword?" The Feybrind handed his to her. The weight was exquisite, and with a flash of guilt she wondered if it was Requiem's equal. *No, it's just a good sword. Requiem was made by the greatest Smith to walk our world.* She flourished the blade to find its balance, then leveled it at the Precept. "It's time."

"So eager for death," he murmured. "Always the folly of your race. You carry the glimmer of stars inside you but toss it into the darkest hole you can find." He heaved a great sigh, tapped Requiem twice on the floor, then charged.

Geneve ran to meet him. She led with Brilliance, Sight of Day's steel trailing behind, a perfect start to Cophine's *Stormfront*. The hoarse whisper of a thousand wings followed her, demons surging at her back, a thousand foes behind and a greater one in front. She felt sick, tired and weak from days of little sleep and seeing comrades die like mayflies in the summer. But she also felt sick because she knew Wincuf was right. She'd beaten him first time because she cheated, and there were no tricks up her sleeve this time. The second time he'd tossed her from a building like used bathwater.

Beside her she imagined a hint of Israel, the Valiant's memory bringing him to life in her mind. For a moment she saw how he would lead this charge, lifting Brilliance a little higher, dropping her sword point a little lower. Not by much, a half centimeter at best, but perfection was everything to the Storm.

As she ran she saw fallen Tilly, trapped Eleni, and remembered her crumpled Meri. She screamed, pushing her body harder, a little more, just a fraction extra for this last fight. As she reached the demon, she raised Brilliance and lowered her sword. Exhaustion warred with anger, and anger won.

Brilliance flared, a starbright disc, and her blade borrowed lighting from the heavens. Geneve caught the Precept's blow on her shield, sparks and fire roaring from the impact. The second step of *Stormfront* took her blade through the Precept and out the other side. Thunder roiled, the heavens opening, and the Three's justice hammered Wincuf from above.

Geneve spun, expecting a smoking ruin, and almost lost her life as the Precept swung Requiem at her head. *It can't be! I ... I hit him!*

The demon hammered her shield four times, each blow ringing sparks and fury to the ground. He tested his will on hers, and for the moment she held.

They stepped apart, circling. The demon host swarmed about them, a blotting tornado of leathery wings and teeth. She caught flashes of Yasmine's glitterbright through the claws, thought she might have seen Mazin's bulk, both standing by the traitor Lily.

The Precept smiled. "It's not so easy to kill a god."

"You're no god," she spat.

"Oh? This is the third time you've fought me. First two times, you failed. No, I see you mean to remind me of the first, but admit it—*you* did *nothing*. That was the most perfect execution of *Stormfront* I've seen, and yet here I stand. Tresward, your *eyes* are glowing. The Storm lives within you, and yet I abide. You can't hurt me." He padded to the left, and she followed his movement.

"Won't stop me from trying again," she growled.

"Aye, no doubt. But think a moment. My offer stands. A throne shared. A world at peace. We want so little from you. Just the starlight you carry. We can wait until the old are ready, taking them from pain and suffering. Your Smith—"

"Do not speak his name!"

"Or what?" He smirked. "Let's be honest. It's not like you can stop me. Kytto died a cripple and in pain. Oh, I can see your surprise even through that mothballed helmet. It wasn't hard to watch his agony. If we ruled, we'd have taken that from him. Where the Sway fails, we remain. Death, but without pain. Service, but without suffering. Your friends will live. Your lover will survive. The ever-hungry dragon at your beck and call lives." His smile broadened. "All you must do is kneel."

Geneve thought about it as they circled like starving wolves. She felt Israel's doubt. Wondered at Meri's disappointment if she crawled before this thing. Touched Tilly's anger and remembered a thousand wars beyond ending these creatures perpetuated. *They drive us against ourselves. Turn the good into bad. I'm so tired ... but I'm not ready to yield.*

She straightened, feeling the weight of her Smithsteel anew. Geneve knew its metal embrace. She felt the point where it chafed her neck, and the tight spot at the base of her spine. But now, it felt heavy, cloying, a too-tight glove around injured fingers. Her eyes went to fallen Vertiline, stark red matting her platinum-white hair, and wondered if the Valiant felt the same before exposing her weak flesh.

That's what we are. The ancients felt our frailty too, and built cities, weapons, and armor to keep death at bay a few more minutes. Geneve looked at Vertiline's metal hand. *They replaced their very selves to be stronger. Look what it cost.*

"I will not kneel." Geneve felt wonder at her words, because she hadn't thought of speaking, yet spoke truth. "Not to you, or your kind."

"Ah, well." Wincuf shrugged. "It's what I thought you'd say. Now ... die."

He flew at her, feet leaving the ground, body weightless, to swing Requiem overhand. Geneve took the blow on Brilliance, then hunkered behind her shield as the second and third strikes landed in less time than an eye blink. The demon was relentless, hammering her guard. Geneve stepped into *Grace's Retreat*, desperate for a little space, a little fucking *time* to breathe.

He uses no pattern, yet his perfect strikes call the Light all the same. She had a hot memory of Mazin throwing a blade as clumsy steps took him through a patchwork of patterns. But this was different. The demon used *no* pattern, just the beauty of the bladework. He was tireless, unlike her.

The Precept also has no elbows. She leaned back as he swung past her face in a way mortal arms could never manage. *How can I kill a thing with no body?*

She stepped into the next movement, and her leading right leg trembled with exhaustion. It wasn't much, the barest ripple in her muscles, but the patterns demanded perfection. Too many hours without sleep, too many fights against so very many foes. Wincuf swung overhand, face impassive, no hate or pity there, just the blank canvass of a thing wearing a human skin. His blow hit Brilliance, and he used the rebounding force of Light on Light to swing the sword around in an arc.

Geneve staggered, then the pain hit. The Precept cut through her weak right leg, severing it just above the knee. She lost her balance, her precious balance, the essence of her perfect strikes. Light left Brilliance, and the demon repeated his overhand swing. Requiem bit, shattering the glass shield into glittering, stinging rain, and through her raised arm.

She screamed, falling on the floor, smoke trailing from the cauterized stumps of her left arm and right leg. Her armor *clanked* as she hit. The Precept's circling, swirling host hissed in excitement, pulling back to the walls of the room. Waiting. *Hungering.* The Precept stepped forward to finish her, Requiem raised in a final reminder of her weakness.

Hissing, spitting sparks rained on him. He raised his arm, covering his eyes as Yasmine screamed forward, tiny lances of fairy light stabbing at the demon. She was so fierce, but so very tiny. The Builder zipped about the demon, relentless to the point where Requiem found her. She died against skymetal, two halves falling to his feet.

Mazin roared forward, rage and pain on his face. He held a massive piece of broken stone overhead as a club, bringing it down on the Precept. The demon gave a slight smile as the stone passed through his not-body, then sliced Mazin in half from shoulder to hip. The wine merchant from Tebrani died, no more stories or fine liquors left to give.

Last came treacherous Lily, the older woman carrying nothing but a smile. "Ho, monster."

"You fucker," he sneered, and ran her through. The bloody steel tip of Requiem tore out her back. She sighed forward, collapsing like an abandoned puppet, hand reaching to touch his not-face, but never making it. Lily landed next to Mazin.

Geneve dragged herself forward by one hand and foot, clawed fingers reaching for the demon. The pain in her severed limbs was exquisite. *How did Tilly bear it?* The Light was lost to her, but she wasn't dead yet. *I can finish this. I can still finish this.* "I'll kill you!"

"Ah, no," he said, and speared her good arm to the floor with Requiem. She felt the pain anew, tried to grab the blade with fingers she no longer had at the end of a ruined stump.

Then Van arrived. The boy yelled, lunging with his spear. It passed through the Precept's body. The demon snatched the weapon from the boy, hefted it for a moment, then swung the end in a savage arc. The blade whipped through Van's throat, and just like that, there was one less dragonrider left. The demon tossed the spear aside.

Balefire blasted the demon. He fell back, lost in a column of unending fiery rage. Heavy feet shook the cobbles, and Ormeon stood astride Geneve. The dragon's scaled hide was above her as she crouched like a guard dog. *//NOT TODAY, DEMON.//*

The Precept patted down his not-clothes. "You can't kill me, Redeemer."

//I CAN HAVE FUN TRYING.//

"Maybe." He considered, then snapped his fingers twice. "But it's even more fun to watch you eaten alive. If you leave the Knight, you may live. Stay there, and you'll die."

The swirling demon host surged from the walls, descending on Ormeon all at once. Dragonfire blasted from her jaws, incinerating ten, a hundred demons, but there were always more, and she could only face one way at once. Demons raked her hide, tore scales free, reached for the delicate meat within.

Ormeon did not retreat. She roared in pain, snatching demons from the air, but she was just one dragon, and already injured.

Run, love. Geneve gave her thoughts to the dragon through her ancient helm.

//NEVER.// Dragon blood smoked against the stone floor, as, little by little, the demons began to feast.

Rainbow light emerged from her hide, hardening as starlight and memory became real. Demons screamed, scorched, and fell back. Ormeon panted above Geneve, blood making its slow *drip, drip* against the stone floor, but she did not leave or fall.

The Precept and Geneve both looked up at Ormeon as wonderful, beautiful armor of light wove about her body. Geneve had seen this once before, armor made of light and hope, cast against the weapons of the Artifices. Armor made by a holomancer.

Meri's broken, hurt voice came from behind her. "I think it's time to break the rules."

Chapter Forty-Two

The floor tasted of a three-day hangover. *Or, maybe that's my mouth.* Meriwether scrabbled on the stone, trying to work out how he got here. *I'm sure I was standing but a moment ago.* The stone was well-swept; it wasn't the worst place he'd woken after a binge.

It's not a tavern. The floor is glowing purple.

Meriwether croaked, eyes traveling the uncomfortable distance to the purple light. Yep, sure as rain was wet, the floor glowed. *My chin hurts. Did I hit it when I fell?*

He craned his neck, feeling an uncomfortable *pop*, and took in the sight of a flock of demons swirling a cloud of hate around the love of his life. She fought with a borrowed blade—*where does she keep finding those?*—against a man with a slightly better chin than Meriwether's.

It all came back in a rush. The Precept, the Guides, and Lily socking him upside the chin. He tried to get up, because the floor was no place to be at a time like this. Meriwether made his knees, then threw up. *I don't feel amazing. She hit me really hard. Maybe I should hit her back.*

Meriwether surged up, staggered, and tried to call out to Geneve. A wave of exhaustion, nausea, and pain rolled over him. *I'm done, son. I'm done as done. I've nothing left, not even a clever comeback.* What was a man like him going to do in a fight like this? He made pretty pictures. Geneve was the one who did the hard work. She made everything real.

Wait. There's something there. A thought he tried to grasp, but it was like herding white cats in snow.

"Wait," he croaked. No one waited. No one appeared to hear him. The Precept hammered Geneve with a flurry of golden strikes. She gave back, but the same exhaustion he felt dogged her steps. Meriwether thought of conjuring help, but there were a few problems. The rules said he couldn't make something real, summon the gods, or bring back the dead. Only the Three could make a thing, he couldn't ask them here, and vile necromancy was the only path left to the everliving.

While he struggled to come up with a catchy idea, the Precept took off Geneve's leg, then her arm, and stole her Light forever. He choked at Yasmine's fall, the best blue bird he'd ever known, reached out at the death of Mazin, but let his hand fall at the ruin of Lily—*one less problem.* But when the Vhemin boy died, a little piece of Meriwether broke inside.

Meriwether took a half-dozen stumbling steps toward them, but the dragon beat him by a country mile. Ormeon's rage and grief was real in a way no illusion could be. She threw fire at the Precept, then died by degrees as demons hove into her hide. They tore scales away, hungering for the flesh within.

The plan hit him all at once, like all his bad ideas. He threw his hand out toward Ormeon, remembering the armor he'd given her outside Ravenswall. Not just remembering, but *creating* the plates of starlight his kind had ever given hers.

Massive plates of blue and orange slammed against her scaled hide. It almost ended him right then to pull the magic together, but only with Ormeon was Geneve getting out alive. The demon host shrieked, pulling away from the incandescent, burning holomancy. He caught Sight of Day's golden gaze and gestured behind his back to a fallen form.

Sight of Day's eyes widened and he scampered across the floor to Eleni's side. The cat fussed with the Justiciar, bringing her around. *Will it be soon enough?* Meriwether straightened his jacket, aware the Precept turned that perfect gaze on him. He offered a tiny smile, but it couldn't shore up the well of loss inside him. It was soft like wet paper, a fragile thing that wouldn't last. Not with his friends dead and his love crippled. *But it only has to last just long enough.* "I think it's time to break the rules."

The Precept manufactured surprise the way a puppet would—exaggerated raised eyebrows, too-wide eyes. "You're still alive! I can fix that."

"Hold a moment." Meriwether stamped the floor, because he was right over the top of the purple glow. His mad rush to help Geneve took him right where he needed to be. "This is the doorway to a demon realm, yes?"

"*The* demon realm," the Precept corrected. "There is only one."

"Good." Meriwether glanced to Geneve. "You should go, love."

//HOLOMANCER,// Ormeon rumbled, brilliance sparkling rainbows to the floor. Where the light touched demons, they hissed, trying to escape the glimmer. *It reminds me of Yasmine,* Meriwether realized. *The beauty of her wings. //I'M NOT SURE I CAN—//*

"Hold up." Meriwether touched the ground beneath him. "All of us are so sure of the things we can't, we don't wonder what we can. And what *I* can do is break the rules." He straightened. "There are three rules. A last cast of the dice. The long throw, tall odds, and—"

"Yes, yes," the Precept hissed. "You're pretty sure whatever it is won't work. Look! I beat the best swordswoman in all the world. With her own blade, no less. Your frail light armor only lasts as long as you do. A snap of my fingers, and the demon host tears you away."

"Meri," Geneve croaked. She tried to shift toward him, but Requiem pinned her in place. "Meri, *run*. Run while you can."

"No, love. Not this time." He shook his head. "You've been the shield of the world so long it broke you. Just this once, let someone else do what must be done."

"And what's that?" The Precept's voice was golden honey. A cat's purr, a Justiciar's benediction. He stalked closer, taking his time, because now Geneve lay dying—

Don't look. Be strong for her.

The monster held all the power in the world. "If you think to leave here alive—"

"No." Meriwether felt his smile take on a little more spice. "There are a few people getting out alive, but I'm not one of them." He pitched his voice. "Eleni! Attend."

The old woman struggled upright on Sight of Day's arm. "I am here, holomancer."

"Ormeon! Stand back."

The dragon turned an ember gaze on him, considering, calculating. She looked at the demon host and her fallen rider. *//ARE YOU SURE?//*

"Nope." Meriwether turned to the Precept, hoping the dragon would—just this once—do as asked. "There are Three rules." He counted them on his fingers. "Make nothing real. Do not raise the dead. And never, ever call the Three." He grinned, borrowing all he knew from the Vhemin's shark-toothed smile. "By my power, I call the dead! Israel, Knight Valiant of the Tresward, come forth."

Meriwether closed his eyes and ... *remembered* the old bastard. His careful manner, his honey-bark colored skin, and the love he held for his daughter. Israel's strength, the will it took to hold a terrible secret for years to save the life of his child. The way the bastard looked at Meriwether as a sinner, his dedication to the Three, and his unwavering faith. How he held a greatsword like it weighed less than a twig. The way his armor encased his frame.

And then, with a breath, made him real. Meriwether opened his eyes. He didn't see the dead Knight at first, because Meriwether looked to the Precept and expected locked blades. But the Precept wasn't fighting—he stared at Geneve, her dragon, and the ghostly form crouching by her side.

Death hadn't been kind to Israel. He wasn't solid, his ghostly form doing little to hide the cobbles beneath him. The Champion's face was haggard, as if he'd fought a great battle lasting days just to be here. *And maybe he has.*

Israel touched Geneve's face, fingertips grazing her jaw, then he stood, swung the greatsword from his back, and faced the Precept. *The dead do not speak. They have nothing to say to the living.*

The floor shook, starting as a gentle rumble, then escalating to a roar of tortured stone as the world cried out at Meriwether's first great sin. *This is what they meant when they called me sinner. Not the rest of my kind, because they can't break the Three's laws, but this ... thing I've done. I made a man alive again after his death, and the world will punish me for it.* Meriwether's doom crackled toward him, the floor splintering stone chips in an encroaching spiral toward him.

Eleni flung out an old, withered hand. *//HOLD!//* And immediately sank to her knees as she burned her life through Sway, holding Meriwether's doom on a leash. The floor churned, angry, a thousand stone teeth hungering for sinner's flesh, but held at bay for the moment.

I'm not done. When you break eggs, break 'em all. "By my power, I call the forces of creation! Geneve, Knight Champion of the Tresward ... let me show you how I see you once again."

The Precept stopped fucking around at this point, breaking into a run toward Meriwether. Israel slipped through the space between them, slid right *into* the demon's body, and ... held him like stone. The Precept shrieked, his form slipping to mist, but Israel stood, his last, perfect stance anchoring him and creature both.

Meriwether closed his eyes, remembering the angel's wings he's gifted Geneve with. Similar to the armor Ormeon had, but this time it needed to be *more*. Live, without belief. Without *him*. He reached trembling fingers to the sky, then clenched into a fist, dragging reality to him. He felt years pile on his young frame, the withering of time as he burned himself from the inside out to make a last, wonderful thing for the woman who'd given everything for him.

The sky opened, night blasted by brilliant gold. Twin pillars of fire lanced through the ceiling, shattering rock as they struck by Geneve. Smoke and flame cleared. Two figures knelt by Geneve. They glowed like hot glass, but even with the heat peeling off them like waves on a storm-tossed sea, the likeness was unmistakable. By Geneve stood two *other* Geneves, both made of glass. With a snap, both flexed angel's wings from behind them, then stood either side of the fallen Champion, sapphire blades in high guard.

The floor bucked, a massive crack sundering the room north to south. Fire belched from beneath the earth as doom hungered for

Meriwether. Eleni screamed, collapsing as she held back Meriwether's second great sin. But even collapsed and in agony, the old woman kept one hand raised, fingers splayed, as she forced back the Three's justice.

Eleni wasn't just in pain, though. Her flesh withered, lines deepening as her remaining life burned like paper in a bonfire. *I don't have much time left.*

"How is this possible?" the Precept hissed. "I don't believe in your fakery!"

"You haven't worked it out?" Meriwether almost collapsed, but he was *damned* if he'd do that in front of the demon. "All I needed was *her* to believe in me. You also haven't guessed what you've done, have you? You killed three gods on the edge of skymetal. Anointed the blade, and sealed your fate. By my power, I call them back. Cophine, Ikmae, and Khiton. I *demand* you answer me. I summon you now, here, and bind you to your people. You may *not* forsake them!"

Eleni trembled, then collapsed. Whether the Sway burned her out or it was shock at the sacrilege, Meriwether would never know, because he dropped his fingers to the floor, tickled the lock of a demon gate, and fell into another world without scream or cry.

His sins screamed enough for all as they came after him. Three dooms fit to break a world howled into the breach on his heels, hungering for everything he'd done. The Three's justice, paid for three times, and come for an accounting.

Chapter Forty-Three

Geneve tried to reach for Meri, but she had nothing but a stump where her arm used to be. She saw her love fall in a pillar of purple fire as the demon gate opened. The floor erupted beside the gate, a massive snaking monster of stone and fire hungering into the breach. It went on and on as the world screamed its pain.

She remembered the withering of his skin as he called his magic to him for one last push. There was no way a man could survive such a thing. It made her sick, her heart limping a crippled rhythm inside her chest.

And she remembered the cold burn of her father's fingertips on her jaw.

"Meri," she croaked. "My love, what have you done?" Emotion strangled her words, throat closing. *I'm maimed! I'm no use to anyone.* She felt heartsick because she'd spent her entire *life* broken like this. *Why did Meri burn his life away? It makes no sense.*

What had he said before he left? *Anointed the blade, and sealed your fate.* Her eyes moved past her glass guards to see Yasmine, Lily, and Mazin's remains. The fairy's blood glittered with golden flecks, but the other two were just ... people. Just like her, spent, used up. Further afield lay Eleni, the Justiciar still as old bones. Wincuf trembled, fighting Israel's grip on his body.

I must get up. I must *fight until I'm dead, and I'm not dead yet.* Geneve glanced to a glass statue beside her. "What are you?"

"Not very smart," the left one said.

"But made of iron and spite," the other countered. They had Geneve's voice, just like they wore her face. Even their glassy haircuts were the same as hers, minted when she and Meri were in Parneer Harbor.

"Enough riddles," Geneve hissed. "My love is dead and gone, and the monster lives."

"Dead? Not ... yet." Left smiled at Right, then they both looked down at her. "We are you."

Geneve spat grit. "Then you know what I must do. Help me up, damn you!"

Right turned a placid stare on her, then grabbed Requiem and yanked it free. Geneve screamed as the blade left her arm. She felt hard hands under her shoulders as they lifted. The stump of her missing leg scraped the ground and she almost blacked out from the pain.

Blackness didn't take her.

Hard hands left her shoulders.

The warmth of summer sun on leaving shadow filled her. Like when the wind outside is cold, but you step inside a room filled with hearth and song. The pain left her arm and leg, replaced by a feeling of soft hands about swaddling, the embrace of love. The noise of Meri's doom faded to a brook's burble.

Do you see it? Left spoke into her ear.

Do you feel it? Right held her hand.

No, Geneve thought. *Yes.* She felt like she was dreaming, held up by the hands of the Three, or maybe just buoyed in that warm bath she shared with Meri yesterday. Floating free through his last gift to her. *He's given me a way to die in peace. No fear. No pain.*

No, Right scolded.

He doesn't want us to die at all. That's our body your talking about. Left bared glass teeth that would have scared a Vhemin.

We're here to win, Right affirmed. *Are you ready?*

Geneve stumbled, swinging Requiem for balance, and—

Swinging Requiem for balance?

Where her arm was a horrific absence, her missing leg a message of how she'd failed, she saw ... *glass. My arm and leg are glass!* She held Requiem before her, the blade's red wet an angry reminder of Mazin, Yasmine, and Lily. The hand holding the blade was a gift, though, a crystal promise from a man she never deserved. *There was a time I looked to see him dead.* Geneve tossed the blade from glowing shield to flesh sword arm, then rounded on the Precept. She had to scream over the noise of Meri's doom. "It's time for you to fucking *die.*"

The Precept twitched in Israel's grip. "It's not possible!"

"You keep talking about what's possible." Geneve stalked toward him, blade low. "The world has changed, demon. We *know* you now. And we're tired of the hand about our throat."

"It's not possible," the Precept said again, as if repetition would make it so. "He's a ... a *holomancer.* He makes fairytales and moonbeams."

Geneve saw his fingers wriggle. *Iz's grip is loosening.* Geneve glanced to Jasmine's remains. "Fairytales come from fairies, and they're real enough. Moonbeams come from the gods, and they're real too. And the gods put me here, because they're tired of your shit."

His face split into a manic grin. The expression made Geneve pause. "See? Not everything he said came to pass. He called on your precious gods, and they didn't answer. If you kneel to me, you'll find I'm a much more practical savior. Safety. Security. All you have to do is think about this the *right* way."

The floor cracked a second time, a cherry-red glow coming from within. The doom cascading into the gateway to the demon world picked up steam. Fragments of masonry, wood, and dirt were sucked into the demon world. Geneve saw a man flail past as the Three's judgment hungered after one brave sinner.

The Precept strained, breaking free with a mad cackle. Israel bared his ghostly blade in cross guard, the ghost standing between Geneve and the enemy who beat her moments before. But the Precept wasn't interested in the ghost of her dead father. Hands clawed the sky. He bellowed, //COME! TO ME!//

The demon's voice rang across Imshir. Geneve was certain they'd have heard it half a world away in Ravenswall. Wincuf spun back to her, face still manic but now with delight. It was hard to hear him over the shrieking, keening scream of the world, but she thought he said, "All my slaves will come here, and we will beat you."

Geneve looked at the hole in the floor. *I must kill this creature, and then I must find my love.* She eyed the sky as a shroud of winged shapes coalesced overheard. The demons clinging to the walls or circling inside the room fluttered, then surged for her.

There are so many. There is no pattern for this. Despair filled her, a well so deep she feared she could never fill it, not with all the training in the world. Iz's ghost threw his greatsword at a clump seething for her. The ghostly blade passed right through them, then appeared back in his hand in an eye blink.

Geneve wondered for a moment why the dead Valiant did that, then something in her brain ... *clicked.* She had a flash of memory of dear Mazin throwing a sword, stumbling through a parody of a handful of different patterns. Israel's ghostly eyes on her, returned greatsword in hand. Her mind's eye showed her where to put her fury, all her pain and loss. Across the cracked floor, on the side where the Precept stood, a glassy mirror of her appeared, one of Meri's last gifts. Geneve took a breath, felt for the beginning of *Stormdance*, and threw Requiem.

The blade spun through the air faster than thought. So much Light infused the blade it hurt to look at. As it turned through the cloud of demons, the sky answered her call. Pillars of lightning touched demons, turning them to wisps of vapor and char. Blue-white light arced from where the lightning touched, linking a dozen, fifty, a *hundred* monsters in brilliant godsrage.

Her glass copy caught Requiem, and as Geneve turned into the third step of *Answering Call*, she stepped into her crystal shadow across the room. She felt no sensation of distance, but now she was closer to the Precept.

The demon grinned like a dingo, flipped a discarded sword into his hand, and came at her. She sidestepped his swing, red hair following, felt an answering smile on her face. He had no elbows, no spine, not really, and moved like the laws of the world were made for other people. A Knight obeying the laws of the Three and following their patterns wouldn't, *couldn't* beat him. Someone like her had tried eight hundred years ago and died.

I'm done following the rules. She spun on her glass leg, Requiem flashing Light and silver. The demon slid back from the force of the blow, feet tearing up the flooring stones. Her sword followed no pattern but the perfect symmetry of movement she'd learned her entire life. Brick by brick she'd built her skills with a blade when the Storm stayed silent. She'd fought with *this* steel, oh yes, this beautiful, wonderful skymetal sword handed to her through eight hundred years. Her friend Kytto found the metal and poured his life, his Smithcraft, and his love into a blade for a foundling child who couldn't use the barest hint of the Tresward's gifts.

Geneve knew Requiem, and the blade answered her call like none other ever would.

A flock of demons came at her back, but she didn't bother looking. *Go*, she urged, and crystal erupted from her, a hard, transparent form raising glass to cut them down. There, a hulking monster with three heads charged, and her second glass guardian met it with Stormy resolve.

Ormeon raged fire, battling a hundred demons while her holomancy armor glowed angry blue. On two sides of the rift in the floor they made the last stand for this world.

Geneve fought without pattern, perfect strike after strike. She fought with the Storm inside her, the glass holding her, and the skymetal in her hand. Where the Precept had no mass to fight, she had no rules to care about. He swung at her head, and she caught on her blade, feeling the weight of her steel. Butterflies shimmered into life from her blade, a flight of wonderful blue mingling with the dark wings above. Her next swing called the north wind, and the third the ocean's roar. She borrowed strikes from *Last Memory* and *Autumn's Call*, tossed them into *Nightfall* and felt how *right* they worked together.

But try as she might, she wasn't as fast as Tilly, and even Tilly wasn't as fast as this creature. *It's lucky I don't need to be fast. It's lucky I've got family*. Geneve halted her advance, blade in cross guard, and let her smile grow. "It's almost time."

The Precept didn't even have the courtesy to pretend to pant. "You're getting tired, Knight."

"Aye." She nodded, red hair sticking to her face. Geneve didn't brush it aside, letting the wolf into her smile.

"Why are you smiling?" He smashed her guard with an overhand strike. Geneve caught it on Requiem's edge as another flurry of demons came for her. *Steel in front, glass in back*. "You're ... you know you're about to *die*, right?"

Another one, two, three against her guard, high-low-high. Ice crystals formed on Requiem, shattering into motes of light that hurried west. The Precept had the grace of every fencer who'd come before, all those he'd watched through his tireless time on this world. Wincuf used his sword as if it weighed less than a blade of grass. Geneve caught each strike with skymetal, feeling the strength of the ancients in her hand. Music left Requiem's edge, an angel's harp mixed with wordless song. "Someone's going to die. It's not going to be me." Her smile widened as she met the Precept's lunge with cross guard, and ran Requiem sparking and shrieking up his blade. Rainbows shimmered in its wake.

The Precept danced away, light as air. "*Why are you smiling?!*"

Geneve stepped back, sucking air, and grinning like the sun. "Because of *that*."

The front of the demon's chest tented, bulging out to a point. Geneve felt the cool wind of the hunt, the leathery touch on her shoulder of an elder pointing to where the buck hid in a thicket. Felt the bowstring against her fingers, and the perfect release as the shaft flew.

Van's spear erupted from the Precept's chest, carrying Vhemin dreams with it. Meri's magic imprinted on a crude weapon, but full of the heart of the downtrodden. A shark-toothed grin leered past the Precept's face, snake eyes holding the anger of an entire people. Armitage twisted the spear in the Precept, then yanked it free. "How's that, fucker?"

Geneve stepped past the Precept's wide-eyed astonishment, batted aside his blade, and sank Requiem into his chest up to the hilt. Her strike was true, front foot holding two-thirds of her weight. The blade entered exactly horizontal to the floor, carved through the dark stuff of the creature, and exited at the same angle. The best strike made by any Knight, delivered here, now, at the right time.

Red hair fell over her face. She held the pose for a heartbeat as the Precept looked at her hand by his chest, astonished. Then he giggled. "You fool. You can't—"

Sunfire blasted through the ruined ceiling, lightning curling along its length all the way to the heavens. It hit the Precept, true as Geneve's strike. She screwed her eyes against the Light, but the brilliance of the Precept's death was visible through her lids. After, she might have said he looked ... surprised.

The pillar of Light continued on, burning into the earth, turning the rock at her feet sluggish and molten. Lightning leaped from the pillar, striking the demons in the room, tearing them from this world forever.

Silence. Geneve opened her eyes, Requiem still in hand. The blade glowed not with yellow Light but brilliant heat, so white it hurt to look at, but the hilt was cool in her hand. Kytto had done his work well. Beyond the blade's sunsmile, Armitage.

"Oh," she sighed, moving around the crumbling, glowing hole in the earth to the monster's side. He was terribly wounded, a massive piece of him missing. It looked as if something very much like a dragon had taken a bite, missing his neck by a whisker, but taking his arm, ribcage, and most other useful things behind it. "My brother."

She caught him as he fell, coughing red, Van's spear falling to the ground. There wasn't much left of it, just a charred twig, a memory of the dragonrider who almost was. She lay Armitage against the ground. He hissed. "Careful, Red. It fucken hurts."

Geneve laughed, brushing wet from her face. "Tell me what you need." Her glass hand found his.

"One of those glass arms would be good." He chuckled, then coughed more red. She tried not to look at the innards working through the rent in his side, the muscles visible as he swallowed. "Always said, you got to go for the head. Anything else is amateur hour."

Chapter Forty-Four

When Vertiline woke, it wasn't because she wanted to. She wanted to sleep, or die, or some other damn thing, but there was so much noise and light. Sparkling lightning, fire, and *harps* if you'd believe that.

She raised her groggy head, taking in the scene. It was a mistake, because she threw up immediately, her body somehow made of nausea so pure it left no room for thought.

Be still. What did I see?

She wiped a string of bile from her lips, remembering. *Geneve by Armitage. Don't think about what he looks like. About how hurt he is. The dragon waits, bleeding but alive. Eleni slumps, but not dead yet I think. The cat is with her. The sinner's gone. Four lie dead, and the demon too. There is the ghost of a dead man watching all.*

Did we win? This doesn't feel like we won. Up, Vertiline. I'm not done.

She made her feet one jerky movement at a time. Vertiline was tempted to lean on her sword, but glass wasn't made for that. The point rested on the ground, sharp as a broken promise. *Now, move.* Tilly walked to Geneve, to Armitage, saw—

Don't look. Not yet.

"Sister," she croaked. "You won."

"No." Geneve stood, slicking back red hair. She looked about, then strode to her helmet. She leveled Requiem—*by the Three, the sword is glowing like the sun*—at the gaping maw of the demon gate. "That's a problem that needs solving."

"I was wondering why it didn't feel like we won."

{Probably because you weren't involved.} Sight of Day slipped to the space on her left. *{You slept for most of it.}*

"I must close the gate." Geneve gave a tiny nod, like she was trying to talk herself into it.

"They're coming," Eleni croaked. The once-old woman looked ancient, eyes milky blind, the lines on her face deep enough to make a crevasse blush. "They're coming home."

Vertiline turned a circle. "All the demons are dead."

"The demons *here*," Geneve corrected. "There are thousands in Imshir. Maybe more across the world."

"The gate can be closed." Eleni groped for her staff, then hauled herself upright. "It will close by itself, given enough time."

The gaping wound in the floor did seem a little smaller. Geneve shook her head. "Meri is in there."

"And his threefold doom," Eleni nodded. "I'd imagine the demon world is a smoking ruin."

"*Meri is in there!*" Geneve shouted.

"Aye, child." Eleni sighed. "Or, he was."

She raised a glass arm. "While this is whole, he lives."

"No." She shambled closer, robes whispering on the ground. "He broke a rule, Geneve. He made something real. Your arm and leg will last until the sun grows dark and the seas dry up. Only when sand turns to rock and rock to dust, the sun's fire dims, the stars darken, and no wind blows will the glass break. I'm sorry. I know it's not what you wanted to hear. But I fear he's dead."

//THERE IS A CHANCE?// Ormeon crunched toward the demon gate, massive head nosing the edge. *//HE MIGHT LIVE?//*

Eleni shrugged. "Tuesday might become Monday."

Ormeon looked into the pit, the runes along her face dimming for a moment. Then she looked at Geneve. *//DRAGONS ARE NOT*

GOOD AT SAYING SORRY.// She put a massive clawed hand on the edge.

Geneve threw out her hand. "Ormeon!"

The dragon offered a final look at her rider. *//HE WAS A VERY GOOD HORSE.//* Then she forced herself into the demon realm.

Geneve staggered toward the gate, but Eleni's arm caught hers. "No, child. You must guard the gate. The demons will return home. You must keep the gate clear of reinforcements until the dragon returns."

Vertiline found her voice. "Or dies."

"Or that." Eleni didn't sound happy about it.

Geneve turned to the gate, then back to Vertiline, then to the gate. "I..." Her face crumpled.

I know what she feels. She is afraid to go into the gate not because of what she might find, but because of what she knows she'll leave. If the best of the demon's fighters regroup into their world, they'll try again, over and over, until the end of time. "I'll do it."

Geneve froze, then her shoulders sagged. "Tilly, you're..." She raised a hand to the back of Vertiline's head. Her fingers came back red and sticky. "You can't."

Vertiline flourished her blade, fought the nausea down, and held cross guard. "I said I will hold this line."

"And what if I lose you too?" Geneve's voice cracked, and she looked away from Israel's ghostly frown. "You're all that's left. I *can't.*"

"And yet I will hold." Vertiline stared down the long length of her glass blade. "I will hold this point until ... what was it?" She glanced at Eleni. "I will hold until the sun grows dark and the seas dry up. When sand turns to rock and rock to dust, the stars grow dark, and no winds blow I will break. Until then," she spun, grabbing Eleni's arm, "*you* will hold the gate open. I've no skill with Sway."

{Good plan.} Sight of Day walked to Armitage, bow ready, golden eyes on the rent in the ceiling. *{This is where we wait until the sun grows dark and the seas dry up. When sand turns to rock and rock to dust, the stars grow dark, and no winds blow I will leave my brother's side.}*

"Cat," the monster croaked. "Go."

{It is cool here, before the storm breaks. The winds are easy on my face. I've

known love and faith, and all the feelings the gods hide in our hearts.} The Feybrind's fingers stilled for a moment. *{I have never met a man as true as you. I will hold.}*

Vertiline faced Geneve as the whisper of something more than wind stirred the air. The beating of a thousand, thousand wings. The hissing promise of demons hungering for revenge for their fallen king. "They want revenge because we sent the doom of our world to theirs. They want a piece of us, and a piece they shall have. Geneve, your lover yet lives. Go find him," she glanced to Israel's ghost, "before it's too late."

Eleni croaked, "He might be—"

"The dragon's armor, witch," Vertiline snapped. "I'm the one with the head injury, but you fools missed her armor of light."

Geneve's expression passed through terror to guilt. Anger flashed, then self-doubt, finally hardening into resolve. "I *will* return. I swear it."

Vertiline spat bile. "Geneve, we have ever doubted you. We thought you too weak to handle the truth, so we hid it from you in a chain around your father's neck. We meant to protect, but we did more harm than good. Then we tried to kill the man you love and didn't listen when you found the weakness in the Tresward." Her eyes found Eleni. "Too little, too late? It doesn't matter. We will hold."

Geneve nodded, spun, and came face to face with Israel. He raised ghostly fingers to her face. Tilly wanted to turn away, because the dead never had kind words for the living. But Israel's voice came through time and the long lands of death, holding something that sounded like broken love. "*I wish I'd said those things too.*"

"Father," Geneve croaked, her fingers rising to touch his but finding nothing but air. Then he was gone, out like a candle in a stiff breeze. Her back straightened, then she slapped her helmet on, and ran for the portal. Knight Champion Geneve jumped high, torqued her body, then straightened her dive into the purple gate.

SIGHT OF DAY HADN'T LIED. VERTILINE CLOSED HER EYES, FEELING the cool wind on her face. *One wounded cat. A dried-up Justiciar. And a dying monster.* She opened them, feeling her heart thrill as the first demons flocked through the open ceiling. More burst through the door at the end of the room, fluttering darkness like water from a burst dam.

Don't forget the injured Knight Valiant Vertiline. The woman who lacks courage, left to defend the breach. She glanced at Eleni. "Will you keep the gate open?"

"Aye." Eleni turned blind eyes to the purple glowing hole. *//HOLD!//*

The room creaked like breaking granite. Then the demons hit them like a hurricane.

Vertiline leaped, turning her body around its axis, blade flashing with light. She parted wing from body, head from shoulders. As she landed, her feet cracked the ground, the rumble of thunder answering her call.

A swarm found Sight of Day. The Feybrind never left his guard of Armitage, turning left to stab, returning to center to block, then lunging to tear the heart from a demon. But he was slowed by pain, his movements brittle like old wood. His sword lodged, was lost. Vertiline saw golden eyes wide with fear, then he was hidden as the deluge of demons swarmed him.

No! Vertiline sprinted to the pair. She shoulder-barged the mass of leathery wings that hid Sight of Day. She hit something that felt like an angry cat, all teeth and spite, then the demons burst free as her armored shoulder glowed with scalding Light.

Sight of Day bled anew from what looked like a hundred places. Demons surged away. Vertiline offered her hand. "Back up, cat."

He gave a half-smile, all teeth, then kipped up beside her. He unshouldered his bow, nocking an arrow. Then the demons came again.

A mass broke free, turning for Eleni. Vertiline feared for the old woman, but lightning pounded the ground as they approached, incinerating twenty in an eye blink. Eleni groaned, raising her hand to the gate. *//HOLD, I SAID!//*

Vertiline stepped in front of Sight of Day, sword finding demon flesh. An arrow passed her ear, tearing a horror from the air. She let it fall past, took a step behind the cat, and felled a fearsome brute the size of a horse with a single swing. As glass bit, she heard the sound of breakers falling. The blade entered, a terrible red glow emerging from the wound. The creature shrieked, then fire burst from its eyes. It lurched away, mewling, and Vertiline spun back to guard.

"There are too many." Her stomach heaved, but she clamped down on it. "It won't be long now."

{Long until we win?} Sight of Day raised an eyebrow.

"Sure," she said absently. "I mean, until it doesn't matter anymore. Win or lose, we'll stop caring, right?" Vertiline wiped sweaty platinum hair from her forehead. "Right?"

{I might care, a little.} Sight of Day bowed his head for a moment, perhaps to hide the dimming light in his gaze. *{You could run.}*

She snorted. "And you keep saying you're the smart one."

"You could both run," Armitage croaked. "Please. For me."

The Feybrind turned golden eyes on his friend, then shook his head once before readying his bow. Vertiline heard the flutter of a thousand wings, the hush of wind, the nightmare of death approaching, and closed her eyes. She imagined a flowing cape of demons coating the city, flowing toward the gate like the tide coming in. *I will hold. I can't break.* "Please don't ask again. For me."

She spun at the soft sound of cloth and the clatter of wood. Eleni lay face down, hand clasping her staff. The demon gate shuddered, then closed faster, purple light dwindling like the dusk sun. "No," Vertiline whispered. "They *must* come back."

She heard a new sound over the onrush of demons swarming toward them. It was like a forge's bellows, the rush of flame, but from a great distance. *What fresh hell is this?* She looked up, and saw the demons circling like a swarm of starlings. *So many. So many!*

The strange forge-like sound loudened. Vertiline thought she glimpsed three points of firebright light in through the demon swarm, new stars birthed, except... *By the Three. Those are huge stars.*

Demons rushed through the broken ceiling, and she had no more time to think. Blade and bared teeth. *Be the wind. Move like the water.* Vertiline reached for a pattern, held onto *Battle of the Endless.* Stepped there, blade striking. Felt a cut on her cheek but ignored it. Her shoulder guard tore free as a demon hungered for her, then staggered back as Sight of Day put a feathered shaft into its eye.

She put glass through the neck of a human-sized snake, then split a two-headed creature in half. Sight of Day shot three shafts past her face, then lost his bow as a monster took it on the wing. The cat drew a knife, golden eyes flashing. A demon lunged at his back, driving a horned spike through. Vertiline twisted, glass flashing crystal and red, cutting off the spike. The Feybrind staggered, then yanked the spike free, tossing it aside.

Vertiline stepped to his back, forgetting the pattern for a moment, because there were so many enemies, and no pattern could beat them. She turned in time to take claws to her gut and screamed. Black shapes were everywhere. She couldn't see the walls. Vertiline couldn't see Armitage.

Sight of Day left her back, dragged away, kicking and clawing. She tried to follow, then screamed again as something sliced her leg. Vertiline stumbled, but didn't kneel, because Tresward only kneeled to the Three.

The forge-like sound was so loud.

"Run!" roared Armitage, then he was gone as leathery forms swarmed over him. Vertiline tried to work back to him but lost her sword. She heard breaking glass and waited for the end.

Vertiline was knocked from the ground as it shook, a titan's fist hammering stone. The walls of the room blasted to dust and rubble. The ceiling fell in, a thousand hungry knives. Light, and heat, and the brilliance of day made her cover her eyes with a bloody hand, made her mewl in fear.

The demons on her broke away, tried for sky, and turned to ash in a flash of brilliant golden light. Vertiline hugged her stomach, trying to hold the blood inside with her metal hand, but crimson leaked all the same. She staggered, then fell next to her broken sword. She grabbed the hilt, trying to find her feet, and another impact hammered the ground. A third, and it was all she could do to curl into a ball, covering her head.

Silence. Warmth, light so bright she could see it through closed eyelids. She peeked and saw a giantess. A young woman, but the size of a three-story house. She *glowed* with Light. This was no maiden of the dawn, but a warrior queen, broad shoulders covered in armor familiar enough to be called Tresward. She held a sword low and ready, scanning the room slowly, paying Vertiline absolutely no attention at all.

A demon leaped from the wall, hungering for the giant, and was met by an arc of purest Light. The titan didn't even have the courtesy to look.

Vertiline crawled, trying to get away, and came up against a massive foot. She raised her eyes, looking into a curious expression another three stories up. This one had a face that changed as frequently as most people blinked, old here, now a baby. A woman, now a man. Changeable as the weather, fickle as the seasons.

She whimpered, scrabbling away. She found her feet, keening at her stomach wound. *Where is Sight of Day? Where is Armitage? We must get away.* Vertiline spun, and saw the third giant. This one looked a little like Israel, if Iz was the size of a mansion. Weathered, stern, and armored. He carried a massive greatsword of light and fire.

Vertiline looked past him at the ruined walls, the glowing super-heated stones, and wanted to cry. *I can't fight this. I can't win against this.* She raised her broken blade anyway, holding it in crippled cross guard. "Come die," she hissed.

The changeable one laughed, voice turned from young to old in the space of a heartbeat. *//ONE OF YOURS, I THINK, SISTER.//*

The giantess raised an eyebrow. *//ONE OF OURS. ALL OF OURS.//* She crunched toward Vertiline, room shaking with each footstep. *//PUT UP YOUR SWORD, VERTILINE.//*

Vertiline sobbed. "What are you?"

The man grinned like a chasm. *//YOU CALLED US. YOU SHOULD KNOW.//* He looked at the closing demon gate. *//AH. THAT'S WHERE HE WENT.//*

"I need to hold," Vertiline said. "I need to hold here until they come back."

The giantess rummaged in the rubble, emerging with a limp cat. She paced to Vertiline, laying Sight of Day at her feet.

The man who looked so much like Israel knocked aside a pillar, brushing bricks from his shoulders as if they were dust. He hefted a broken body, then returned it to Vertiline. *Armitage. //YOU HAVE HELD THEM UP FOR SO LONG. REST, NOW. LET US GUARD YOU AS WE SHOULD HAVE.//*

"*Who* are you?" Vertiline whispered.

Summer wind tickled the giantess's hair. *//I AM COPHINE. THIS IS IKMAE. KHITON IS THE UGLY ONE.//*

Vertiline clattered to her knees, bowing her head to hide her eyes. "My Lords."

A finger the width of a beam touched her chin. Soft, warm. Her pain eased, and she looked into the eyes of the goddess. *Three's mercy. It's Cophine. What did that sinner do?!* No time for thought, because Cophine spoke with a voice of oceans, mountains, thunder, and the deep rumble of the earth. *//WE HEARD YOUR VOICE IN THE WIND. WE HEARD IT IN THE STARS, AND THE BLACK WORLD BEYOND. YOUR HEART WAS BROKEN, BODY MAIMED, AND STILL YOU SAID YOU WOULD HOLD.//* She straightened, eyes painted like the sky, and looked about. *//REST, VERTILINE. WE WILL HOLD IT FOR YOU.//*

Ikmae grinned, old teeth, young eyes. Sober as an ancient, steady as a youth. *//WE WILL HOLD.//* His grin widened, showing shark teeth. *//WE WILL ALSO KICK SOME ASS.//*

//THIS IS YOUR WORLD.// Khiton nodded, rumbling like a mountain. *//IT IS OUR WORLD. IT IS TIME FOR ALL TO REMEMBER.//*

The god held his greatsword in a cross guard so perfect it made Vertiline's broken heart ache anew. And then the demons came.

Cophine led the charge, long hair flowing like a river, eyes holding the forge of the stars. Ikmae loped at her heels, armor smooth and silent. Perfect. Mighty Khiton held the rear, steady as time.

The goddess smashed through the remains of the palace wall, a cascade of brickwork thrown in an arc like a wave. A rush of monsters came right for her.

She clenched her fists, stepping into a forward-leaning stance as perfect as dawn lovemaking. Twin beams of Light lanced from her eyes, raking the demons, turning them to crumbling ash and smoke and bitter memory.

Ikmae put a hand on her braced shoulder, pirouetting through the air, bastard sword cutting through the fabric of the world. Behind the crescent wound in the sky glimmered an ocean of purest Light. It blasted forth, turning night to a summer's day. First warmth like hearthstones, then blazing fire. Demons screamed, struggling to run or fly as their forms dictated, but none were fast enough.

A cunning clutch crept about the broken walls of the palace, seeking the gate, or weak mortal flesh, and met Khiton's will. He swung his greatsword in a massive uppercut, a storm of fury knocking the demons away. They scattered like thrown pebbles, some bouncing at least half a klick away. He raised his open hand to the sky, clenched his fist, and yanked.

The sky roiled, curling into a tempest. A circle of cloud formed in an eye blink, the center angry red like a dragon's grin. The sky spat burning rocks the size of houses, five, ten, twenty, then too many to count. The meteors hit the ground. The world shook as demons screamed, burning in the angelfire of a god's wrath.

Demons called from across the seas arrived. Those within the city gave up their hosts, yanking soul and life as they went, empowering themselves, hungering for the victory they were promised eight hundred years ago. They had the numbers. They were made strong by the weak-willed. And the loss of their Precept made them angry.

A winged horror larger than Ormeon banked across the sky, screaming rage. Cophine's blade turned to a spear, and she threw, turning away before it hit. Hit it did, the not-dragon exploding as the spear went through without slowing in the slightest.

Ikmae stood at Cophine's back, leaning an old body on a staff, an ancient man now. Demons sensed weakness, rushing forth, and Ikmae shifted like the clouds, becoming young, a maiden in the prime of youth. She clenched fingers low, lifting as if shouldering a great weight. The ground heaved, ruptured, rocks closing like jaws, and the monsters were swallowed by the hungry land.

More flying creatures approached in a V formation. Khiton turned, rocks the size of wagons tearing from the earth to hover behind him. He swung his *arm forward, and the rocks shot across the sky, tearing demon from sky, shattering bone, breaking resolve.*

The Three used Storm as a weapon, Sway as a shield. Reality shifted ten times in a second, night to day, day to the black beyond the stars. The ground shook, then settled, then became the stormy sea. Seconds turned to hours, and all passed in a heartbeat. Cophine used sword and spear, shield and will. Everychanging Ikmae became whatever they wanted to be, crone one moment, dragon the next. Khiton held the end of all things in his heart, greatsword steady, never moving from the closing demon gate.

The battle raged, angry demons against angrier gods. But the outcome was certain. The demons had the numbers. They'd prepared for eight hundred years, biding their time, building their strength. They knew the hearts of humans, how they worked, and how to make them change.

But the Three were gods. May as well throw stones at the lightning.

The battle was over before it began. The demon gate closed to a twinkle of purple light, then snapped shut with a tiny pop. The runes went dark. Silence held counsel, waited for the world to take a breath, to see its victory.

Sobbing interrupted silence's decree. Gods turned, backs straight, unbowed, feeling no weariness, ready for another fight, ready for another eight hundred years if need be. They walked through the ruins of Imshir to the demon gate, trying to find the source of the tears.

Laying against the ground, metal fingers clawing broken stone, nub of a shattered glass sword gouging dirt, Knight Valiant Vertiline wept. The demon gate was gone, runes absent. No purple light. No hole. No Geneve, Meriwether, or mighty Ormeon.

"They're gone," she said. "They're gone."

Chapter Forty-Five

Vertiline haunted Imshir, the only living human soul in a city of dead. The demons had taken everything. *Every child that ever bounced a ball, every person who baked bread, sang songs, or told tall tales.* Her pale hair was matted, grime on her face, but she didn't care. *Everything is ash, even my heart. I failed.* Two nights passed since the Three broke the demon army on the wheel of their will. Two long days, where she thought she saw people out of the corner of her eye.

She'd imagined Geneve bursting forth from the ground, the sinner right behind her on that ridiculous disc he rode. Vertiline looked for the red grin of a dragon.

There was nothing.

Ahead, a massive fire burned even during midmorning. There was plenty of fuel by way of fallen buildings. She'd walked their perimeter of silent houses, looking for anyone who still drew breath. She found fallen Knights, and plenty of dead people. The fire was a beacon to draw survivors in, but no one came. *We'll have to do something about the dead soon. Disease won't be far behind.* She almost laughed, because disease was a worry for the living. This city of the damned had nothing to fear.

She stalked to the warm circle of firelight, welcoming the crackle of flames, the kiss on her face, and felt guilty for being alive. Sight of Day crouched by a sleeping—or unconscious—Armitage. The monster was a ruin, but his wounds were already scabbing over. The cat looked worse, if it were possible, golden eyes heavy as the leaden sky above. She kept her voice low. "Has anyone come?"

Sight of Day frowned. *{I know you're trying to stay positive, but that was a stupid question.}* His frown deepened. *{Scratch that. There are no stupid questions, only stupid people.}*

Vertiline snorted despite herself. "Stop your babbling. You'll wake the monster."

The Feybrind glanced at his silent fingers, then steepled them with a half-smile. *{The gods came earlier.}*

"Still here?" She heard the bitterness in her words. "What did they want?"

{You.}

Vertiline eyed the Precept's palace, dark and silent. Much of it still loomed above the city, despite the damage done in the battle. *Broken teeth in a rotted jaw.* She sighed. "I'd best go see what they want."

{Not taking a sword?}

"What for? There's no one alive to fight."

SHE FOUND COPHINE BY GLOW, CHARTING HER COURSE TO WHERE the goddess crouched on the eastern slope leading to the palace. Cophine stared at an unlit pyre made from mighty beams scrounged from the palace. On the pyre lay five bodies.

Eleni was easiest to make out. Her withered skin was stretched over tired bones. There were no eyes in her head, her body giving the appearance of an ancient mummy. The Sway she'd drawn to hold the demon gate open took life, then more, and put her ledger in the red. Her cloak was stripped of color, her hair mangy and brittle as if in the grave for a hundred years already.

Van, novice dragonrider, lay next to her. His body was clean, and he'd been dressed in borrowed Tresward armor. Not all fit, but the burnished sun sat well on his chest. He seemed so young, so peaceful, and so very dead.

Beside the Vhemin lad was the bulk of Mazin. Like Lily beside him, his body was wrapped in a shroud, no doubt to keep the pieces together. He sold no more wine, or told any tales.

Lily seemed brittle, already old when this started, her body made of sticks inside a fragile shell. She was a prisoner of a demon tyrant no more. She would never see Omrar again. Vertiline wasn't sure if she would've wanted to, but the option was closed off for all time.

Vertiline almost missed the last body at first pass. Tiny, gossamer wings no longer sparkling. Builder Yasmine, over eight hundred years old, trapped in the body of a blue bird for most of that time until a sinner set her free. The tiniest shroud Vertiline had ever seen wrapped the small body.

Tilly looked away, finding the giant eyes of Cophine looking down at her. Those eyes were ancient beyond reckoning, all the secrets of the stars and universe beyond in them. They held understanding of the world's pain. *//WELCOME, VERTILINE.//*

"I..." Vertiline trailed off. "I don't know what to do."

The goddess pointed to an unlit torch beside the pyre. *//YOU MUST SAY GOODBYE.//*

Vertiline fielded the torch, considering the oil soaked head. She smelled the richness of it, the promise of a final flight to the heavens. "I want to go with them."

//WHICH IS WHY YOU MUST SAY GOODBYE.// Cophine rose. *//YOUR JOB ISN'T DONE.//*

Vertiline rounded on the goddess, staring up, forgetting who she spoke to for a moment. "What more could you want of me?" She pointed at Cophine with the torch. "Want me to die too? The last Tresward, on bent knee, waiting for the godless to cast me into the pit? Wasn't the dragon a big enough sacrifice? What about the sinner? Or, or..." She choked, thinking of red hair.

//YOU HAVE THE HARDEST JOB OF ALL,// Cophine said. *//YOU MUST REMEMBER WHAT HAPPENED. TEACH IT TO THOSE WHO WANT TO LEARN. FIND A WAY FOR THOSE WHO DON'T, TO LISTEN. YOU MUST LIVE.//*

Vertiline sagged. "What if I don't want to?"

//WE DON'T ALWAYS GET WHAT WE WANT.// Cophine looked at the cloud cloaked sky. *//I DIDN'T WANT TO BE A MOON FOR EIGHT HUNDRED YEARS, BUT HERE WE ARE.//*

Vertiline looked to the pyre, then to the torch. "What will you do?"

//I WILL SAY GOODBYE WITH YOU.//

"After that, I mean."

//WHAT WOULD YOU DO IF YOU WERE A GOD?//

Vertiline teased matted hair with a metal hand. *Unlimited power. A world to oversee. People to save. A new Tresward, or let it die? Bless a kingdom, or step aside while they work it out?* "I don't know."

//NEITHER DO I.// Cophine offered a tiny smile, but even that was like the purest dawn over snow-dusted mountains. *//WILL YOU SAY GOODBYE WITH ME?//*

"I have no flint."

//YOU HAVE A GODDESS.// Cophine snapped giant fingers with the crack of breaking timber, and the torch flickered to life.

Vertiline frowned. "You must teach me how to do that."

//PERHAPS I SHALL.// Cophine shrugged. *//DO YOU WANT TO LEARN?//*

Vertiline thrust the torch into the pyre. Dry wood crackled, coughed, caught. Red flames snaked through the timbers, then reached yellow fingers to the sky. Smoke rose to the sky as five brave dead rose for the last time.

The sky huddled closer, raindrops spattering the ground. The fire responded, reaching higher. Vertiline stepped back, running a smudged finger under her eyes. *I'm crying. I barely knew these people and I'm crying.* She faced the goddess as the rain turned to a torrent, hiding Vertiline's tears. "Do mortals mean so little to you? Why aren't you *crying?*"

Cophine stared at her with those eternal eyes, then turned away as the heavens broke open.

V ERTILINE FOUND I KMAE LAYING IN THE MARKET SQUARE. T HE GOD was untouched by the rain, an island of dry warm light around them. They were in the form of a young man, bare-chested, well-muscled without showing off. Ikmae opened an eye as she stamped forward, rain sluicing from pale lank hair. *//YOU SHOULD WEAR A HAT.//*

She spat rainwater. "I can't believe—"

//MEETING YOUR IDOLS NEVER WORKS OUT WELL FOR EITHER SIDE.// Ikmae stretched, then shrank to an older man. *//YOU CAN'T BELIEVE YOU USED TO WORSHIP US. THAT THE STARS DANCED TO OUR WHIM, AND YET WE CAN'T DO THE THING YOU MOST WANT.//* The man shrugged, then shrank into an older woman of plain ol' regular size. There was still a god in those eternal, nightmare-or-dream eyes.

Vertiline blinked. "Lily?"

Ikmae-as-Lily nodded. "Do you like it?" She gestured to her body.

"I see we're nothing but costumes to you." Vertiline's metal hand flexed as if hungry for the blade. "Toys, on a tiny battlefield."

Ikmae's eyes glowed for a moment, and she looked at the dry cobbles at her feet. "You are more than nightshirts, Knight Valiant. You are what we wanted to do, or be, while we were trapped in the sky. It's easy to fight a demon horde when you're a god. That's why the Precept spent so much time getting *you* to lock *us* up."

"Wait, what?" Vertiline blinked. "Fuck this rain!"

Ikmae nodded as if agreeing. "The rain is tiresome, but Cophine's agony knows no end. She was always the soft one."

"Wait, what?" Vertiline said again. "Cophine cares *nothing* for us. Just like you."

Lily—*no, that's Ikmae, keep it straight*—Ikmae sighed. "It is raining over the entire world right now. The seas are drenched. The deserts weep. Trees shoulder the tears of heaven. From this sadness, new life springs forth. Crops grow. The blasted plaguelands might see a bloom."

Vertiline looked up. "These are Cophine's tears?"

"How else would a god cry?" Ikmae kicked a pebble. "What will dawn on you soon is that you're standing in a steady torrent of heavenly snot."

Vertiline blinked rain, or god snot, or whatever. "You're not like her. Or him."

"Not really." Ikmae sighed, heavier than last time. "But is anyone like their siblings?" She flashed a wolfish grin. "Does anyone want to be? What we share is our love for you."

"And yet you wear a dead woman's shape like an overcoat." The words were out before Vertiline could pull them back. "I'm sorry, Lord, but—"

"Words can't hurt me, Tilly. I've listened to all the words ever said. Different tongues spoke them. They said them in different ways across the oceans of time. I'm so used to them I don't really understand what all the fuss is about." Ikmae looked at the sky. "She's really going for it this time."

"Why did you choose Lily?"

"Because she died for you." Ikmae's voice became flat and hard as new steel. "She died, at the same moment the demons broke our prison. They tried to kill us, you see. It was a good try, but we've a trick or two left. We squirreled away our power for eight hundred years for one shot. And when it came, we reached down, and..." He sighed. "Took it. We took what wasn't ours, because we needed it more."

"Sounds about right." Vertiline turned away, boots sloshing through puddles.

"I WONDERED WHEN YOU'D MAKE IT." NOT-MAZIN BECKONED HER inside an old taverna. Vertiline followed him inside, smelling roast lamb with rosemary, buttered potatoes, and hearty ale. Her stomach growled, and she called it traitor. "You must be hungry."

"I'm also angry. But I'll settle for hungry," admitted Vertiline.

He set her up at the otherwise empty common table, then bustled to the back. Out of tune humming came from the kitchen for a while, then Mazin reemerged carrying a large platter heaped with lamb, suedes, bacon, potatoes, beans, and bread. He pushed this in front of her, then deposited a sweating pitcher of ale beside it. "Eat."

"Is this guilt food?"

"Food is food," he said. "Also, it's guilt food."

Vertiline speared a strip of lamb. It was warm and succulent, the juices running down her chin. She had to fight the urge to embrace the wolf and put her face into the platter. "If Geneve were here, she'd eat all this. She'd..." Her voice died, the lamb tasting more of guilt than food.

"She'd eat it and tell you to stop fussing." Mazin helped himself to a slice of bread, spreading butter almost as thick as the slice. "Ask your questions."

Vertiline pushed a fork between her hands, hunting for the right words. "Was it Mazin, or was it Khiton?"

Mazin sighed. "We are the same. We fell from the sky, Tilly. It took a long time to get here. We landed in a person, thinking and real. We brought the heavens with us and merged them with the real. Mazin is me, and I am Mazin."

"But the real Mazin died."

"He did." Mazin nodded, hangdog. "And he won't ever come back. I'm wearing his shape because it is ... kinder."

"To you?" She bridled.

"No." The god turned away. "You can say what you need to say to Mazin. You can't to Khiton."

Vertiline made herself eat a suede. *It's ... really tasty, and I hate suedes.* "We tried so hard."

"Hear me, Vertiline. We *all* tried hard. The Three are gods, but we're not infallible. We made a deal eight hundred years ago to guard you. We agreed to enter stone temples in the sky to watch the world. All of us were tricked. We can balance a sword on its point for eternity, but we couldn't ... *see.* Do you understand?"

"You couldn't get here fast enough, or be strong enough, to save my sister." *There. I've said it. I accused a god of being just like me.*

Mazin looked away, then wiped his eyes. "Aye. I own that. I will for all time. The thing about you is you'll forget as the years pass. Memory will fade, and so will your pain. We can't forget. It never passes. Today will be with us forever." His hand found hers across the table. "I promise we will do better. *Be* better."

Vertiline looked at his hand, then lay down her fork and enclosed it with her metal one. "I promise the same, Lord."

"I'm just Mazin today." The god retrieved his hand and brushed his stomach. "Mazin was a good man. He loved to laugh. He traded joy, not wine. His stories were kind on the ears and heart. I wish he were here to see what his kindness bought."

"You're not much of a god of war."

"You're not much of a good listener."

She snorted. "Fair."

"What will you do?"

Vertiline retrieved her fork. "I'm going to eat. I feel like I haven't been this hungry in all my life."

VERTILINE MET THE *CHIMERA* AT THE DOCKS. IMSHIR'S WHARFS were full of bobbing, empty hulls. Fish rotted in holds, cargo and riches unplundered. She waited, arms crossed, as a lone vessel tacked into the harbor.

The ship was brutalized from her crash against the rocks of Ravenswall. Hasty repairs were evident, insufficient even to Vertiline's untrained eye for any captain but the bravest or stupidest to take her to deep water. Yet here she was, a diminutive captain gesturing at an unready crew. On her deck stood a pale woman in a red cloak. The Raven Queen had come. Vertiline spied aged Barret and earnest Heser the Cheg. They no longer argued with each other, quiet as they saw dead Imshir close up.

The ship moored, sailors doing their best to tether the *Chimera*. The crew was inexperienced, the too old and far too young working cheek by jowl to make her secure. They got the job done, the plank made ready. Morgan strode from the ship and put feet on a foreign kingdom's soil. "Knight Vertiline."

Vertiline walked to the queen, then clasped her hands. "Thank you for coming."

The small captain walked the gangway behind Morgan. Vertiline remembered this one: only fourteen or fifteen summers, but with her mother's eyes and black hair. Ekua glanced around, eyes haunted, seeking a person who wouldn't ever be there again. Tilly pushed past Morgan, but with a gentle touch. Morgan was here to help, and there were precious few left with the will or means.

Ekua's gaze locked with Vertiline's, a hard question there. Tilly gave a tiny, sad nod, and wanted to look away as something in Ekua broke. Her face was still hard like a pirate captain's daughter's would be, but her shoulders dropped a fraction, her face paler by degrees.

"Ekua du Parneer. I'm sorry for your loss." Vertiline pulled the girl into a gentle embrace and put her lips next to her ear. "You know the what already. But you don't know the how or the why." She pulled back, holding Ekua at arm's length. "I will share her story with you."

The queen's retinue began unloading supplies. Food and cloth, medicines and bundles that might become tents. All for a people who were already dead. Morgan joined them, and the three watched. The Raven Queen cleared her throat. "The world weeps without end, and it isn't enough."

"Why did she come?" Ekua's voice was rigid, ice on the verge of breaking.

"The same reason we all did." Morgan glanced to the sky. "Because the world needed mending, and we had the needle and thread."

Vertiline found her voice. "Why are you here?"

"Because someone had to be."

"Your kingdom—"

"Is fine," Morgan spat. "We bleed red, but we live. Imshir is..." She trailed off. "I don't know what to do."

"Perhaps you don't have to know what to do. Maybe you need to ask what's needed."

Morgan glanced sidelong at her. "We are not good at asking."

"We don't always get put in situations we're good at." Vertiline kicked a coil of rope. "But we don't have to be. We just have to do it together."

IT WAS STILL RAINING THE NEXT DAY, SO VERTILINE MOVED Armitage—and, by proxy, Sight of Day—to the taverna. The monster healed, but slowly. *He should be dead. Another man would be, if a dragon took a bite out of his hide.* Vertiline, Armitage, and Sight of Day shared another excellent platter of breakfast sausage, eggs, and buttered toast. The monster ate like six ordinary men. "This is good food."

"Thanks," Mazin said from his mug-polishing duties behind the bar.

Armitage glared snake eyes. "Was I fucking talking to you?"

"I—"

"Exactly." Armitage swiveled back to the platter, then his eyes found Vertiline's. "So. No hope for Red?"

{We should open the gate.} The Feybrind nibbled sausage. *{Go after them. They would, for us.}*

"There is no gate." Vertiline sighed. "It was built with sinner's magic, and we're all out of sinners."

"There are no sinners," Mazin said. "That's all a big—"

"Still not talking to you," Armitage rumbled, then coughed. Vertiline's eyes shied away from the grievous wound where his shoulder and half his chest had been. *Like a bite out of a gingerbread man.* "So, can't go in?"

"No," Vertiline agreed.

"Then we wait." Armitage gave a lopsided shrug. "We wait for a hundred years if we have to."

{You won't live for a hundred years.} Sight of Day's golden eyes found Armitage's. *{You weren't made that way.}*

"Then we wait for as long as we've got." He looked at Vertiline, then his remaining hand found hers. "It's all anyone can do."

They sat like that, Vertiline holding his cool hand in hers, and liking how it felt. Minutes past, or it might have been hours. It didn't matter. "I've got to go." Tilly pushed her chair back.

The monster glanced up at her. "Where are you going?"

"To find someone."

THE RAIN STOPPED AS SHE HEADED UPHILL. SHE FOUND YASMINE BY the burned-out pyre. The fairy twinkled at her approach. "Hello, big person."

"It's like you're her," Vertiline breathed. "I ... I don't know if I like it."

"I'm not her," Yasmine glittered. "I can't be all the wonderful things she was. She was brave despite her size. Yasmine lived as a blue-feathered bird since we fell, because she refused to finish our prison. Did you know that? They tried to kill her, but couldn't, so they cursed her to live in a shape that couldn't speak. She carried that anger forward. Yasmine promised to see us back. Then she died." Yasmine flitted to Vertiline's eye height. "Then she lived again for a tiny moment, and met a wonderful man, who worked with a fantastic woman to save you all. She delivered on her promise."

"Tell me of the Boundless," Vertiline said. "I thought it was some Three thing. You know, get a dragon, a Knight, and a sinner, and ... boom."

"Boom?"

"Boom," Tilly agreed.

"Well, it did go boom." Yasmine looked at the Precept's crumbling palace. "But that's not what the Boundless are. They're ... *you*. When you put aside the dumb things you think about each other and work together, you are truly magical. You don't need a goddess to light the way. You make us ... unimportant."

"I'm Boundless?" Vertiline blinked.

Yasmine gave her a little side-eye. "Maybe not you *specifically*."

Tilly laughed. *Oh, that feels good.* Her chest unlocked, and she laughed louder. "Thank you."

"No problem. That's not what you walked all this way on those big, heavy feet to say."

"No." Vertiline looked at those same big, heavy feet. "I'm sorry. I ... wasn't good enough, and I blamed you for it."

"Not bad." The fairy shimmered, stardust falling to the wet pavement. "Only took you a day to get your head out of your—"

"Don't push it," Vertiline warned. They stood in silence for a while, looking at the deserted city. *It felt dead before, but now it's ... waiting.* "I think I'd like to live here."

"It's full of bodies."

"They need someone to put them to rest. And ... I've had enough of everyone for a while."

"Everyone?" The fairy landed on her shoulder, hanging on to a strand of hair like a rope. "You need someone."

"I have all the people I need," Vertiline breathed. "And now I need to tell someone how important they are to me. I need to be better. I need to start again." She teased her hair with metal fingers. *Everything is hard.* "How do I do that?"

"Beats me," Yasmine said. "I Build things."

"Can you build me hope?"

Yasmine's eyes glimmered with eternal god Light for a moment. "I think you've found that already."

Epilogue

Geneve fell for a long time. It felt like days as she plummeted through dark skies filled with … *nothing*.

She saw no ground below. Requiem glowed with the heat of a thousand suns, still white-hot from her battle with the Precept Wincuf. *I hold a falling star.*

Her eyes didn't stream, because it wasn't wind on her face, something close but not quite real enough. She blinked them anyway, trying to make out something in the deep dark. Requiem's brilliance lit the way, but it made for lousy night blindness.

"Meri?" Her words were lost behind her. Geneve reached thought through her ancient helmet. *Ormeon?*

There was nothing but darkness.

AT FIRST SHE THOUGHT THE RED-TINGED GROUND WAS HER EYES playing more tricks on her. She'd seen splashes of color as her mind tried to make sense of the nothing. *No, this is real. There is earth below, and it is on fire.*

She approached fast, wondering if she would die as she hit. Her feet touched rock, but her legs didn't shatter. It was as if she was made of nothing at all in this place.

The world about her glowed with remembered heat, embers sullen against the dark. Within the char were misshapen bodies. She spied something with five heads, and another that might have been an alligator if created by a drunk god. Geneve turned a slow circle, Requiem pushing bright light about her. *There are so many.* But all the demons were dead.

"Meri?" Still nothing. *Ormeon?*

Geneve thought she heard a murmur in her mind from ahead. *It's not north or south, it's just 'that way.'* She held skymetal as she tramped broken ground.

THE HORIZON SPARKLED. GENEVE SHIFTED TO A JOG, SMITHSTEEL clanking as she ran. Bright lances made of vermillion spat across the ground, and from the same direction a mighty gout of roiling fire. She broke into a run, head down. *Ormeon?*

//HURRY.//

Geneve vaulted a piece of ancient stone, black and rotted. Ash puffed in her wake. She crested a rise and saw Meri and Ormeon. The holomancer still stood but was bent with fatigue. The dragon curled protectively at his back, a red grin waiting, but she was ... flat, used up, the runes about her face dim.

Demons swarmed from the other side of Meri and Ormeon's position. They clawed ground, night black eyes mirroring the starless sky.

Geneve screamed challenge and raised Requiem. Then she charged.

GENEVE REMOVED HER HELMET, SUCKING NOT-REALLY-AIR. HER

skymetal sword smoked as demon ichor burned from the blade. The dead were a wall before them, Light-struck and charred.

//THEY WILL COME AGAIN.// Ormeon growled low. *//THEY ALWAYS COME.//*

She put a hand on the dragon's flank, then turned to Meri. He was sweaty, tired, hollow-eyed, but the smile he gave her made her forget about everything else for just a moment. She grabbed him in a fierce hug. "I thought I'd lost you."

"I tried to be lost," he admitted. "Did you see what happened here?"

Geneve let him go, glancing around. "It looks like you did a number on this place."

"No." His grinned widened. "I brought my doom with me. *That* did a number on this place. I'm a real grown-up sinner now, and I brought my hate to the place it would help the most."

She touched his chin. "I thought I'd lost you," she said again.

He looked away. "I thought I'd lost you too. It was a price I was willing to pay—"

"So the world could be safe?" she spat, anger rising. "You stupid, lovely fool."

"No." He glanced at the black heavens. "So *you* could be safe. And here you are, not safe at all."

"Oh, love." She put Requiem's tip to the ground, stone glowing under the tip, and leaned on it. "I'm nothing without you. I need someone to see me. I need *you* to see me. Not the armor and the sword. What's beyond that, and what's inside."

Silence held for a moment. "I see you. I've always seen you. Ever since you tried to kill me."

Geneve laughed, then trickled to silence. "I think we're screwed. There's no way out of here."

"It's okay." He put hands on hips. "You make it possible for me to look amazing. I'm sure we'll figure something out."

//THEY COME AGAIN,// Ormeon growled. *//I DON'T KNOW HOW MUCH LONGER I CAN HOLD.//*

"Ormeon the Redeemer," Geneve whispered. "Rest, dragon. You've redeemed one world. Your work is done."

//ALL THAT IS DEAR TO ME IS HERE. I CAN'T REST.// The dragon looked up. *//ALMOST EVERYTHING. I'M QUITE FOND OF THE CAT.//*

"They come because of us." Meri tapped the burnished sun on her breastplate. "They see what's in you too. At the end, all we are is stardust. We brought it to them."

"We need higher ground." Geneve looked about, then headed maybe-east. "Coming?"

"What for?" Meri leaned against the dragon, weary.

"We're not stuck here with them. They're stuck here with us." She slammed her helmet on. "They want *my* stardust? They'll have to fight me for it."

THE END.

A NEW SONG RISES. A NEW WAR BECKONS.

Sixteen years have passed since Geneve's final battle. The world she saved still bears its scars, and the war she ended left echoes that refuse to fade.

In the heart of Imshir, a bard sings of heroes long gone. Evanne carries the weight of her legacy in her hands—a song, a blade, and the blood of two worlds in her veins. But the past has a way of catching up, and what was buried will not stay forgotten.

The world is shifting once more. The gods are silent. And an old enemy is waking.

Turn the page to meet Evanne.

A bard. A warrior's heir. A woman who was never meant to survive.

The next chapter begins now.

THE COPPER BARD

A DARK FANTASY ADVENTURE

Damn Lies

The miracle arrived in the usual way.

The world didn't notice. Not immediately, and not before it was too late.

Sixteen summers passed in Imshir. The long days grew fat and heavy as the people who came to test themselves against the Platinum Warrior decided to settle down instead. This wasn't because they failed against her; it was because Vertiline was completely uninterested in cutting down imbeciles.

Imshir welcomed all who came. How could it not? Its streets were haunted and empty. It's no wonder, then, that the miracle favoured death. They called her Evanne, and this is her story.

THE MARKET'S CACOPHONY MADE EVANNE'S TEETH VIBRATE, AND the mélange of scents made her want to sneeze. Colourful tents and stalls stretched as far as she could see, each one offering wares that ranged from the mundane to the apparently magical. *I haven't seen any real magic here, except when Meefe outran the guard for selling 'lucky coins'.*

Towering over the crowd atop its hill was the school's tower, its disapproving shadow falling over Evanne. She ignored it, because the tower was just stone. What was inside it? Another matter entirely.

"I need twelve copper barons, and you need your strings fixed." Old Merle's voice carried above the market's hubbub. He fixed Evanne with a steely gaze, gnarled hand of iron on the neck of her instrument. If you called him wizened to his face, you'd get a punching, because despite washing out at the school, his right cross was epic.

"I need my strings fixed because I broke them—"

"I know. Beating someone's head in." Old Merle's sigh was one for the ages, almost loud enough to echo through the market and be heard across the seas in Or'sen. His stall was a treasure trove of musical wonders, strings of all kinds suspended like shimmering vines in the breeze. "Did your father put you up to it?"

Evanne looked at her hands. Bigger than they should be, and weaker too. Her shirt was pulled down below her elbows so the scales weren't so visible. "Dad is—"

"He's gone soft in the head, is what—"

"Let me finish!" Evanne glared. "Just because you're the only one with lute strings for a thousand klicks in any direction doesn't mean you can be a total dick."

That sat between them for a spell, just like Evanne's damaged lute. Or was it her damaged pride? Hitch touched icy fingers against her elbow. "It kind of does. Basic supply and demand economics. Merle—"

"You shut up," Evanne said.

"You what now?" Old Merle looked to the empty air at Evanne's elbow. "Is that boy troubling you again? Tell him to find someone else to haunt. No place for the likes of him around you."

"He said you could charge what you liked because you're the only one with strings. He took your side."

"I didn't—"

"Well, that's different then." Old Merle stroked his beard, trying to look upset and pleased at the same time. "How many did you say you beat down with the lute?"

Evanne sighed, putting a little Trick into it. "Here's the tale of it."

"The truth?"

"Would you like it?"

Old Merle snorted. "Would I get it even if I wanted it?"

Evanne let her fingers rest on the lute strings. Hitch hovered at her elbow, his not-quite-there face soft in the candlelight. Fui gave her a nod from his place behind the bar. He knew they'd come to listen to the Girl With Two Souls play. It was a nicer name than others she'd been given.

Fui's was a haven for the mysterious and the lost. The walls sported tapestries he claimed were gathered during the fall of Ravenswall, but Evanne didn't think battlefields went big on tapestry. It didn't matter; the tapestries worked with torches to lend a smoky tone to the air and soul alike.

The tune she struck up was merry. It suited the rich, thick air like a good whiskey might suit the throat. A crowd of regulars were littered about. These people came to Imshir from all parts of the world and preferred to leave their past in the past. Some even from far off Or'sen, paler than the local stock, all those strong arms put to better use these days than wielding swords.

The door slammed wide, six newcomers—

"Six? Even the Platinum Warrior would have trouble with that." Old Merle squinted. "Truth, now."

Evanne snorted. "She wouldn't. At six she wouldn't even break a sweat." This with a little pride, and perhaps some regret. The Storm lived in the Platinum Warrior, but not in her daughter.

"Sweat or no, you're barely competent with a lute. I can't see you—"

"Aye, *aye*. Get your hand off it, Merle." Evanne bunched her shoulders, then let out a breath. "Three it is."

THE DOOR SLAMMED WIDE, THREE NEWCOMERS CHASED IN BY HOT DESERT wind. They were cloaked in tattered, darkened robes, lending an unfriendly aura of dark foreboding. Their presence sent shivers through the room, like a sudden gust of icy wind. They wore hooded masks, concealing their faces in a veil of enigma. The tavern's regulars exchanged knowing glances, recognising that these newcomers were no ordinary travellers.

The sun had dipped from the sky but the sands outside Imshir remembered its heat well enough. Two men, one woman, all tough and gnarled in the way a hundred-year oak was. They'd come to test steel against the Platinum Warrior. See if the Storm still answered her call, or argue with the Sway that sometimes worked, other times behaved like a worn-out old nag.

Evanne didn't recognise them, but she knew their type. She fingered the brim of her hat, tugging it lower, hiding her face. She was a monster, and monsters weren't welcome in the light. That she had the voice of angels didn't matter. People didn't give her a chance to speak before they raised a blade or fist.

Hitch breathed on her neck. "It will be okay."

"Easy for you to say. You're already dead."

"Today isn't your day." He seemed confident, but the dead always did about her.

Fui gave her a little side-eye, because he wasn't paying her to talk to the air. Everyone knew the dead had nothing to say to the living, so most thought her borderline mad. Evanne wasn't mad, though. Uncle Day asked her once what she thought she was, and she'd said cursed. *He'd mock-laughed at her, despite the poetic ring her voice gave the word.*

Evanne strummed, hunching closer to the shadows beside the big hearth. It wouldn't be lit for a time yet, so it was good she didn't feel the cold like her father. All seemed well as she played, the crowd murmuring, until Fui's girl Kabili brought her mead. It was good, and took the rasp from her voice. But as she drank, her face caught light, and the three newcomers chose that moment to look over to see why the music stopped.

It might've been because they wanted to check out Kabili. Evanne had done her share of that already. They were close enough in age, but no one would want to tousle in the hay with a monster. Whatever the reason, they saw Evanne, and her face. The hard line of her jaw, the teeth that weren't quite right, and the lavender snake eyes.

Then it was shouting, and hands on weapons, and before Evanne knew it she was surrounded by six—

"THREE," CORRECTED OLD MERLE.

"Three gods, or—"

"Three people beset you," Old Merle said.

"Of course," Evanne sighed. "No room for creative license?"

"None."

EVANNE WAS SURROUNDED BY THE THREE NEW TO IMSHIR'S WONDERS AND terrors. The woman stood back a pace or two, leaving room for her steel if it came to that. Her companions weren't so patient, one hauling Evanne from her stool. "A ... Vhemin?" His tone was confused.

Hitch shrugged. "Always they go there first."

"I'm not Vhemin," Evanne said. "I'm not anything, really. You should put me down." Because for all she was half of one world and half of another, blood warm and cold, consorting with the living and the dead, she was still a sixteen-year-old young woman and weighed as much. A bushel lighter or heavier, depending on whether you used the human or Vhemin scales.

"I'll put you down when you're dead," the man hissed. Evanne didn't think his breath started out great, and the ale hadn't improved it.

"Take her outside," the other man snarled. "We'll show these Vhemin scum what attacking our homes brings. Justice!"

Fui hollered from behind the bar, but no one seemed to care. Kabili was gone, the door to the yard slamming in her wake. Gone to get aid, or just to flee. Help wouldn't arrive in time. Evanne looked to Hitch. "You said today wasn't my day!"

"Who you talking to?" The man with his hand bunched in her shirt looked at the empty air beside the hearth.

"I didn't say you would get a free ride," the ghost said. "Work a little."

Evanne kicked the man in the shins. She had no leverage, but he startled well enough. She grabbed his shirt in turn, then slammed the lute into his head. It was a sloppy blow, and if the Storm could love a half-breed like her it wouldn't have answered her call at the abortive attempt. It bought her a little more time, the man flinching, so she kneed him in the balls with enthusiasm.

He let her go, sucking air while trying to throw up, and Evanne grabbed the lute's neck with both hands, stepped to the left to avoid the chair his friend swung at her, and clobbered the man in the face.

The lute gave up at that point, pieces of delicate wood hitting the floor, strings broken. The woman drew steel, lamplight orange carried on the blade, snarled, and ... stopped. Evanne's scattergun was pointed at the woman's face.

The moment held. The woman looked at her companions, then the scattergun. "But ... that's a holy weapon."

"And I'm a holy person," Evanne nodded. "Now get out."

OLD MERLE STROKED HIS BEARD. "YOU GOT YOUR MOTHER'S scattergun?"

"And if I did?" Evanne felt the jut of her chin, but liked the look well enough.

The shopkeeper trailed his fingers over Evanne's lute. "And you've repaired the lute well enough since just last night! That Feybrind of yours—"

"He's not mine. Uncle Day is—"

"Peace!" Old Merle raised his hands in surrender. "Was but a trick of the lips. There's no owning here, and never will be, despite what might be fashionable in Or'sen." It was difficult to tell with the beard but Evanne thought Old Merle might have the hint of a smile about him. "We also haven't discussed how this is my problem. Why this lute, magnificently repaired, needs new strings that *I* must pay for."

"Ah. That's the best part of the story." Evanne hitched her hip next to the counter top. "The story alone is worth a regal."

"A regal!" The old man burst out laughing, then wiped a crinkled eye. "Let's hear it then."

Evanne raced after the thugs. The air outside was trending cooler now, and there was no Kabili in sight to heat up her thoughts. She could see the faint heat footprints left by her assailants. They were warm to her half-Vhemin eyes. She'd have satisfaction before the night was out, and damn her human weakness.

A crash from ahead. She slowed her roll, hand going to her holster. The lute hung from her other arm, neck clenched in her fingers, ready to strike. She heard muted whispers, wishing for a moment some half of her was Feybrind, so's to get the cat people's hearing.

That's Old Merle's shop. *Now what would six assailants—*

"Blessed Cophine," said Merle. "It's back to six? And when did the lute get repaired?"

"You said it yourself. Couldn't have gone down that way. Now hush." Evanne grinned her pointed teeth. "We're getting to the finale."

Perhaps three people could make noise enough for six. Evanne sneaked closer, scattergun drawn, wearing shadows as her armour. She arrived at the broken door leading to Old Merle's storage room. Evanne had no idea why three down and out hoodlums would want to hide among sealing wax and drum skins but there was no accounting for taste.

She poked her head around the jamb. Inside: the three stooges, working with a hooded lantern. The man she'd kneed in the groin looked uncomfortable as he rooted about, but the other two were in fine form. The woman held up her prize: a small box with a metal clasp. "I have it!"

Evanne squinted. She'd not seen the box before, but that wasn't surprising. Old Merle was miserly with access to his storeroom—

"'WARE," SAID OLD MERLE. "DANGEROUS GROUND."

OLD MERLE HAD NO OCCASION TO OFFER HER ACCESS TO THE ROOM, EVEN when she'd offered to help him store the heaviest boxes inside. He wasn't here, but she was, and it was time to stop the thieves once and for all. She stood, stepped into the doorway, and shouted, "Drop it!"

Three sets of eyes moved to her. The woman did not, in point of fact, drop the box. The thieves as one marked her drawn scattergun. The man she'd kneed in the best place ever spat. "You've only two rounds in that weapon. There are three of us, monster."

"Hard for one to carry two coffins though." Evanne considered the man, sniffed, then showed her pointed teeth. Some might call it a smile, and the darkness would keep the lie well enough. "You can go. If you like, that is."

"I can what?"

"Go. Out." She stepped aside. "That way you won't be shot and I can kill the other two and be done."

"What kind of freak show are you?" hissed the woman. "Clyde is my brother true."

"I'm out," said Clyde, who stepped past Evanne with a protective hand in front of his nethers. Evanne heard the beating of his feet as he tried to distance himself from his mistakes.

"Fuck," offered the other man.

"Not you, not ever," Evanne countered. "Now Clyde's gone, who wants it?"

The woman hurled the box at Evanne, then rushed her, sword savaging the night as it hungered from its scabbard. Evanne fired, but the box collided with the scattergun, and she hit nothing but air. The lantern's light would've night-blinded a human but her Vhemin eyes saw true. She crouched, the woman's swing missing her neck and overbalancing her assailant. Evanne straightened with gusto, putting her shoulder into the woman. As the air left her Evanne hit her upside the jaw with her lute.

Down, and out, just in time for the man to come at her with a wicked-looking knife. Evanne heard tales of Vide assassins with similar weapons: the blade black as night, sharp as sin. Where a two-baron thug would get a blade like that was anyone's guess, but the question could wait. She pivoted about the thrust, her lute clutched close. Evanne heard the cry as strings died against the steel's edge. She snarled, all bared fangs and lavender snake eyes, then head butted the man.

Her father would've been proud. The man dropped like a two-baron doxy at the wharfs with a new ship in port. And she still had one round in her gun. She holstered it, fingered broken strings, then fetched the box. "Ah," she breathed. "Now what's inside you then?"

O<small>LD</small> M<small>ERLE</small> <small>LEANED FORWARD.</small> "A <small>BOX, YOU SAY?</small>"

"A box," Evanne confirmed. She swung her satchel in front of her, rummaged inside, and drew forth the box. "Here you go. Metal clasp. Sorry about the chipping on the corner. I think the scattergun caught it and—"

"Fuck me," Old Merle said. "You found my wife's old keep chest."

"Not you either, not ever," Evanne said. "The story is worth a regal, and the box two. But all I want is new strings for my lute."

The shopkeeper leaned close, beckoning her with a weathered hand. She leaned in, companionable-like, and tried on a conspiratorial smile. Old Merle stayed quiet for a spell, long enough she wondered if he'd had a stroke, then he said, "Did you break into my storeroom trying to find strings?"

"I'm shocked and offended by the allegation." Evanne kept her smile up, but it felt a heavier lift. "That's a libellous thing to say."

"It's not libel if it's true."

Hitch drifted through the counter top. "He's not wrong."

"Strings, Merle. Can I have them or not?"

The moment held, then the old man showed teeth that could've been in better condition. "You were right, Evanne. It was a regal-worthy story. For this chest, here are your strings." She snatched them as he put them down. "Break into my storeroom again and I'll have you flayed."

"Fair," Evanne admitted. "Good day, sir."

He barked a laugh. "Good day, m'lady. Try not to get killed by someone less understanding before dinner."

Chapter One

Tarragon Greyflight wanted to die. The thing stopping her was being in a very small cage, a very long way below ground, without her sword. She was a fairy and had been here for seven or eight hundred years. Keeping count was *hard* without the sun. The cage was in a prison that doubled as a laboratory, a dark space that brimmed with forgotten experiments and decaying machinery. The walls were still strong, which was part of the problem, but a little moss found root about a hundred years past and lingered still.

Helio died six months earlier. He'd been in the cage beside her, always quick with a joke, but his feeding tube stopped working. His glimmer died, and took Tarragon's will to live with it. The view didn't help; the floor was a mishmash of grime and crumbling tiles, with scattered debris from centuries-old equipment strewn about. Broken glass vials and beakers lay in jagged piles, their contents long since evaporated or turned to a sticky residue.

The two of them lived here—*if you could call it living*—since they'd been captured. Itikari sent them on a mission, and somewhere along that mission someone captured her in a net, and then: surprise! Small cage for all eternity. It sucked. Sucked! And when Helio left with his jokes, leaving a crumpled, desiccated pile in the bottom of his cage, Tarragon was left with no one to talk to.

No one to remind her of why life was worth living.

"I wish I had my sword," she said to no one in particular, but mostly to the dead woman lolling at a table three meters away. The woman had died slightly less than seven hundred years ago, because she'd been shot in the head. She had been nice enough for a sociopath, all smiles when there was no need for needles, and might have let Tarragon and Helio free.

Her name was Meredith or Mazretha, or perhaps Mawisroh. It didn't matter much, not now and not before, because she was a scientist who worked for Vehement Systems, and Vehement were the sworn enemies of Itikari. Tarragon was a spy for Itikari, and that meant she and Mefothah—*who names their baby Mefothah, anyway?*—could never be friends.

But even an enemy would be good about now, because Tarragon hadn't spoken to anyone in six months, and for seven hundred years before that, no one but Helio.

The monster who'd shot Minah—*that's it! Her name was Minah!*—had been a smaller-than-usual brute. He'd looked at the fairies, his gun, sniffed, and walked away. When Helio asked *what about us* the thug had sighed, and said, *they don't pay me enough to kill the pretty things.* And like that, he'd left them, and no one had been here since.

She rattled the bars of her cage. They were good steel, built in a way that a tiny person like Tarragon couldn't open. With enough of a run up she might use her glimmer to melt through, but the cage was only about two humans' hand spans across. If she had a sword, it'd be different.

"I'm sorry you died, Minah." The woman didn't answer of course. Her skin was long gone, the skeleton beneath a misery of off white. The lab coat remained, untouched by time, clean as if newly spun. Minah had worn glasses, an interesting affectation from a time when such things were fixable, and those glasses had slipped from her sloughing face about a hundred years into Tarragon's imprisonment to lie on the edge of the table.

The table was a bit more average than the rest. It was made of actual wood, which meant it was having a rough time of things about now. A few longhorn borers had made their way in here and spent a lovely time in the table until some long-dormant system had sprayed the room with poison. It'd made Tarragon sneeze—Helio hadn't minded it—and then the borers were dead too.

Tarragon eyed the glasses. The arms looked like they could hold an edge if you had time to carve such. They could be, in a certain light, swords. If only they were two metres closer. Ah, well. It was time for lunch anyway.

She ambled to her feeding tube, giving it a kick. It spat out a small blob of paste which tasted like peanut butter, in a good enough way, but peanut butter for seven hundred years was getting old. Tarragon munched without much interest, then stopped chewing as a thought hit her.

Borer. Table. Glasses. Feeding tube.

She wished she was a Builder like the rest of her kind. She'd not been good with metal things. Sure, better than the Bigs, but the same could be said about rock apes. Helio sucked too, which is why they were Itikari spies and not Builders. But: the feeding tube. The table! And the glasses.

She kicked the tube, got more not-quite-peanut-butter, and hurled it through the bars of the cage. It flew, trailing some of her glitterdust, to *splat* on the table.

The table didn't seem to care.

Tarragon went to work with great industry. She threw hunk after miniature hunk of paste on the table. After a puff of dust, she knew she was onto a good thing. Seven tiny heartbeats later, the table gave up its seven-hundred-year vigil, slumping in a brown eddy of wood dust.

The glasses fell. Bounced. Tumbled toward the cage.

Tarragon hurled herself toward the bars, wings aglow, arm outstretched. The cold steel against her face smelled of old metal and ill remembered hate. Her fingers clutched nothing, grasping for something, *anything*, and then: she had them.

The glasses were in her hand. Tarragon breathed for a moment, hand trembling, the glasses over a fall to the floor, then very slowly pulled them back to her. It took a bit of doing and a lot of swearing, but she got the glasses into the cage. The lenses got scratched, but she didn't need those, and Minah wouldn't care.

Tarragon flicked a wing, motes of emberbright tumbling to the floor, before slicing the arms of the glasses free. A little elbow grease, and yes, more swearing, and she had two oddly shaped plastic swords with a heart of what was probably iron.

"Here we go, Minah. Time to go." Tarragon fluttered, struck a pose, then swung with all her minute might. She gave as much of her ember as she dared to her weapons, the let's-call-them-blades glimmering with fairy might, and managed to cut through the bars of the cage in two strikes. The swords didn't like this much, sloughing apart, but their work was done.

Tarragon spent a moment or two catching her breath, because ember made her live, and she'd used most of what she had. Then she burst free of the cage and flitted to hover before Minah. The dead woman had a rectangle of plastic above her breast pocket. Tarragon stole it, then headed for the door that hadn't opened in seven hundred years.

She was free.

Chapter Two

Evanne spent time with the dead. It was what she did every morning.

She and Hitch slouched by a low stone wall that had seen better days, away from the market proper. This path was a backstreet of a backstreet, useful to know if you were the kind of person with sticky fingers and low means. It fed into a ruined square which used to be the market, before Evanne was born, and before Mama and Papa saved the world.

Living up to that legacy is a chore. The dead don't want anything from me. So, Evanne hung out with them.

For their part, the dead didn't mind. The dead didn't do much of anything except pretend to live lives they lost long ago. There, a farrier, putting shoes on a horse. Except there was no horse, not even the ghost of one. Just the farrier, a little fatter and shorter than most she'd seen, wrestling with a beast that was long gone.

Across the market, a hawker trying to sell... She squinted. "Cabbages? Flowers? What's he on about?"

"Rutabagas," Hitch suggested.

"I see." Evanne nodded. "Yes, there's no one buying, because everyone hates rutabaga. It makes sense."

"You could ask him," her ghostly companion wisped. "Try just one more. For luck."

She glared at Hitch, but couldn't tell if he glared back, which spoiled the effect. He was mostly translucent, faded and tattered at the edges like an old cloak, and let the daylight through. She didn't know what his face looked like. "They never talk. The dead have nothing to say to the living."

"Except me."

"Except you," Evanne allowed with a growl. "He's been trying to sell rutabagas forever. You'd think he'd get the idea by now."

"It's only sixteen years." Hitch walked with her toward the maybe-rutabaga seller. Or, at least she thought it was walking. He didn't have legs, not all the way down, just wafting along as if a good breeze could take him. But the weather didn't move Hitch any more than her glare. "That's when they all died. When Imshir fell, right before you were born."

She shored up beside the rutabaga hawker. "Hey! No one's buying today." She waved her arm in front of the ghost's face as he earnestly entreated someone who wasn't there anymore to buy something. It was a shame no one was left to buy. The man looked so earnest. "*I'd* buy a rutabaga from this man." Evanne rummaged in her satchel for a small notebook, and a little longer for the pencil she could never find. *If your eyes show belief, then the other person will want the same thing*, she wrote. "And I wasn't born straight away. You make it sound like Mama and Papa had a scattergun wedding."

Ignoring the remark, Hitch looked over her shoulder. "What are you writing? More Tricks?"

"Piss off," Evanne suggested, snapping the book closed. "I can give you directions, if you need them." She pointed with her pencil toward the destroyed castle at the top of the big hill overlooking the city. "Up there, maybe."

Her companion gave a shrug, drifting through the hawker as he did so. The hawker didn't seem to mind. He had nothing to say to the dead either, it seemed. "It's a long way."

Evanne tossed her Tricks notebook into the bag, slapped the flap closed, and ground out a glare. "Best you get started then."

"I'd get so lonely without the warm blanket of your sarcasm," Hitch said. "I'll stay. You need company while you restring that lute you broke robbing Old Merle last night."

"I did no such thing!" Evanne's voice rose, and she wound it back down. "I interrupted the robbers myself. You were there!"

"Hmm," said Hitch, which didn't sound like agreement. "Make sure you don't drink too deeply from your own Tricks."

The hawker stilled for a moment, then swung his ghostly gaze north. All the ghosts in the market did the same thing, a ripple spreading through them like rings in a pond. Toward the broken tower, then they yearned forward a stumble step at a time.

"Great," Hitch said. "The fucking cat."

"Uncle Day!" Evanne squealed. She broke into a run, and damn how tired she'd be at the end. Her body was as broken as her soul, but she couldn't stop her heart from wanting to see the Feybrind.

DAMN THESE LEGS. SHE STAGGERED UP THE HILL TOWARD THE school's tower, breath rasping un-Vheminlike in her chest. The lute banged against her bag, unsettling her balance, and making a difficult job harder. At least there weren't people here. The noise of the market fell behind, taking the musky smell with it. Warm wind touched her, ruffling rust locks, plastering them to her face.

Hitch ghosted by her side. "You could just walk. He'll still be there if you don't run."

"Spoken like someone with no flair for the dramatic." Evanne wheezed around a corner, hand outstretched, the pale human skin of her forearms disappearing into her shirt. Her hand left a sweat print against the old stone in a way her Vhemin scales couldn't.

"Spoken like someone who doesn't like cats," Hitch argued.

"I don't know why I keep you around." Evanne braced her hands on knees, sucking like a bellows.

"Because you can't get rid of me. Believe me, if I could leave I would have. You're slower than a wet April. Put some back into it."

Hitch bobbed encouragingly, voice turning sonorous. "You can do it. I believe in you."

"Eat a big bowl of dicks." Evanne spared Hitch another glance, then lurched on. Her breath came in fits and starts, heart hammering its uneven rhythm, but she kept going. She scampered through the Craftsman's District, ignoring the allure of Whitetower Ward in favour of the school's keep.

Ghosts she left behind. She might be slow, the unkind calling her feeble, but she at least had a pulse. The ghosts didn't like leaving where they'd anchored in death, or life, or whatever made them do what they did. But they always came for Sight of Day.

She burst through the shattered keep gate, winding up the hill toward the broken palace. It'd gone to seed since Imshir fell, but since the city was in the middle of a desert nature had not laid claim to it again. It was just busted old rocks and bad memories.

At the steps leading to the keep's main doors: a Feybrind. He sprawled on the steps, basking in the summer sun, eyes closed. His horse nosed the ground in a way that implied it was used to disappointment. She ignored the fat saddlebags, putting on a last burst of speed. "Uncle Day!"

The Feybrind opened a glorious golden eye, stretched, and stood just in time for her to cannon into him. Evanne wrapped him in a hug, panting into the cinnamon sweet smell of his fur. The cat put a hand on the back of her head, stroked her hair, then slipped free. His hands moved, Handspeak clear and slow for those without the People's speed and grace. *{You need to work on your approach. You are not stealthy at all.}*

Evanne snorted, ignoring the tell-tale twinge in her stomach at the closeness of the Feybrind. It'd always been there. Her father said he had it too, maybe worse, but said it'd been a small price to pay for *a friend worth all the Vhemin in the world.* "It's been *ages.*"

{It's been four months. I've had longer naps.} The cat half smiled, ignoring her breathlessness as if her feebleness was what everyone was like. *{Are you well? Have you managed to lose that peskersome ghost?}*

Hitch sighed. "Tell him—"

"The peskersome ghost ... *lingers,*" Evanne said. "Once, a long time ago, Imshir had an outbreak of yellow fever. It swept from Crimsonfair to Whitetower. They barricaded the streets, waiting for people to die. And they died! A lot. But the plague spread from Imshir to the surrounding lands. People died of yellow fever for years. They called it the Twenty-Year Plague. I think Hitch is my own personal Twenty-Year Plague."

"I resemble that remark," the ghost said.

Sigh of Day's wonderful golden eyes roamed. *{He's here, isn't he?}*

"Like syphilis, he never really leaves."

{I see.} The cat's eyes grew sad for a moment as he gazed down at Imshir. *{And the rest?}*

Evanne turned toward the city. The legion of ghostly forms stagger-stepped up the hill toward them, looking through her and toward the Feybrind. "Aye. They're coming."

{I wish I could tell them...} The cat's hands stilled. *{It doesn't matter.}*

"They know." Evanne clasped the Feybrind's hands in her own. "They know you're sorry. They come to thank you."

THE KEEP HELD ALL THE SECRETS. EVANNE WASN'T SUPPOSED TO GO in there, which was a fight her parents lost before she was five years old. The Platinum Warrior, wise to the ways of battle, set her sights on a new challenge: educating her daughter about the perils of demons. *Don't touch, hot* was the basic lesson, and Evanne was fine with that. Demons seemed to suck the joy out of just about everything, almost broke the world—*twice!*—and she lived on the edge of a city literally killed by their last invasion attempt.

She *wanted* to touch, though. The inside of Imshir's dilapidated keep-turned-school was a wonder. The walls held carvings depicting ancient battles between people, Vhemin, Feybrind, and devices too devilish to understand. A scrabbling climbing grass like ivy's buck-toothed cousin tried to scale the walls but couldn't really stick the landing. The doors they passed were heavy, still standing after years of existence.

The air was cooler here, thicker, *closer*. It smelled like nothing else, and Evanne wondered if that was dead demon musk, or something brought on by the Sway. Mama didn't use the Sway often.

Much of the wreckage of the battle *slightly* before her birth had been cleared up. No broken chandeliers littered their path. No broken benches or corpses littered the way. But no one had spared time in here dicking about putting on a fresh lick of paint, because it felt like things lived in the walls. Watched, and waited.

Mama said it kept her sharp. For Evanne? Yeah, it was all *don't touch, hot.*

So, to the keep they went, but she kept her hands (mostly) to herself. Sight of Day strolled at her side, golden eyes everywhere without seeming to be, hand a careful close distance from his sword.

Evanne cleared her throat. "They're all dead. Your sword. You won't need it."

{You tend to need a weapon when you least want to hold it.} The Feybrind relaxed a micron despite his words, Handspeak flowing like visual music. *{How is the village?}*

"It is full of petty people."

{Who did you try stealing from this time?}

"The cat's not stupid," Hitch allowed.

"I hope you both have a horrible accident." Evanne swept her rust locks aside. She liked it shoulder length, but it didn't always agree. Her mother's platinum tresses seemed to yearn for the ground. Her father's short hair didn't need cutting. She was lost somewhere in the middle ground of not quite long enough, not quite short enough. Not platinum, not dark as rock. *Muddy*, perhaps, with a heavy lacing of saffron. "Anyway, the settlement is *fine*."

{Fine never means that.} The Feybrind paused at an intersection. Crumbling mortar salted the ground around a massive stone block that lay in the middle. *{The keep is dying, too.}*

"We had another five come to test their luck and steel against 'the Platinum Warrior'." Evanne gave a few air quotes for good measure. "So, we now have five new students."

Sight of Day half smiled at that. *{It seems the deluge is slowing. Good. News is getting out that she can't be beaten.}*

Evanne snorted. "She can be beaten. I beat her!"

{One time! And you cheated.}

"'There is no cheating in war'," Evanne quoted. "Who said that?"

The cat's tail lashed. *{I forget.}*

"That's right! It was *you*." She dimpled impishly at him because she knew he claimed to hate it but didn't really, pointed teeth peeking out, before leading Sight of Day past the fallen stone. The sound of steel on stone came, faint as a lark on the wind. "We're almost there."

A short walk took them closer to the sound of violence. A double door waited, closed, perhaps even sullen. Evanne shouldered it aside to take in a room about twenty meters a side, complete with pillars and high-set windows. Also, there were ten people trying to murder her mother.

The Platinum Warrior stood in the middle of the room. She didn't even have the grace to breathe hard. Vertiline held a crooked stick like a sword, her posture achingly perfect. Five people were already on the ground, one out for the count, the other four clutching various parts of their anatomy and groaning. Their metal weapons lay on the pavers, not having made a nick in the stick Vertiline held.

A woman with jet hair and a good eye shadow game turned at Evanne's entrance. Vertiline stepped forward three steps and tapped her on the back of the head with her stick. The stick glowed as she swung, hit with a *crack*, and the raccoon-faced woman dropped like a bad rhyme. "Sloppy." Vertiline's voice was cool, calm, almost ... *bored*. "Never lose your focus."

Two rushed her, and she just ... wasn't there anymore, sidestepping like she was made of air. Evanne had little skill with a blade, but she loved watching her mother play at war. She was just so damn beautiful at it. *Unlike me*, a voice in her mind said. Evanne gritted her not-quite-shark-teeth. *But I make better music.*

A door at the far end opened, a brute the size of four ordinary men striding through. Armitage wore knee-length shorts but no shirt. His muscled torso didn't wear time like most men's despite the creases holding counsel with his eyes. Vhemin didn't wrinkle like people, but snakes still aged. Evanne looked at the pale scales over his shoulder and most of his chest. An old injury. She knew it still pained him. He admitted it in the quiet of their home, but let none of it show here.

Vertiline turned, a smile warm as the sun touching her lips. No longer *bored*, but *radiant*. His voice was comforting, like warm sand beneath your feet. "You fuckers still haven't dropped her?"

Vertiline's smile dimmed somewhat at that. Four of the Platinum Warrior's opponents took that moment to rush her from behind. She swept to the side, stick blazing like a falling star, breaking a leg, arm, sword, and shield, leaving four more on the ground. Vertiline pointed her stick at Armitage. "Ho, monster. I expected you to be on my side."

"Eh," Armitage said. "Cat?"

{Brother.} Sight of Day slipped across the floor, giving a cautious berth to Vertiline's opponents. He made Armitage, slipped inside the big Vhemin's arms, and embraced him.

"Take five." Vertiline lowered her stick as Armitage disentangled from fur, heading toward her. Evanne's father grabbed her mother, kissing her deep and long.

A man with an ugly scar on his forearm took that moment to rush Vertiline's back. Armitage swung her aside with the same ease an ox would move an ant, wound up, and punched the man so hard his legs and head reversed heights. "The boss said 'take five.' She didn't mean five more beatings. Fuck off."

Vertiline brushed platinum hair back. "Love. You say the sweetest things."

{He's barely literate. This is not poetry.}

Evanne held by the door. No matter how often her mother said she was welcome here, she didn't feel at home in the world of steel. That place was for the Platinum Warrior, not Evanne the Half-Made.

Sight of Day stood next to a fallen student. *{What of these?}*

"Cartessa will be along." Vertiline tossed her makeshift weapon to the ground. The golden glow left it as it dropped, an ordinary stick again, not a weapon of the gods. "She needs to practice Sway."

Armitage grunted. "Who needs a beer?"

"It's eleven in the morning!" Vertiline linked an arm with his.

"I'm sure there's a point there, but I can't work it out." Armitage dragged Vertiline along, collecting Evanne in his other arm as they reached the door. "C'mon, kid."

Her father was big, sure. Gruff, to a certainty. Strong like the core of the world. She leaned into his cool embrace, feeling warmed by it despite his cold blood. Evanne smiled up at him, because although she was tall for a human woman, she was nothing on her father's massive size. "I'll take a beer."

Vertiline frowned across her father's chest at her. "You will—"

"Fine by me," Armitage rumbled, hefting them both along. "Beer all around."

"I don't know why I bother." The Platinum Warrior rolled her eyes, but smiled all the same.

"It's because beer is so good," Evanne offered. "And it's an excuse for an early lunch."

"WE SHOULD GO TO CRIMSONFAIR FARTHING." VERTILINE'S LONG legs kept her at the front, hair flowing like a wave. Evanne thought she was beautiful. Always had, and always wanted to look like her. Long-legged, blonde, strong and lean, and perfect. Not a ... *half.*

{I wish you wouldn't call it that.} Uncle Day strode backward so they could see his Handspeak, making it look easy like he did with anything and everything. *{We don't know what they called it.}*

"We kinda do," Armitage argued, hefting their picnic basket. It gave a happy *clink* as bottles within huddled closer. "There are books." He waved his hand, as if *books* were like *diseases.*

"The books are in Tebrani," Evanne said. "They are so unemotional. 'This is the farrier's district' is not as poetic as Crimsonfair Farthing." She tried not to look at the bundle Sight of Day carried. It looked like, *maybe,* an axe, except the Feybrind carried it as if it weighed nothing at all. He'd tied it with a bright silk bow.

"It's less honest," Hitch offered. "The people of Imshir wanted a farrier's district, not a Crimsonfair Farthing."

"Well, they're dead, so they don't get a vote." Evanne looked down before raising a fist. "Hear me, ghosts! If you speak, I will listen!"

{The dead have nothing to say to the living.}

"Aye, aye." Evanne waved the cat's comment off. "And yet, they follow." The cluster of shades about them would have been cloying if she hadn't been used to it. *I grew up with the dead as companions.* "And yet they love you."

Vertiline sighed. "I wish I could make them ... stop. The world is saved, and yet the dead linger with their tasks not yet done."

"Fuck 'em," suggested Armitage.

"Not today, not ever," Evanne said. She ducked a good-natured cuff from her father and dodged an eye roll from her mother. "What's in the package?"

Sight of Day glanced down at the ribbon-bound bundle. *{A surprise.}*

"For me?"

{Who it's for is part of the surprise.}

They found an old broken down taverna by the waterfront. Her mother said it used to smell bad by the docks in the first days they kept vigil, but without people or fishing boats the sea reclaimed all, leaving a salty freshness. The rest of Imshir's folk didn't come into the old, dead city proper. The Platinum Warrior hadn't forbidden it, because her mother had no time for rules or ruling. But people didn't come here. Maybe it was the ghosts. While Evanne was the only one who could see them, people claimed a chill at odds with the hot desert air when the dead clustered close.

Her father's picnic basket yielded rich booty: home brewed beer for all, good crusty bread, salted pork, desert stone fruits, and a half wheel of soft cheese in a grease paper wrap. Uncle Day sliced pork while Evanne stole a plum. They four ate in companionable silence, broken by Evanne's beery burp.

"Keep it classy." Vertiline didn't sound like her heart was in it. Her gaze rested on the water, or perhaps the horizon far beyond.

Armitage shifted his weight. "You're just jealous you can't compete with Vhemin majesty."

{That was not majestic.}

The Platinum Warrior put her bottle down, then reached across the table and took Sight of Day's hands in hers. "Dear heart. Why have you come?"

The Feybrind held still for a moment, then freed his hands. *{To* *bring a gift.}* He lifted the bundle from beneath the table, handing it to Evanne. *{For you.}*

She took it, eyes wide. It was the work of a moment to free the silken cords and lift the paper. As she opened the present, she smelled sandalwood and a hint of fresh lacquer. Red-stained wood glinted under the sun. Evanne lifted her prize free, holding it up to the noonday light.

"Very nice," Armitage growled. "What is it?"

"Can't you tell, Papa?" Evanne held it to her chest. "It is love. It is distance and time brought close. It's the nearest city, holding your furthest heart. It is myth and rhyme. Rhythm and hope."

The big man looked at what she held, then to Evanne, and finally to Vertiline. "Did you understand that?"

{It is an instrument of the ancients,} Uncle Day said. *{I found it below the earth. I believe it is called a,}* and here he spelled the word letter by letter, *{guitar.}*

Vertiline looked at Evanne's guitar, then Uncle Day. "A what?"

"It's a lute with six strings, Mama."

"I thought it was love. Distance and time." She brushed back hair. "Hearts and hope."

"I *knew* you were listening." Evanne brushed the strings with human-enough fingers. The guitar didn't sound like a lute. Richer, perhaps, or sadder, as if it remembered the ancient dead, but was too polite to make a fuss.

Vertiline looked to Sight of Day. "You've been hunting again?"

The cat spread his hands. *{As you've been holding vigil, I've been seeking. It is what we do, the three of us. For our honoured friends.}*

"That's not why you're here," Armitage said. "We know Red and the runt went away. The dragon too." He scratched at the seam of his scar, Vhemin-strong fingers rasping at scale. "It's what we said we'd do. Tilly, to mind the gate. Me, to mind the people. And you, to hunt. Until the end of time, when the seas dry up, or some such."

"I will hold," Vertiline whispered. She shook herself. "But you are not hunting. You are here. And while your company warms my bitter, twisted heart in a way the sun can't, I am suspicious."

{I'm not a thief! Look to the fruits of your loins.}

"What did you steal this time?" Armitage growled.

Evanne bridled. "I think we're getting off track. This isn't about *me*. It's about Uncle Day and why he's not doing whatever the desert asks of him."

Her father gave her a flat stare before turning back to the Feybrind. "She's got a point. The thievery will keep."

"Hey! I didn't—"

"What I want to know is whether trouble's on your heels." Her father sipped beer, then leaned back. His chair gave an ominous *creak*. "About time I had an honest fight. All these new Supplicants are a waste of good air."

Vertiline leaned forward. "Rebuilding the Tresward isn't easy—"

"That shouldn't be your job, either." Armitage shrugged. "I didn't say your fancy school was a problem. It's nice to have a hobby."

"A *hobby?*" Vertiline's voice rose at least two octaves.

{*I found a place,*} Sight of Day said. {*I found a place of devils, and they are waking up.*}

The Past is Not Done With Her.

A LEGACY FORGED IN BLOOD NEVER FADES.

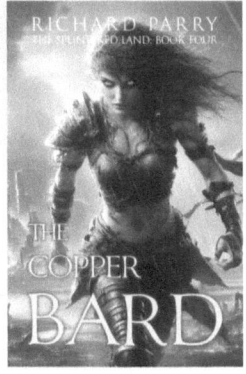

Sixteen years have passed since the war, but peace was never meant to last.

Evanne sings of heroes long gone, carrying their stories in verse and memory. But the past she honors is not finished with her, and neither are the enemies her bloodline left behind.

A song. A blade. A legacy not yet fulfilled. **Grab *The Copper Bard* now!**

https://www.books2read.com/TheCopperBard

Because some wars don't end. They just wait.

About the Author

Richard Parry worked as a senior marketing manager in one of the world's top tech companies. It sounds cool, but it wasn't all cocaine parties. He lives in Wellington with the love of his life, Rae. They have two cats, Harry and Friday, who chase birds. The birds, who have the power of flight, don't seem to mind.

WAIT. DON'T GO!

Thanks for reading my book. If you enjoyed it, let's keep the party going:

📖 Join *Roll for Narrative* for reviews, storytelling breakdowns, and writing misadventures:

https://rollfornarrative.parrydox.com

✍ Lurk, judge, or say hi:

https://www.parrydox.com

P.S. An angel still gets its wings for every five-star review, but I'm told they're on backorder.

Also by Richard Parry

DAWN'S WARDEN

The Three Faces of Fate

The Undefeated Throne

The Fury of the Betrayed

THE SPLINTERED LAND

Tomb of the Six

Blade of Glass

The Storm Within

Requiem's Justice

The Copper Bard

Heartsong

The Hymn of All

THE EZEROC WARS

The Ezeroc Wars universe is big (and growing!). Get the reading guide here: https:// www.parrydox.com/ezeroc-wars-reading-guide/

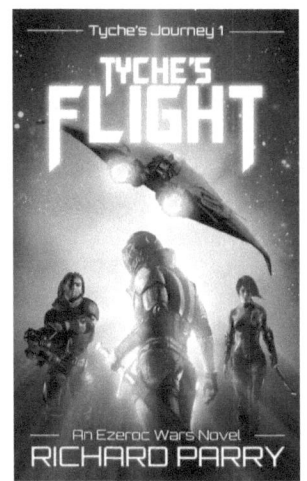

The Empire's Rogues: Volume 1

FUTURE FORFEIT

Not sure where to start? Get the reading guide here: https://www.parrydox.com/future-forfeit-reading-guide/

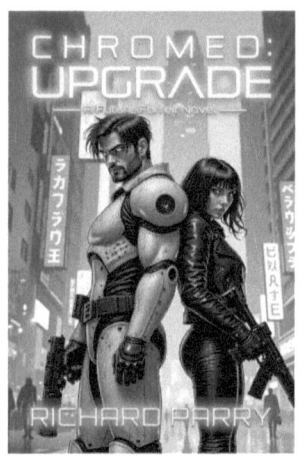

Chromed: Upgrade

Chromed: Rogue

Chromed: Restore

City Stories

Chromed: Consensus

Chromed: Delilah

Chromed: Meltdown

NIGHT'S CHAMPION

Night's Favor

Night's Fall

Night's End

www.ingramcontent.com/pod-product-compliance
Lightning Source LLC
Chambersburg PA
CBHW060242030726

47493CB00024B/1539